R. M. Ballantyne

Under the Waves

Or, Diving in Deep Waters, a Tale

R. M. Ballantyne

Under the Waves
Or, Diving in Deep Waters, a Tale

ISBN/EAN: 9783337100360

Printed in Europe, USA, Canada, Australia, Japan

Cover: Foto ©Andreas Hilbeck / pixelio.de

More available books at **www.hansebooks.com**

UNDER THE WAVES

OR

DIVING IN DEEP WATERS

A Tale

BY R. M. BALLANTYNE,

AUTHOR OF "POST HASTE;" "IN THE TRACK OF THE TROOPS;" "THE SETTLER AND
THE SAVAGE;" "RIVERS OF ICE;" "BLACK IVORY;" "THE PIRATE CITY;"
"ERLING THE BOLD;" "THE NORSEMEN IN THE WEST;" "THE FLOATING
LIGHT;" "THE IRON HORSE;" "FIGHTING THE FLAMES;" "SHIFTING
WINDS;" "DEEP DOWN;" "THE LIGHTHOUSE;" "THE
LIFEBOAT;" "GASCOYNE;" "THE GOLDEN
DREAM;" ETC. ETC.

With Illustrations

LONDON:

JAMES NISBET & CO., 21 BERNERS STREET

PREFACE.

THIS tale makes no claim to the character of an exhaustive illustration of all that belongs to the art of diving. It merely deals with the most important points, and some of the most interesting incidents connected therewith. In writing it I have sought carefully to exhibit the true and to ignore the false or improbable.

I have to acknowledge myself indebted to the well-known submarine engineers Messrs. Siebe and Gorman, and Messrs. Heinke and Davis, of London, for much valuable information; and to Messrs. Denayrouze, of Paris, for permitting me to go under water in one of their diving-dresses. Also—among many others—to Captain John Hewat, formerly Commander in the service of the Rajah of Sarawak, for much interesting material respecting the pirates of the Eastern Seas.

R. M. B.

EDINBURGH, 1876.

CONTENTS.

LIST OF ILLUSTRATIONS.

UNDER THE WAVES

OR

DIVING IN DEEP WATERS.

———◆———

CHAPTER I.

INTRODUCES OUR HERO, ONE OF HIS ADVISERS, AND SOME OF HIS
DIFFICULTIES.

"So, sir, it seems that you've set your heart on
learning something of everything?"

The man who said this was a tall and rugged professional diver. He to whom it was said was Edgar
Berrington, our hero, a strapping youth of twenty-one.

"Well—yes, I have set my heart upon something
of that sort, Baldwin," answered the youth. "You
see, I hold that an engineer ought to be practically
acquainted, more or less, with everything that bears,
even remotely, on his profession; therefore I have
come to you for some instruction in the noble art of
diving."

"You've come to the right shop, Mister Edgar,"

▲

replied Baldwin, with a gratified look. "I taught you to swim when you wasn't much bigger than a marlinespike, an' to make boats a'most before you could handle a clasp-knife without cuttin' your fingers, an' now that you 've come to man's estate nothin'll please me more than to make a diver of you. But," continued Baldwin, while a shade clouded his wrinkled and weatherbeaten visage, " I can't let you go down in the dress without leave. I 'm under authority, you know, and durstn't overstep—"

"Don't let that trouble you," interrupted his companion, drawing a letter from his pocket; "I had anticipated that difficulty, and wrote to your employers. Here is their answer, granting me permission to use their dresses."

"All right, sir," said Baldwin, returning the letter without looking at it; "I 'll take your word for it, sir, as it 's not much in my line to make out the meanin' o' pot-hooks and hangers.—Now, then, when will you have your first lesson ?"

"The sooner the better."

"Just so," said the diver, looking about him with a thoughtful air.

The apartment in which the man and the youth conversed was a species of outhouse or lumber-room which had been selected by Baldwin for the stowing away of his diving apparatus and stores while these were not in use at the new pier which was in process

of erection in the neighbouring harbour. Its floor
was littered with snaky coils of indiarubber tubing;
enormous boots with leaden soles upwards of an
inch thick; several diving helmets, two of which
were of brightly polished metal, while the others
were more or less battered, dulled, and dinted by
hard service in the deep. The walls were adorned
with large damp indiarubber dresses, which suggested the idea of baby-giants who had fallen
into the water and been sent off to bed while their
costumes were hung up to dry. In one corner lay
several of the massive breast and back weights by
which divers manage to sink themselves to the
bottom of the sea; in another stood the chest containing the air-pump by means of which they are
enabled to maintain themselves alive in that uncomfortable position; while in a third and very dark
corner, an old worn-out helmet, catching a gleam
from the solitary window by which the place was
insufficiently lighted, seemed to glare enviously out
of its goggle-eyes at its glittering successors.
Altogether, what with the strange spectral objects
and the dim light, there was something weird in the
aspect of the place, that accorded well with the
spirit of young Berrington, who, being a hero and
twenty-one, was naturally romantic.

But let us pause here to assert that he was also
practical—eminently so. Practicality is compatible

with romance as well as with rascality. If we be right in holding that romance is gushing enthusiasm, then are we entitled to hold that many methodical and practical men have been, are, and ever will be, romantic. Time sobers their enthusiasm a little, no doubt, but does by no means abate it, unless the object on which it is expended be unworthy.

Recovering from his thoughtful air, and repeating "Just so," the diver added, "Well, I suppose we'd better begin wi' them 'ere odds an' ends about us."

"Not so," returned the youth quickly ; "I have often seen the apparatus, and am quite familiar with it. Let us rather go to the pier at once. I'm anxious to go down."

"Ah! Mister Edgar—hasty *as* usual," said Baldwin, shaking his head slowly. "It's two years since I last saw you, and I *had* hoped to find that time had quieted you a bit, but—. Well, well—now, look here : you think you've seen all my apparatus, an' know all about it ?"

"Not exactly all," returned the youth, with a smile; "but you know I've often been in this store of yours, and heard you enlarge on most if not all of the things in it."

"Yes—most, but not *all*, that's where it lies, sir. You've often seen Siebe and Gorman's dresses, but did you ever see this helmet made by Heinke and Davis ?"

" No, I don't think I ever did."

" Or that noo helmet wi' the speakin'-toobe made by Denayrouze and Co., an' this dress made by the same ? "

" No, I've seen none of these things, and certainly this is the first time I have heard of a speaking-tube for divers."

" Well then, you see, Mister Edgar, you have something to larn here after all ; among other things, that Denayrouze's is *not* the first speakin'-toobe," said Baldwin, who thereupon proceeded with the most impressive manner and earnest voice to explain minutely to his no less earnest pupil the various clever contrivances by which the several makers sought to render their apparatus perfect.

With all this, however, we will not trouble the reader, but proceed at once to the port, where diving operations were being carried on in connection with repairs to the breakwater.

On their way thither the diver and his young companion continued their conversation.

" Which of the various dresses do you think the best ? " asked Edgar.

" I don't know," answered Baldwin.

" Ah, ther J u are not bigotedly attached to that of your employer—like some of your fraternity with whom I have conversed ? "

" I *am* attached to Siebe and Gorman's dress,"

returned Baldwin, "but I am no bigot. I believe in
every thing and every creature having good and bad
points. The dress I wear and the apparatus I work
seem to me as near perfection as may be, but I've
lived too long in this world to suppose nobody can
improve on 'em. I've heard men who go down in
the dresses of other makers praise 'em just as much
as I do mine, an' maybe with as good reason.
I believe 'em all to be serviceable. When I've
had more experience of 'em I'll be able to say
which I think the best.—I've got a noo hand
on to-day," continued Baldwin, "an' as he's goin'
down this afternoon for the first time, so you've
come at a good time. He's a smart young man,
but I'm not very hopeful of him, for he's an Irishman."

"Come, old fellow," said Edgar, with a laugh,
"mind what you say about Irishmen. I've got a
dash of Irish blood in me through my mother, and
won't hear her countrymen spoken of with disre-
spect. Why should not an Irishman make a good
diver?"

"Because he's too excitable, as a rule," replied
Baldwin. "You see, Mister Edgar, it takes a cool,
quiet, collected sort of man to make a good diver,
and Irishmen ain't so cool as I should wish.
Englishmen are better, but the best of all are
Scotchmen. Give me a good, heavy, raw-boned

lump of a Scotchman, who'll believe nothin' till he's convinced, and accept nothin' till it's proved, who'll argue with a stone wall, if he's got nobody else to dispute with, in that slow sedate humdrum way that drives everybody wild but himself, who's got an amazin' conscience, but no nerves whatever to speak of—ah, that's the man to go under water, an' crawl about by the hour among mud and wreckage without gittin' excited or makin' a fuss about it if he should get his life-line or air-toobe entangled among iron bolts, smashed-up timbers, twisted wire-ropes, or such like."

"Scotchmen should feel complimented by your opinion of them," said Edgar.

"So they should, for I mean it," replied Baldwin, "but I hope the Irishman will turn up a trump this time.—May I take the liberty of askin' how you're gittin' on wi' the engineering, Mister Edgar?"

"Oh, famously. That is to say, I've just finished my engagement with the firm of Steel, Bolt, Hardy, and Co., and am now on the point of going to sea."

Baldwin looked at his companion in surprise. "Going to sea!" he repeated, "why, I thought you didn't like the sea?"

"You thought right, Baldwin, but men are sometimes under the necessity of submitting to what they don't like. I have no love for the sea, except, indeed, as a beautiful object to be admired from the shore, but, you see, I want to finish my education by going a voyage as one of the subordinate engineers in an ocean steamer, so as to get some practical acquaintance with marine engineering. Besides, I have taken a fancy to see something of foreign parts before settling down vigorously to my profession, and—"

"Well?" said Baldwin, as the youth made rather a long pause.

"Can you keep a secret, Baldwin, and give advice to a fellow who stands sorely in need of it?"

The youth said this so earnestly that the huge diver, who was a sympathetic soul, declared with much fervour that he could do both.

"You must know, then," began Edgar with some hesitation, "the fact is—you're such an old friend, Baldwin, and took such care of me when I was a boy up to that sad time when I lost my father, and you lost an employer—"

"Ay, the best master I ever had," interrupted the diver.

"That—that I think I may trust you; in short, Baldwin, I'm over head and ears with a young girl, and—and—"

"An' your love ain't requited—eh?" said Baldwin interrogatively, while his weatherbeaten face elongated.

"No, not exactly that," rejoined Edgar, with a

laugh. "Aileen loves me almost, I believe, as well as I love her, but her father is dead against us. He scorns me because I am not a man of wealth."

"What is *he*?" demanded Baldwin.

"A rich China merchant."

"He's more than that," said Baldwin.

"Indeed!" said Edgar, with a surprised look; "what more is he?"

"He's a goose!" returned the diver stoutly.

"Don't be too hard on him, Baldwin. Remember, I hope some day to call him father-in-law. But why do you hold so low an opinion of him?"

"Why, because he forgets that riches may, and often do, take to themselves wings and fly away, whereas broad shoulders, and deep chest, and sound limbs, and a good brain, usually last the better part of a lifetime; and a brave heart will last for ever."

"I am afraid that I have yet to prove, to myself as well as to the old gentleman, that the brave heart is mine," returned Edgar. "As to the physique —you may be so far right, but he evidently under-values that."

"I said nothing about physic," returned Baldwin, who still frowned as he thought of the China merchant, "and the less that you and I have to do wi' that the better. But what are you goin' to do, sir?"

"That is just the point on which I want to have your advice. What ought I to do?"

"Don't run away with her, whatever you do," said Baldwin emphatically.

The youth laughed slightly as he explained that there was no chance whatever of his doing that, because Aileen would never consent to run away or to disobey her father.

"Good—good," said the diver, with still greater emphasis than before, "I like that. The gal that would sacrifice herself and her lover sooner than disobey her father—even though he *is* a goose—is made o' the right stuff. If it's not takin' too great a liberty, Mister Edgar, may I ask what she's like?"

"What she's like—eh?" murmured the other, dropping his head as if in reverie, and stroking the dark shadow on his chin which was beginning to do duty for a beard. "Why, she—she's like nothing that I ever saw on earth before."

"No!" ejaculated Baldwin, elevating his eyebrows a little, as he said gravely, "what, not even like an angel?"

"Well, yes; but even that does not sufficiently describe her. She's fair"—he waxed enthusiastic here,—"surpassingly fair, with wavy golden tresses and blue eyes, and a bright complexion and a winning voice, and a sylph-like figure and a thinnish but remarkably pretty face—"

"Ah!" interrupted Baldwin, with a sigh, "I know: just like my missus."

"Why, my good fellow," cried Edgar, unable to restrain a fit of laughter, "I do not wish to deny the good looks of Mrs. Baldwin, but you know that she's uncommonly ruddy and fat and heavy, as well as fair."

"Ay, an' forty, if you come to that," said the diver. "She's fourteen stun if she's an ounce; but let me tell you, Mister Edgar, she wasn't always heavy. There *was* a time when my Susan was as trim and taut and clipper-built as any Aileen that ever was born."

"I have no doubt of it whatever," returned the youth, "but I was going to say, when you interrupted me, it is her eyes that are her strong point—her deep, liquid, melting blue eyes, that look at you so earnestly, and seem to pierce—"

"Ay, just so," interrupted the diver; "pierce into you like a gimblet, goin' slap agin the retina, turnin' short down the jugular, right into the heart, where they create an agreeable sort o' fermentation. Oh! don't I know?—my Susan all over!"

Edgar's amusement was tinged slightly with disgust at the diver's persistent comparisons. However, mastering his feelings, he again demanded advice as to what he should do in the circumstances.

"You han't told me the circumstances yet," said the diver quietly.

"Well, here they are. Old Mr. Hazlit—"

" What! Hazlit? Miss Hazlit, is *that* her name?"
cried Baldwin, with a look of pleased surprise.

" Yes, do you know her ?"

" Know her? Of course I do. Why, she visits the
poor in my district o' the old town—you know I'm
a local preacher among the Wesleyans—an' she's
one o' the best an' sweetest—ha! angel indeed! I'm
glad she wasn't made an angel of, for it would have
bin the spoilin' of a splendid woman. Bless her !"

The diver spoke with much enthusiasm, and the
young man smiled as he said, " Of course I add
Amen to your last words.—Well then," he continued,
" Aileen's father has refused to allow me to pay my
addresses to his daughter. He has even forbidden
me to enter his house, or to hold any intercourse
whatever with her. This unhappy state of things
has induced me to hasten my departure from
England. My intention is to go abroad, make a
fortune, and then return to claim my bride, for the
want of money is all that the old gentleman objects
to. I cannot bear the thought of going away without saying goodbye, but that seems now unavoidable,
for he has, as I have said, forbidden me the house."

Edgar looked anxiously at his companion's face,
but received no encouragement there, for Baldwin
kept his eyes on the ground, and shook his head
slowly.

" If the old gentleman has forbid you his house, of

course you mustn't go into it. However, it seems to me that you might cruise about the house and watch till Sus—Aileen, I mean—comes out ; but I don't myself quite like the notion of that either, it don't seem fair an' above-board like."

"You are right," returned Edgar. "I cannot consent to hang about a man's door, like a thief waiting to pounce on his treasure when it opens. Besides, he has forbidden Aileen to hold any intercourse with me, and I know her dear nature too well to subject it to a useless struggle between duty and inclination. She is certain to obey her father's orders at any cost."

"Then, sir," said Baldwin decidedly, "you'll just have to go afloat without sayin' goodbye. There's no help for it, but there's this comfort, that, bein' what she is, she'll like you all the better for it.—Now, here we are at the pier. Boat a-ho-o-y !"

In reply to the diver's hail a man in a punt waved his hand, and pulled for the landing-place.

A few strokes of the oar soon placed them on the deck of a large clumsy vessel which lay anchored off the entrance to the harbour. This was the diver's barge, which exhibited a ponderous crane with a pendulous hook and chain in the place where its fore-mast should have been. Several men were busied about the deck, one of whom sat clothed in the full dress of a diver, with the exception of the helmet, which was unscrewed and lay on the deck near his heavily-weighted feet. The dress was wet, and the man was enjoying a quiet pipe, from all which Edgar judged that he was resting after a dive. Near to the plank on which the diver was seated there stood the chest containing the air-pumps. It was open, the pumps were in working order, with two men standing by to work them. Coils of india-rubber tubing lay beside it. Elsewhere were strewn about stones for repairing the pier, and various building tools.

"Has Machowl come on board yet?" asked Baldwin, as he stepped on the deck. "Ah, I see he has.—Well, Rooney lad, are you prepared to go down?"

"Yis, sur, I am."

Rooney Machowl, who stepped forward as he spoke, was a fine specimen of a man, and would have done credit to any nationality. He was about the middle height, very broad and muscular, and apparently twenty-three years of age. His countenance was open, good-humoured, and good-looking, though by no means classic—the nose being turned up, the eyes small and twinkling, and the mouth large.

"Have you ever seen anything of this sort before?" asked Baldwin, with a motion of his hand towards the diving apparatus scattered on the deck.

"No sur, nothin'.'"

"Was you bred to any trade?"

"Yis, sur, I'm a ship-carpenter."

"An' why don't you stick to that?"

"Bekase, sur, it won't stick to me. There's nothin' doin' apparently in this poort. Annyhow I can't git work, an' I've a wife an' chick at home, who've bin so long used to praties and bacon that their stummicks don't take kindly to fresh air fried in nothin'. So ye see, sur, findin' it difficult to make a livin' above ground, I'm disposed to try to make it under water."

While Rooney Machowl was speaking Baldwin regarded him with a fixed and critical gaze. What his opinion of the recruit was did not, however, appear on his countenance or in his reply, for he merely said, "Humph! well, we'll see. You'll begin your education in your noo profession by payin' partikler attention to all that is said an' done around you."

"Yis, sur," returned Machowl, respectfully touching the peak of his cap and wrinkling his forehead very much, while he looked on at the further proceedings of the divers with that expression of deep earnest sincerity of attention which—whether assumed or genuine—is only possible to the countenance of an Irishman.

During this colloquy the two men standing by the pump-case, and two other men who appeared to be supernumeraries, listened with much interest, but the diver seated on the plank, resting and calmly smoking his pipe, gazed with apparent indifference at the sea, from which he had recently emerged.

This man was a very large fellow, with a dark surly countenance—not exactly bad in expression, but rather ill-tempered-looking. His diving dress being necessarily very wide and baggy, made him seem larger than he really was—indeed, quite gigantic. The dress was made of very thick indiarubber cloth, and all—feet, legs, body, and arms—was of one piece, so perfectly secured at the seams as to be thoroughly impervious to air or water. To get into it was a matter of some difficulty, the entrance being effected at the neck. When this neck is properly attached to the helmet, the diver is thoroughly cut off from the external world, except through the air-tube communicating with his helmet and the pump afore mentioned.

"Have ye got the hole finished, Maxwell?" said Baldwin, turning to the surly diver.

"Yes," he replied shortly.

"Well, then, go down and fix the charge. Here it is," said Baldwin, taking from a wooden case an object about eighteen inches long, which resembled a large office-ruler that had been coated thickly with pitch. It was an elongated shell filled to the muzzle with gunpowder. To one end of it was fastened the end of a coil of wire which was also coated with some protecting substance.

As Baldwin spoke Maxwell slowly puffed the last "draw" from his lips and knocked the ashes out of his pipe on the plank, on which he still remained seated while the two supernumeraries busied themselves in completing his toilet for him; one screwing on his helmet, which appeared ridiculously large, the other loading his breast and back with two heavy leaden weights. When fully equipped, the diver carried on his person a weight fully equal to that of his own bulky person.

"Now look here, Mister Edgar, an' pay partikler attention, Rooney Machowl. This here toobe, made of indyrubber, d'ee see? ('Yis, sur,' from Rooney) I fix on, as you perceive, to the back of Maxwell's helmet. It communicates with that there pump, and when these two men work the pump, air will be forced into the helmet and into the dress down to his very toes. We could bu'st him, if we were so disposed, if it wasn't for an escape-valve, here close beside the air-toobe, at the back of the helmet, which keeps lettin' off the surplus air. Moreover, there is another valve, here in front of the breast-plate, which is under the control of the diver, so that he can let air escape by givin' it a half-turn when the men at the pumps are givin' him too much, or he can keep it in when they're givin' him enough."

B

"An' what does he do," asked Rooney, with an anxious expression, "whin they give him too little?"

"He pulls on the air pipe,—as I'll explain to you in good time—the proper signal for 'more air.'"

"But what if he forgits, or misremimbers the signal?" asked the inquisitive recruit.

"Why then," replied Baldwin, "he suffocates, and we pull him up dead, an' give him decent burial. Keep yourself easy, my lad, an' you'll know all about it in good time. I'll soon give 'ee the chance to suffocate or bu'st yourself accordin' to taste."

"Come, cut it short and look alive," said Maxwell gruffly, as he stood up to permit of a stout rope being fastened to his waist.

"You shut up!" retorted Baldwin.

Having exchanged these little civilities the two divers moved to the side of the barge—Maxwell with a slow ponderous tread.

A short iron ladder dipped from the gunwale of the barge a few feet down into the sea. The diver stepped upon this, turning with his face inwards, descended knee-deep into the water, and then stopped. Baldwin handed him the blasting-charge. At the same moment one of the supernumeraries advanced with the front-glass or bull's-eye in his hand, and the men at the pumps gave a turn or two to see that all was working well.

"All right ?" demanded the supernumerary.

"Right," responded Maxwell, in a voice which issued sepulchrally from the iron globe.

There are three round windows fitted with thick plate-glass in the helmets to which we refer. The front one is made to screw off and on, and the fixing of this is always the last operation in completing a diver's toilet.

"Pump away," said the man, holding the round glass in front of Maxwell's nose, and looking over his shoulder to see that the order was obeyed. The glass was screwed on, and the man finished off by gravely patting Maxwell in an affectionate manner on the head.

"Why does he pat him so ?" asked Edgar, with a laugh at the apparent tenderness of the act.

"It's a tinder farewell, I suppose," murmured Rooney, "in case he niver comes up again."

"It is to let him know that he may now descend in safety," answered Baldwin. "The pump there is kep' goin' from a few moments before the front glass is screwed on till the diver shows his head above water again—which he'll do in quarter of an hour or so, for it don't take long to lay a charge; but our ordinary spell under water, when work is steady, is about four hours—more or less—with perhaps a breath of ten minutes once or twice at the surface when they're working deep."

"But why a breath at the surface?" asked Edgar. "Isn't the air sent down fresh enough?"

"Quite fresh enough, Mister Edgar, but the pressure when we go deep—say ten or fifteen fathoms —is severe on a man if long continued, so that he needs a little relief now and then. Some need more and some less relief, accordin' to their strength. Maxwell has only gone down fifteen feet, so that he wouldn't need to come up at all durin' a spell of work. We're goin' to blast a big rock that has bin' troublesome to us at low water. The hole was driven in it last week. We moored a raft over it and kep' men at work with a long iron jumper that reached from the rock to the surface of the sea. It was finished last night, and now he's gone to fix the charge."

"But I don't understand about the pressure, sur, at all at all," said Machowl, with a complicated look of puzzlement; "sure whin I putt my hand in wather I don't feel no pressure whatsomediver."

"Of course not," responded Baldwin, "because you don't put it deep enough. You must know that our atmosphere presses on our bodies with a weight of about 20,000 lbs. Well, if you go thirty-two feet deep in the sea you get the pressure of exactly another atmosphere, which means that you've got to stand a pressure all over your body of 40,000 when you've got down as deep as thirty-two feet.

"But," objected Rooney, "I don't feel no pressure of the atmosphere on me body at all."

"That's because you're squeezed by the air inside of you, man, as well as by the atmosphere outside, which takes off the *feelin'* of it, an', moreover, you're used to it. If the weight of our atmosphere was took off your outside and not took off your inside—your lungs an' the like,—you'd come to feel it pretty strong, for you'd swell like a balloon an' bu'st a'most, if not altogether."

Baldwin paused a moment and regarded the puzzled countenance of his pupil with an air of pity.

"Contrairywise," he continued, "if the air was all took out of your inside an' allowed to remain on your outside, you'd go squash together like a collapsed indyrubber ball. Well then, if that be so with one atmosphere, what must it be with a pressure equal to two, which you have when you go down to thirty-two feet deep in the sea? An' if you go down to twenty-five fathoms, or 150 feet, which is often done, what must the pressure be there?"

"Tightish, no doubt," said Rooney.

"True, lad," continued Joe. "Of course, to counteract this we must force more air down to you the deeper you go, so that the pressure inside of you may be a little more than the pressure outside, in order to force the foul air out of the dress through the escape valve ; and what between the one an' the other your sensations are peculiar, you may be sure.—But come, young man, don't be alarmed. We'll not send you down very deep at first. If some divers go down as deep as twenty-five fathoms, surely you'll not be frightened to try two and a half."

Whatever Rooney's feelings might have been, the judicious allusion to the possibility of his being frightened was sufficient to call forth the emphatic assertion that he was ready to go down two thousand fathoms if they had ropes long enough and weights heavy enough to sink him !

While the recruit is preparing for his sub-aqueous experiments, you and I, reader, will go see what Maxwell is about at the bottom of the sea.

CHAPTER II.

DESCRIBES A FIRST VISIT TO THE BOTTOM OF THE SEA.

WHEN the diver received the encouraging pat on the head, as already related, he descended the ladder to its lowest round. Here, being a few feet below the surface, the buoyancy of the water relieved him of much of the oppression caused by the great weights with which he was loaded. He was in a semi-floating condition, hence the ladder, being no longer necessary, was made to terminate at that point. He let go his hold of it and sank gently to the bottom, regulating his pace by a rope which descended from the foot of the ladder to the mud, on which in a few seconds his leaden soles softly rested. A continuous stream of air-bubbles from the safety-valve behind the helmet indicated to those above that the pumps were doing their duty, and at the same time hid the diver entirely from their sight.

Meanwhile the two men who acted as signalman and assistant stood near the head of the ladder, the first holding the life-line, the assistant the coil of air-tubing. Their duty was to stand by and pay out or haul in tubing and line according as the diver's movements and necessities should require. They were to attend also to his signals—some of which were transmitted by the line and some by the air-tube. These signals vary among divers. With Baldwin and his party one pull on the *life-line* meant " All right ;" four pulls, " I 'm coming up." One pull on the air-pipe signified " Sufficient air ;" two pulls, " More air (pump faster)." Four pulls was an alarm, and signified " Haul me up." The aspect of Rooney Machowl's face when endeavouring to understand Baldwin's explanation of these signals was a sight worth seeing !

But to return to our diver. On reaching the bottom, Maxwell took a coil of small line which hung on his left arm, and attached one end of it to a stone or sinker which kept taut the ladder-line by which he had descended. This was his clew to guide him back to the ladder. Not only is the light under water very dim—varying of course, according to depth, until total darkness ensues—but a diver's vision is much weakened by the muddy state of the water at river-mouths and in harbours, so that he is usually obliged to depend more on feeling than on sight. If he were to leave the foot of his ladder without the guiding-coil, it would be difficult if not impossible to find it again, and his only resource

would be to signal " Haul me up," which would be
undignified, to say the least of it! By means of this
coil he can wander about at will—within the limits
of his air-tube tether of course,—and be certain to
find his way back to the ladder-foot in the darkest
or muddiest water.

Having fastened the line, the diver walked in the
direction of the rock on which he had to operate,
dropping gradually the coils of the guiding-line as
he proceeded. His progress was very slow, for water
is a dense medium, and man's form is not well
adapted for walking in it—as every bather knows
who has attempted to walk when up to his neck in
it. He soon found the object of his search, and
went down on his knees beside the hole already
driven into the rock. Even this process of going
on his knees was not so simple as it sounds, for the
men above were sending down more air than could
escape by the valve behind the helmet, and thus were
filling his dress to such an extent that he had a
tendency to rise off the ground despite his weights.
To counteract this he opened the valve in front,
let out the superabundant air, got on his knees,
and was soon busy at work inserting the charge-
tube into the hole and tamping it well home,
taking care that the fine wire with which it communicated with the party in the barge should not be
injured.

While thus engaged he was watched, apparently with deep interest, by a small crab, a shrimp, and several little fish of various kinds, all of which we may add, seemed to have various degrees of curiosity. One particular little fish, named a goby, and celebrated for its wide-awake nature and impudence, actually came to the front glass of the helmet and looked in. But the diver was too busy to pay attention to it. Nothing abashed, the goby went to each of the side-windows, but, receiving no encouragement, it made for a convenient ledge of the rock, where, resting its fore-fins on a barnacle, it turned its head a little on one side and looked on in silence. Finding this rather tedious, after a time it went, with much of the spirit of a London street-boy, and, passing close to the shrimp, tweaked the end of one of its feelers, causing that volatile creature to vanish. It then made a demonstration of attack on the crab, but that crustaceous worthy, sitting up on its hind-legs and expanding both claws with a very "come-on-if-you-dare" aspect, bid it defiance.

Meanwhile the charge was laid, and Maxwell rose to return to the world above. Feeling a certain uncomfortable hotness in the air he breathed, and observing that his legs were remarkably thin, and that his dress was clasped somewhat too lovingly about his person, he became aware of the fact that, having neglected to reclose the front-valve, his supply of air was now insufficient. He therefore shut the valve and began to wend his way back to the ladder. By the time he reached it the air in his dress had swelled him out to aldermanic dimensions, so that he pulled himself up the ladder-rope, hand over hand, with the utmost ease—having previously given four pulls on his life-line to signal "coming up." A few seconds more and his head was seen to emerge from the surface, like some goggle-eyed monster of the briny deep.

A comrade at once advanced and unscrewed his front glass, and then, but not till then, did the men at the pumps cease their labours.

"All right," said Maxwell, stepping over the side and seating himself on his plank.

"Stand by," said Baldwin.

The two satellites did not require that order, for they were already standing by with a small electrical machine. The wire before mentioned as being connected with the charge of powder, now safely lodged in the hole at the bottom of the sea, was connected with the electrical machine, and a few vigorous turns of its handle were given, while every eye was turned expectantly on the surface of the sea.

That magic spark which now circles round the world, annihilating time and space, was evolved; it flashed down the wire; the ocean could not put it out; the dry powder received it; the massive rock burst into fragments; a decided shock was felt on board the barge, and a turmoil of gas-bubbles and dead or dying fish came to the surface, in the midst of which turmoil the shrimp, the crab, and the goby doubtless came to an untimely end.

Thus was cleared out of the way an obstruction which had from time immemorial been a serious inconvenience to that port; and thus every year serious inconveniences and obstructions that most people know very little about are cleared out of the way by our bold, steady, and daring divers, through the wisdom and the wonderful appliances of our submarine engineers.

"Now then, Rooney, come an' we'll dress you," said Baldwin. "As you're goin' to be a professional diver it's right that you should have the first chance and set a good example to Mister Berrington here, who's only what we may call an amateur."

"Faix, I'd rather that Mister Berrington shud go first," said Rooney, who, as he spoke, however, stripped himself of his coat, vest, and trousers preparatory to putting on the costume.

"I'll be glad to go first, Rooney, if you're afraid," said Edgar.

Rooney's annoyance at being thought afraid was increased to indignation by a contemptuous guffaw from Maxwell.

Flushing deeply and casting a glance of anger at

Maxwell, the young Irishman crushed down his feelings and said—

"Sure, I'm only jokin'. Put on the dress Mister Baldwin av ye plaze."

A diver, like a too high-bred lady, cannot well dress himself. He requires two assistants. Rooney Machowl sat down on the plank beside Maxwell, who was busy taking off his dress, and acted according to orders.

First of all they brought him a thick guernsey shirt, a pair of drawers and pair of *inside* stockings, which he put on and fastened securely. Sometimes a "crinoline" to afford protection to the stomach in deep water is put on, but on the present occasion it was omitted, the water being shallow. Then Baldwin put on him a "shoulder-pad" to bear the weight of the helmet, etc., and prevent chafing.

"If it was cold, Rooney," said his instructor, "I'd put two guernseys and pairs of drawers and stockin's on you, but, as it's warm, one set'll do. Moreover, if you was goin' deep you'd have the option of stuffin' your ears with cotton soaked in oil, to relieve the pressure; some do an' some don't. I never do myself. It's said to relieve the pressure of air on the ears, but my ears are strong. Anyway you won't want it in this water.—Now for the dress, boys."

The two assistants—with mouths expanded from ear to ear— here advanced with the strong indiarubber garment whose legs, feet, body, and arms are, as we have already said, all in one piece. Pushing his feet in at the upper opening, Rooney writhed, thrust, and wriggled himself into it, being ably assisted by his attendants, who held open the sleeves for him and expanded the tight elastic cuffs, and, catching the dress at the neck, hitched it upwards so powerfully as almost to lift their patient off his legs. Next, came a pair of *outside* stockings and canvas overalls or short trousers, both of which were meant to preserve the dress-proper from injury. Having been got into all these things, Rooney was allowed to sit down while his attendants each put on and buckled a boot with leaden soles—each boot weighing about twenty pounds.

"A purty pair of dancin' pumps!" remarked Rooney, turning out his toes, while Baldwin put on his breast-plate, after having drawn up the inner collar of the dress and tied it round his neck with a piece of spare yarn.

The breast-plate was made of tinned copper. It covered part of the back, breast, and shoulders of the diver, and had a circular neck, to which the helmet was to be ultimately screwed. It rested on the *inner* collar of the dress, and the *outer* collar—of stout indiarubber—was drawn over it. In this outer collar were twelve holes, corresponding to twelve screws round the edge of the breast-plate. When these

holes had been fitted over their respective screws, a
breast-plate-band, in four pieces, was placed over
them and screwed tight by means of nuts—thus
rendering the connection between the dress and the
breast-plate perfectly water-tight. It now only remained to screw the helmet to the circular neck of the
breast-plate. Previously, however, a woollen night-
cap was drawn over the poor man's head, well down
on his ears, and Rooney looked—as indeed he afterwards admitted that he felt—as if he were going to be
nanged. He thought, however, of the proverb, that a
man who is born to be drowned never can be hanged,
and somehow felt comforted.

The diving helmet is made of tinned copper, and
much too large for the largest human head, in order
that the wearer may have room to move his head
freely about inside of it. It should not touch the
head in any part, but is fixed rigidly to the breast-
plate, resting on the shoulders, and does not partake
of the motions of the head. In it are three
round openings filled with the thickest plate-glass,
and protected by brass bars or guards; also an
outlet-valve to allow the foul air to escape; a short
metal tube with an inlet-valve, to which the air-
pump is screwed; and a regulating cock for getting
rid of excess of air. The arrangement is such, that
the fresh air enters, and is spread over the front of
the diver's face, while the foul escapes at the back

of his head.   By a clever contrivance—a segmental
screw—the helmet can be fixed to its neck with one-
eighth of a turn, instead of having to be twisted
round several times.   To various hooks and studs
on the helmet and breast-plate are hung two leaden
masses weighing about forty pounds each.

These weights having been attached, and a waist-
belt with a knife in it put round Rooney's waist,
along with the life-line, the air-tube was affixed,
and he was asked by Baldwin how he felt.

" A trifle heavy," replied the pupil, through the
front hole of the helmet, which was not yet closed.

" That feeling will go off entirely when you're
under water," said Baldwin.   " Now, remember, if
you want more air, just give two pulls on the air-
pipe—an' don't pull as if you was tryin' to haul down
the barge ; we'll be sure to feel you.   Be gentle and
quiet, whatever ye do.   Gettin' flurried never does
any good whatever.   D'ee hear ?"

" Yis, sur," answered Rooney, and his voice sounded
metallic and hollow, even to those outside—much
more so to himself !

" Well, then, if we give you too much air, you've
only got to open the front-valve—so, and, when you're
easy, shut it.   When you get down to the bottom,
give one—only one—pull on the life-line, which
means ' All right,' and I'll give one pull in reply.
We must always reply to each other, d'ee see ?

because if you don't answer, of course we'll think you've been suffocated, or entangled at the bottom among wreckage and what-not, or been took with a fit, an' we'll haul you up, as hard as we can; so you'll have to be particular. D'ee understand?"

Again the learner replied "Yis, sur," but less confidently than before, for Baldwin's cautions, although meant to have an encouraging effect, proved rather to be alarming.

"Now," continued the teacher, leading his pupil to the side of the barge, "be sure to go down slow, and come up slow. Whatever you do, do it slow, for if you do it fast—especially in comin' up—you'll come to grief. If a man comes up too fast from deep water, the condensed air inside of him is apt to swell him out, and the brain bein' relieved too suddenly from the pressure, there's a rush of blood to it, and a singin' in the ears, and a pain in the head, with other unpleasant symptoms. Why," continued Baldwin, growing energetic, "I've actually known a man killed outright by bein' pulled up too quick from a depth of twenty fathoms. So mark my words, lad, and take it easy. If you get nervous, just stop a bit an' amuse yourself with thinkin' over what I've told you, and then go on with your descent."

At this point Rooney's heart almost failed him, but, catching sight of Maxwell's half-amused, half-contemptuous face, he stepped resolutely on the ladder, and began to descend in haste.

" Hold on !" roared Baldwin, laying hold of the life-line. " Why, man alive, you 're off without the front glass !"

" Och ! whirra ! so I am," said Rooney, pausing.

" Pump away, lads," cried Baldwin, looking back at his assistants.

" Whist ! what 's that ?" asked the pupil excitedly, as a hissing sound buzzed round his head.

" Why, that 's the air coming in. Now then, I 'll screw on the glass. Are you all right ?"

" All right," replied Rooney, telling, as he said himself afterwards, " one of the biggist lies he iver towld in his life !"

The glass was screwed on, and the learner was effectually cut off from all connection with the outer air, save through the slight medium of an indiarubber pipe.

Having thus screwed him up—or in—Baldwin gave him the patronising pat on the helmet, as a signal for him to descend, but Rooney stood tightly fixed to the ladder, and motionless.

Again Baldwin patted his head encouragingly, but still Rooney stood as motionless as one of the iron-clad warriors in the Tower of London. The fact was, his courage had totally failed him. He was ashamed to come up, and could not by any effort of will force himself to go down.

"Why, what's wrong?" demanded Baldwin, looking in at the glass, which, however, was so clouded with the inmate's breath that he could only be seen dimly. It was evident that Rooney was speaking in an excited voice, but no sound was audible through that impervious mass of metal and glass. Baldwin was therefore about to unscrew the mouth-glass, when accident brought about what Rooney's will could not accomplish. In attempting to move, the poor pupil missed his hold, or slipped somehow, and fell into the sea with a sounding splash.

"Let him go, boys—gently, or he'll break everything. A dip'll do him no harm," cried Baldwin to the alarmed assistants.

The men let the life-line and air-tube slip, until the rushing descent was somewhat abated, and then, checking the involuntary diver, they hauled him slowly to the surface, where his arms and open palms went swaying wildly round until they came in contact with the ladder, on which they fastened with a grip that was sufficient to have squeezed the life out of a gorilla.

In a few seconds he ascended a step, and his head emerged, then another step, and Baldwin was able to unscrew the glass.

The first word that the poor man uttered through his port-hole was "Och!" the next, "Musha!"

A burst of laughter from his friends above some-

what reassured him, and again the tinge of contempt
in Maxwell's voice reinfused courage and desperate
resolve.

"Why, man, what was your haste?" said Baldwin.

"Sure the rounds o' yer ladder was slippy,"
answered Rooney, with some indignation. "Didn't
ye see, I lost me howld? Come, putt on the glass
an' I'll try again. Never say die was a motto of
me owld father, an' it was the only legacy he left
me.—I'm ready, sur."

It is right here to remark that something of the
pupil's return of courage and resolution was due to
his quick perception. He had time to reflect that
he really had been at, or near, the bottom of the sea—
at all events over head and ears in water—for several
minutes without being drowned, even without being
moistened, and his faith in the diving-dress, though
still weak, had dawned sufficiently to assert itself as
a power.

"Ha! my lad, you'll do. You'll make a diver
yet," said Baldwin, when about to readjust the
glass. "I forgot to tell you that when your breath
clouds the front glass, you've only got to bend your
head down, and wipe it off with your nightcap.
Now, then, down you go once more."

This time the pat on the head was followed by a
descending motion. The mailed figure was feeling
with its right foot for the next round of the ladder.

Then slowly—very slowly—the left foot was let down, while the two hands held on with a tenacity that caused all the muscles and sinews to stand out rigidly. Then one hand was loosened, and caught nervously at a lower round—then the other hand followed, and thus by degrees the pupil went under the surface, when his helmet appeared like a large round ball of light enveloped in the milky-way of air-bubbles that rose from it.

"You'd better give the signal to ask if all's right," said Edgar, who felt a little anxious.

"Do so," said Baldwin, nodding to the assistant.

The man obeyed, but no answering signal was returned.

According to rule they should instantly have hauled the diver up, but Baldwin bade them delay a moment.

"I'm quite sure there's nothing wrong," he said, stooping over the side of the barge, and gazing into the water, "it's only another touch of nervousness. —Ah! I see him, holdin' on like a barnacle to the ladder, afraid to let go. He'll soon tire of kickin' there—that's it: there he goes down the rope like the best of us."

In another moment the life-line and air-pipe ceased to run out, and then the assistant gave one pull on the line. Immediately there came back *one pull*—all right.

" *That's* all right," repeated Baldwin ; " now the ice is fairly broken, and we'll soon see how he's going to get on."

In order that we too may see that more comfortably, you and I, reader, will again go under water and watch him. We will also listen to him, for Rooney has a convenient habit of talking to himself, and neither water nor helmet can prevent *us* from overhearing.

True to his instructions, the pupil proceeded to fasten his clew-line to the stone at the foot of the ladder-rope, and attempted to kneel.

" Well, well," he said, " did ye iver ! What would me mother say if she heard I couldn't git on my knees whin I tried to ?"

Rooney began this remark aloud, but the sound of his own voice was so horribly loud and unnaturally near that he finished off in a whisper, and continued his observations in that confidential tone.

" Och ! is it dancin' yer goin' to do, Rooney ?—in the day-time too!" he whispered, as his feet slowly left the bottom. " Howld on, man !"

He made a futile effort to stoop and grasp the mud, then, bethinking himself of Baldwin's instructions, he remembered that too much air had a tendency to bring him to the surface, and that opening the front valve was the remedy. He was not much too soon in recollecting this, for, besides rising, he was

beginning to feel a singing in his head and a disagreeable pressure on the ears, caused by the ever
increasing density of the air. The moment the
valve was fully opened, a rush out of air occurred
which immediately sank him again, and he had now
no difficulty in getting on his knees.

"There's little enough light down here, anyhow,"
he muttered, as he fumbled about the stone sinker
in a vain attempt to fasten his line to it, "sure the
windy must be dirty."

The thought reminded him of Baldwin's teaching.
He bent forward his head and wiped the glass with
his nightcap, but without much advantage, for the
dimness was caused by the muddiness of the water.

Just then he began to experience uncomfortable
sensations; he felt a tendency to gasp for air, and
became very hot, while his garments clasped his
limbs very tightly. He had, like Maxwell, forgotten
to re-close the breast-valve, but, unlike the more
experienced diver, he had failed to discover his
omission. He became flurried and anxious, and
getting, more and more confused, fumbled nervously at his helmet to ascertain that all was
right there. In so doing he opened the little
regulating cock, which served to form an additional
outlet to foul air. This of course made matters
worse. The pressure of air in the dress was barely
sufficient to prevent the water from entering by the

breast-valve and regulating cock. Perspiration burst out on his forehead. He naturally raised his hand to wipe it away, but was prevented by the helmet.

Rooney possessed an active mind. His thoughts flew fast. This check induced the following ideas—

"What if I shud want to scratch me head or blow me nose ? or what if an earwig shud chance to have got inside this iron pot, and take a fancy to go into my ear ?"

His right ear became itchy at the bare idea. He made a desperate blow at it, and skinned his knuckles, while a hitherto unconceived intensity of desire to scratch his head and blow his nose took violent possession of him.

Just then a dead cat, that had been flung into the harbour the night before, and had not been immersed long enough to rise to the surface, floated past with the tide, and its sightless eye-balls and ghastly row of teeth glared and glistened on him, as it surged against his front glass. A slight spirt of water came through the regulating cock at the same instant, as if the dead cat had spit in his face.

"Hooroo ! haul up !" shouted Rooney, following the order with a yell that sounded like the concentrated voice of infuriated Ireland. At the same time he seized the life-line and air-tube, and tugged at both, not four times, but nigh forty times four, and never ceased to tug until he found himself gasping on the deck of the barge with his helmet off, and his comrades laughing round him.

"It's not a bad beginning," said Baldwin, as he assisted his pupil to unrobe; "you'll make a good diver in course o' time."

Baldwin was right in this prophecy, for in a few months Rooney Machowl became one of the best and coolest divers on his staff.

We need not try the reader's patience with an account of Edgar's descent, which immediately followed that of the Irishman. Let it suffice to say that he too accomplished, with credit and with less demonstration, his first descent to the bottom of the sea.

CHAPTER III.

REFERS TO A SMALL TEA-PARTY, AND TOUCHES VERY MILDLY
ON LOVE.

MISS PRITTY was a good soul, but weak. She
was Edgar Berrington's maiden aunt—of an uncertain
age—on the mother's side. Her chief characteristic
was delicacy—delicacy of health, delicacy of sentiment, delicacy of intellect—general delicacy, in fact,
all over. She was slight too—slightly made, slightly
educated, slightly pretty, and slightly cracked. But
there were a few things in regard to which Miss
Laura Pritty was strong. She was strong in her
affections, strong in her reverence for all good
things (including a few bad things which in her
innocence she thought good), strong in her prejudices
and impulses, and strong—remarkably strong—in
parentheses. Her speech was eminently parentheti-
cal, insomuch that the range of her ideas was wholly
untrammelled by the proprieties of subject or
language. Given a point to be aimed at in conversation, Miss Pritty *never* aimed at it. She
invariably began with it, and, parting finally from it

at the outset, diverged to any or every other point in nature. Perplexity, as a matter of course, was the usual result both in speaker and hearer, but then that mattered little, for Miss Pritty was also strong in easy-going good-nature.

On the evening in which we introduce her, Miss Pritty was going to have her dear and intimate friend Aileen Hazlit to tea, and she laid out her little tea-table with as much care as an engineer might have taken in drawing a mathematical problem. The tea-pot was placed in the exact centre of the tray, with its spout and handle pointing so that a line drawn through them would have been parallel to the sides of her little "boudoir." The urn stood exactly behind it. The sugar-basin formed, on one side of the tray, a *pendant* to the cream-jug on the other, and inasmuch as the cream-jug was small, a toast-rack was coupled with it to constitute the necessary balance. So, too, with the cups: they were placed equidistant from the tea-pot, the sides of the tray, and each other, while a salver of cake on one side of the table was scrupulously balanced by a plate of buns on the other side.

"There she is—the *darling!*" exclaimed Miss Pritty, with a little skip and (excuse the word) a giggle as the bell rang.

"Miss Aileen Hazlit," announced Miss Pritty's small and only domestic, who flung wide open the door of the boudoir, as its owner was fond of styling it.

Whereupon there entered "an angel in blue, with a straw hat and ostrich feather."

We quote from the last, almost dying, speech of a hopeless youth in the town—a lawyer's clerk—whose heart was stamped over so completely with the word "Aileen" that it was unrecognisable, and practically useless for any purpose except beating—which it did, hard, at all times.

Aileen was beautiful beyond compare, because, in her case, extreme beauty of face and feature was coupled with rare beauty of expression, indicating fine qualities of mind. She was quiet in demeanour, grave in speech, serious and very earnest in thought, enthusiastic in action, unconscious and unselfish.

"Pooh! perfection!" I hear some lady reader ejaculate.

No, fair one, not quite that, but as near it as was compatible with humanity. Happily there are many such in the world—some with more and some with less of the external beauty—and man is blessed and the world upheld by them.

The chief bond that bound Aileen and Miss Pritty together was a text of Scripture, "Consider the poor." The latter had strong sympathy with the poor, being herself one of the number. The former, being rich in faith as well as in means, "considered" them.

The two laid their heads together and concerted plans
for the "raising of the masses," which might have
been food for study to *some* statesmen. For instance,
they fed the hungry and clothed the naked; they
encouraged the well-disposed and reproved the evil;
they "scattered seeds of kindness" wherever they
went; they sowed the precious Word of God in all
kinds of ground—good and bad; they comforted the
sorrowing; they visited the sick and the prisoner;
they refused to help, or, in any way to encourage, the
idle; they handed the obstreperous and violent over to
the police, with the hope—if not the recommendation
—that the rod should not be spared; and in all cases
they prayed for them. The results were considerable, but, not being ostentatiously trumpeted, were
not always recognised or traced to their true cause.

"Come away, darling," exclaimed Miss Pritty,
eagerly embracing and kissing her friend, who
accepted, but did not return, the embrace, though
she did the kiss. "I thought you were not coming
at all, and I have not seen you for a whole week!
What has kept you? There, put off your hat. I'm
so glad to see you, dear Aileen. Isn't it strange
that I'm so fond of you? They say that people who
are contrasts generally draw together—at least I've
often heard Mrs. Boxer, the wife of Captain Boxer,
you know, of the navy, who used to swear so dreadfully before he was married, but, I am happy to say,

has quite given it up now, which says a great deal for wedded life, though it's a state that I don't quite believe in myself, for if Adam had never married Eve he would not have been tempted to eat the forbidden fruit, and so there would have been no sin and no sorrow or poverty—no poor ! Only think of that."

"So that our chief occupation would have been gone," said Aileen, with a slight twinkle of her lustrous blue eyes, "and perhaps you and I might never have met."

Miss Pritty replied to this something very much to the effect that she would have preferred the entrance of sin and all its consequences—poverty included—into the world, rather than have missed making the friendship of Miss Hazlit. At least her words might have borne that interpretation—or any other !

"My father detained me," said Aileen, seating herself at the table, while her volatile friend put lumps of sugar into the cups, with a tender yet sprightly motion of the hand, as if she were doing the cups a special kindness—as indeed she was, when preparing one of them to touch the lips of Aileen.

"Naughty man, why did he detain you ?" said Miss Pritty.

"Only to write one or two notes, his right hand being disabled at present by rheumatism."

" A gentleman, Miss, in the dinin'-room," said the small domestic, suddenly opening a chink of the door for the admission of her somewhat dishevelled head. " He won't send his name up—says he wants to see you."

" How vexing !" exclaimed Miss Pritty, " but I 'll go down.   I 'm determined that he shan't interrupt our *tête-à-tête.*"

Miss Pritty uttered a little scream of surprise on entering the dining-room.

" Well, aunt," said Edgar Berrington, with a hearty smile, as he extended his hand, " you are surprised to see me ? "

" Of course I am, dear Eddy," cried Miss Pritty, holding up her cheek for a kiss. " Sit down. Why, you were in London when I last heard of you."

" True, but I 'm not in London now, as you see. I 've been a week here."

" A week, Eddy ! and you did not come to see me till now ? "

" Well, I ought to apologise," replied the youth, with a slight look of confusion, " but—the fact is, I came down partly on business, and—and—so you see I 've been very busy."

" Of course," laughed Miss Pritty ; " people who have business to do are usually very busy ! Well, I forgive you, and am glad to see you—but—"

" Well, aunt—but what ? "

"In short, Eddy, I happen to be particularly engaged this evening—on *business*, too, like yourself; but, after all, why should I not introduce you to my friend? You might help us in our discussion—it is to be about the poor. Do you know much about the poor and their miseries?"

Edgar smiled sadly as he replied —

"Yes, I have had some experimental knowledge of the poor—being one of them myself, and my poverty too has made me inconceivably miserable."

"Come, Eddy, don't talk nonsense. You know I mean the *very* poor, the destitute. But let us go up-stairs and have a cup of tea."

The idea of discussing the condition of the poor over a cup of tea with two ladies was not attractive to our hero in his then state of mind, and he was beginning to excuse himself when his aunt stopped him :—

"Now, don't say you can't, or won't, for you must. And I shall introduce you to a very pretty girl—oh! *such* a pretty one—you 've no idea—and *so* sweet !"

Miss Pritty spoke impressively and with enthusiasm, but as the youth knew himself to be already acquainted with and beloved by the prettiest girl in the town he was not so much impressed as he might have been. However, being a good-natured fellow, he was easily persuaded.

All the way up-stairs, and while they were entering the boudoir, little Miss Pritty's tongue never
ceased to vibrate, but when she observed her nephew
gazing in surprise at her friend, whose usually calm
and self-possessed face was covered with confusion,
she stopped suddenly.

" Good-evening, Miss Hazlit," said Edgar, recovering himself, and holding out his hand as he advanced
towards her; "I did not anticipate the pleasure of
meeting *you* here."

"Then you are acquainted already!" exclaimed
Miss Pritty, looking as much amazed as if the
accident of two young people being acquainted
without her knowledge were something tantamount
to a miracle.

"Yes, I have met Mr. Berrington at my father's
several times," said Aileen, resuming her seat, and
bestowing a minute examination on the corner of
her handkerchief.

If Aileen had added that she had met Mr. Berrington every evening for a week past at her father's,
had there renewed the acquaintance begun in London
a year before, and had been wooed and won by him
before his stern repulse by her father, she would
have said nothing beyond the bare truth; but she
thought, no doubt, that it was not necessary to add
all that.

"Well, well, what strange things do happen !" said

Miss Pritty, resuming her duties at the tea-table. "Sugar, Eddy? and cream?—Only to think that Aileen and I have known each other so well, and she did not know that you were my nephew; but after all it could not well be otherwise, for now I think of it, I never mentioned your name to her. Out of sight, out of mind, Eddy, you know, and indeed you don't deserve to be remembered. If we all had our deserts, some people that I know of would be in a very different position from what they are, and some people wouldn't *be* at all."

"Why, aunt," said Edgar, laughing. "Would **you—**"

"Some more cake, Eddy?"

"No, thank you. I was going to say—"

"Have you enough cream? Allow me to—"

"*Quite* enough, thanks. I was about to remark—"

"Some sugar, Aileen?—I beg your pardon—yes—you were about to say—"

"Oh! nothing," replied Edgar, half exasperated by these frequent interruptions, but laughing in spite of himself; "only I'm surprised that sentence of annihilation should be passed on 'some people' by one so amiable as you are."

"Oh! I didn't exactly mean annihilation," returned Miss Pritty, with a pitiful smile; "I only mean that I wouldn't have had them come into existence, they seem to be so utterly useless in the world, and *so* interfering, too, with those who *want* to be useful."

"Surely that quality, or capacity of interference, proves them to be not *utterly* useless," said Edgar, "for does it not give occasion for the exercise of patience and forbearance?"

"Ah!" replied Miss Pritty, with an arch smile, shaking her finger at her nephew, "you are a fallacious reasoner. Do you know what that means? I can't help laughing still at the trouble I used to have in trying to find out the meaning of that word fallacious, when I was at Miss Dullandoor's seminary for young ladies—hi! hi! some of us were excessively *young* ladies, and we were taught everything by rote, explanations of meanings of anything being quite ignored by Miss Dullandoor. Do you remember her sister? Oh! I'm so stupid to forget that it's exactly thirty years to-day since she died, and you can't be quite that age yet; besides, even if you were, it would require that you should have seen, and recognised, and remembered her on her deathbed about the time of your own birth. Oh! she *was* so funny, both in face and figure. One of the older girls made a portrait of her for me which I have yet. I'll go fetch it; the expression is irresistible—it is killing. Excuse me a minute."

Miss Pritty rose and tripped—she never walked—from the room. During much of the previous con-

versation our hero had been sorely perplexed in his
mind as to his duty in present circumstances.
Having been forbidden to hold any intercourse with
Aileen, he questioned the propriety of his remaining
to spend the evening with her, and had made up his
mind to rise and tear himself away when this
unlooked-for opportunity for a *téte-à-téte* occurred.
Being a man of quick wit and strong will, he did
not neglect it. Turning suddenly to the fair girl,
he said, in a voice low and measured—

"Aileen, your father commanded me to have no
further intercourse with you, and he made me aware
that he had laid a similar injunction on yourself.
I know full well your true-hearted loyalty to him,
and do not intend to induce you to disobey. I ask
you to make no reply to what I say that is not consistent with your promise to your father. For
myself, common courtesy tells me that I may not
leave your presence for a distant land without
saying at least goodbye. Nay, more, I feel that I
break no command in making to you a simple
deliberate statement."

Edgar paused for a moment, for, in spite of the
powerful restraint put on himself, and the intended
sedateness of his words, his feelings were almost too
strong for him.

"Aileen," he resumed, "I may never see you
again. Your father intends that I shall not. Your

looks seem to say that you fear as much. Now, my heart tells me that I *shall*; but, whatever betide, or wherever I go, let me assure you that I will continue to love you with unalterable fidelity. More than this I shall not say, less I could not. You said that these New Testaments"—pointing to a pile of four or five which lay on the table—" are meant to be given to poor men. *I* am a poor man: will you give me one ?"

" Willingly," said Aileen, taking one from the pile.

She handed it to her lover without a single word, but with a tender anxious look that went straight to his heart, and took up its lodging there—to abide for ever !

The youth grasped the book and the hand at once, and, stooping, pressed the latter fervently to his lips.

At that moment Miss Pritty was heard tripping along the passage.

Edgar sprang to intercept her, and closed the door of the boudoir behind him.

" Why, Edgar, you seem in haste !"

" I am, dear aunt ; circumstances require that I should be. Come down-stairs with me. I have stayed too long already. I am going abroad, and may not spend more time with you this evening."

" Going abroad !" exclaimed Miss Pritty, in breathless surprise, " where ? "

" I don't know. To China, Japan, New Zealand,

the North Pole—anywhere. In fact, I've not quite
fixed. Goodbye, dear aunt. Sorry to have seen so
little of you. Goodbye."

He stooped, printed a gentle kiss between Miss
Pritty's wondering eyes, and vanished.

"A most remarkable boy," said the disconcerted
lady, resuming her seat at the tea-table—"so
impulsive and volatile. But he's a dear good boy
nevertheless—was so kind to his mother while she
was alive, and ran away from school when quite
young—and no wonder, for it was a dreadful school,
where they used to torture the boys,—absolutely
tortured them. The head-master and ushers were
tried for it afterwards, I'm told. At all events,
Eddy ran away from it after pulling the master's
nose and kicking the head usher—so it is said,
though I cannot believe it, he is usually so gentle
and courteous.—*Do* have a little more tea. No?
A piece of bun? No? Why, you seem quite
flushed, my love. Not unwell, I trust? No?
Well, then, let us proceed to business."

CHAPTER IV.

DIVERS MATTERS.

CHARLES HAZLIT, Esquire, was a merchant and a
shipowner, a landed proprietor, a manager of banks,
a member of numerous boards and committees, a
guardian of the poor, a volunteer colonel, and a good-
humoured man on the whole, but purse-proud and
pompous. He was also the father of Aileen.

Behold him seated in an elegant drawing-room, in
a splendid mansion at the " west end " (strange that
all aristocratic ends would appear to be west ends!) of
the seaport town which owned him. His blooming
daughter sat beside him at a table, on which lay a
small, peculiar, box. He doated on his daughter,
and with good reason. Their attention was so ex-
clusively taken up with the peculiar box that they
had failed to observe the entrance, unannounced, of
a man of rough exterior, who stood at the door, hat
in hand, bowing and coughing attractively, but without success.

"My darling," said Mr. Hazlit, stooping to kiss
his child—his only child—who raised her pretty little

three-cornered mouth to receive it, "this being your twenty-first birthday, I have at last brought myself to look once again on your sainted mother's jewel-case, in order that I may present it to you. I have not opened it since the day she died. It is now yours, my child."

Aileen opened her eyes in mute amazement. It would seem as though there had been some secret sympathy between her and the man at the door, for he did precisely the same thing. He also crushed his hat somewhat convulsively with both hands, but without doing it any damage, as it was a very hard sailor-like hat. He also did something to his lips with his tongue, which looked a little like licking them.

"Oh papa !" exclaimed Aileen, seizing his hand, "how kind; how—"

"Nay, love, no thanks are due to me. It is your mother's gift. On her deathbed she made me promise to give it you when you came of age, and to train you, up to that age, as far as possible, with a disregard for dress and show. I think your dear mother was wrong," continued Mr. Hazlit, with a mournful smile, "but, whether right or wrong, you can bear me witness that I have sought to fulfil the second part of her dying request, and I now accomplish the first."

He proceeded to unlock the fastenings of the little

box, which was made of some dark metal resembling iron, and was deeply as well as richly embossed on the lid and sides with quaint figures and devices.

Mr. Hazlit had acquired a grand, free-handed way of manipulating treasure. Instead of lifting the magnificent jewels carefully from the casket, he tumbled them out like a gorgeous cataract of light and colour, by the simple process of turning the box upside down.

"Oh papa, take care!" exclaimed Aileen, spreading her little hands in front of the cataract to stem its progress to the floor, while her two eyes opened in surprise, and shone with a lustre that might have made the insensate gems envious. "How exquisite! how inexpressibly beautiful!—oh my dear, darling mother!"—

She stopped abruptly, and tears fluttered from her eyes. In a few seconds she continued, pushing the gems away, almost passionately—

"But I cannot wear them, papa. They are worthless to me."

She was right. She had no need of such gems. Was not her hair golden and her skin alabaster? were not her lips coral and her teeth pearls? and were not diamonds of the purest water dropping at that moment from her down-cast eyes?

"True, my child, and the sentiment does your heart credit; they are worthless, utterly worthless—

mere paste "—at this point the face of the man at
the door visibly changed for the worse—" mere paste,
as regards their power to bring back to us the dear
one who wore them. Nevertheless, in a commercial
point of view "—here the ears of the man at the
door cocked— "they are worth some eight or nine
thousand pounds sterling, so they may as well be
taken care of."

The tongue and lips of the man at the door again
became active. He attempted—unsuccessfully, as
before—to crush his hat, and inadvertently coughed.

Mr. Hazlit's usually pale countenance flushed, and
he started up.

"Hallo ! my man, how came *you* here ?"

The man looked at the door and hesitated in his
attempt to reply to so useless a question.

"How comes it that you enter my house and
drawing-room without being announced ?" asked Mr.
Hazlit, drawing himself up.

"'Cause I wanted to see you, an' I found the
door open, an' there warn't nobody down stair to
announce me," answered the man in a rather surly
tone.

"Oh, indeed ?—ah," said Mr. Hazlit, drawing out a
large silk handkerchief with a flourish, blowing his
nose therewith, and casting it carelessly on the table
so as to cover the jewel-box. "Well, as you are now
here, pray what have you got to say to me ?"

"Your ship the *Seagull* has bin' wrecked, sir, on Toosday night on the coast of Wales."

"I received that unpleasant piece of news on Wednesday morning. What has *that* to do with your visit?"

"Only that I thought you might want divers for to go to the wreck, an' *I'm* a diver—that's all."

The man at the door said this in a very surly tone, for the slight tendency to politeness which had begun to manifest itself while the prospect of "a job" was hopeful, vanished before the haughty manner of the merchant.

"Well, it is just possible that I may require the assistance of divers," said Mr. Hazlit, ringing the bell; "when I do, I can send for you.—John, show this person out."

The hall-footman, who had been listening attentively at the key-hole, and allowed a second or two to elapse before opening the door, bowed with a guilty flush on his face and held the door wide open.

David Maxwell—for it was he—passed out with an angry scowl, and as he strode with noisy tread across the hall, said something uncommonly pithy to the footman about "upstarts" and "puppies," and "people who thought they was made o' different dirt from others," accompanied with many other words and expressions which we may not repeat.

To all of this John replied with bland smiles and

polite bows, hoping that the effects of the interview
might not render him feverish, and reminding him
that if it did he was in a better position than most
men for cooling himself at the bottom of the sea.

"Farewell," said John earnestly; "and if you should
take a fancy to honour us any day with your company
to dinner, *do* send a line to say you're coming."

John did not indulge in this pleasantry until the
exasperated diver was just outside of the house, and
it was well that he was so prudent, for Maxwell
turned round like a tiger and struck with tremendous
force at his face. His hard knuckles met the panel
of the door, in which they left an indelible print, and
at the same time sent a sound like a distant cannon
shot into the library.

"I'm afraid I have been a little too sharp with
him," said Mr. Hazlit, assisting his daughter to re-
place the jewels.

Aileen agreed with him, but as nothing could
induce her to condemn her father with her lips she
made no reply.

"But," continued the old gentleman, "the rascal
had no right to enter my house without ringing. He
might have been a thief, you know. He looked
rough and coarse enough to be one."

"Oh papa," said Aileen entreatingly, "don't be too
hasty in judging those who are sometimes called
rough and coarse. I do assure you I've met many

men in my district who are big and rough and coarse
to look at, but who have the feelings and hearts of
tender women."

"I know it, simple one; you must not suppose
that I judged him by his exterior; I judged him by his
rude manner and conduct, and I do not extend my
opinion of him to the whole class to which he belongs."

It is strange—and illustrative of the occasional
perversity of human reasoning—that Mr. Hazlit did
not perceive that he himself had given the diver cause
to judge him, Mr. Hazlit, very harshly, and the worst
of it was that Maxwell *did*, in his wrath, extend his
opinion of the merchant to the entire class to which
he belonged, expressing a deep undertoned hope that
the "whole bilin' of 'em" might end their days in a
place where he spent many of his own, namely, at
the bottom of the sea. It is to be presumed that he
wished them to be there without the benefit of
diving-dresses!

"It is curious, however," continued Mr. Hazlit,
"that I had been thinking this very morning about
making inquiries after a diver, one whom I have
frequently heard spoken of as an exceedingly able
and respectable man—Balding or Bolding or some
such name, I think."

"Oh! Baldwin, Joe Baldwin, as his intimate
friends call him," said Aileen eagerly. "I know
him well; he is in my district."

" What !" exclaimed Mr. Hazlit, " not one of your paupers ?"

Aileen burst into a merry laugh. " No, papa, no ; not a pauper certainly. He's a well-off diver, and a Wesleyan—a local preacher, I believe—but he lives in my district, and is one of the most zealous labourers in it. Oh ! if you saw him, papa, with his large burly frame and his rough bronzed kindly face, and broad shoulders, and deep bass voice and hearty laugh."

The word suggested the act, for Aileen went off again at the bare idea of Joe Baldwin being a pauper —one at whose feet, she said, she delighted to sit and learn.

" Well, I'm glad to have such a good account of him from one so well able to judge," rejoined her father ; " and as I mean to go visit him without delay I'll be obliged if you'll give me his address."

Having received it, the merchant sallied forth into those regions of the town where, albeit she was not a guardian of the poor, his daughter's light figure was a much more familiar object than his own.

" Does a diver named Baldwin live here ?" asked Mr. Hazlit of a figure which he found standing in a doorway near the end of a narrow passage.

The figure was hazy and indistinct by reason of the heavy wreaths of tobacco-smoke wherewith it was enveloped.

" Yis, sur," replied the figure; " he lives in the door
at the other ind o' the passage. It's not over-light
here, sur; mind yer feet as ye go, an' pay attintion to
your head, for what betune holes in the floor an'
beams in the ceilin', tall gintlemen like you, sur,
come to grief sometimes."

Thanking the figure for its civility, Mr. Hazlit
knocked at the door indicated, but there was no
response.

" Sure it's out they are !" cried the figure from the
other end of the passage. " Joe Baldwin's layin' a
charge under the wreck off the jetty to-day—no
doubt that's what's kep' 'im, and it's washin'-day
with Mrs. Joe, I belave; but I'm his pardner, sur,
an' if ye'll step this way, Mrs. Machowl 'll be only
too glad to see ye, sur, an' I can take yer orders."

Not a little amused by this free-and-easy invitation, Mr. Hazlit entered a small apartment, which
surprised him by its clean and tidy appearance. A
pretty little Irishwoman, with a pert little turned-up
nose, auburn hair so luxuriant that it *could* not be
kept in order, and a set of teeth that glistened in
their purity, invited him to sit down, and wiped a
chair with her apron for his accommodation.

" You've got a nice little place here," remarked
the visitor, looking round him.

" Troth, sur, ye wouldn't have said that if you'd
seen it whin we first came to it. Of all the dirty

places I iver saw! I belave an Irish pig would have scunnered at it, an' held his nose till he got out. It's very well for England, but we was used to cleaner places in the owld country. Hows'iver we've got it made respictable now, and we're not hard to plaze."

This was a crushing reply. It upset Mr. Hazlit's preconceived ideas regarding the two countries so completely that he was perplexed. Not being a man of rapid thought he changed the subject :—

"You are a diver, you say?"

"I am, sur."

"And Mr. Baldwin's partner—if I understand you correctly?"

"Well, we work together—whin we're not workin' apart—pritty regular. He took in hand to train me some months gone by, an' as our two missuses has took a fancy to aich other, we're likely to hold on for some time—barrin' accidents, av coorse."

"Well, then," said Mr. Hazlit, "I came to see Mr. Baldwin about a vessel of mine, which was wrecked a few days ago on the coast of Wales—"

"Och! the *Seagull* it is." exclaimed Rooney.

"The same ; and as it is a matter of importance that I should have the wreck visited without delay, I shall be obliged by your sending your partner to my house this evening."

Rooney promised to send Baldwin up, and took his wife Molly to witness, with much solemnity, that he would not lose a single minute. Thereafter the conversation became general, and at last the merchant left the place much shaken in his previous opinion of Irish character, and deeply impressed with the sagacity of Rooney Machowl.

The result of this visit was that Baldwin was engaged to dive for the cargo of the *Seagull*, and found himself, a few days later, busy at work on the Welsh coast with a staff of men under him, among whom were our friends Rooney Machowl and surly David Maxwell. The latter had at first declined to have anything to do with the job, but, on consideration of the wages, he changed his mind.

CHAPTER V.

TREATS OF PLOTS AND PLANS, ENGINEERING AND OTHERWISE

THE spot where the wreck of the *Seagull* lay was a peaceful sequestered cove or bay on the coast of Anglesea. The general aspect of the neighbouring land was bleak. There were no trees, and few bushes. Indeed, the spire of a solitary little church on an adjoining hill was the most prominent object in the scene. The parsonage belonging to it was concealed by a rise in the ground, and the very small hamlet connected with it was hid like a rabbit in the clefts of some rugged cliffs. The little church was one of those temples which are meant to meet the wants of a rural district, and which cause a feeling of surprise in the minds of town visitors as to where the congregation can come from that fills them.

But, bleak though the country was, the immediate shore was interesting and romantic in its form. In one place perpendicular cliffs, cut up by ragged gorges, descended sheer down into deep water, and

meeting the constant roll of the Irish Channel, even
in calm weather, fringed themselves with lace-work
of foam, as if in cool defiance of the ocean. In another
place a mass of boulders and shattered rocks
stretched out into the sea as if still resistant though
for the time subdued. Elsewhere a half-moon of
yellow sand received the ripples with a kiss, suggestive of utter conquest and the end of strife.

As we have said, the spot was peaceful, for, at the
time to which we refer, ocean and air were still, but
ah! those who have not dwelt near the great deep
and beheld its fury when roused can form but a
faint conception of the scene that occurred there on
the night in which the *Seagull* went down!

Mr. Hazlit thought of the place as something like
the region of a " bad debt,"—where a portion of his
wealth had been wrecked. Some knew it as the
hated spot where they had suffered the loss of all
their fortune ; but others there were, who, untouched
by the thought of material gain or loss, knew it as the
scene of the wreck of all their earthly hopes—for the
Seagull had been a passenger ship, and in that quiet
bay God in His providence had dealt some of the
most awful blows that human beings are capable
of bearing.

Close to a bald cliff on the northern shore the
foretopmast of the wreck rose a few feet above the
calm water. In a cove of the cliff the remains of a

mast or yard lay parallel with a deep and thick
mass of wreckage, which had surged out and into
that cove on the fatal night with such violence that
it now lay in small pieces, like giant matchwood. On
a patch of gravel not far from that cliff a husband
and father had wandered for many days, after being
saved—he knew not how—gazing wistfully, hopelessly at the sea which had swallowed up wife and
children and fortune. He had been a "successful"
gold-digger! On that patch of gravel scenes of
terrible suspense had been enacted. Expectant ones
had come to inquire whether those whom they
sought had *really* embarked in that vessel, while
grave and sympathetic but worn-out or weary men
of the Coast-guard, stood ready to give information
or to defend the wreck.

In the church on the hill there were dreadful
marks on the floor, where the recovered bodies had
lain for a time, while frantic relations came and
went day by day to search for and claim their dead.
Ah, reader, we are not mocking you with fiction.
What we refer to is fact. We saw it with our eyes.
Peaceful though that spot looked—and often looks
—it was once the scene of the wildest of storms, the
most terrible of mercantile disasters, and the deepest
of human woe.

But we are mingling thoughts with memories.
The wreck which has crept into our mind is that of

the *Royal Charter*. The *Seagull*, although a passenger ship, and wrecked near the same region, does not resemble *that!*

At the time of which we write, Joe Baldwin and his men had already saved a considerable portion of the cargo, but during his submarine explorations and meditations Joe had conceived the idea that there was some possibility of saving the vessel itself, for, having recoiled from its first shock and sunk in deep water, the hull was comparatively uninjured.

But Joe, although a good diver, was not a practical engineer. He knew himself to be not a very good judge of such matters, and was too modest to suggest anything to competent submarine engineers. He could not, however, help casting the thing about in his mind for some time. At last, one evening while reading a newspaper that had been got from a passing boat, he observed the return of the ship in which his young friend Edgar Berrington had gone to India. At once he wrote the following letter:—

"MY DEAR MISTER EDGAR,—I'm in a fix here. It's my opinion there's a chance of savin' a wreck if only good brains was set to work to do it. It would pay if we was to succeed. If you happen to be on the loose just now, as is likely, run over an' see what you think of it.—Yours to command,

"J. B."

Our hero received the letter, at once acted on it, and in a few days was on the spot.

"What a change there is in you, my dear sir!' said Joe, looking with admiration at the browned, stalwart youth before him; "why, you've grown mustaches!"

"I couldn't help it, Joe," replied Edgar; "they *would* come, and I had no time to shave on board. —But now, tell me about this wreck."

When Edgar heard that the vessel belonged to Mr. Hazlit his first impulse was to have nothing to do with it. He felt that any interference in regard to it would seem like a desire to thrust himself before the merchant's notice—and that, too, in a needy manner, as if he sought employment at his hands; but on consideration he came to the conclusion that he might act as a wire-puller, give Baldwin the benefit of his knowledge, and allow him to reap the credit and the emoluments. But for a long time the honest diver would not listen to such a suggestion, and was only constrained to give in at last when Edgar threatened to leave him altogether.

"By the way, have you seen Miss Aileen since you came home?" asked Baldwin, while the two friends were seated in the cabin of the diver's vessel poring, pencil in hand, over several sheets of paper on which were sundry mysterious designs.

"No; I was on the point of paying a visit to my good aunt Miss Pritty, with ulterior ends in view, when your letter reached me and brought me here. To say truth, your note arrived very opportunely, for I was engaged at the time in rather a hard struggle between inclination and duty—not feeling quite sure whether it was right or wise to throw myself in her way just now, for, as you may easily believe, I have not, during my comparatively short absence, made a fortune that is at all likely to satisfy the requirements of her father."

"I suppose not," returned the diver. "No doubt, at gold-diggin's an' diamond-fields an' such-like one does hear of a man makin' a find that enables him to set up his carriage an' four, and ride, mayhap at a tremendous pace, straight on to ruin by means of it, but as a rule people don't pick up sovereigns like stones either at home or abroad. It's the experience of most men, that steady perseverance leads by the shortest road to competence, if not to wealth.—But that's beside the question. I think you did right, Mister Eddy—excuse an old servant, sir, if it's taking too much liberty to use the old familiar name,—you did right in coming here instead of going there."

"So thought I, Baldy—you see that I too can take liberties,—else I should not have come. Your letter solved the difficulty, for, when I was at the very height of the struggle before mentioned—at equipoise so to speak,—and knew not whether to go to the right or to the left, *that* decided me. I regarded it as a leading of Providence."

Baldwin turned a rather sudden look of surprise on his young companion.

"A leading of Providence, Mr. Eddy! I never heard you use such an expression before."

"True, but I have learned to use it since I went to sea," replied our hero quietly.

"That's strange," rejoined the diver in a low voice, as if he feared to scare the young man from a subject that was very near his own heart, "very strange, for goin' to sea has not often the effect of makin' careless young fellows serious—though it sometimes has, no doubt. How was it, if I—"

"Yes, Baldy," interrupted Edgar, with a pleasant smile, laying his hand on the diver's huge shoulder, "I don't mind making a confidant of you in this as in other matters. I'll tell you,—the story is short enough. When I parted from Aileen, she made me a present of a New Testament from a pile that she happened to have by her to give to the poor people. To be more particular, I asked for one, and she consented to let me have it. You see I wanted a keepsake! Well, when at sea, I read the Testament regularly, night and morning, for Aileen's sake, but God in His great love led me at last to read it for the sake of Him whose blessed life and death it records."

"Then you've fairly hauled down the enemy's colours and hoisted those of the Lord?" asked Baldwin.

"I have been led to do so," replied the youth modestly but firmly.

"Bless the Lord!" said the diver in a low tone as he grasped Edgar's hand, while he bowed his head for a moment.

Presently he looked up, and seemed about to resume the subject of conversation when Edgar interrupted him—

"Have you seen or heard anything of Aileen since I left?"

"Nothing, except that she's been somewhat out of sorts, and her father has sent her up to London for a change."

"Has he gone to London with her?"

"No, I believe not; he's taken up a good deal wi' the cargo o' this ship, and comes down to see us now and then, but for the most part he remains at home attendin' to business."

"Have you spoken to him about raising the hull of the ship?"

"Not yet. He evidently thinks the thing impossible—besides, I wanted to hear your opinion on the matter before sayin' anything about it."

"Well, come, let us go into it at once," said the youth, turning to the sheets of paper before him and taking up a pencil. "You see, Baldwin, this trip of mine as second engineer has been of good service to me in many ways, for, besides becoming practically acquainted with everything connected with marine engines, I have acquired considerable knowledge of things relating to ships in general, and am all the more able to afford you some help in this matter of raising the ship. I've been studying a book written by a member of the firm whose dresses you patronise,[1] which gives a thorough account in detail of everything connected with diving, and in it there is reference to the various modes that have hitherto been successful in the raising of sunken vessels."

"I've heard of it, but not seen it," said Baldwin. "Of course I know somewhat about raisin' ships, havin' once or twice lent a hand, but I've no head for engineerin'. What are the various modes you speak of? *That's* not one of 'em, is it?"

He pointed, with a grave smile as he spoke, to the outline of a female head which Edgar had been absently tracing on the paper.

"Well, no," replied the youth, scribbling out the head, "that's not one of Siebe and Gorman's appliances and yet I venture to prophesy that that head will have a good deal to do with the raising of

---

[1] *The Conquest of the Sea,* by Henry Siebe.

the *Seagull!* However, don't let's waste more time. Here you are. The first method,—that of putting empty casks in the hold so as to give the hull a floating tendency, and then mooring lighters over it and pushing chains under it,—we may dismiss at once, as being suitable only for small vessels; but the second method is worth considering, namely, that of fixing air-bags of indiarubber in the hold, attaching them to the sides, and then inflating them all at the same time by means of a powerful air-pump. We could get your divers to pass chains under her, and, when she began to rise could haul on these chains by means of lighters moored above, and so move the wreck inshore till she grounded. What say you to that?"

Baldwin shook his head. "She's too big, I fear, for such treatment."

"Good-sized vessels have been raised by these air-bags of late," said Edgar. "Let me see: there were the brig *Ridesdale*, of 170 tons burthen, sunk off Calshot Castle, and Her Majesty's gun-brig *Partridge*, 180 tons, and the brig *Dauntless*, 179 tons, and last, but not least, the *Prince Consort*, at Aberdeen, an iron paddle-steamer of 607 tons, and the dead weight lifted was 560 tons, including engines and boilers."

Still Baldwin shook his head, remarking that the *Seagull* was full 900 tons.

"Well, then," resumed the young engineer, "here is still another method. We might send down your men to make all the openings,—ports, windows, etc. —water-tight, fix a shield over the hole she knocked in her bottom on the cliffs, and then, by means of several water-pumps reaching from above the surface to the hold, clear her of water. When sufficiently floated by such means a steam-tug could haul her into port. The iron steamship *London* was, not long ago, raised and saved at Dundee in that way. She rose four feet after the pumps had been worked only two hours, and while she was being towed into dock the pumps were still kept going. It was a great success—and so may it be in this case. Then, you know, we might construct a pontoon by making a raft to float on a multitude of empty barrels, pass chains under the *Seagull* and fix them to this pontoon at low water, so that when the tide rose she would rise perforce along with the pontoon and tide, and could be moved inshore till she grounded ; then, waiting for low tide, we could taughten the chains again, and repeat the process till we got her ashore. Or, better still, we could hire Siebe and Gorman's patent pontoon, which, if I mistake not, is much the same thing that I now suggest carried out to perfection."

"I'm not sure that the pontoon you speak of has been launched yet. I'm afraid it's only in model," said Baldwin.

" More 's the pity," rejoined Edgar, " but I can go to London and ascertain. In any case, I shall have to go to London to make inquiries, and secure the necessary apparatus."

" Are you sure," said Baldwin, with a look of great solemnity, " that your going to London has nothing whatever to do with apparatus of *that* sort ? "

He placed a blunt forefinger, as he spoke, on the obliterated sketch of the female head.

" Oh you suspicious old fellow ! " replied Edgar ; " come, you *are* presuming now.—We will change the subject, and go on deck."

" Human natur 's the same everywhere," observed Baldwin, with a quiet laugh as he rose. " Same with me exactly when I was after Susan. For one glance of her black eye I 'd have gone straight off to China or Timbuctoo at half-an-hour's notice. Well, well ! —Now, Mister Eddy, don't you think it would be as well for you to go down and have a look at the wreck ? You 'll then be better able to judge as to what 's best to be done, an' I 've got a noo dress by the firm of Denayrouze, with a speakin'-apparatus, which 'll fit you. I got it for myself, and we 're much about a size—barrin' the waist, in which I have the advantage of you as to girth. Their noo pump and lamp, too, will interest you. See, here is the pump."

As he spoke, the diver pointed to a pump which commended itself at first sight by its extreme simplicity. Whether or not it was better than the more complex, but well-tried, pumps of other makers, our hero was well aware could only be proved by time and experience. Meanwhile he was favourably impressed with it.

The peculiarities of the pump referred to were, first, and most obvious, that it had no outer wooden case or box, and the parts were exceedingly few and simple. It was on the lever principle, the cylinders, instead of the pistons, being movable. The pistons were fixed to a bed-plate and pointed upwards, so that the pump was, as it were, turned upside down, a position which, among other advantages, allowed of the plungers being covered with water, through which the air was forced and partially cooled. Another and important peculiarity was an air-reservoir which received air from the pump direct, and then passed it on to the diver, so that even if the pumps should stop working there would still be a supply of air flowing down to the diver for several minutes. The lamp referred to was also a novelty, inasmuch as it was supplied with air by a separate tube from the reservoir in the same way as if it were a separate human diver. The Henkie and Davis lamp burns, on the other hand, entirely without air, by means of certain acids. That of Siebe and Gorman is an electric lamp. Both are said to be effective and economical.

Putting on the new dress, our hero was soon ready
to descend, with the lamp burning in his hand.

"There are three men down just now," said Baldwin as he was about to screw on the mouth-piece,
"two of 'em bein' your old friends Maxwell and
Rooney Machowl. They've been down about three
hours, and won't be up for an hour yet. See that
you don't foul them in your wanderings below. The
other man, Jem Hogg—an' he's well named—is the
laziest chap I ever had to do with. I do believe he
sometimes goes to sleep under water!"

"Is that possible?" asked Edgar.

"Possible? ay, I've caught 'em takin' a snooze
before now. Why, I've known a man *smoke* under
water. There was one of our fellows once got a
comrade to let him keep his pipe in his mouth while
he screwed on the front glass; you see he couldn't
have put it in his mouth *after* that was fixed; but
he was well paid. For a time he smoked away well
enough, and the draught of air carried off the smoke
through the escape-valve, but an extra strong puff
sent a spark out o' the bowl, which went straight into
his eye. He spat out the pipe, and nearly drove in
the glasses in his useless efforts to get at his eye, and
then he tugged at the lines like fury, and, when
we got him on deck he danced about like wildfire, as
if he'd been shod with indyrubber instead of bein'
weighted with lead. We thought he had gone mad,

and held him fast till we got his helmet off. It
cost him a month in hospital before that eye was
cured."

"That being the case, I won't smoke while below,
said Edgar, laughing; "screw away."

The glass was fastened, and our hero quickly disappeared under the sea.

CHAPTER VI.

A SUNKEN WRECK INSPECTED, SUNDRY WONDERFUL DOINGS UNDER WATER RECORDED, AND VARIOUS PLANS SUCCESSFULLY CARRIED OUT.

THE vessel which Edgar Berrington had left his native element to inspect was a large barque. It had gone to the bottom only a few months after having been launched. The cargo, being intended for the Cape of Good Hope colony, was of a miscellaneous character, and some of it was of course ruined by water, but much remained almost uninjured, or only a little damaged.

It was for the purpose of raising the latter portion of the cargo that Baldwin and his men had been engaged by Mr. Hazlit. Hitherto the divers had been extremely successful. With the usual appliances of slings, chains, shears and windlasses, etc., they had already recovered a large quantity of goods, and were still busy in the hold when Edgar went down.

As we have said, the wreck lay in comparatively deep water—about ten fathoms. The ladder which descended from the side of the diver's vessel was not

F

two fathoms in length, so that after reaching the
lowest round, Edgar had to continue his descent by
slipping down the rope which hung from the ladder
and was weighted at the bottom with a stone.

On reaching the ground he knelt, set down the
lamp, and attached his guide-line to the stone.
While thus engaged he looked with much interest at
his little lamp, which burned as brightly and steadily
down in the depths of ocean as if on land, while
from its chimney the air which gave it life rose
upwards in a constant stream of bubbles. The water
being dense and very dark its light did not penetrate
far, but close to the bull's-eye it was sufficiently
strong to enable our hero to see what he was about.
Having fixed the line, he was about to move in the
direction of the wreck when he received one pull on
his life-line. Replying to it with one pull—" all
right "—he was again about to move, when a strange
unearthly sound filled his ears, and he smiled to
think that in his interest about the lamp and fastening his guide-line he had totally forgotten the
speaking apparatus connected with his helmet.

" How d'ee git on down there ? " inquired the
voice, which sounded strangely mysterious, not to
say unpleasant, in his confined metal head-piece.

" Splendidly," he replied, not applying his mouth
to any orifice in his helmet—for there *was* no opening into the speaking-tube—but simply giving

utterance to the word in his usual manner. "I've just fixed my line and am going to move on."

"Go ahead, and luck go with 'ee," was the prompt reply from Joe Baldwin.

We have said that there was no opening into the helmet in connection with the speaking apparatus, such not being necessary. It was quite sufficient that the speaking-tube was fastened to the outside of the helmet, just over a sort of cavity formed inside by means of what we may style an interior patch of metal. The sound passed *through* the head-piece and up the tube—or *vice versa*—and thus even though the tube should get broken and filled with water, no evil result could follow to the diver.

Suddenly Berrington was again arrested.

"Hallo!" shouted Baldwin.

"Hallo! well?" was sent up in reply, and the voice that came from below came out at the mouth-piece above, so soft and faint and far-far-away-like that it seemed to Joe to belong to another world, and had to be listened to attentively to be understood.

"D' you think you could read by the light of your lamp?"

"Yes, I'm sure I could."

"Look out then; I'm sending you down a copy o' the *Times*."

The youth looked up, and now perceived the advantage of the *fourth* hole or window, just

over the forehead, which is peculiar to the Denayrouze helmet, most others having only three openings. He could look up by merely raising his eyes,
whereas with the other helmets it is necessary to
bend well back in order to get the front glass to
face upwards. Afterwards he found that there were
some who objected to this glass on the ground that
as divers when below, and in total or partial darkness, are constantly butting their heads against
beams and other portions of wrecks, the upper glass
would be in frequent danger of being broken, but to
this it was replied that it might be well guarded by
powerful cross-bars. The point we believe is still an
open question. At all events the upper glass was
found useful on the occasion to which we refer, for,
looking up through it, our amateur diver saw a stone
coming down to him. It was lowered by a piece of
twine, and tied to it was an old *Times* newspaper.
Detaching and unfolding it Berrington set his lamp
on the sand, and, seating himself beside it, found
that he could read with perfect ease!

Intimating the fact to his friend above, he returned the paper and began his explorations.

He had been lowered close beside the stern of the
wreck, that he might be as far as possible from the
divers who were at work in the hold, and had taken
only half a dozen steps in the direction of it when
its vast bulk appeared above him, looming through

the dark water like a darker cloud. For some time he went carefully round it, minutely examining the rudder and stern-post and the parts connected therewith, all of which he found to be uninjured. Then, passing along the starboard side, he proceeded in his inspection until he reached a point which he judged to be nearly amidships. Glancing upwards, he thought he could see the life-lines and air-pipes of the other divers. To make sure he signalled for more air. This he did by means of the air-pipe— two pulls—instead of using the speaking-tube, because the air-pipe and life-line are never for a single instant let go or neglected by the attendants above, whereas the speaking-tube, on that occasion, was merely tried for the first time by these divers as an experiment. Immediately the puffing at the airhole showed that the men at the pumps were on the alert. Edgar now closed his front valve so that no air at all was suffered to escape through it; the dress began to inflate, and in a few seconds was swelled out pretty tightly.

Up to that period he had felt no further inconvenience than a slight pressure on the drums of his ears, which was relieved by the usual method of swallowing the saliva, which action has the effect of opening a small, and not *easily* opened, internal orifice or passage to the drum, and thus, by admitting the condensed air to the interior of the ear, enables it to resist the pressure on the outside. Each inspiration of air has the same effect on the lungs, and the pressure, inside and outside, being *at once* equalised, is in their case unfelt, although it remains and tests the strength of the animal tissues. Hence it is a recognised rule that a man who has at any time spat blood is unsuited to a diver's work, as his weak blood-vessels are apt to burst. But now, under the increased pressure, our hero felt his ears affected considerably, and other disagreeable sensations came on —such as singing in the head, etc.; nevertheless, confident in his strength, he persevered.

Presently the amount of air in his dress more than counterbalanced the weight of lead about him— great though it was—and he began to rise like a cork—slowly. In a few seconds his head was close to the lines and air-pipes which he observed passing over the bulwarks of the wreck and down into the hold. Afraid lest he should get entangled in them he caught hold of the end of a piece of iron which projected near him and checked his upward rise. At the same time he opened his valves ; the air rushed out, and he immediately descended. On reaching the bottom he regulated the valves so as to give himself just enough of air to permit of his *keeping* the ground, and moving about as before.

He had observed, while up, that one set of lines diverged away from the wreck, but this did not

strike him at the time as being noteworthy. After
a few minutes he signalled his friends above, and
shouted by means of the speaking-tube—

" Pay out the air-pipe and life-lines and give me
free play."

This being done he could pass under the lines of
the other divers, and examined the wreck as far as
the bow, where he found an immense hole, partially
filled by a mass of the rock which had originally
driven it in. This of itself was sufficient to have
sunk the vessel. In order to examine the port side
of the wreck he returned towards the stern and
signalled for more air. As before, he rose to the
bulwarks, over which he passed by a slight effort, and,
opening the valves, dropt gently, like a bird, upon
the deck. Walking across it slowly, and with some
difficulty, owing to the broken spars and cordage with
which it was encumbered, he passed over the port
bulwarks and lowered himself again to the bottom.
A careful examination showed him that no injury
worth mentioning had been sustained on that side,
and he finally came to the conclusion that the large
hole in the starboard bow was the only serious
damage done to the hull.

To make sure of this he returned to it, and
satisfied himself as to its exact nature and extent.
While thus engaged, his attention was again directed
to the diverging line and air-pipe before referred to.

Following these up he came to a mass of rocks, in a
snug corner of which he found a diver fast asleep.
At first he could scarcely believe his eyes, but when
he cautiously held the lantern close to the man's
front glass all doubt was removed, for not only were
the eyes of the sleeper tightly closed, but the opening and shutting of his nostrils, coupled with certain
regular motions about the lips, gave unquestionable
evidence that the man was snoring vigorously,
although, of course, no sound passed the metal
covering that hermetically sealed his head.

While Edgar gazed at the slumberer, around whose
form a number of small fish were prying inquiringly,
he observed that his life-line received a jerk, and
came to the correct conclusion that the attendants
above, alarmed at the absense of motion in the diver's
life-line and air-pipe, had signalled to know if all was
right.   Of course he expected that the sleeper would
give no reply, and would, according to rule in such
cases, be hauled up without delay.   What then was his
astonishment to see the man slowly lay hold of his life-
line with his left hand, give it a single tug to indicate
that all was right, and then settle himself more
comfortably to continue his submarine slumbers !

Our hero gave vent to an uncontrollable burst of
laughter, which, however, resounded so horribly in his
ears that he checked it suddenly and began to consider what he should do in order to punish the idler

Remembering to have heard it said that divers might communicate with each other with their voices by bringing their helmets into contact, so that the sound should vibrate through both, he resolved to test this and try an effect. Hooking the lantern to his belt behind, in such a way that its light was concealed, he kneeled down beside the diver—who, he had no doubt, was the Jem Hogg mentioned to him by Baldwin—and rested his helmet on the rock, in such a way that the side of it was brought into contact with the back of Jem's head-piece. No sooner did it touch than the snoring became audible. Feeling assured, therefore, of success, our hero drew in a long breath and gave vent to a Red-Indian yell that rendered himself completely deaf. Its effect on the sleeper was electric. Edgar could just hear the beginning of a responsive yell of terror when Jem's springing up separated the helmets and produced silence. At first the scared man stood up and stared right before him in a state of wild amazement, while Edgar took care to stand directly behind him, out of sight. A man in a diving dress cannot turn his head round so as to look over his shoulder. When he wishes to see behind him he must needs turn round. Seeing nothing in front to account for the alarming sound, Jem began to turn, but Edgar knew that this motion would have the effect of twisting their lines and pipes together. He therefore seized Jem sud-

denly round the chest, and, being a much larger and
stronger man, held him like a vice in the grasp of
his left arm while he pommelled him heartily with
his right all over the back and ribs. At the same
time he punished him considerably with his knees,
and then, a sudden fancy striking him, he placed his
helmet against that of Jem, and began to laugh,
howl, and yell like a maniac, the laughter being
rendered very real and particularly effective owing
to the shrieks of terror which he then heard issuing
from the horrified diver. Not content with this he
seized his lantern and passed it smartly in front of
his victim's front glass, in the hope that the unwonted
and unaccountable glare might add to his consternation. That he had not failed in his intention was
made plain by the shock which he immediately felt
thrilling Jem's frame from head to foot.

Strong though he was, however, our hero was not
powerful enough to prevent the struggle from agitat-
ing the air-pipes and lines to such an extent that
those in charge above became alarmed, and signalled
down to Jem to know if all was right. Edgar
observed the jerk, and felt the diver make a violent
effort to disengage one hand, with the intention, no
doubt, of replying; he therefore held him all the
tighter, and seizing the line replied for him—" All
right." At the same moment his own line received
one jerk, to which he quickly replied in the same

CAUGHT NAPPING.—PAGE 90.

manner, and then resumed his belabouring, which, being delivered under water, required to be done vigorously in order to have any satisfactory effect. While thus engaged, and during a momentary pause in his howlings, he heard a faint voice come down his speaking-tube, and instantly removed his head from Jim's in order to prevent the latter hearing it.

"What on earth are you about down there?"

"Never mind; all right; attend to signals!" answered Edgar sharply; then, being pretty well fatigued with his exertions, he suddenly gave four pulls at Jem's line with such good-will as almost to haul the attendant at the other end into the sea. At the same instant he relaxed his grip and Jem Hogg shot upwards like a submarine rocket!

While this struggle was going on at the bottom, the attendants above were, as we have said, greatly perplexed, and it is certain that they would have hauled both divers up but for the reassuring signals of young Berrington.

"I say, Bill," remarked one of the couple who held Jem Hogg's lines, "Jem seems to be doin' somethin' uncommon queer—he's either got hold of a conger-eel by the tail, or he's amoosin himself by dancin' a hornpipe."

"Why, boys," answered Bill, who was one of the attendants on Edgar, "I do believe Mr. Berrington has got hold o' somethin' o' the same sort. See here:

his line is quiverin' as if a grampus was nibblin' at
the end of it.   Hadn't we better haul 'im up, sir?"

He addressed Joe Baldwin, who chanced to come
on deck at t'ie moment.

" Haul 'im up—no, why?"

" Why, sir, just look at the lines an' pipes."

" Have you signalled down?" asked Joe.

" Yes, sir, an' he 's answered ' all right.'"

" So 's Jem, sir, signalled the same," said one of
the latter's attendants.

Baldwin looked anxiously at the lines, and went
quickly to the speaking-tube, to which he applied
his ear. A look of surprise mingled with the
anxiety as he put his lips to the tube.

It was at this moment that he sent down the
message before referred to, and received Edgar's
prompt reply.

" All right," said Baldwin, turning gravely to his
men, while a little gleam of intelligence and humour
twinkled in his grey eyes.   " When a man signals
' all right,' he *must* be all right, you know.   Let 'em
alone, but stand by and mind your signals."

He had scarcely finished speaking when the man
at Jem's life-line gave a shout, and held on, as if to
an angry shark.

" Hallo! hi! haul in.   Lend a hand!"

He said no more, and did not require to, for
willing hands came to the rescue.

In a few seconds poor Jem Hogg was hauled inboard, and tumbled on the deck, where he lay rolling about for some time, and kicking as if in a fit.

"Hold him fast, Bill! Off with his mouth-piece," cried Baldwin, kneeling on the writhing diver; "why, what's wrong, Jem?"

"Wrong?" gasped Jem, as soon as his glass was off; "wrong? hey!—haul me up! hi!—"

These exclamations terminated in a fearful yell, and it was plain that Jem was about to relapse into hysterics or a fit, when Baldwin, lifting him in his arms, planted him sitting-wise, and with some violence, on a seat.

"Come, none o' *that*," he said sternly. "Off with his helmet, Bill. If you don't quiet yourself, I'll chuck you overboard—d'ee hear?"

Somewhat reassured by this remark, and having his helmet and weights removed, Jem Hogg looked about him with bloodshot eyes and a countenance that was almost sea-green with terror.

"There's nothin' bu'st about your dress," said Baldwin, examining it, "nor broken about the helmet. What on earth's wrong with you?"

"Wrong?" shouted Jem again, while a horrible grin distorted his unhandsome visage; "wrong? hey! oh! I've seen—seen the—ho!—'

Another relapse seemed imminent, but Baldwin held up a warning finger, which restored him, and

then the poor man went on by slow degrees, and
with many gasping interruptions, to tell how, when
busily engaged at work in the hold of the wreck, he
had been suddenly seized by a " Zanthripologus," or
some such hideous creature, with only one eye, like
a glaring carbuncle in its stomach, and dragged right
out o' the hold, overboard, taken to the bottom, and
there bashed and battered among the rocks, until
all his bones were smashed; squeezed by the
monster's tentacles—sixteen feet long at the very
least—until all his ribs were broke, and his heart
nigh forced out of his mouth, and finally pitched
right up to the surface with one tremendous swing
of its mighty tail !

All this and a great deal more was related by the
unfortunate diver, while having his dress removed,
his volubility increasing as his fears were allayed,
but he was not fairly restored to his wonted stateof
mind until he had swallowed a stiff glass of grog,
and been put into his hammock, where, in his sleep,
he was heard to protest with great fervour that he
wouldn't go under water again for any sum short of
ten hundred thousand million pounds !

Meanwhile our amateur diver continued his
inspection of the wreck.   Returning to the deck he
went down into the hold.

The idea occurred to him that the other divers
might also be indulging in a siesta.   He therefore

left his lamp on the deck behind him. The hold was very dark, and at first he could see nothing. As he could hear nothing, he fancied that the men could not be there, but he was somewhat rudely corrected in this error by receiving a severe blow on the helmet from a large box which, having just been attached to the slings, was being hauled up by the men at the windlass overhead. The blow knocked him off a beam on which he stood, and he fell on the cargo below, fortunately, however, without evil result, owing to the medium in which he half-floated. Presently his eyes became accustomed to the faint light that penetrated from above, and he saw an indistinct figure moving slowly towards him, with a sprawling motion. As it drew near, the huge head and distended form proved it to be a diver. He was guiding the box above mentioned, and had let it slip, when it came so violently against Edgar's helmet. Not wishing to be recognised at first, our amateur drew back into a darker spot and watched.

The diver bent his head close to the slings, apparently to see that all was secure, and gave a signal with his line on which the box moved slowly up. A few minutes later it was deposited on the deck of the vessel overhead, and added to the heap of goods which had previously been recovered from the deep.

The diver sprawled slowly back into darkness again. As he disappeared, a similar figure became faintly visible, guiding another box of goods. The box was sent up as before, and now Edgar was convinced that Rooney Machowl and his comrade David Maxwell—unlike their sleepy-headed companion— were busy at work.

Thousands of pounds' worth of property is saved in this manner by divers every year—not only on the coasts of England, but all over the world, whereever human enterprise and commerce have touched, or costly ships gone down.

As we have said, a large portion of the cargo of the *Seagull* had already been recovered. During the process a healthy spirit of emulation had arisen among the men as to which of them should send up most of the sunken property. Rooney and Maxwell were confessedly the best divers among them, but the rivalry between these two had degenerated, on the part of Maxwell, into a spirit of jealousy. Under the influence of this, even Rooney's good-nature had to some extent given way, and frequent disputes and semi-quarrels were the result. But these quarrels were always made up, and the two were soon as good friends as ever.

At this time, however, while Edgar Berrington stood watching them, these two men seemed to have found an apple of discord of unusual size—to judge from the energetic display of feeling which it occasioned. Edgar never ascertained what the bale in dispute contained, but he saw them appear rather suddenly and simultaneously, dragging it between them. The violent gesticulations of the two showed that their spirits were greatly roused, both having evidently resolved to claim and keep possession of the bale. At last one of them struck the other a severe blow on the chest, which, though it did not hurt him, caused him to stumble and fall. From his smaller size Edgar judged the striker to be Rooney. Before the other could recover, he had fastened his slings to the bale, and given the signal to hoist—intending to go up with it, but Maxwel caught him by the legs and attempted to drag him off, whereupon Rooney kicked as hard as his suspended position would admit of, and in his struggles kicked in one of the glasses of his comrade's helmet. The water instantly began to rush in, and he would certainly have been suffocated had he not signalled quickly, and been hauled up to the surface without delay. At the same time Rooney Machowl signalled to be hauled up in haste, and appeared on deck of the attendant vessel, in dreadful anxiety as to the consequence of his violent conduct under water.

But Maxwell was not seriously injured. He had indeed been half-suffocated, and had to be invalided for a few days, but soon he and Rooney were at work again, as good—or, if you will, as bad—friends as ever!

After this incident Edgar received a pull on his life-line, to which he replied "All right." Immediately after, and while he was in the act of rising from the hold of the wreck by the process of retaining his air until it floated him, he heard Baldwin's voice saying—

"You've kicked up a pretty shindy among my men, Mister Edgar, since you went under. Don't you think you'd better come up?"

"Yes, I'm coming directly," he replied.

"There's a letter here for you—just brought off by a boat."

"All right; send me more air."

While this order was being obeyed, Edgar made his way to the ladder-line, being guided thereto by his guide-line, and then, shutting his valves, he quickly inflated his dress which soon floated him, so that he used the rope depending from the ladder merely to guide him upwards. As he ascended the light became gradually stronger, the pressure of water also decreased, obliging him to open his valves and let out air which was becoming superabundant. At last he emerged from the sea, was assisted over the side, and two men began to divest him of his dress.

While thus occupied he read his letter. It was from the owners of the steamer in which he had made his recent voyage. Not being aware of his distance from London they merely asked him to call, as they wished to talk with him on a matter of importance.

"I wish they had mentioned what the matter was," said Edgar, with a troubled look, as he and Baldwin descended to the cabin. "It may be important enough to justify my returning to London at once, and yet may not be worth more than a walk of half a mile."

"True, Mister Edgar," said Baldwin. "However, as you say you 've examined the hull well, and feel sure it can be raised, there 's no reason why you shouldn't go see about the apparatus required, and so kill two birds with one stone. Meanwhile, I 'll write to Mr. Hazlit, recommending him to try to raise the wreck, and he 's pretty sure to take my advice."

In accordance with this plan Edgar returned to London. We will not however trace his future steps in regard to the *Seagull*. It is sufficient to say that his advice was acted on. The divers tightly closed the hole in the bow of the wreck, they also stopped up every other orifice in her, and then pumped her out until at last she floated, was towed into dock, and finally repaired.

Thus were several thousands of pounds saved to Mr. Hazlit, and not only to him, but to the world, for a lost ship—unlike a dropt purse—is a *total* loss to the human race.

CHAPTER VII.

HISTORICAL BUT NOT HEAVY.

THERE can be no question of the fact that authentic history sends its roots into the subsoil of fabulous antiquity. In turning to the records of submarine exploration we are staggered on the very threshold of the question with obvious absurdity. We are depressed. We seek to dive into our subject, but find it too deep for us. If we were to put on the latest "patent improved diving-dress," with all its accompaniments of double-extra pumps, pipes, powers, and purchases, and descend to a depth of antiquity that would suffice to collapse a whale, we should find nothing but idiotic speculation in the midst of chaotic darkness.

In this chapter we shall give a mere outline, and even that somewhat disjointed, of the subject of diving. We feel tempted to pass by the fabulous period altogether, but fear lest, in our effort to eschew the false, we do damage to the true. Perhaps, therefore, it were well to walk humbly in the beaten path of our forefathers, and begin at the beginning.

It is not certain whether Adam was a diver. There is reason to believe that he wore no "dress" of any kind at first, so that, if he dived at all, he must have used his natural powers alone. These powers, we learn from the best authorities, are barely sufficient to enable a man to stay under water for two minutes at the furthest. Experience corroborates these "best authorities." It has been asserted that pearl-divers can sometimes stay under water as long as three, four, and even five minutes, but we don't believe the assertion. If the reader does, we have no hesitation in pronouncing him—or her—credulous.

To return to Adam. We have no doubt whatever that he—perhaps Eve also—could dive. It is possible, though not probable, that they "guddled" small trout in the streams of Paradise, and dived for the big ones in the deeper pools. We *may* be wrong in supposing that they did, but he would certainly be bold who should assert that they did *not*. Unfortunately neither Adam nor Eve used the pen, therefore we have no authentic records as to the art of diving at that period of the world's history.

The first writer who makes reference to diving is Homer, who is supposed to have lived somewhere about a thousand years before the Christian era, and he refers to it not as a novelty but in an off-hand way that proves it to have been at that time a well-known art, practised for the purpose of obtaining oysters. Then we find Æschylus comparing mental vision to the strong natural eye of the "deep diver." But Thucydides speaks more definitely of divers having been employed at the siege of Syracuse to cut down barriers which had been constructed below water; to damage the Grecian vessels while attempting to enter the harbour, and, generally, to go under and injure the enemy's ships. All this inclines us to think they must at that time have learned to supplement their natural powers with artificial.

Livy mentions the fact that the ancients employed divers for the purpose of recovering property from the sea. The Rhodians had a law fixing the share of the recovered treasure which was due to the divers who saved it. According to this law the remuneration was in proportion to the depth from which it was brought up, and the risk incurred. But as these divers considered four fathoms or thereabouts an extreme and dangerous depth, it is probable that they did their work in the natural way without the aid of apparatus.

For the benefit of the credulous we may mention several statements which have been more or less received. The Dutch were once celebrated divers, and it is reported that some of them have remained under water more than an hour! From this report some have argued that these Dutchmen must have possessed artificial means of maintaining life below water. To this we reply, if that were so, is it likely that the reporter who made reference to the length of time spent below water was ignorant as to the means—if any—by which this apparent miracle was accomplished? and if he was not ignorant, would he have passed over such means in silence? The idea is absurd. The probability is rather that the reporter had been gulled, or was fond of drawing the " long bow."

Again, mention is made by one Mersennius of a man who could remain six hours under water! If Mersennius were in a position to become acquainted with that diver's powers, how comes it that he failed to become acquainted with his apparatus? Simply because there was no such apparatus, and the whole affair is a fable.

But the most remarkable of these stories is recorded by a certain Father Kircher, who might appropriately be styled a father of lies! Here is *his* fabrication :—

In the time of Frederick of Sicily there lived a man named Nicolo Pesce,—Nicholas the Fish. This man's powers seem to have been decidedly superhuman. He was evidently an amphibious animal. He appears to have acted the part of ocean-postman in these old times, for it is related of him that he used to carry letters for the king far and wide about the Mediterranean. On one occasion a vessel found him out of sight of land in the discharge of ocean-postal duty—bearing despatches of the king from Sicily to Calabria. They took him on board and had a chat with him. It is not said that they smoked a friendly pipe with him or gave him a glass of grog, but we think it probable that they did! After a little rest and refreshment Nicholas the Fish bade them good-bye, jumped overboard, and continued his voyage. The end of this poor man was very sad. The king, being seized with an insane desire to know something about the depths of the terrible gulf of Charybdis, offered Nicholas a golden cup if he would dive down and explore them. He dived accordingly, remained below nearly an hour, and brought back a glowing account of the wonders and horrors of the seething whirlpool. The king, far from being satisfied, became more than ever desirous of knowledge. He asked Nicholas to dive again, and tempted him with the offer of another and larger cup, as well as a purse of gold. The poor Fish, after some hesitation, again dived into the gulf and was never more heard of!

We don't wonder at it. The greatest wonder is, that Nicolo Pesce ever obtained a place in the encyclopædias of the world. From the fact, however, that he has been thus rescued from oblivion, we conclude, that although much that is said of him is false, the man himself was not a myth, but a fact;

that he was a man of the Captain Webb type, who possessed extraordinary powers of swimming, perhaps of diving, to the extent, it may be, of nearly three minutes, and that he possibly lost his life by rashly venturing into the vortex of some dangerous whirlpool. That he did not use diving apparatus of any kind is clear from the fact that nothing is said about such apparatus, which, had it really existed, would have claimed as much attention and caused as much talk as did the man himself.

The earliest authentic records we have of the use of diving apparatus belong to the beginning of the sixteenth century. In an edition of Vegetius on the *Art of War*, published in 1511, there is an engraving of a diver walking in the sea with a cap over his head and shoulders, from which a flexible tube rises to the surface. This was, no doubt, the embryo of our "diving-dress." John Taisner, in 1538, says that he saw two Greeks, at Toledo in Spain, make experiments with diving apparatus, in presence of the Emperor Charles V. and ten thousand spectators. Gaspar Schott of Nurnberg, in 1664, refers to this Greek machine as an "aquatic kettle;" but mentions, as preferable in his estimation, a species of "aquatic armour," which enabled those who wore it to walk under water. The "aquatic kettle" was doubtless the embryo of the diving-bell.

From that time onward inventive minds have been
turned, with more or less success, towards the subject
of submarine operations, and many are the contrivances—clever, queer, absurd, and useful—which
have been the outcome.   Not content with " kettles "
and " bells," by means of which they could descend
into the deep and remain there for an hour or
more at a time, and with " armour " and " dresses '
with which they could walk about at the bottom of
the sea, men have constructed several submarine
boats and machines, in which, shut up like Jonah in
the whale, they purposed to move about from place
to place, sink to the bottom and rise to the surface,
at will, or go under the bottoms of enemy's ships
and fix torpedoes wherewith to blow them up, and
otherwise do them damage.   These latter machines
have not attained to any noteworthy degree of success
—at least they have not yet done either much good
or much harm to the human race ; but the former—
the "kettles" and the " armour,"—in other words, the
" diving-bells " and " dresses "—have attained to a
high degree of perfection and efficiency, and have
done incalculable good service.

The diving-bell was so styled owing to the first
machines being made in the shape of a gigantic bell.
An inverted wine-glass, thrust mouth downwards
into water, will not fill with water, owing to the air
which it contains keeping the water out.   It will

partially fill, however, because air is compressible, and the deeper down it is thrust the more will the air be compressed. At a depth of thirty-three feet the air will be compressed to half its bulk—in other words, the glass will be half-full of water. It is clear that a fly or any small insect could live in the air thus confined although thrust to great depths under water. But it could not live long, because air becomes unfit for use after being breathed a certain time, and cannot sustain life. Hence, if we are to preserve the life of our fly, we must send fresh air down to it.

The first diving-bells were made so large that the air contained in them sufficed for a considerable period—an hour or more. When this air had lost its life-sustaining qualities, the bell had to be drawn up and the air renewed. This was so inconvenient that ingenious men soon hit on various plans to renew the air without raising the bells. One plan, that of Dr. Halley, was to send air down in tight casks, which were emptied into the bell and then sent up, full of water, for a fresh supply of air, while the foul air was let out of the bell by a valve in the top. Another plan was to have tubes from the bell to the surface by which air was made to circulate downwards, at first being forced down by a pair of bellows, and afterwards by means of air-pumps.

Round the inside of the bell ran a seat for the

divers. One or more holes fitted with thick plate-glass, gave them light and enabled them to use the various tools and implements required in their voca-tion. From some of these bells, a man could be sent out, when at or near the bottom, having on a water-tight head-piece connected by a tube with the air inside the bell. He could thus move about with more freedom than his comrades inside, but of course could not travel further than the length of his tube, while, being wet, he could not endure the cold for any great length of time.

As time went on the form of the bell was improved until that of a square or oblong box of iron came to be generally adopted. The bell now in use is that which was made in 1788 by the celebrated engineer Smeaton, who applied the air forcing-pump to it, and otherwise brought the machine to a high degree of perfection. He used it with great advantage in the works at Ramsgate harbour, and Smeaton's diving-bell, improved by Rennie, has continued in constant and general use on all submarine works until a very recent period. It has now been almost entirely super-seded—except in the case of some special kinds of work—by the diving dress—the value and the use of which it is the province of our tale to illustrate and expound.

In regard to the diving dress, we may say that it has grown out of the "aquatic armour" of the olden

time, but no great advance in its improvement was
made until the end of the eighteenth and beginning
of the present centuries, when the names of Rowe,
Halley, Spalding, Bushwell, and Colt, appear in connection with various clever contrivances to facilitate
diving operations. Benjamin Martin, a London
optician, made a dress of strong leather in 1778
which fitted his arms and legs as well as his trunk,
and held half a hogshead of air. With this he could
enter the hold of a sunk vessel, and he is said to have
been very successful in the use of it. Mr. Kleingert
of Breslau, in 1798, designed a dress somewhat like
the above, part of which, however, was made of tin-
plate. The diving dress was greatly improved by Mr.
Deane, and in the recovery of guns, etc., from the
wreck of the *Royal George*, in 1834-36, as well as in
many other operations, this dress—much improved,
and made by Mr. Siebe, under Deane's directions—
did signal service.

It has now been brought to a high state of perfection by the well-known submarine engineers Siebe
and Gorman, Heinke and Davis, and others, of London, and Denayrouze of Paris. It encases the diver
completely from head to foot, is perfectly water-tight,
and is made of thick sheet indiarubber covered on
both sides with tanned twill—the helmet and breast-
plate being metal.

For further information on this subject we refer

the inquisitive reader to the *Encyclopædia Britannica*, to the descriptive pamphlets of the submarine engineers above named, and to an admirable little book styled *The Conquest of the Sea*, by Henry Siebe, which contains a full and graphic account in detail of almost everything connected with diving and submarine engineering.[1]

[1] It may interest practical spirits to know that they can *see* the diving dress and apparatus in operation, by going to No. 17 Mason Street, Westminster Bridge Road, London, where Messrs. Siebe and Gorman have erected a large Tank for the purpose of illustrating their apparatus.   At the Alexandra Palace, also, Messrs. Denayrouze and Co. have a tank for the same purpose.

CHAPTER VIIL.

THE GRINDING OF THE SCREW.

IT is proverbial that incidents in themselves trivial frequently form the hinges on which great events turn. When Edgar Berrington went to London he learned that the owners of the fine ocean-steamer the *Warrior* wished him to become their chief engineer for that voyage, the previous chief having been suddenly taken ill and obliged to leave them. Although flattered by the proposal, and the terms in which it was made, Edgar declined it, for, having acquired all the knowledge he desired about marine engines during the voyage out and home, he did not wish to waste more time at sea. The owner, however, being aware of his worth, was not to be put off with a first refusal. He took Edgar into his private room and reasoned with him.

"Come now, Mr. Berrington, consider my proposal again. You'll go, won't you?"

"Impossible," replied Edgar. "You are very

kind, and I assure you that I fully appreciate your offer, but—"

He was interrupted by a clerk who entered at the moment and spoke a few words in an under tone to the owner.

"Excuse me one minute, Mr. Berrington," said the latter, rising quickly. "I shall return immediately. There is a newspaper, to look—no—where is it? Ah! no matter: here is a list of the passengers going out to China in the *Warrior*. It may amuse you. Perhaps you may find a friend amongst them."

Left alone, Edgar ran his eye carelessly over the names—thinking the while of the disagreeables of another long sea-voyage, and strengthening his resolves not to be tempted to go.

Now, the careless glance at this passenger-list was the apparently trifling incident on which hinged the whole of our hero's future career; his careless glance became suddenly fixed and attentive; his eyebrows lifted to their utmost elevation and his face flushed crimson, for there he beheld the names of Charles Hazlit, Esq., and his daughter, Miss Aileen Hazlit.

Just at that moment the owner of the *Warrior* returned. This owner was an intelligent, shrewd man—quick to observe. He noted the flush on Edgar's countenance, and Edgar immediately blew his nose with violence to account for the flush.

"Well now, Mr. Berrington, what say you?" he resumed.

Poor Edgar knew not what to say. A reply had to be given at once. He had no time to think. Aileen going to China! An offer of a situation in the same vessel!

"Well, sir," said our hero, with sudden decision, " I will go."

Of course the owner expressed himself well pleased, and then there followed a deal of nautico-scientific talk, after which Edgar ventured to say—

"I observe the name of Mr. Charles Hazlit on your list. He is an acquaintance of mine. Do you happen to know what takes him so far from home?"

"Can't say exactly," replied the other. " I think some one told me his affairs in China require looking after, and his daughter's health necessitates a long sea-voyage."

"Health!" exclaimed Edgar, striving to look and speak in a comparatively indifferent manner. "She was quite well when I saw her last."

"Very likely," said the owner, with a smile, " but it does not take long to make a young lady ill—especially when her heart is touched. Some sort of rumour floats in my mind to the effect that Miss

Hazlit is going out to China to be married, or requires to go out because she doesn't want to be married—I forget which. But it comes pretty much to the same thing in the end!"

"Hah!" said Edgar shortly.

If he had said "Oh!" in tones of agony, it would have been more truly expressive of his feelings.

The moment he got out of the office and felt the cool air of the street he repented of his decision and pronounced himself to be a consummate donkey!

"There," thought he, "I've made a fool of myself. I've engaged for a long voyage in a capacity which precludes the possibility of my associating with the passengers, for not only must nearly all my waking hours be spent down beside the engine, but when I come up to cool myself I must perforce do so in dirty costume, with oily hands and face, quite in an unfit state to be seen by Aileen, and without the slightest right to take any notice of her. Oh! donkey—goose that you are, Eddy! But you've done it now, and can't undo it, therefore you must go through with it."

Thinking of himself in this lowly strain he went home to the solitude of his lodging, sat down before his tea-table, thrust both hands into his pockets, and, in a by no means unhappy frame of mind, brooded over his trials and sorrows.

Let us change the scene now. We are out upon

the sea—in a floating palace. And oh how that palace rushes onward, ever onward, without rest, without check, night and day, cleaving its **way** irresistibly through the mighty deep. Mighty! ah! *how* mighty no one on board can tell so well as that thin, gentle, evidently dying youth who leans over the stern watching the screws and the "wake" that seems to rush behind, marking off, as it were mile by mile, the vast and ever increasing space—never to be re-traversed he knows full well—that separates him from home and all that is dear to him on earth.

The palace is made of iron—hard, unyielding, unbeautiful, uncompromising iron,—but her cushions are soft, her gilding is gorgeous, her fittings are elegant, her food is sumptuous, her society—at least much of it—is refined. Of course representatives of the unrefined are also there—in the after-cabin too— just as there are specimens of the refined in the fore-cabin. But, taking them all in all, they are a remarkably harmonious band, the inhabitants of this iron palace, from the captain to the cabin-boy inclusive. The latter is a sprightly imp; the former is—to use the expression of one of the unrefined— "a brick." He is not tall—few sea-captains seem to be so—but he is very broad, and manly, and as strong as an elephant. He is a pattern captain. Gallant to the lady passengers, chatty with the gentlemen, polite to the unrefined, sedately grave

among the officers and crew, and jocular to the
children; in short, he is all things to all men—and
much of the harmony on board is due to his unconscious influence. He has a handsome face, glittering black eyes, an aquiline nose that commands
respect, and a black beard and moustache that
covered a firm mouth and chin.

Grinding is one of the prominent ideas that are
suggested on board the iron palace. There are
many other ideas, no doubt. Among seventy or
eighty educated and intelligent human beings of
both sexes and all ages it could not be otherwise.
We allude, however, to the boat—not to the
passengers. The screw grinds and the engine grinds
incessantly. When one thinks of a thing, or things,
going round and round, or up and down, regularly,
uninterruptedly, vigorously, doggedly, obstinately,
hour after hour, one is impressed, to say the least; and
when one thinks of the said thing, or things, going on
thus, night and day without rest, one is solemnised;
but when one meditates on these motions being
continued for many weeks together, one has a
tendency to feel mentally overwhelmed.

The great crank that grinds the screw, and is
itself ground by the piston—not to mention the
cylinder and boiler—works in a dark place deep
down in the engine-room, like a giant hand constantly engaged on deeds of violence and evil.

Here Edgar Berrington, clothed in white canvas and oil, finds genial companionship. He dotes on the great crank. It is a sympathetic thing. It represents his feelings wonderfully. Returning from the deck after inhaling a little fresh air, he leans against the iron bulkhead in these clanking depths and gazes gloomily and for prolonged periods at the crank while it grinds with a sort of vicious energy that seems in strange harmony with his soul. Sometimes he grinds his teeth as a sort of obbligato accompaniment—especially if he has while on deck, during a wistful gaze at the distant perspective of the aft-regions, beheld (or fancied he has beheld) a familiar and adored form.

At first the passengers were sick—very sick, most of them—insomuch that there were some who would gladly, if possible, have surrendered their lives with their dinners ; but by degrees they began to improve, and to regard meals with anticipation instead of loathing. When the sunny and calm latitudes near the line were reached, every one grew well and hearty, and at last there was not a sad soul on board except the poor sick lad who studied the screw and measured the ever increasing distance from home. One of the first evidences of the return of health was the sound of song. When the nights were clear and calm, and naught was audible save the grinding of the screw, the passengers crystallised naturally into

groups in the same way that ice-particles arrange
themselves in sympathetic stars; and from several
such constellations the music of the spheres was
naturally evolved.

One of these crystals was formed, usually in a
tent on deck, by the attractive influence of smoke.
It was consequently not a bright crystal, and
included particles both refined and otherwise. Its
music was gruff for the most part, sometimes growly.
There was another crystal which varied its position occasionally—according to the position of the
moon, for it was a crystal formed of romantic
elements. One of its parts was a Scottish maiden
whose voice was melodious, flexible, and very sweet.
Her face and spirit had been made to match. She
had many admirers, and a bosom-friend of kindly
heart and aspect, with wealth of golden hair, in
some respects like herself.

Our heroine Aileen, being passionately fond of
music, and herself a sweet singer, attached herself
to this crystal, and became as it were another bosom-
friend.

Two bearded men were also much given to seek
attachment to this crystal. They also seemed knit to
each other in bosom-friendship—if we may venture
to use such a term with reference to bearded men.
One was amateurly musical, the other powerfully
sympathetic. A pastor, of unusually stalwart pro-

portions, with a gentle pretty wife and lovable family, also had a decided leaning to this crystal.

One evening the group, finding its favourite part of the deck occupied, was driven to a position near the tent of the smoky crystal, and, sitting down not far from the engineer's quarters, began to indulge in song. Grave and gay alternated. Duets followed; trios ensued, and miscellaneous new forms of harmony sometimes intervened.

"Do sing a solo, Miss Hazlit," said the Scottish maiden. "I like your voice *so* much, and want to hear it alone. Will you sing?"

Aileen had an obliging spirit. She at once began, in a low contralto voice, "I cannot sing the old songs."

Sometimes in private life one hears a voice so sweet, so thrilling, with a "something" so powerful in it, that one feels, amid other sensations of pleasure, great satisfaction to think that none of the public singers in the world could "bat that" if they were to try their best, and that few of them could equal it!

Such a voice was that of our heroine. It drew towards her the soul, body, and spirit of the music-lovers who listened. Of course we do not deny that there were some who could not be drawn thus. There were a few, among the smoky crystals, for whom a draw of the pipe or a mildly drawn pot of bitter beer had greater charms than sweet sounds, however melting. With the exceptions of these,

nearly all who chanced to be within hearing drew
near to the musical group, and listened while that
most beautiful of songs was being warbled in tones
not loud but inexpressibly pathetic.

Among the listeners was our friend Edgar Berrington.   Seated, as usual, in front of the great crank,
with bare muscular arms folded on his broad chest
and a dark frown on his forehead, he riveted his eyes
on the crank as if it were the author of all his
anxieties.   Suddenly the terminating lines, " I cannot
sing the old songs, they are too dear to me," rising
above the din of machinery, floated gently down
through iron lattice-work, beams, rods, cranks, and
bars, and smote upon his ear.

Like a galvanised man he sprang on his legs and
stood erect.   Then, if we may say so, like a human
rocket, he shot upwards and stood on the margin of
the crowd.   Being head and shoulders over most of
them he observed a clear space beside the singer.   The
night was dark, features could not be discerned, even
forms were not easily recognisable.   He glided into
the open space, and silently but promply sat down
on the deck beside Aileen.   His elbow even touched
one of the folds of her garment.   He went straight
into paradise and remained there !

As for Aileen, if she observed the action at all, she
probably set it down to the enthusiasm of a more
than usually musical member of the ship's crew.

While she was still dwelling on the last note, a grinding sound was heard and a slight tremor felt that not only stopped the song abruptly but checked the applause that was ready to burst from every lip and hand. Edgar vanished from the spot where he sat quite as quickly as he had appeared, and in a moment was at his station. The captain's voice was heard on the bridge. The signal was given to stop the engines—to back them—to stop again. Eager inquiries followed—" What's that? Did you feel it? hear it? Could it be a rock? Impossible, surely?" No one could answer with knowledge or authority, save those who were too busy to be spoken to. Accustomed as they all were for many weeks past to the ceaseless motion of the engines, the sudden stoppage had a strange and solemnising effect on most of the passengers. Presently the order was given to steam ahead, and once more they breathed more freely on hearing again the familar grinding of the screw.

To the anxious inquiries afterwards made of him, the captain only smiled and said he could not tell what it was—perhaps it might have been a piece of wreck. "But it did not feel like that, captain," objected one of the passengers, who, having frequently been to sea before, was regarded as being semi-nautical; "it was too like a touch on something solid. You've heard, I suppose, of coral

reefs growing in places where none are marked on
our charts ?"

"I have," answered the captain drily.

"Might it not be something of the kind ?"

"It might," replied the captain.

"We are not far from the coast of China, are
we ?" asked the semi-nautical passenger.

"Not very far."

Seeing that the captain was not disposed to be
communicative, the semi-nautical passenger retired
to persecute and terrify some of the ladies with his
surmises. Meanwhile the well was sounded and a
slight increase of water ascertained, but nothing
worth speaking of, and the pumps were set to
work.

The anxiety of the passengers was soon allayed,
everything going on as smoothly as before. The
evening merged into night. The moon rose slowly
and spread a path of rippling silver from the ship
to the horizon. The various groups began to un-
crystallise. Sleepy ones went below and melted away
somehow. Sleepless ones went to their great panacea,
smoke. Lights were put out everywhere save where
the duties of the ship required them to burn continually. At last the latest of the sleepless turned
in, and none were wakeful through the iron palace
except the poor youth who mentally measured the
distance from home, and the officers and men on

duty.   Among the latter was Edgar Berrington, who, standing at his accustomed post down in his own iron depths, pondered the events of the evening while he watched the motions of the great crank and listened to the grinding of the screw.

CHAPTER IX.

TREATS OF A LEAK AND CONSEQUENT DIFFICULTIES.

IT turned out, on investigation, that, whatever the object by which the vessel had been touched, some degree of injury had been done to her iron-plating, for the pumps were found to be insufficient to prevent the rising of water in the hold. This was a serious matter, because although the rise was very slow, it was steady, and if not checked would sooner or later sink the ship. Everything that could be done was attempted in order to discover and stop the leak, but without success.

Fortunately it happened that the *Warrior* had among her other goods a quantity of diving apparatus on board, consigned to a firm in Hong-Kong that had lost valuable property in a wreck, and meant to attempt the recovery of it by means of divers. The men had gone out by a previous vessel, but their dresses, having been accidentally delayed, had been sent after them in the *Warrior*. Bethinking himself of these dresses, the captain conceived that he was justified, in the circumstances, in making temporary use of them; but he was disappointed to find, on inquiry, that not a man of his ordinary crew had ever seen a diving-dress put on, or its attendant air-pumps worked. In these circumstances he sent for the chief engineer.

Edgar Berrington was busy about some trifling repairs to the machinery when the message reached him. The place being very hot, he was clad only in shirt and trousers, with a belt round his waist—a by no means unbecoming costume for a well-made figure! His shirt-sleeves were rolled up to the shoulders, displaying a pair of very muscular and elegantly moulded arms—such as Hercules might have been pleased with, and Apollo would not have disdained. His hands were black and oily, and his face was similarly affected.

Expecting to meet the captain at the entrance to his domains, Edgar merely rolled down his sleeves, and seized a bundle of waste with which he hastily wiped his hands and face, thereby drawing on the latter, which had previously been spotty, a series of varied streaks and blotches that might have raised the envy of a Querikoboo savage. But the captain was not where he expected to find him, and on looking aft he saw him on the quarter-deck in converse with one of the passengers. Edgar would rather not have appeared in public in such guise, but being in haste to return to the work from which he had been called, he pulled on a light linen jacket and forage-cap, and walked quickly aft. To his horror he saw Aileen seated on a basket-work easy-chair close to the captain. It was too late, however, to retreat, for the latter had already observed him. Fortunately Aileen was deeply engaged with a book. Edgar quickly advanced and took such a position that his back was turned to her.

"Excuse my appearance, sir," he said in a low voice, touching his cap to the captain; "I am in the midst of a job that requires to be—"

"No matter," interrupted the captain, with a laugh, "you look very well in your war-paint. We'll excuse you."

Attracted by the laugh, Aileen looked up at the tall form in front of her.

"What a *very* handsome figure!" she whispered to her bosom-friend, who sat beside her reading.

The bosom-friend put her book in front of her mouth and whispered—

"Yes, *very*. I wish he would turn round and show his face."

But her wish was not granted, for the captain walked slowly forward in conversation with the "*very* handsome figure," which obstinately,—we might almost say carefully,—kept its back turned towards them.

Great was the satisfaction of the captain when he found not only that one of the subordinate engineers understood a good deal about diving, but that the chief himself was a diver! It was accordingly arranged that a descent should be made without delay. The dresses were got up and unpacked, and one was found suitable for a large man.

Soon the air-pumps were set up and rigged on deck. One of the sub-engineers was set to work them, with one of the crew, while another sub and an officer, having been previously instructed by our hero, were detailed to the important duty of holding the life-line and air-pipe. Thereafter the engines were stopped, and the dead-calm that followed,— that feeling of unnatural quietude to which we have referred elsewhere,—did more perhaps to arouse all the sleepers, readers, and dreamers on board, than if a cannon had been fired. Of course the descent of a diver over the side was a point of great interest to the passengers, coupled as it was with some anxiety as to the leak, of the existence of which all were fully aware, though only a select few had been informed of its serious nature—if not checked. They crowded round the apparatus therefore, and regarded its arrangement with the deepest interest.

When all was ready Edgar issued from the deck-cabin, in which he meant to dress, to take a final look at the air-pumps. In the flutter of excitement he had for one moment, and for the first time since the beginning of the voyage, totally forgotten the existence of Aileen.   Now, she and Lintie, the Scottish maiden who sang so well, chanced to be looking with much interest at the helmet which lay on the deck, when his eye fell on them.   At once he turned on his heel and retreated towards his cabin.

"That's the man who is to go down, I believe," observed one of the passengers, pointing to him.

Lintie looked up and saw his back.

"Oh !" she whispered to Aileen, "it is the *very* handsome man !"

"Is it ?" replied **Aileen**, with indifference, for she was engrossed with the helmet just then.

Greatly perplexed as to how he should escape observation, poor Edgar began to dress—or, rather, to be dressed by his assistants,--delaying the operation as long as possible ; but delay did not seem to increase his inventive powers, and could not prevent the completion of the process.

The guernsey, drawers, and outside stockings were drawn on, and Edgar's brain worked the while like the great crank of his own engine ; but no feasible plan of escape was evolved.   Then the "crinoline" was drawn on, but it added no feminine sharpness to his wits, though it seriously modified and damaged the shape of his person.   The crinoline, as we have said elsewhere, is seldom used except at great depths.

where the pressure of water is excessive. It was put on Edgar at this time partly because it formed a portion of the dress, and partly because, his mind being preoccupied, he did not observe with sufficient care what his attendants were about.

After this came the shoulder-pad, and then the thick dress itself was drawn on, and the attendants hitched it up with difficulty over his spreading shoulders, but they could not hitch up an idea along with it. The forcing of his hands through the tight indiarubber wrists of the sleeves was done with tremendous power, but it was nothing compared with the energy he put forth to force himself through his mental difficulty—yet all in vain! The outside stockings and the canvas "overalls" followed, and he finally put on the red night-cap, which seemed to extinguish all capacity for thought.

"You seem to be a little nervous, sir," remarked one of the attendants, as he affixed the back and chest weights, while the other put on his ponderous boots.

"Am I,—eh!" said Edgar, with a grim smile; then he added, as a sudden idea flashed on him; "go fetch me the dirtiest bundle of waste you can find below, and give it a good scrape on the blackest part of the boiler as you pass."

"Sir!" exclaimed the attendant.

"Go; do what I bid you," said Edgar, in a tone that did not brook delay.

1

The attendant vanished and speedily returned with the desired piece of waste.

Edgar at once rubbed it over his face and became so piebald and hideous that both the attendants laughed.

Not heeding them, and only half sure of the completeness of the disguise, Edgar issued boldly from his cabin, and walked with heavy tread towards the place where he had to sit down to have the helmet screwed on.

A loud roar of laughter greeted him.

" Why, you 've been kissing the funnel," exclaimed one of the mates.

" That 'll do me no harm," growled Edgar, stooping to catch hold of the air-tube, and making an excuse for sidling and backing towards his seat.

" Oh ! what a fright ! and *such* a figure !" exclaimed Lintie ; " come round, let us try to get a nearer view of him."

She dragged the laughing Aileen with her, for she was an impulsive little woman ; but at whatever opening in the crowd she and her friend presented themselves, they were sure to find the diver's ridiculously broad and now inelegant back turned towards them.

" Plague on him !" she exclaimed, for she was an impatient little woman, just then, " I don't believe he 's got a front at all ! Come round again—quick."

" Why, what are you turning about like that for?" exclaimed one of the exasperated attendants, who stood ready with the helmet.

" His head 's turned wi' fear, an' he 's a-follerin of 't," growled the boatswain.

" Why don't you sit down ?" said the attendant.

" Are you ready ?" asked Edgar, in a low gruff voice.

" Of course I am—don't you see me ?"

Another happy idea came into Edgar's head at that moment. He pulled his red night-cap well down over his eyes, and sat down with a crash, while another hearty laugh greeted his supposed eccentricity.

" Hallo, I say, you 're not going to be hanged—no need to draw it down like that," said the first officer.

" Drowning comes much to the same thing ; let 's do it decently—according to rule," retorted Edgar, with a grin that displayed a brilliant set of teeth.

" H'm ! we shan't see him *now*," whispered Lintie, in disappointment, forcing her way once more to the front.

This time there was no reply from Aileen, for a strange shock passed through her as she observed the momentary smile—and no wonder, for many a time had that same mouth smiled upon her with winning tenderness.

Of course she did not for a moment suspect the truth, but she thought it strange, nevertheless, that the diver's mouth should have such a strong resemblance to—she knew not precisely what! Afterwards she confided to Lintie that it had struck her as bearing a faint—very faint—resemblance to the mouth of a friend.

"Of a very particular friend?" inquired Lintie, who was sharp-witted.

Aileen blushed and hid her face on the neck of her friend, and suddenly poured out her soul, which the other drank up with avidity.

That same night, lying in her berth, which was a top one, and looking languidly over the side at her friend, who lay in the berth below looking sympathetically up, she revealed her hopes and fears and sentiments, to the edification (it is to be hoped) of a mean-spirited passenger in the saloon, who stood on the other side of the very thin partition, and tried to overhear. If he succeeded it must have been a new sensation to him to listen to the gentle streams of hope and love that flowed through to him—for Aileen's thoughts were gems, as pure and beautiful as the casket which contained them. We are not quite sure, but we more than half suspect that if his presence there had been discovered, and himself had been within easy reach, the casket's palm would have evoked something resembling a pistol-shot from his dirty cheek!

But to return to our diver. The moment his

helmet was on he breathed freely, recovered his equanimity, and went down the rope-ladder that hung over the side, with an air of easy decision that checked the criticisms of the men and aroused the admiration—not to mention the alarm—of the women.

" The puir felly'll be droon'd," pitifully observed a fore-cabin passenger from Edinburgh, as she gazed at the mass of air-bubbles that arose when Edgar's iron head had disappeared.

"Nothink of the sort," responded a fore-cabin passenger from London, who had taken an immense liking to the fore-cabin passenger from Edinburgh, in virtue of their total mental, moral, and physical dissimilarity; " divers are never drownded."

We need scarcely observe to the intelligent reader that both females were wrong—as such females, in regard to such matters, usually are. Edgar was *not* " droon'd," and divers *are* sometimes " drownded."

So far from being drowned, he was remarkably successful in discovering the leak on his first descent.

It was caused by one of the iron plates near the keel having been badly torn by a coral rock.

Thoroughly to repair this was a difficulty. Our diver did indeed stuff it with oakum in a way that at once diminished the influx of water; but this was merely a makeshift. It now became a question whether it were possible to effect the necessary repairs while at sea. Our young engineer removed the difficulty. He undertook to rivet an iron plate over the hole—at least to make the attempt.

In order to effect this, a rope-ladder was constructed long enough to pass entirely under the ship's bottom, to which it was tightly pressed by means of tackle at both ends. The rounds of this ladder were made of wood, and all along its course were fastened rough balls or blocks of wood about four inches in diameter, which prevented it coming too close to the ship's bottom. Thus there was secured space for the diver to place his feet on the rounds. This ladder having been affixed, so as to pass close to the injured plate, a boat was lowered, and from this boat descended a small ladder, hung in such a way that the diver, when a few feet under water, could easily step from it to the fixed rope-ladder. In addition to this, a small plank suspended to a rope, somewhat after the fashion of a familiar style of bed-room bookshelf, was taken down by the diver and hung to the rope-ladder by a hook, so that he could sit on it while at work, and move it about at pleasure.

All having been prepared, our engineer descended with the necessary tools, and, to make a long story short, riveted a new plate over the old one in such a way as effectually to close the leak, so that thereafter it gave no further trouble or anxiety.

But for this the vessel would certainly have been

lost, unless they had succeeded in beaching her, before the final catastrophe, on some part of the neighbouring coast; in which case they would have run the chance of being taken by the pirates who at that time infested the China seas.

Delivered from this threatened danger, the good ship sped merrily on her course; most of the crystallised groups grew closer together—in some instances, however, they burst asunder! Musical tendencies also developed, though in some cases the sublime gave place to the ridiculous, and music actually, once or twice, became a nuisance. As the end of the voyage drew near, the hearty captain grew heartier; the bosom-friends drew closer; the shy passengers opened up; the congenial passengers began to grieve over the thought of parting; charades were acted; concerts were given: the mean-spirited passenger became a little less vile; the fore-cabin passenger from Edinburgh observed to her friend that the "goin's on a'boord were wonderfu';" to which the fore-cabin passenger from London replied that "they certainly was;" flying-fish and porpoises, and sharks and albatrosses, and tropical heat, ceased to furnish topics of interest, and men and women were thrown back on their mental resources, which were, among other things, largely and pleasantly—sometimes even hotly!—exercised on religious discussion. In short the little community, thus temporarily thrown together, became an epitome of human life. As calm and storm alternated outside the iron palace, so, inside, there was mingled joy and sorrow. Friendships were formed and cemented. Love and folly, and hate and pride, and all the passions, were represented—ay, and Death was also there.

In the silent night, when nothing was heard save that ceaseless music of the screw, the destroying angel came—so silently that only a few were aware of his dread presence—and took away the youth whose sole occupation seemed to have been the watching of the ever-increasing distance from that home which he was destined never again to see. It was inexpressibly sad to those left behind when his coffin was committed to the deep amid the solemn silence that once again ensued on the stoppage of the engines, while the low voice of a pastor prayed for those who wept his departure ; but it was not sad for him who had been taken—he had reached the " better home," and, sitting by the side of Jesus, could doubtless afford to think, at last without longing, of the old home beyond the sea.

CHAPTER X.

ANXIETIES ; DISASTERS ; HOPES.

STANDING in his accustomed place on the iron floor of the iron chamber, Edgar Berrington watched the grinding of the great crank, and pondered.

He had now been many weeks at sea, and had not once spoken a word to Aileen—had not even seen her more than half-a-dozen times in the far vista of the quarter-deck. Each Sabbath-day, indeed, dressed like his former self, he had worshipped with her in the same saloon, but on these occasions he had kept carefully in the background, had crept quietly down after the others had assembled, had kept in the shadow of the door, and had left before the worshippers had time to rise.

An event, however, was now pending, which was destined to remove his present difficulties in a very unexpected manner, and to saddle on the shoulders of Charles Hazlit, Esquire, difficulties which he had never in all his previous business calculations taken into account.

During most part of the voyage out to China Mr. Hazlit's visage had presented a sea-green aspect, edged with yellow. The great Demon of the sea had seized upon and held him with unwonted avidity and perseverance. It appeared to regard him as fair game—as one whose life had been largely devoted to ploughing up its peculiar domain—or rather, inducing others to plough there—and who was therefore worthy of special attention. At all events, the wealthy merchant did not appear above-board until the lapse of two weeks after leaving his native land. At the end of that period something like the ghost of him crawled on deck one rather fine day, but a demoniac squall rudely sent him below, where he remained until those charming regions of the Equatorial calms were entered. Here a bad likeness—a sort of spoiled photograph—of him again made its appearance, and lay down helplessly on a mattress, or smiled with pathetic sarcasm when food was offered. But soon the calm regions were passed ; the Cape of Storms was doubled, and the fierce " south-easters " of the Indian seas were encountered, during which period Mr. Hazlit passed away, as one of the things that *had* been, from the memory of all on board, with the exception of Aileen, the captain, the bed-room steward, and a Christian pastor, who, with his amiable wife, had done much during the voyage for their fellow-passengers.

At last, when the shores of China were approached, and people began to talk earnestly about the end of the voyage, Mr. Hazlit's shade once more made its appearance, with a spot of dark red on each cheek and on the point of his nose. These spots were hopefully regarded as signs of returning health. They did not appear too soon, for the shade would infallibly have vanished altogether if it had been subjected to further attenuation.

"Oh, papa dear, you look so *much* better to-day !" said Aileen, arranging his shawls as he lay on deck —"quite rosy."

If she had said port-winy it would have been more in accordance with truth, but Aileen was rather apt to diverge from truth, unintentionally, in speaking of her father.

"I am thankful, dear," replied the shade in a faint voice, and with a fainter smile. "The captain says we shall be in port in a few days, and then we shall be all right, and—"

"Ha ! shall you ?" exclaimed the Demon of the sea, giving the ship a little lurch to starboard, which cut short the merchant's remarks abruptly; "you think so, do you ? ho ! we shall see !"

Following up this inaudible speech with one of those audible howls for which demons are so justly celebrated, he went off in a gust of wind, and summoned to his aid one of those simooms, or monsoons, or typhoons which are in the habit of ravaging the southern seas.

These spirits, quickly obeying the summons, sent not only Mr. Hazlit but many of the other passengers to their berths, blew into ribbons the few sails that chanced to be hoisted, boiled up the sea as if in a huge caldron, caused the blackened sky to mingle with the world of waters, rent the firmament with gleaming fire and crashing thunder, and hissed or yelled everywhere in the spirit of wildest revelry.

The *Warrior* was a splendid steamer, and her commander an able seaman, but neither splendour of material nor power of mind can avert what is decreed.

The storm was prolonged, and raged with unwonted fury, the captain did his best, the good ship behaved nobly, and things went well until the night of the third day. It was at that time so very dark that nothing could be seen farther off than a few yards beyond the bulwarks, where the white-crested waves loomed high in air in a sort of ghostly fashion as if they meant to fall on the deck unawares and sink the ship.

The passengers had by degrees got used to the mad plunging and rolling of their iron home, and even the timid among them began to feel hopeful that after all the gale would be weathered, and the harbour gained.

What the captain thought no one could tell. He remained on the bridge night and day, clad from head to foot in oil-skin garments, facing the furious blast as if it were his native air, watching every motion of his vessel, and gazing intently into the world of ebony ahead as if trying to read his fate there.

The darkness around was almost palpable. Sometimes it seemed as if the vessel were rushing against a mighty rock, that towered high above the masts, but this was only optical illusion, or, perhaps, a denser storm-cloud than usual passing by, for the steamer continued to plough her onward way unchecked, save, now and then, by the bursting on her bows of a monster billow, which caused her to quiver from stem to stern, and swept the decks with green seas fore and aft. One such sea had carried away part of the bulwarks, and swept overboard all the loose material on the decks. Presently, there was a slight diminution in the force of the seas. The captain noted this, and gave orders to get the lead ready to heave.

Deep in the iron chambers below, Edgar Berrington stood—not in his wonted dreamy mood, beside the great crank, but close to the directing-wheel of the engine,—alert, steady, with his hand on the wheel, his eye on the index.

Suddenly the order came, "Half-speed,"—then abruptly followed, "Stop."

These orders were obeyed instantly.

The lead was hove—the result, "no bottom at thirty fathoms."

Again Edgar was signalled—"Half-speed," then— as the captain looked into the darkness ahead, and saw, or thought he saw, it deepen horribly—came the sharp order, "Astern, full-speed!"

Full well did Edgar know that this implied imminent danger. Quick as lightning he reversed the engines.

Next moment there was an appalling crash that overturned everything in the vessel. Our hero was himself wrenched from his position, and hurled against the bulkhead of the boiler-room; the masts went over the sides as if they had been pipe-stems, and the wire-ropes snapt like pack-thread. A moment of appalling silence followed, as if the very elements had suspended their strife, then there came shriek and cry from fore and aft as the passengers rushed frantically about, while above all yelled the escaping steam when Edgar opened the safety-valves.

The spot where they had struck was partially protected by cliffs, that rose like a wall in front. These cliffs turned off the direct force of the gale, but the general turmoil of the sea raised a surf around them which rendered the prospect of effecting a landing a very poor one, even if the vessel should hold together for any length of time. They had not struck on the shore of the mainland, but on a solitary islet or rock, not far from the coast, which rose abruptly out of deep water. Hence the silence of "the lead" as to its presence.

It were vain to attempt a description of the confusion that followed. The few cool and collected men in the ship were powerless at first, but gradually they succeeded in restoring some degree of order. Then the captain explained that being hard and fast on the rocks they could not sink, and that the vessel being strong was likely to hold together, perhaps, for several hours.

"We're *not* hard and fast, captain," said the semi-nautical passenger in an undertone, as he stood by the after-hatch, where most of the cabin passengers were assembled.

He referred to a swinging motion of the wreck, which, however, was so very slight as to be almost imperceptible.

"I know that," replied the captain, also in an undertone, but somewhat sternly, "we *may* slip back into deep water, but we're hard and fast *just now*, and I shall do my best to keep her so. Don't you go, sir, and raise needless alarm in the minds of the passengers. See," he added aloud, pointing towards the east, "day is already breaking; we shall soon have light enough to commence landing. Go below, ladies, and get your bonnet-boxes packed."

The captain's mind was far enough from jesting at that moment, but he knew that a quiet joke, possessing a modicum of truth in it, would do more to calm the fears of the timid than solemn advice or reasoning. He was right. Many went to their cabins to look after their most precious treasures, while the officers and men commenced active preparations for escaping to the islet, whose towering cliffs now began to loom heavily through the driving mist and foam.

From the first it was evident that only one mode of escape offered, namely, by means of a rope to the shore, and a running tackle. This material was easily procured and arranged, but the connecting of the rope with the shore was another question. As daylight increased, the island was recognised as a mere uninhabited rock, from which, therefore, no assistance could be expected, and the terrible turmoil of waters that leaped and seethed between the wreck and the cliffs, seemed to all on board, including the captain himself, to be impassable.

At last it became necessary to make an effort, for it was soon discovered that the vessel hung on the edge of a ledge, outside of which the water deepened suddenly to twenty fathoms, and a slip back into that would have been equivalent to certain and immediate death to all on board.

"My lads," said the captain to the crew, most of

whom were assembled with the passengers near the port bow, where the preparations for escaping were going on, " we must have a man to go ashore with that line. I cannot swim myself, else I would not ask for a volunteer. Come; who has got the heart to do a gallant deed, and save these women and children ?"

He turned as he spoke, and glanced at the female passengers and children, who crowded under the lee of the cook-house, wet, dishevelled, and terrified, Aileen and her musical friend being among them.

There was no response at first. The men turned with doubtful looks at the furious sea, in the midst of whose white surges black forbidding rocks seemed to rise and disappear, and the surface of which had by that time become much cumbered with portions of wreckage.

" If I could only swim," growled the boatswain, " I 'd try, but I can't float no more than a stone."

Others, who looked stout and bold enough to make the venture, seemed to think it might be better to stick to the ship until the sea should go down. Indeed one of them said as much, but the captain interrupted him, and was about to make another appeal, when there was a movement in the crowd, and one of the sub-engineers pushed towards him with the information that a volunteer was ready, and would appear immediately.

" Who is it ?" asked the captain.

K

"Mr. Berrington, sir; he's getting ready."

"The chief engineer!" exclaimed the captain. "Good; if there's a man in the ship can do it, he is the man."

Aileen, standing somewhat back in the crowd, thought she had caught a familiar sound!

"Who is going to make the venture?" she inquired of a man near her.

"The chief engineer, Miss, I believe."

At the moment the crowd opened and our hero came forward, clothed only in a shirt and duck trousers. His face was not streaked with professional paint on *this* occasion. It beamed with the flush and the latent fire of one who feels that he has made up his mind deliberately to face death.

"Oh! it's the man with the handsome figure," gasped Lintie, with a wild look of surprise.

Aileen did not now require to be told who it was. Unlike heroines, she neither screamed nor fainted, but through the wonder which shone in her eyes she shot forth another look,—one of proud confidence,—which Edgar caught in passing, and it rendered his power and purpose irresistible. The stern work before him, however, was not compatible with soft emotions. Seizing the end of the light line which was ready, he tied it firmly round his waist and leaped into the raging sea, while an enthusiastic cheer burst from the crew

At first it seemed as if the youth had been endowed with superhuman powers, so vigorously and with such ease did he push through the surf and spurn aside the pieces of wreck that came in his way; but as his distance from the vessel increased, and the surging foam bore him in among the rocks, he received several blows from a piece of the floating bulwarks. Once also he was launched with terrible violence against a rock. This checked him a little. Still, however, he swam on, apparently unhurt, while the people on board the wreck gazed after him with inexpressible eagerness. They not only thought of the imminent danger of the gallant youth, but fully realised the probability that his failure would be the sealing of their own doom.

As he drew near to the rocks on shore, a mass of wreck was seen to rise on the crest of the surf close to the swimmer's side and fall on him. An irresistible cry of despair burst from those in the ship. Some one shouted to haul on the line and pull him on board, and several seamen sprang to do so, but the captain checked them, for through his glass he could see Edgar struggling to free himself from the wreck. In a few minutes he succeeded, and the next wave hurled him on the rocky shore, to which he clung until the retreating water had lost its power. Then he rose, and struggling upwards, gained a ledge of rock where he was safe from the violence of the waves.

It need scarcely be said that his success was hailed with three tremendous cheers, and not a few deep and fervent exclamations of "Thank God" from some who regarded the young engineer's safety as a foretaste of their own. Some there were, however, who knew that the work which yet remained to be done was fraught with danger as well as difficulty. This work was commenced without delay.

By means of the light line which he had carried ashore, Edgar hauled the two ends of a stouter line or small rope from the wreck. These two ends he quickly spliced together, thus making the rope an endless one, or, as seamen have it, an endless fall. The other loop, or bight, of this endless double-rope was retained on the wreck, having been previously rove through a block or pulley which was attached to the broken fore-mast about ten feet above the deck —in accordance with our "rocket apparatus" directions. In fact, the whole contrivance, got up so hastily at this time, was just an extemporised rocket apparatus without the rocket—Edgar having already performed the duty of that projectile, which is to effect communication between wreck and shore.

By means of the endless fall our hero now hauled a heavy rope or cable from the wreck, the end of which he fastened round a large boulder. This rope, being hauled taut, remained suspended between the wreck

and the cliffs some feet above the sea. Previous
to fixing it a large block had been run upon it,
and to this block was suspended one of those
circular cork life-preservers which one usually sees
attached to the bulwarks of ships. It was made into
a sort of bag by means of a piece of canvas. The
endless fall was then attached to this bag so that
it could travel with its block backwards and forwards
on the thick cable.

The first who passed from the wreck to the shore
by means of this contrivance was a stout seaman
with two very small children in charge. The man
was sent partly to give the passengers confidence in
the safety of the mode of transit, and partly that he
might aid Edgar in the working of the tackle. The
next who passed was the mother of the children.
Then followed Aileen, and after her the sweet
singer. Thus, one by one, all the females and
children on board were borne in safety to land.

After these the male passengers commenced to go
ashore. A few of the older men were sent first.
Among them was Mr. Hazlit.

The unfortunate merchant was so weak as to be
scarcely equal to the exertion of getting over the side
into the life-buoy or bag, and he was so tall that, despite the efforts he made to double himself together,
there was so much of him above the machine
that he had a tendency to topple over. This

would have mattered nothing if he had possessed even a moderate degree of power to hold on, but his hands were as weak as those of a child. However, the case being desperate, he made the attempt, and was sent away from the wreck with many earnest cautions to "hold on tight and keep cool."

You may be sure that his progress was watched with intense anxiety by Aileen, who stood close to Edgar as he hauled in the rope carefully.

"Oh! he will fall out," she cried in an agony as the rope dipped a little, and let him just touch the roaring surf, when he was somewhat more than half way over.

Edgar saw that her fears were not unlikely to be realised. He therefore gave the rope to the seaman who had first come ashore, with orders to haul steadily.

Owing to its position and the dipping of the life-buoy with its burden, the cable formed a pretty steep slope from the shore. Throwing himself on the cable, Edgar slid swiftly down this incline until stopped by the buoy. The effect of course was to sink the machine deeper than ever, insomuch that poor Mr. Hazlit, unable any longer to withstand the buffeting, threw up his arms with a cry of despair. Edgar caught him as he was falling over.

"Here, put your arms round my neck," he cried, struggling violently to fix himself firmly to the life-buoy.

The merchant obeyed instantly, giving the youth an embrace such as he had never expected to receive at his hands! Even in that moment of danger and anxiety, Edgar could not help smiling at the gaze of unutterable wonder which Mr. Hazlit cast on him through the salt water—if not tears—that filled his eyes, for he had not seen the youth when he jumped overboard.

"Haul away!" shouted our hero; but the words were stifled by a sea which at the moment overwhelmed them.

The man at the line, however, knew what to do. He and some of the passengers hauled steadily but swiftly on the line, and in a few seconds the buoy, with its double freight, was brought safe to land. Mr. Hazlit was carried at once by his rescuer to a recess in the cliffs which was partially protected from the storm, and Edgar, after doing what he could to place him comfortably on the ground, left him to the care of his daughter.

On his return to the beach he found the passengers who had been saved in a state of great alarm because of the slipping backwards of the wreck, which strained the cable so much that it had become as rigid as a bar of iron. He began, therefore, to ply the means of rescue with redoubled energy, for there were still some of the passengers and all the crew on board; but suddenly, while the buoy was being sent out for another freight, the cable snapt, the wreck slid off the shelf or ledge on which it had hung so long, and sank in deep water, leaving nothing save a momentary whirlpool in the surf to tell where the splendid ocean palace had gone down.

The horror that filled the minds of those who witnessed the catastrophe cannot be described. A feeling of dreary desolation and helplessness followed the sudden cessation of violent energy and hopeful toil in which most of them had been previously engaged. This was in some degree changed, if not relieved, by the necessity which lay on all to face the vicissitudes of their new position.

That these were neither few nor light soon became apparent, for Edgar and the seaman, after an hour's investigation, returned to their friends with the information that they had been cast on a small rocky islet, which was uninhabited, and contained not a vestige of wood or of anything that could sustain the life of man. Thus they were left without shelter or food, or the means of quitting the inhospitable spot —not, however, without hope, for one of the seamen said that he knew it to be an isle lying not very far from the mainland, and that it was almost certain to be passed ere long by ships or native boats.

On further search, too, a spring of fresh water was discovered, with sufficient grass growing near it to make comfortable beds for the women and children.

The grass was spread under the shelter of an over-hanging cliff, and as the weather was warm, though stormy, the feelings of despair that had at first over-whelmed young and old soon began to abate. During the day the gale decreased and a hot sun came out at intervals, enabling them to dry their soaking garments.

That night, taking Edgar aside, Mr. Hazlit thanked him warmly for preserving his life.

" But," said he, seriously, " forgive me if I at once broach a painful subject, and point out that our posi-tions are not changed by this disaster. Much though I love my life I love my daughter's happiness more, and I would rather die than allow her to marry—excuse me, Mr. Berrington—a penniless man. Of course," continued the merchant, with a sad smile as he looked around him, " it would be ridiculous as well as ungrateful were I to forbid your holding ordinary converse with her *here*, but I trust to your honour that nothing more than *ordinary* converse shall pass between you."

" My dear sir," replied the youth, " you greatly mistake my spirit if you imagine that I would for one moment take advantage of the position in which I am now placed. I thank God for having permitted me to be the means of rendering aid to you and Ai—your daughter. Depend upon it I will not give you reason to regret having trusted my honour. But "

(he hesitated here) " you have referred to my position. If, in time and through God's goodness, I
succeed in improving my position; in gaining by
industry a sufficiency of this world's pelf to maintain
Aileen in a condition of comfort approaching in
some degree that in which she has been brought up,
may I hope—may I—"

Mr. Hazlit took the young man's hand and said,
" You may;" but he said it sadly, and with a look
that seemed to imply that he had no expectation of
Edgar ever attaining to the required position.

Satisfied with the shake of the hand, our hero
turned abruptly away, and went off to ruminate by
the sea-shore. At first he was filled with hope;
then, as he thought of his being penniless and without influential friends, and of the immense amount
of money that would have to be made in order to
meet the wealthy merchant's idea of comfort, he
began to despair. Presently the words came to
his mind—" Commit thy way unto the Lord; trust
also in Him, and He shall bring it to pass." This
revived him, and he began to run over in his mind
all sorts of wild plans of making a huge fortune
quickly! Again a word came to him—" Make not
haste to be rich."

" But what *is* making haste?" he thought, and his
conscience at once replied, " Taking illegitimate
courses—venturesome speculation without means—

devotion of the soul and body to business in such a way as to demoralise the one and deteriorate the other—engaging in the pursuit of wealth hastily and with eager anxieties, which imply that you doubt God's promise to direct and prosper all works committed to Him."

"My plan, then," thought Edgar, "is to maintain a calm and trusting mind; to be diligent in fulfilling *present* duty, whatever that may be; to look about for the direction that is promised, and take prompt advantage of any clear opportunity that offers. God helping me, I 'll try."

Strong in his resolves, but, happily, stronger in his trust, he returned to the cavern in which his companions in misfortune had already laid them down to rest, and throwing himself on a bed of grass near the entrance, quickly fell into that profound slumber which is the perquisite of those who unite a healthy mind to a sound body.

CHAPTER XI.

TELLS OF BOLD PLANS, FOLLOWED BY BOLDER DEEDS.

MONTHS passed away, and Miss Pritty, sitting in her little boudoir sipping a cup of that which cheers, received a letter.

" I know that hand, of course I do. How strange it is there should be such a variety of hands—no two alike, just like faces; though for my part I think that some faces are quite alike, so much so that there are one or two people who are always mistaken for each other, so that people don't know which is which. Dear me! what an awful thing it would be if these people were so like that each should forget which was the other! Nobody else being able to put them right, there would be irretrievable confusion. What do you want, eh ? "

The first part of Miss Pritty's mutterances was a soliloquy; the query was addressed to her small and only domestic with the dishevelled head, who lingered at the door from motives of curiosity.

"Nothink, ma'am. Do you wish me to wait, ma'am?"

" No ;—go."

She went, and Miss Pritty, opening the letter, exclaimed, "From my nephew, Edgar! I knew it. Dear fellow! I wonder why he writes to *me*."

The letter ran as follows :—

"DEAR AUNT,—You will doubtless be surprised to receive a letter from me. It must be brief; the post leaves in an hour. Since I saw you we have had a charming voyage out, but at the last we ran on a rocky island off the coast of China, and became a total wreck in a few minutes."

At this point Miss Pritty gasped "oh!" and fainted—at least she went into a perfect semblance of the state of coma, but as she recovered suddenly, and appealed to the letter again with intense earnestness, it may have been something else that was the matter. She resumed her perusal :—

" We succeeded in getting a hawser on shore, by means of which, through God's mercy, nearly all the passengers were saved, including, of course, your friend Miss Hazlit and her father. It is mournful to have to add, however, that before the work was finished the wreck slipped into deep water and sank with all her crew on board. We remained only one day on the rock, when a passing ship observed our signals, took us off, and carried us safely into Hong-Kong.

"Mr. Hazlit and his daughter immediately left for —I know not where! I remained here to make some

inquiries about the wreck, which I am told contains
a large amount of gold coin. Now, I want you to
take the enclosed letter to my father's old servant,
Joe Baldwin; help him to read it, if necessary, and to
answer it by return of post. It is important; therefore, dear aunt, don't delay. I think you know
Baldwin's address, as I've been told he lives in the
district of the town which you are wont to visit.
Excuse this shabby scrawl, and the trouble I ask
you to take, and believe me to be your loving
nephew,   EDGAR BERRINGTON."

Miss Pritty was a prompt little woman. Instead
of finishing her tea she postponed that meal to an
indefinite season, threw on her bonnet and shawl,
and left her humble abode abruptly.

Joe Baldwin was enjoying a quiet pipe at his
own fireside—in company with his buxom wife and
his friends Mr. and Mrs. Rooney Machowl—when
Miss Pritty tripped up to his door and knocked.

She was received warmly, for Joe sympathised
with her affectionate and self-denying spirit, and
Mrs. Joe believed in her. Woe to the unfortunate in
whom Mrs. Joe—*alias* Susan—did *not* believe.

" Come away, Miss,—glad to see you—always so,"
said Joe, wiping a chair with his cap and extinguish-
ing his pipe out of deference; "sit down, Miss."

Miss Pritty bowed all round, wished each of the

party good evening by name, and seating herself beside the little fire as easily and unceremoniously as though it had been her own, drew forth her letter.

"This is for you, Mr. Baldwin," she said; "it came enclosed in one to me, and is from my nephew, Edgar Berrington, who says it is important."

"Thank you, ma'am," said Joe, taking the letter, opening it, and looking at it inquiringly.

"Now Miss," said he, "it's of no manner o' use my tryin' to make it out. You musn't suppose, Miss, that divers can't read. There's many of 'em who have got a good education in the three *rs*, an' some who have gone further. For the matter of that I can read print easy enough, as you know, but I never *was* good at pot-hooks and hangers, d'ee see; therefore I'll be obliged, Miss, if you'll read it to me."

Miss Pritty graciously acceded to the request, and read:—

"DEAR BALDWIN,—My aunt, Miss Pritty, who will hand this letter to you, will tell you about our being wrecked. Now, in regard to that I have a proposal to make. First, let me explain. The wreck of the *Warrior*, after slipping off the ledge on which she struck, sank in twenty fathoms water. On our arrival at Hong-Kong, the agent of the owners sent off to see what could be done in the way of recovering the treasure on board—there being no less than fifty thousand pounds sterling in gold in her treasure-

room, besides valuables belonging to passengers.
Lloyds' agent also visited the place, and both came
to the conclusion that it was utterly impossible to
recover anything from such a depth by means of
divers.   This being so, and I happening to be on the
spot, offered to purchase the right to recover and
appropriate all the gold I could fish up.   They
laughed at me as a wild enthusiast, but, regarding the thing as hopeless themselves, were quite
willing to let me have the wreck, etc., for what you
would call 'an old song.'   Now, although nominally
a 'penniless man,' I do happen to possess a small
property, in the form of a block of old houses in
Newcastle, which were left to me by an uncle, and
which I have never seen.   On these I have raised
sufficient money for my purpose, and I intend to
make the venture, being convinced that with the
new and almost perfect apparatus now turned out in
London by our submarine engineers, bold divers may
reach even a greater depth than twenty fathoms.
My proposal then is, that you should come to my
aid.   I will divide all we bring up into three equal
portions.   One of these you shall have, one I'll keep
to myself, and the third shall be shared equally by
such divers as you think it advisable to employ.
What say you?   Do the prospects and terms suit,
and will you come without delay?   If so, reply at
once, and send all the requisite material to this place.

Be particular to bring dresses made by the first makers in London. I wish this to be a sort of semi-scientific experiment—to recover property from a great depth, to test the powers and properties of the various apparatus now in use and recently invented, and, while so doing, to make my fortune as well as yours, and that of all concerned! Perhaps you think the idea a wild one. Well, it may be so, but wilder ideas than this have been realised. Remember the noble house of Mulgrave!—Yours truly,

" Edgar Berrington."

The last sentence in the letter referred to a fact in the history of diving which is worthy of mention. In or about the year 1683 a man named Phipps, the son of an American blacksmith, was smitten with a mania, then prevalent, for recovering treasure from sunken wrecks by means of diving. He succeeded in fishing up a small amount from the wreck of a Spanish galleon off the coast of Hispaniola, which, however, did not pay expenses. Being a man of indomitable perseverance as well as enthusiasm, Phipps continued his experiments with varying success, and on one occasion—if not more—succeeded in reducing himself to poverty. But the blacksmith's son was made of tough material—as though he had been carefully fashioned on his father's anvil. He was a man of strong faith, and this, in material as well as spiritual affairs, can remove mountains. He was invincibly convinced of the practicability of his schemes. As is usual in such men, he had the power to impart his faith to others. He had moved Charles the Second to assist him in his first efforts, which had failed, but was unable to similarly influence the cautious—not to say close-fisted—James the Second. The Duke of Albemarle, however, proved more tractable. Through his aid and influence, and with funds obtained from the public, Phipps was enabled in 1687 once more to try his fortune. He set sail in a 200-ton vessel, and after many fruitless efforts succeeded in raising from a depth of between six and seven fathoms (considered but a small depth now-a-days) property to the value of about £300,000. Of this sum the usurious Earl obtained as his share £90,000 while Phipps received £20,000. Although James the Second had refused to aid in the expedition, he had the wisdom to recognise the good service done to mankind in the saving of so much valuable property at so great personal risk. He knighted Phipps, who thus became the founder of the house of Mulgrave—now represented by the Marquis of Normanby.

When Miss Pritty had concluded the letter, Joe Baldwin turned to Rooney Machowl:—

"What think you, lad," he said, "would you venture down to twenty fathom?"

"To twenty thousand fathom, if you'll consint to watch the pumps and howld the life-line," replied the daring son of Erin.

"Will you let me go, Susan?" said Baldwin, turning to his wife.

"How could I hinder you, Joe?" answered Mrs. Baldwin, with a face reddened by suppressed emotion at the bare idea.

"And will you go with me, Susan?"

"I'd sooner go to the—" she stopped, unable to decide as to what part of earth she would not sooner go to than China, but not being versed in geography she finished by asserting that she'd sooner go to the moon!

Pretty little Mrs. Machowl, on the contrary, vowed that no power on earth should separate between her and her Rooney, and that if he went she should go, and the baby too.

"Well then, Miss," said Baldwin to his visitor, "if you'll be so kind as to write for me I'll be obliged. Say to Mister Eddy—I can't forget the old name, you see—that I'm agreeable; that I'll undertake the job, along with Rooney Machowl here, and mayhap another man or two. I'll get all the dresses and apparatus he requires, and will set sail as soon as I can; but, you see, I can't well start right off, because I've a job or two on hand. I've a well to go down an' putt right, an' I've some dock repairs to finish.

However, to save time I'll send Rooney off at once with one dress and apparatus, so that they can be tryin' experiments till I arrive—which will be by the following steamer. Now, Miss, d'you think you can tell him all that?"

"I will try," said Miss Pritty, making rapid entries in a small note-book, after completing which and putting a few more questions she hurried home.

Meanwhile Rooney's wife went off to make arrangements for a long voyage, and a probably prolonged residence in foreign parts, and Joe Baldwin went to visit the well he had engaged to descend, taking Rooney as his assistant. During his visit to this well, Joe underwent some experiences, both physical and mental, which tried his nerve and courage more severely than any descent he had ever made in the open sea.

It is a well-known fact among divers that various temperaments are suited to various works, and that, among other things, many men who are bold enough in open water lose courage in confined places such as wells. They say—so powerful is imagination!— that they "cannot breathe" down in a well, though, of course, the means of breathing is the same in all cases. Joe Baldwin, being gifted with cool blood and strong nerves, and possessing very little imagination, was noted among his fellows for his readiness and ability to venture anywhere under water and do anything.

The well in question was connected with the water-works of a neighbouring town. Having got himself and his apparatus conveyed thither he spent the night in the town and proceeded on the following morning at day-break to inspect the scene of his operations.

The well was an old one and very deep—about fifteen fathoms. That, however, was a matter of small importance to our diver. What concerned him most was the narrowness of the manhole or entrance at the top, and the generally dilapidated state of the whole affair.

The well, instead of being a circular hole in the ground lined with brick, like ordinary wells, was composed of huge iron cylinders four feet in diameter, fitted together and sunk ninety feet into the ground. This vast tube or circular iron well rested on a foundation of brickwork. When sunk to its foundation its upper edge was just level with the ground. Inside of this tube there were a variety of cross-beams, and a succession of iron ladders zigzagging from top to bottom, so that it could be descended when empty. At the time of Joe's visit it was found nearly full of water. Down the centre of the well ran two iron pipes, or pumps, each having a "rose" at its lower end, through which the water could be sucked and pumped up to a reservoir a hundred feet high for the supply of the town. These two pumps were worked by an engine whose distinguishing features were noise and rickets. It could, however, just do its work; but, recently, something had gone wrong with one of the pumps—no water was thrown up by it. Two results followed. On the one hand the water-supply to the town became insufficient, and, on the other, the surplus water in the well could not be pumped out so as to permit of a man descending to effect repairs. In these circumstances a diver became absolutely necessary. Hence the visit of Baldwin and Machowl.

"Now then, diver," said the managing engineer of the works to Joe, after he had examined everything above ground with care, "you see it is impossible to pump the well dry, because of the defective pump and the strength of the spring which feeds it. Water is admitted into the great cylinder through a number of holes in the bottom. These holes therefore must be stopped. In order to this, you will have to descend in the water with a bag of wooden pegs and a hammer—all of which are ready for you—and plug up these holes. You see, the work to be done is simple enough."

"Ay," asserted Baldwin, "but the way how to set about it ain't so simple or clear. How, for instance, is a man of my size to squeeze through that hole at the top?"

"You *are* large," said the engineer, regarding the diver for a moment, "but not too large, I should think, to squeeze through."

" What ! with a divin' dress on ? "

" Ah, true ; I fear that is a puzzling difficulty at the outset, for you see the well is frail, and we dare not venture to enlarge the hole by cutting the beams that support the pumps."

While he was speaking the diver put his head through the hole in question, and gazed down into darkness visible where water was dripping and gurgling, and hissing a sort of accompaniment to the discordant clanking and jarring of the pump-rods. The rickety engine that worked them kept puffing close alongside—grinding out a horrible addition to the din. As his eyes became more accustomed to the subdued light, Baldwin could see that there was an empty space between the surface of the water and the top of the well, great part of the first length of zigzag ladder being visible, and also the cross beams on which its foot rested. He also observed various green slimy beams, which being perpetually moistened by droppings from the pumps, seemed alive like water snakes.

" Well," said the diver, withdrawing his head, "I'll try it. I'll dress inside there. You're sure o' the old ingine, I fancy ?"

"It has not yet failed us," answered the engineer, with a smile.

"What would happen if it broke or stopped working?" asked Joe.

"The well would fill to the brim and overflow in a minute or two."

"So that," rejoined the diver, "if it caught me in the middle o' dressin', me and my mate would be drownded."

"You'd stand a good chance of coming to that end," replied the engineer, with a laugh. "Your mate might get out in time, but as you say the dress would prevent you getting back through the hole, there would be no hope for *you*."

"Well then, we'll begin," said Baldwin ; "come, Rooney, get the gear in order." So saying, the adventurous man went to work with his wonted energy. The air-pumps were set up, and two men of the works instructed in the use of them. Then Baldwin squeezed himself with difficulty through the manhole, and 'the dress was passed down to him. Rooney then squeezed himself through, and both went a few steps down the iron ladder until they stood on the cross-beams behind and underneath it. The position was exceedingly awkward, for the ladder obliged them to stoop, and they did not dare to move their feet except with caution, for fear of slipping off the beams into the water—in which, even as it was, they were ankle-deep while standing on the beams. They were soon soaked to the skin by the drippings and spirtings from the pipes, and almost incapable of hearing each other speak, owing to the din. If Rooney had dropped the lead-soled boots or the shoulder-weights, they would have sunk at once beyond recovery, and have rendered the descent of the diver very difficult if not impossible.

Realising all this, the two comrades proceeded with great care and slowness. Dressing a diver in the most favourable circumstances involves a considerable amount of physical exertion and violence of action. It may therefore be well believed that in the case of which we write, a long time elapsed before Baldwin got the length of putting on his helmet. At last it was screwed on. Then a hammer and a bagful of wooden pins were placed in his hands.

"Now, Joe, are ye aisy?" asked Rooney, holding the front glass in his hand, preparatory to sealing his friend up.

"All right," answered Baldwin.

"Set agoin' the air-pumps up there," shouted Rooney, from whose face the perspiration flowed freely, as much from anxiety about his friend as from prolonged exertion in a constrained attitude.

In a few seconds the air came hissing into the

helmet, showing that the two men who wrought it were equal to their duty, though inexperienced.

" All right ?" asked Rooney a second time.

The reply was given, " Yes," and the bull's-eye was screwed on.

Rooney then sprang up the ladder and through the manhole ; took his station at the signal-line and air-pipe, while the engineer of the works watched the air-pump. The rickety steam-engine was then stopped, and, as had been predicted, the water rose quickly. It rose over Baldwin's knees, waist, and head, and, finally, rushed out at the manhole, deluging Rooney's legs.

Our diver was now fairly imprisoned ; an accident, however trifling in itself, that should stop the air-pump would have been his death-knell. Fully impressed with this uncomfortable assurance, he felt his way slowly down the second ladder, knocking his head slightly against cross-beams as he went, holding on tightly to his bag and hammer, and getting down into darkness so profound as to be "felt." He soon reached the head of the third ladder, and then the fourth.

But here, at a depth of about thirty feet, an unexpected difficulty occurred which had well-nigh caused a failure. The head of the fourth ladder was covered with wood, through which a square manhole led to the bottom of the well. Of course Joe

Baldwin discovered this only by touch, and great was his anxiety when, passing his hand round it, he found the hole to be too small for his broad shoulders to pass. At this point, he afterwards admitted, he "felt rather curious," the whole structure being very frail. However, with characteristic determination he muttered to himself, " never mind, Joe, do it if you can," and down he went through the hole, putting one arm down with his body, and holding the other up and drawing it down after him, by which process he squeezed his shoulders through at an angle. After reaching the bottom of the well, a feeling of alarm seized him lest he should be unable to force his way upwards through the hole. To settle this question at once he ascended to it, forced himself through, and then, being easy in mind, he redescended to the bottom and went to work with the hammer and wooden pegs.

At first he had some difficulty in finding the holes in the great cylinder, but after a dozen of them had been plugged it became easier, as the water rushed in through the remaining holes with greater force. While thus engaged his foot suddenly slipped. To save himself from falling—he knew not whither—he let go the bag of pegs and the hammer —the first of which went upwards and the latter down. To find the hammer in total darkness among the brick-work at the bottom was hopeless, therefore

Joe signalled that he was coming up, and started for the top after the bag, but failed to find it. In much perplexity he went to the upper manhole and put up one of his hands.

To those who were inexperienced it was somewhat alarming to see the hand of an apparently drowning man with the fingers wriggling violently, but Rooney understood matters.

"Arrah, now," said he, giving the hand a friendly shake, "it's somethin' you're wantin', sure. What a pity it is wan can't spake wid his fingers!"

Presently the hand shut itself as if grasping something, and moved in a distinct and steady manner.

"Och! it's a hammer he wants. He's gone an' lost it. Here you are, boy—there's another."

The hand disappeared, transferred the implement to the left hand, and reappeared, evidently asking for more.

"What now, boy?" muttered Rooney, with a perplexed look.

"Doubtless he wants more pegs," said the engineer of the works, coming up at the moment.

"Sure, sur, that can't be it, for if he'd lost his pegs wouldn't they have comed up an' floated?"

"They've caught somewhere, no doubt, among the timbers on the way up. Anyhow, I had provided against such an accident," said the engineer,

DOWN THE WELL.—Page 172.

putting another bag of pegs into the impatient hand.

It seemed satisfied, and disappeared at once.

Joe returned to the bottom, and succeeded in plugging every hole, so that the water from the outside spring could not enter. That done, he ascended, and signalled to the engineer to begin pumping. The rickety engine was set to work, and soon reduced the water so much that Rooney was able to re-descend and undress his friend. Thereafter, in about five hours, the well was pumped dry. The engineer then went down, and soon discovered that one of the pump-rods had been broken near the foot, and that its bucket lay useless at the bottom of the pipe. The repairs could now be easily made, and our divers, having finished their difficult and somewhat dangerous job, returned home.[1]

Next day Joe Baldwin paid a visit to the neighbouring harbour, where a new part of the pier was being built by divers. His object was to sound our surly friend David Maxwell about joining him in his intended trip to the antipodes, for Maxwell was a first-rate diver, though a somewhat cross-grained man.

---

[1] A "job" precisely similar to this was undertaken, and successfully accomplished by Corporal Falconer of the Royal Engineers, and assistant-instructor in diving, from whom we received the details. The gallant corporal was publicly thanked and promoted for his courage and daring in this and other diving operations.

Maxwell was under water when he arrived. It was Baldwin's duty to superintend part of the works. He therefore went down, and met his man at the bottom of the sea. Joe took a small school-slate with him, and a piece of pencil—for, the depth being not more than a couple of fathoms, it was possible to see to read and write there.

The spot where Maxwell wrought was at the extreme end of the unfinished part of the break-water. He was busily engaged at the time in laying a large stone which hung suspended to a travelling-crane connected with the temporary works overhead. Joe refrained from interrupting him. Another man assisted him. In the diver fraternity, there are men who thoroughly understand all sorts of handicrafts—there are blacksmiths, carpenters, stone-masons, etc. Maxwell was a skilled mechanic, and could do his work as well under water as many a man does above it—perhaps better than some! The bed for the stone had been carefully prepared on a mass of solid masonry which had been already laid. By means of the signal-line Maxwell directed the men in charge of the crane to move it forward, backward, to the right or to the left, as required. At last it hung precisely over the required spot, and was lowered into its final resting-place.

Then Baldwin tapped Maxwell on the shoulder. The latter looked earnestly in at the window—if we may so call it—of his visitor, and, recognising Joe, shook hands with him. Joe pointed to a rock, and sat down. Maxwell sat down beside him, and then ensued the following conversation. Using the slate, Baldwin wrote in large printed letters :—

" I 've got a splendid offer to go out to dive in the China seas. Are you game to go ?"

Taking the slate and pencil, Maxwell wrote— " Game for anything !"

" We must finish this job first," wrote Joe, " and I shall send Rooney out before us with some of the gear—to be ready."

" All right," was Mawell's laconic answer.

Baldwin nodded approval of this, but the nod was lost on his comrade owing to the fact that his helmet was immovably fixed to his shoulders. Maxwell evidently understood it, however, for he replied with a nod which was equally lost on his comrade. They then shook hands on it, and Joe, touching his signal-line four times, spurned the ground with a light fantastic toe, and shot to the realms above like a colossal cherub.

CHAPTER XII.

DIVING PRACTICE EXTRAORDINARY IN THE EAST.

In a certain street of Hong-Kong there stands one of those temples in which men devote themselves to the consumption of opium, that terrible drug which is said to destroy the natives of the celestial empire more fatally than " strong drink " does the peoples of the west. In various little compartments of this temple, many celestials lay in various conditions of debauch. Among them was a stout youth of twenty or so. He was in the act of lighting the little pipe from which the noxious vapour is inhaled. His fat and healthy visage proved that he had only commenced his downward career.

He had scarce drawn a single whiff, however, when a burly sailor-like man in an English garb entered the temple, went straight to the compartment where our beginner reclined, plucked the pipe from his hand, and dashed it on the ground.

"I *know'd* ye was here," said the man, sternly, "an' I *said* you was here, an' sure haven't I *found* you here—you spalpeen! you pig-faced bag o' fat! What d'ee mane by it, Chok-foo? Didn't I say I'd give you as much baccy as ye could chaw or smoke an ye'd only kape out o' this place? Come along wid ye!"

It is perhaps scarcely necessary to say that the man who spoke, and who immediately collared and dragged Chok-foo away, was none other than our friend Rooney Machowl. That worthy had been sent to China in advance of the party of divers with his wife and baby—for in the event of success he said he'd be able to "affoord it," and in the event of failure he meant to try his luck in " furrin' parts," and would on no account leave either wife or chick behind him.

On his arrival a double misfortune awaited him. First he found that his employer, Edgar Berrington, was laid up with fever, in the house of an English friend, and could not be spoken to, or even seen; and second, the lodging in which he had put up caught fire the second night after his arrival, and was burnt to the ground, with all its contents, including nearly the whole of his diving apparatus. Fortunately, the unlucky Irishman saved his wife and child and money, the last having been placed in a leathern belt made for the purpose, and worn night and day round his waist. Being a resolute and hopeful man, Rooney determined to hunt up a diving apparatus

M

of some sort, if such was to be found in China, and he succeeded. He found, in an old iron-and-rag-store sort of place, a very ancient head-piece and dress, which were in good repair though of primitive construction. Fortunately, his own pumps and air-pipes, having been deposited in an out-house, had escaped the general conflagration.

Rooney was a man of contrivance and resource. He soon fitted the pump to the new dress and found that it worked well, though the helmet was destitute of the modern regulating valves under the diver's control, and he knew that it must needs therefore leave the diver who should use it very much at the mercy of the men who worked the pumps.

After the fire, Rooney removed with his family to the house of a Chinese labourer named Chok-foo, whose brother, Ram-stam, dwelt with him. They were both honest hard-working men, but Chok-foo was beginning, as we have seen, to fall under the baleful influence of opium-smoking. Ram-stam may be said to have been a teetotaler in this respect. They were both men of humble spirit.

Chok-foo took the destruction of his pipe and the rough collaring that followed in good part, protesting, in an extraordinary jargon, which is styled Pidgin-English, that he had only meant to have a "Very littee smokee," not being able, just then, to resist the temptation.

"Blathers!" said Rooney, as they walked along in the direction of the lower part of the town, "you could resist the timptation aisy av you'd only try, for you're only beginnin', an' it hasn't got howld of 'ee yit. Look at your brother Ram, now; why don't 'ee take example by him?"

"Yis, Ram-stam's first-chop boy," said Chok-foo, with a penitential expression on his fat visage.

"Well, then, you try and be a first-chop boy too, Chok, an' it'll be better for you. Now, you see, you've kep' us all waiting for full half an hour, though we was so anxious to try how the dress answers."

In a few minutes the son of Erin and the China-man entered the half ruinous pagoda which was their habitation. Here little Mrs. Machowl was on her knees before an air-pump, oiling and rubbing up its parts. Ram-stam, with clasped hands, head a little on one side, and a gentle smile of approbation on his lips, admired the progress of the operation.

"Now then, Chok and Ram," said Rooney, sitting down on a stool and making the two men stand before him like a small awkward squad, "I'm goin' to taich you about pumps an' pumpin', so pay attintion av ye plaze. Hids up an' ears on full cock! Now then."

Here the vigorous diver began an elaborate expla-nation which we will spare the reader, and which his pupils evidently did not comprehend, though

they smiled with ineffable sweetness and listened
with close attention. When, however, the teacher
descended from theory to practice, and took the
pump to pieces, put it up again, and showed the
manner of working, the Chinamen became more
intelligent, and soon showed that they could turn
the handles with great vigour. They were hopelessly stupid, however, in regard to the use of
the signal line—insomuch that Rooney began to
despair.

"Niver mind, boys," he cried, hopefully, "we'll
try it."

Accordingly he donned the diving dress, and
teaching his wife how to screw on the bull's-eye, he
gave the signal to "pump away."

Of course Chok-foo and Ram-stam, though anxious
to do well, did ill continually. When Rooney,
standing in the room and looking at them, signalled to give "more air," they became anxious and
gave him less, until his dress was nearly empty.
When he signalled for "less air" they gave him
more, until his dress nearly burst, and then, not
having the breast-valve, he was obliged to unscrew
his front-glass to prevent an explosion! At last the
perplexed man resolved to make his wife do duty as
attender to signals, and was fortunate in this arrangement at first, for Molly was quick of apprehension.
She soon understood all about it, and, receiving her

husband's signals, directed the Chinamen what to do. In order to test his assistants better, he then went out on the verandah of the pagoda, where the pumpers could not see him nor he them. He was, of course, fully dressed, only the bull's-eye was not fixed.

"Now, Molly, dear," said he, "go to work just as if I was goin' under water."

Molly dimpled her cheeks with a smile as she held up the glass, and said, "Are ye ready?"

"Not yet; putt your lips here first."

He stooped; Molly inserted part of her face into the circular hole, and a smack resounded in the helmet.

"Now, cushla, I'm ready."

"Pump away, boys," shouted the energetic little woman.

As soon as she heard the hiss of the air in the helmet, she screwed on the bull's-eye, and our diver was as much shut off from surrounding atmosphere as if he had been twenty fathoms under the sea. Then she went to where the pumpers were at work, and taking the air-pipe in one hand and the life-line in the other, awaited signals. These were soon sent from the verandah. More air was demanded and given; less was asked and the pumpers wrought gently. Molly gave one pull at the life-line, "All right?" Rooney replied, "All right." This was repeated several times. Then came four sharp pulls at the line. Molly was on the alert; she bid Ramstam continue to pump while Chok-foo helped her to pull the diver forcibly out of the verandah into the interior of the pagoda amid shouts of laughter, in which Rooney plainly joined though his voice could not be heard.

"Capital, Molly," exclaimed the delighted husband when his glass was off; "I always belaved—an' I belave it now more than iver—that a purty woman is fit for anything. After a few more experiments like that I'll go down in shallow wather wid an aisy mind."

Rooney kept his word. When he deemed his assistants perfect at their work, he went one morning to the river with all his gear, hired a boat, pushed off till he had got into two fathoms water, and then, dressing himself with the aid of the Chinamen, prepared to descend.

"Are you ready?" asked his wife.

"Yis, cushla, but you've forgot the kiss."

"Am I to kiss *all* the divers we shall have to do with before sending them down?" she asked.

"If you want *all* the divers to be kicked you may," was the reply.

Molly cut short further remark by giving the order to pump, and affixing the glass. For a few seconds the diver looked earnestly at the Chinamen and at his better half, who may have been said to hold his life in her hands. Then he stepped boldly on the short ladder that had been let down outside the boat, and was soon lost to view in the multitude of air-bells that rose above him.

Now, Rooney had neglected to take into his calculations the excitability of female nerves. It was all very well for his wife to remember everything and proceed correctly when he was in the verandah of the pagoda, but when she knew that her best-beloved was at the bottom of the sea, and saw the air-bells rising, her courage vanished, and with her courage went her presence of mind. A rush of alarm entered her soul as she saw the boiling of the water, and fancying she was giving too much air, she said hurriedly, " Pump slow, boys," but immediately conceiving she had done wrong, she said, " Pump harder, boys."

The Chinamen pumped with a will, for they also had become excited, and were only too glad to obey orders.

A signal-pull now came for "Less air," but Molly had taken up an idea, and it could not be dislodged. She thought it must be " More air" that was wanted.

" Pump away, boys—pump," she cried, in rapidly increasing alarm.

Chok-foo and Ram-stam obeyed.

The signal was repeated somewhat impatiently.

"Pump away, boys; for dear life—pump," cried the little woman in desperate anxiety.

Perspiration rolled down the cheeks of Chok-foo and Ram-stam as they gasped for breath and turned the handles with all the strength they possessed.

"Pump—oh! pump—for pity's sake."

She ended with a wild shriek, for at that moment the waves were cleft alongside, and Rooney Machowl came up from the bottom, feet foremost, with a bounce that covered the sea with foam. He had literally been blown up from the bottom—his dress being filled with so much compressed air that he had become like a huge bladder, and despite all his weights, he rolled helplessly on the surface in vain attempts to get his head up and his feet down.

Of course his distracted wife hauled in on the life-line with all her might, and Chok-foo and Ram-stam, forsaking the pump, lent their aid and soon hauled the luckless diver into the boat, when his first act was to deal the Chinamen a cuff each that sent one into the stern-sheets on his nose, and the other into the bow on his back. Immediately thereafter he fell down as if senseless, and Molly, with trembling hands, unscrewed the bull's-eye.

Her horror may be imagined when she beheld the countenance of her husband as pale as death, while blood flowed copiously from his mouth, ears, and nostrils.

"Niver mind, cushla!" he said, faintly, "I'll be all right in a minute. This couldn't have happened if I'd had one o' the noo helmets.—Git off my—"

"Ochone! he's fainted!" cried Mrs. Machowl; "help me, boys."

In a few minutes Rooney's helmet was removed, and he began to recover, but it was not until several days had elapsed that he was completely restored; so severe had been the consequences of the enormous pressure to which his lungs and tissues had been subjected, by the powerful working of the pump on that memorable day by Ram-stam and Chok-foo.

CHAPTER XIII.

TREASURE RECOVERED—ACCIDENTS ENCOUNTERED—AN UNEXPECTED
DISCOVERY—ENEMIES MET AND CIRCUMVENTED.

It is pleasant to loll in the sunshine on a calm day in the stern of a boat and gaze down into un- fathomable depths, as one listens to the slow, regular beating of the oars, and the water rippling against the prow—and especially pleasant is this when one in such circumstances is convalescent after a pro- longed and severe illness.

So thought Edgar Berrington one lovely morning, some months after the events related in the last chapter, as he was being rowed gently over the fair bosom of the China sea. The boat—a large one with a little one towing astern—was so far from the coast that no land could be seen. A few sea-gulls sported round them, dipping their wings in the wave, or putting a plaintive question now and then to the rowers. Nothing else was visible except a rocky isle not far off that rose abruptly from the sea.

" Well, we 're nearing the spot at last," said Edgar, heaving that prolonged sigh which usually indicates one's waking up from a pleasant reverie. "What a glorious world this is, Baldwin! How impressively it speaks to us of its Maker!"

"Ay, whether in the calm or in the storm," responded Joe.

"Yes; it was under a very different aspect I saw this place last," returned Edgar. "Yonder is the cliff now coming into view, where the vessel we are in search of went down."

"An ugly place," remarked Joe, who was steering the boat. "Come boys, give way. The morning's gittin' on, an' we must set to work as soon · ever we can. Time an' tide, you know, etcetera.

Rooney, Maxwell, Chok-foo, and Ram-stam, who were rowing, bent to their work with a will, but the heavy boat did not respond heartily, being weighted with a large amount of diving gear. Just then a light breeze arose, and the boat, obedient to the higher power, bent over and rippled swiftly on.

The only other individual on board was a Malay— the owner of the boat. He sat on the extreme end of the bow looking with a vacant gaze at the island. He was a man of large size and forbidding, though well-formed, features, and was clothed in a costume, half European half Oriental, which gave little clew to the nature of his profession—except that it savoured a good deal of the sea. His name, Dwarro, was, like his person, nondescript. Probably it was a corruption of his eastern cognomen. At all events it suffered further corruption from his companions in the boat, for Baldwin and Maxwell called him Dworro, while Rooney Machowl named him Dwarry. This diversity of pronunciation, however, seemed a matter of no consequence to the stolid boatman, who, when directly addressed, answered to any name that people chose to give him. He was taciturn—never spoke save when spoken to ; and at such times used English so broken that it was difficult to put it together so as to make sense. He was there only in capacity of owner and guardian of the boat. Those who hired it would gladly have dispensed with his services, but he would not let them have it without taking himself into the bargain.

Having reached the scene of the wreck of the *Warrior*, the party at once proceeded to sound and drag for it, and soon discovered its position, for it had not shifted much after slipping off the ledge, where it had met its doom on the night of the storm. Its depth under the surface was exactly twenty-three fathoms, or 138 feet.

"It will try our metal," observed Baldwin, "for the greatest depth that the Admiralty allow their divers to go down is twenty fathom."

"What o' that ?" growled Maxwell, " I 've worked myself many a time in twenty-three fathom water, an 'll do it again any day. *We* don't need to mind

what the Admiralty says. The submarine engineers
of London tell us they limit a man to twenty-five
fathom, an' they ought to know what's possible if
any one should."

"That's true, David," remarked Rooney, as he filled
his pipe, "but I've heard of a man goin' down
twenty-eight fathom, an' comin' up alive."

"Oh, as to that," said Berrington, "*I* have heard
of one man who descended to thirty-four fathom,
at which depth he must have sustained a pressure
of 88½ lbs. on every square inch of his body—
and *he* came up alive, but his case is an exception.
It was fool-hardy, and he could do no effective work
at such a depth. However, here we are, and here
we must go to work with a will, whatever the depth
be. You and I, Joe, shall descend first. The others
will look after us. I'll put on a Siebe and Gorman
dress. You will don one of Heinke and Davis, and
we'll take down with us one of Denayrouze's lamps,
reserving Siebe's electric light for a future occasion."

In pursuance of these plans the boat was moored
over the place where the wreck lay, a short ladder
was hung over the side of a smaller boat they had
in tow with its pendent line and weight, the pumps
were set up and rigged, the dresses were put on, and,
in a short time our hero found himself in his old
quarters down beside the great crank!

But ah! what a change was there! The grinding

had ceased for ever ; the great crank's labours were over, and its surface was covered with mud, sand, barnacles, and sea-weed, and involved in a maze of twisted iron and wrecked timbers—for the ship had broken her back in slipping into deep water, and wrenched her parts asunder into a state of violent confusion. Thick darkness prevailed at that depth, but Denayrouze's lamp rendered the darkness visible, and sufficed to enable the divers to steer clear of bristling rods and twisted iron-bands that might otherwise have torn their dresses and endangered their lives.

The work of inspection was necessarily slow as well as fraught with risk, for great difficulty was experienced while moving about, in preventing the entanglement of air-pipes and life-lines. The two men kept together, partly for company and partly to benefit mutually by the lamp. Presently they came on human bones tightly wedged between masses of timber. Turning from the sad spectacle, they descended into the cabin and made their way towards the place where Berrington knew that the treasure had been stowed. Here he found, with something like a shock of disappointment, that the stern of the vessel had been burst open, and the contents of the cabin swept out.

On further inspection, however, the treasure-room was found to be uninjured. Putting down the lamp on an adjacent beam, Edgar lifted a heavy mass of wreck from the ground, and dashed the door in. The scene that presented itself was interesting. On the floor lay a number of little barrels, which the divers knew contained the gold they were in search of. Most of these were so riddled by worms that they were falling to pieces. Some, indeed, had partially given way, so that the piles of coin could be seen through the staves, and two or three had been so completely eaten away as to have fallen off, leaving the masses of gold in unbroken piles. There were also bags as well as kegs of coin, all more or less in a state of decay.

The divers gazed at this sight for a few moments quite motionless. Then Edgar with one hand turned the lamp full on his companion's front glass so as to see his face, while with the other hand he pointed to the treasure. Joe's eyes expressed surprise, and his mouth smiling satisfaction. Turning the light full on his own face to show his comrade that he was similarly impressed, Edgar motioned to Joe to sit down on an iron chest that stood in a corner, and giving the requisite signal with his life-line, went up to the surface. He did this very slowly in order to accustom his frame to the change of pressure both of air and water, for he was well aware of the danger of rapid ascent from such a depth. Soon after, he redescended, bearing several canvas sacks, some cord, and a couple of

small crowbars. Placing the lamp in a convenient
position, and throwing the bags on the floor of the
treasure-room, Edgar and Baldwin set to work
diligently with the crowbars, broke open the kegs,
and emptied their golden contents into one of the
bags, until it was quite full; tied up the mouth,
fastened it to a rope which communicated with
the boat above, and gave the signal to hoist away.
The bag quickly rose and vanished.

Previous to redescending, our hero had arranged
with Rooney to have pieces of sail-cloth in readiness
to wrap the bags in the instant of their being got
into the small boat, so that when being transferred
to the large boat's locker, their form and contents
might be concealed from the pilot, Dwarro. The
precaution, however, did not seem to be necessary,
for Dwarro was afflicted with laziness, and devoted
himself entirely to the occupations of alternately
smoking, in a dreamy way, and sleeping.

For three hours the divers wrought under great
excitement, as well as pressure, and then, feeling
much exhausted, returned to the surface, having
sent up the contents of about twenty boxes and
kegs of treasure. Rooney and Maxwell then took
their turn under water, and were equally successful.

That night, being very calm and clear, they ran
the boat into a sheltered crevice among the cliffs,
and slept on board of her. Next morning at day-

break they were again at work, but were not equally fortunate, for although plenty of treasure was sent up, several accidents occurred which were severe, though, happily, not fatal.

In the first place, Baldwin tore his left hand badly while attempting to raise a heavy mass of ragged iron-plate that prevented his reaching some loose coin lying under it. This, though painful, did not render him altogether incapable of working. Then, while Edgar Berrington was passing from one part of the wreck to another, threading his way carefully, a mass of wire ropes and other wreckage suddenly dropt from a position where it had been balanced, and felled him to the deck with such violence that for a few moments he was stunned. On recovering, he found to his horror that he was pressed down by the mass, and had got inextricably entangled with it. If his dress had been torn at that time, or his helmet damaged, it is certain that his adventures would have been finally cut short, and there can be no doubt that his preservation was largely owing to the excellence of the material of which his dress was made.

But how to escape from his wire-cage was a difficulty he could not solve, for the lamp had been extinguished, and the entanglement of his line and air-pipe rendered signalling impossible. He continued to struggle helplessly, therefore, in total

N

darkness. That the air-tube continued all right, was evident from the fact that air came down to him as before.

In this dilemma he remained for a short time, occasionally managing to clear himself partially, and at other times becoming more and more involved.

At last Rooney Machowl, who was attending to the lines above, bethought him that he had not received any signals for some time or observed any of those motions which usually indicate that a diver is busy below. He therefore gave a pull to the life-line. Of course no answer was received.

"Hallo!" exclaimed Rooney, with a start, for in diving operations Life and Death frequently stand elbowing each other.

He gave another and still more decided pull, but no answer was returned.

Jumping up in excitement, he attempted to haul on the line, so as to bring Edgar to the surface by force, but to his consternation he found it to be immovably fixed.

"Hooroo! man alive," he yelled, rather than shouted, to Maxwell, who was attending the other line, "signal for Joe to come up—look sharp!"

Maxwell obeyed with four strong quick pulls on Joe's line, and Joe appeared at the surface rather sooner than was consistent with safety. On learning the cause of his being called, he refixed his bull's-eye hastily; went down again with a heavy plunge, and discovering his companion, soon removed the wreck by which he was entangled, and set him free.

Experience, it is said, teaches fools; much more does it instruct wise men. After this event our hero became a little more careful in his movements below.

When a considerable amount of treasure had been recovered, it was thought advisable to return to the shore and place it in security.

"It won't be easy to manage this," said Edgar to Baldwin in a low tone, as they sailed away from the rocky islet, under a light breeze. "I have an uncomfortable belief that that fellow Dwarro suspects the nature of the contents of these bags, despite our efforts at concealment."

"I don't think he does," whispered Baldwin. "He seems to me to be one o' these miserable opium-smokers whose brains get too much fuddled to understand or care for anything."

"Whist now, don't spake so loud," said Rooney, advancing his head closer to his companions, and glancing doubtfully at the object of their suspicion; "sure he's got a sharp countenance, fuddled or not fuddled."

The pilot had indeed an intelligent cast of countenance, but as he sat in a careless attitude in the bow of the boat smoking listlessly and gazing dreamily, almost stupidly, towards the shore, it did seem as though he had indulged too freely in the noxious drug which poisons so many inhabitants of these unhappy lands.

As he was out of earshot, the four adventurers drew their heads still closer together, and talked eagerly about their prospects.

"Sure our fortins is made already," said Rooney; "how much d'ee think we've fished up, Mr. Berrington?"

"I cannot say, but at a rough guess I should think not less than twenty thousand pounds."

"Ye don't main it? Och! Molly astore! ye shall walk in silks an' satins from this day forward—to say nothin' of a carridge an' four, if not six."

"But where'll we putt it, sir?" asked Baldwin.

"I've been thinking of that," replied Edgar. "You see I don't like the notion of running right into port with it, where this pilot has probably numerous friends who would aid him in making a dash for such a prize—supposing he has guessed what we are about. Now, I happen to have a trusty friend here, a young Scotchman, who lives in a quiet out-o'-the-way part. We'll run up to his place, land the gold quickly, and get him to carry it off to some place of security—"

"Whist, not so loud! I do belave," said Rooney, that rascal is cocking his weather ear."

"He don't understand a word of English," muttered Baldwin.

Dwarro looked so intensely absent and sleepy as he sat lounging in the bow, that the divers felt relieved and continued, though in more cautious tones, to discuss their plans.

Meanwhile the boat ran into the Hong-Kong river. As it proceeded, a small light boat or skiff was observed approaching. Baldwin, who steered, sheered out a little in the hope of avoiding her, but the man who sculled her conformed to the movement, and quickly shot past their bow—so closely that he could exchange salutations with the pilot. Nothing more appeared to pass between the two,—indeed there seemed no time for further communication— nevertheless Rooney Machowl declared that some telegraphic signals by means of hands and fingers had certainly been exchanged.

In a short time the boat was turned sharp round by Baldwin, and run into a cove near a wall in which was a little wooden gate. A flight of dilapidated steps led to this gate.

"What if your friend should not be at home?" asked Joe, in a whisper.

"I'll land the bags in any case and await him, while you return to the port with Dwarro," replied Edgar.

If the pilot was interested in their proceedings, he

must have been a consummate actor, for he took no notice whatever of the sudden change of the boat's course, but continued to smoke languidly, and to gaze abstractedly into the water as if trying to read his fortune there, while Edgar and Rooney landed the bags, and carried them through the little gate into the Scotchman's garden. In a few minutes Edgar returned to the boat, stepped in, and pushed off, while the two Chinamen, in obedience to orders, rowed out into the river.

"It's all right," whispered Edgar, sitting down beside Joe, "Wilson is at home, and has undertaken to have the bags carried to a place of safety long before any attempt to capture them could be organised, even if Dwarro knew our secret and were disposed to attempt such a thing. Besides, we will keep him under our eyes to-night as long as possible."

That night, highly elated at the success of their labours, our four friends sat round their evening meal in the pagoda and related their various diving adventures and experiences to the admiring and sympathetic Molly Machowl. They had previously entertained the pilot with unlimited hospitality and tobacco, and that suspected individual, so far from showing any restless anxiety to shorten his stay, had coolly enjoyed himself until they were at last glad when he rose to go away.

On the following morning, too, he was ready with

his boat before day-break, and the party returned to the scene of operations at the wreck in high spirits.

It is certain that their enthusiasm would have been considerably damped had they known that exactly three hours after their gold was landed, a party of six stout nautical-looking Malays entered the residence of Wilson, the Scotchman, knocked down Wilson's servants, gagged Wilson's mouth, drank up the claret with which Wilson had been regaling himself, and carried off the bags of gold before his very eyes! Fortunately for their peace of mind and the success of their labours, our adventurers did *not* know all this, but, descending to the wreck with heavy soles and light hearts, they proceeded to recover and send up additional bags of gold.

That day they were not quite so successful. Unforeseen difficulties lay in their way. Some of the gold had been washed out of the treasure-room in their absence, and was not easily recovered from the sand and sea-weed. In order the better to find this, the electric-lamp was brought into requisition and found to be most effective, its light being very powerful—equal to that of fifteen thousand candles,—and so arranged as to direct the light in four directions, one of these being towards the bottom by means of a reflecting prism. It burned without air, and when at the bottom, could be lighted or extinguished from the boat by means of electricity.

Still, notwithstanding its aid, they had not collected treasure beyond the value of about eight thousand pounds when the time for rest and taking their mid-day meal arrived. This amount was, however, quite sufficient to improve their appetites, and render them sanguine as to the work of the afternoon.

"You'd better signal Mr. Berrington to come up," said Joe, who with all the others of the party were assembled in the stern of the boat, anxiously waiting to begin their dinner.

"Sure I've done it twice a'ready," replied Rooney, who was attending to our hero's life-line while Ramstam and Chok-foo toiled at the air-pumps.

"What does he reply?" asked Joe.

"He replies, 'all right,' but nothin' more. If he knew the imptiness of my—och! there he goes at last, four tugs. Come along, my hearty," said Rooney, coiling away the slack as Edgar rose slowly to the surface.

Presently his helmet appeared like a huge round goblet ascending from the mighty deep. Then the surface was broken with a gurgle, and the goggle eyes appeared. Rooney unscrewed the front glass, and the Chinamen were free to cease their weary pumping. When Edgar was assisted into the boat, it was observed that he had a small peculiarly-shaped box under his arm. He made no reference to this until relieved of his helmet, when he took it up and examined it with much curiosity.

"What have you got there, sir?" asked Joe Baldwin, coming forward.

"That is just what I don't know," answered Edgar. "It seems to me like an iron or steel box much encrusted with rust, and I shouldn't wonder if it contained something of value. One thing is certain, that we have not got the key, and must therefore break it open."

While he was speaking, David Maxwell gazed at the box intently. He did not speak, but there was a peculiar motion about his lips as if he were licking them. A fiend happened just then to stand at Maxwell's ear. It whispered, "You know it."

"Ay," said Maxwell, under his breath, in reply, "*I* knows it—well."

"I wonder if there are valuables in it," said Edgar.

"Shouldn't wonder if there wor," said Rooney.

"Eight or nine thousand pounds, more or less," whispered the fiend, quoting words used by Mr. Hazlit on a former occasion.

"Ah—jis' so," muttered Maxwell.

"Don't you say a word more, David," said the fiend.

"I won't," muttered Maxwell's heart; for the hearts of men are desperately wicked.

"That's right," continued the fiend, "for if you

keep quiet, you know, the contents will fall to be divided among you, and the loss won't be felt by a rich fellow like old Hazlit."

Maxwell's heart approved and applauded the sentiment, but a stronger power moved in the rough man's heart, and softly whispered, "Shame!"

"Why, Maxwell," said Edgar, smiling, "you look at the box as if it were a ghost!"

"An' so it *is*," said Maxwell, with a sudden and unaccountable growl, at the sound of which the fiend sprang overboard, and, diving into the sea, disappeared from Maxwell's view for ever!

"Why, what d'ee mean, David?" asked Baldwin, in surprise.

"I mean, sir," said Maxwell, turning to Edgar with a look of unwonted honesty on his rugged face, "that that box is the ghost of one that belongs to Miss Hazlit, if it ain't the box itself."

"To Miss Hazlit," exclaimed Edgar, in surprise; "explain yourself."

In reply to this the diver told how he had originally become acquainted with the box and its contents, and said that he had more than once searched about the region of Miss Hazlit's cabin while down at the wreck in hope of finding it, but without success.

"Strange," said Edgar, "I too have more than once searched in the same place in the hope of finding something, or anything that might have belonged to her, but everything had been washed away. Of course, knowing nothing about this box, I did not look for *it*, and found it at last, by mere chance, some distance from the berth she occupied. Why did you not mention it before?"

Maxwell was silent, and at that moment the drift of thought and conversation was abruptly turned by Rooney Machowl shouting, "Dinner ahoy!" with impatient asperity.

While engaged in the pleasant duty of appeasing hunger, our divers chatted on many subjects, chiefly professional. Among other things, Rooney remarked that he had heard it said a diving dress contained sufficient air in it to keep a man alive for more than five minutes.

"I have heard the same," said Edgar.

"Come, David," suggested Joe Baldwin, "let's test it on you."

"Ready," said Maxwell, rising and wiping his huge mouth.

The proposal which was made in jest was thereupon carried out in earnest!

Dinner being over, Maxwell put on his diving dress; the Chinamen set the pump going, and the front glass was screwed on. Air was forced into the dress until it was completely inflated and looked as if ready to burst, while Maxwell stood on the deck holding on to a back-stay. At a given signal the pumpers ceased to work, and the adventurous man was thus cut off from all further communication with the outward air.

At first the onlookers were amused ; then they became interested, and as the minutes flew by, a little anxious, but Maxwell's grave countenance, as seen through the bull's-eye, gave no cause for alarm. Thus he stood for full ten minutes, and then opening the escape-valve, signalled for more air.

This was a sufficient evidence that a man might have ample time to return to the surface from great depths, even if the air-pumps should break down.

"But, perhaps," said Edgar, as they conversed on the subject, "you might not be able to hold out so long under water where the pressure would be great."

"Sure that's true.　What d'ee say to try, David ?" said Rooney.

Again Maxwell expressed willingness to risk the attempt.　The glass was once more screwed on, the pumps set agoing, and down the bold diver went to the bottom.　On receiving a pre-arranged signal, the pumps were stopped.

This, let the reader fully understand, is a thing that is never done with the ordinary pumps, which are not permitted to cease working from the time the bull's-eye is fixed on until after it is taken off, on the diver's return to the surface.　It was therefore with much anxiety that the experimenters awaited the result—anxiety that was not allayed by Rooney Machowl's expression of countenance, and his occasional suggestion that "he must be dead by this time," or, "Och! he's gone entirely now!"

For full five minutes Maxwell stayed under water without a fresh supply of air—then he signalled for it, and the anxious pumpers sent it down with a will. Thus it was found that there was still sufficient time for a man to return to the surface with the air contained in his dress, in the event of accident to the pumps.[1]

While the divers were engaged with these experiments, Chok-foo was sent on shore in the small boat for a supply of fresh water from a spring near the top of the island.

Having filled his keg, the Chinaman turned his fat good-humoured countenance toward the sea, for the purpose of taking an amiable view of Nature in general before commencing the descent. As he afterwards gazed in the direction of the mainland, he observed what appeared to be a line of sea-gulls on the horizon. He looked intently at these after shouldering his water-keg. Chok-foo's visage was yellow by nature. It suddenly became pale green.

---

[1] The pump used by Denayrouze of Paris, besides being very simple in its parts and action, possesses an air-reservoir which renders a cessation of the pump-action for a few minutes of no importance.

He dropped his burden and bounded down the hill-side as if he had gone mad. The water-keg followed him. Being small and heavy it overtook him, swept the legs from under him, and preceded him to the beach, where it was dashed to atoms. Chok-foo recovered himself, continued his wild descent, sprang into the boat, rowed out to his companions in furious haste, and breathlessly gave the information that pirates were coming!

Those to whom he said this knew too well what he meant to require explanation. They were aware that many so-called "traders" in the Eastern seas become pirates on the shortest notice when it suits their convenience.

Edgar Berrington immediately drew a revolver from his pocket, and stepping suddenly up to Dwarro, said sternly :—

" Look here !"

The pilot did look, and for the first time his calm, cool, imperturbable expression deserted him, for he saw that he had to deal with a resolute and powerful man. At the same time his right hand moved towards his breast, but it was arrested from behind in the iron grip of Joe Baldwin.

"Now, pilot," said Edgar, " submit, and no one shall harm you. Resist, and you are a dead man. Search him, Joe."

The diver opened Dwarro's pilot-coat, and found

beneath it a brace of pistols and a long sheath knife, which he quietly removed and transferred to his own person. The other men in the boat looked on, meanwhile, in silence.

"Dwarro," continued Edgar, " *you* have planned this, I know, but I'll thwart you. I won't tie or gag you. I'll make you sit at the helm and steer, while we evade your friends. I shall sit beside you, and you may rely on it that if you disobey an order in the slightest degree, or give a signal by word or look to any one, I'll blow out your brains. D' you understand me ?"

The pilot made no reply save by a slight inclina · tion of the head, while a dark frown settled on his features.

It was obvious that fear found no place in the man's breast, for a deep flush of indignation covered his countenance. He merely felt that he must obey or die, and wisely chose the former alternative.

Meanwhile the fleet of boats which had appeared to the Chinaman on the hill-top was now seen by the party in the boat as they drew nearer under the influence of a land breeze—their high sails rendering them visible before the low boat of our divers could be seen by them.

The wind had not yet reached the island, but, even if it had, the divers would not have hoisted sail, lest they should have been seen.

"Ship your oars now, lads, and pull for life," cried Edgar, seizing the tiller with one hand, while with the other he held the revolver. "You take *this* oar, Dwarro, and pull with a will."

In a few seconds the pilot boat was creeping pretty swiftly along the rugged shore of the island, in the direction of the open sea. To lighten her, the little boat astern was cut adrift. Continuing their course, they rowed quite past the island, and then, turning abruptly to the southward, they pulled steadily on until the first "cat's-paw" of the breeze ruffled the glassy sea.

By this time the fleet of boats was distinctly visible, making straight for the island. Edgar now ordered the sails to be set, and bade Dwarro take the helm. The pilot obeyed with the air of a Stoic. It was clear that his mind was made up. This had the effect of calling up a look of settled resolution on Edgar's face.

In a few minutes the sails filled, and then, to the surprise not only of Dwarro but all on board, Edgar ordered the pilot to steer straight for the line of advancing boats.

Two of these had changed their course on first observing the divers' boat, but when they saw it steering straight down, as if to meet or join them, they resumed their course for the island. Presently the breeze increased, and the pilot boat leaped over the waves as if it had received new life.

"It's a bowld thing to try," muttered Rooney Machowl, "but I'm afeard, sir——"

He was silenced by a peremptory "Hush" from Edgar. "Get down so as to be out of sight," he continued, "all of you except the Chinamen.—You two come and sit by Dwarro."

As he spoke, Edgar himself sat down on an oar, so as to be able to see over the gunwale without himself being seen. To those in the fleet it would thus appear that their vessel was a pilot boat returning from sea-ward with its skipper and two Chinamen. Whatever Dwarro's intentions had been, he was evidently somewhat disconcerted, and glanced more than once uneasily at the calm youth who sat pistol in hand at his side directing him how to steer.

Although there was a considerable fleet of the piratical boats, they were spread out so that a space of several hundred yards intervened between each. Edgar steered for the centre of the widest gap, and his bold venture was favoured by a sudden increase of wind, which caused the waves to gurgle from the bow.

Just as they passed between two of the boats they were hailed by one of them. Edgar kept his eyes fixed on Dwarro, who became slightly pale. The click of the pistol at the moment caused the pilot to start.

"You may inform and we may be caught," said

Edgar, sternly; "but whatever happens you shall die if you disobey. Speak not, but wave your hand in reply."

Dwarro obeyed. Those who had hailed him apparently thought the distance too great for speech; they waved their hands in return, and the boat passed on. A few minutes more and our divers were safely beyond the chance of capture, making for the mainland under a steady breeze.

CHAPTER XIV.

MISS PRITTY'S "WORST FEARS" ARE MORE THAN REALISED.

TURN we now to Miss Pritty—and a pretty sight she is when we turn to her! In her normal condition Miss Pritty is the pink of propriety and neatness. At the present moment she lies with her mouth open, and her eyes shut, hair dishevelled, garments disordered, slippers off, and stockings not properly on. Need we say that the sea is at the bottom of it? One of the most modest, gentle, unassuming, amiable of women has been brought to the condition of calmly and deliberately asserting that she "doesn't care!"—doesn't care for appearances; doesn't care for character; doesn't care for past reminiscences or future prospects; doesn't care, in short, for anything—life and death included. It is a sad state of mind and body—happily a transient!

"Stewardess."

"Yes, Miss?"

"I shall die."

"Oh no, Miss, don't say so. You'll be quite well in

a short time" (the stewardess has a pleasant motherly way of encouraging the faint-hearted). "Don't give way to it, Miss. You've no idea what a happytite you'll 'ave in a few days. You'll be soon able to eat hoceans of soup and 'eaps of fat pork, and—"

She stops abruptly, for Miss Pritty has gone into sudden convulsions, in the midst of which she begs the stewardess, quite fiercely, to "Go away."

Let us draw a veil over the scene.

Miss Pritty has been brought to this pass by Mr. Charles Hazlit, whose daughter, Aileen, has been taken ill in China. Being a man of unbounded wealth, and understanding that Miss Pritty is a sympathetic friend of his daughter and an admirable nurse, he has written home to that lady requesting her, in rather peremptory terms, to "come out to them." Miss Pritty, resenting the tone of the request as much as it was in her nature to resent anything, went off instanter, in a gush of tender love and sympathy, and took passage in the first ship that presented itself as being bound for the China seas. She did not know much about ships. Her maritime ideas were vague. If a washing-tub had been advertised just then as being A.1. at Lloyds' and about to put forth for that region of the earth with every possible convenience on board for the delight of human beings, she would have taken a berth in it at once.

We do not intend to inflict Miss Pritty's voyage on our reader. Suffice it to say that she survived it, reached China in robust health, and found her sick friend,—who had recovered,—in a somewhat similar condition.

After an embrace such as women alone can bestow on each other, Miss Pritty, holding her friend's hand, sat down to talk. After an hour of interjectional, exclamatory, disconnected, irrelevant, and largely idiotical converse—sustained chiefly by herself—Miss Pritty said :—

"And oh! the pirates!"

She said this with an expression of such awful solemnity that Aileen could not forbear smiling as she asked—

"Did you see any ?"

"Gracious! No," exclaimed Miss Pritty, with a look of horror, "but we *heard* of them. Only think of that! If I have one horror on earth which transcends all other horrors in horribleness, that horror is—pirates. I once had the misfortune to read of them when quite a girl—they were called Buccaneers, I think, in the book—and I have never got over it. Well, one day when we were sailing past the straits of Malacca,—I think it was,—our captain said they were swarming in these regions, and that he had actually seen them—more than that, had slain them with his own—oh! it is too horrible to think of.

And our captain was *such* a dear good man too. Not fierce one bit, and *so* kind to everybody on board, especially the ladies! I really *cannot* understand it. There are such dreadfully strange mixtures of character in this world. No, he did not say he had slain them, but he used nautical expressions which amount to the same thing, I believe; he said he had spiflicated lots of 'em and sent no end of 'em to somebody's locker. It may be wrong in me even to quote such expressions, dear Aileen, but I cannot explain myself properly if I don't. It is fearful to know there are so many of them, 'swarming,' as our captain said."

"The worst of it is that many of the boatmen and small traders on the coast," said Aileen, "are also pirates, or little better."

"Dreadful!" exclaimed her friend. "Why, oh *why* do people go to sea at all?"

"To transport merchandise, I suppose," said Aileen. "We should be rather badly off without tea, and silk, and spices, and such things—shouldn't we?"

"Tea and silk! Aileen. I would be content to wear cotton and drink coffee or cocoa—which latter I hate—if we only got rid of pirates."

"Even cotton, coffee, and cocoa are imported, I fear," suggested Aileen.

"Then I'd wear wool and drink water—anything

for peace. Oh *how* I wish," said Miss Pritty, with as much solemn enthusiasm as if she were the first who had wished it, "that I were the Queen of England—*then* I'd let the world see something."

"What would you do, dear?" asked Aileen.

"Do! well, I'll tell you. Being the head of the greatest nation of the earth—except, of course, the Americans, who assert their supremacy so constantly that they *must* be right—being the head, I say, of the greatest earthly nation (with that exception), I would order out all my gun-ships and turret-boats, and build new ones, and send them all round to the eastern seas, attack the pirates in their strongholds, and—and—blow them all out o' the water, or send the whole concern to the bottom! You needn't laugh, Aileen. Of course I do not use my own language. I quote from our captain. Really you have no idea what strong, and to me quite new expressions that dear man used. So powerful too, but *never* naughty. No, never. I often felt as if I ought to have been shocked by them, but on consideration I never was, for it was more the manner than the matter that seemed shocking. He was so gentle and kind, too, with it all. I shall *never* forget how he gave me his arm the first day I was able to come on deck, after being reduced to a mere shadow by sea-sickness, and how tenderly he led me up and down, preventing me, as he expressed it, from lurching into the lee-scuppers, or going slap through the quarter-rails into the sea."

After a little more desultory converse, Aileen asked her friend if she were prepared to hear some bad news.

Miss Pritty declared that she was, and evinced the truth of her declaration by looking prematurely horrified.

Aileen, although by no means demonstrative, could not refrain from laying her head on her friend's shoulder as she said, "Well then, dear Laura, we are beggars! Dear papa has failed in business, and we have not a penny in the world!"

Miss Pritty was not nearly so horrified as she had anticipated being. Poor thing, she was so frequently in the condition of being without a penny that she had become accustomed to it. Her face, however, expressed deep sympathy, and her words corresponded therewith.

"How did it happen?" she asked, at the close of a torrent of condolence.

"Indeed I don't know," replied Aileen, looking up with a smile as she brushed away the two tears which the mention of their distress had forced into her eyes. "Papa says it was owing to the mismanagement of a head clerk and the dishonesty of a foreign agent, but whatever the cause, the fact is that we are ruined Of course that means, I suppose, that we shall have **no** more than enough to procure the bare necessaries of life, and shall now, alas! know experimentally what it is to be poor."

Miss Pritty, when in possession of "enough to procure the bare necessaries of life," had been wont to consider herself rich, but her powers of sympathy were great. She scorned petty details, and poured herself out on her *poor* friend as a true comforter— counselled resignation as a matter of course, but suggested such a series of bright impossibilities for the future as caused Aileen to laugh, despite her grief.

In the midst of one of these bursts of hilarity Mr. Hazlit entered the room. The sound seemed to grate on his feelings, for he frowned as he walked, in an absent mood, up to a glass case full of gaudy birds, and turned his back to it under the impression, apparently, that it was a fire.

"Aileen," he said, jingling some loose coin in his pocket with one hand, while with the other he twisted the links of a massive gold chain, "your mirth is ill-timed. I am sorry, Miss Pritty, to have to announce to you, so soon after your arrival, that I am a beggar."

As he spoke he drew himself up to his full height, and looked, on the whole, like an over-fed, highly ornamented, and well-to-do beggar.

"Yes," he said, repeating the word with emphasis as if he were rather proud of it, "a beggar. I have not a possession in the world save the clothes on my back, which common decency demands that my creditors should allow to remain there. Now, I have all my life been a man of action, promptitude, decision. We return to England immediately—I do not mean before luncheon, but as soon as the vessel in which I have taken our passage is ready for sea, which will probably be in a few days. I am sorry, Miss Pritty, that I have put you to so much unnecessary trouble, but of course I could not foresee what was impending. All I can do now is to thank you, and pay your passage back in the same vessel with ourselves if you are disposed to go. That vessel, I may tell you, has been selected by me with strict regard to my altered position. It is a very small one, a mere schooner, in which there are no luxuries though enough of necessaries. You will therefore, my child, prepare for departure without delay."

In accordance with this decision Mr. and Miss Hazlit and Miss Pritty found themselves not long afterwards on board the *Fairy Queen* as the only passengers, and, in process of time, were conveyed by winds and currents to the neighbourhood of the island of Borneo, where we will leave them while we proceed onward to the island of Ceylon. Time and distance are a hindrance to most people. They are fortunately nothing whatever in the way of writers and readers !

Here a strange scene presents itself; numerous pearl-divers are at work—most of them native, some European. But with these we have nothing particular to do, except in so far as they engage the attention of a certain man in a small boat, whose movements we will watch. The man had been rowed to the scene of action by two Malays from a large junk, or Chinese vessel, which lay in the offing. He was himself a Malay—tall, dark, stern, handsome, and of very powerful build. The rowers were perfectly silent and observant of his orders, which were more frequently conveyed by a glance or a nod than by words.

Threading his way among the boats of the divers, the Malay skipper, for such he seemed, signed to the rowers to stop, and directed his attention specially to one boat. In truth this boat seemed worthy of attention because of the energy of the men on board of it. A diver had just leaped from its side into the sea. He was a stalwart man of colour, quite naked, and aided his descent by means of a large stone attached to each of the sandals which he wore. These sandals, on his desiring to return to the surface, could be thrown off, being recoverable by means of cords fastened to them. Just as he went down another naked diver came up from the bottom, and was assisted into the boat. A little blood trickled from his nose and ears, and he appeared altogether much exhausted. No wonder. He had not indeed remained down at any time more than a minute and a half, but he had dived nearly fifty times that day, and sent up a basket containing a hundred pearl oysters each time.

Presently the man who had just descended re-appeared. He also looked fagged, but after a short rest prepared again to descend. He had been under water about ninety seconds. Few divers can remain longer. The average time is one minute and a half, sometimes two minutes. It is said that these men are short-lived, and we can well believe it, for their work, although performed only during a short period of each year, is in violent opposition to the laws of nature.

Directing his men to row on, our skipper soon came to another boat, which not only arrested his attention but aroused his curiosity, for never before had he seen so strange a sight. It was a large boat with novel apparatus on board of it, and white men—in very strange costume. In fact it was a party of European divers using the diving dress among the pearl-fishers of Ceylon, and great was the interest they created, as well as the unbelief, scepticism, misgiving, and doubt which they drew forth—for, although not quite a novelty in those waters, the dress was new to many of the natives present on that occasion, and Easterns, not less than Westerns, are liable to prejudice!

A large concourse of boats watched the costuming of the divers, and breathless interest was aroused as they went calmly over the side and remained down for more than an hour, sending up immense quantities of oysters. Of course liberal-minded men were made converts on the spot, and, equally of course, the narrow-minded remained " of the same opinion still." Nevertheless, that day's trial of Western ingenuity has borne much fruit, for we are now told, by the best authorities, that at the present time the diving dress is very extensively used in sponge, pearl, and coral fisheries in many parts of the world where naked divers alone were employed not many years ago ; and that in the Greek Archipelago and on the Turkish and Barbary coasts alone upwards of three hundred diving apparatuses are employed in the sponge fisheries, with immense advantage to all concerned and to the world at large.

Leaving this interesting sight, our Malay skipper threaded his way through the fleet of boats and made for the shores of the Bay of Condatchy, which was crowded with eager men of many nations.

This bay, on the west coast of Ceylon, is the busy scene of one of the world's great fisheries of the pearl oyster. The fishing, being in the hands of Government, is kept under strict control. It is farmed out. The beds of oysters are annually surveyed and reported on. They are divided into four equal portions, only one of which is worked each year. As the fishing produces vast wealth and affords scope for much speculation during the short period of its exercise, the bay during February, March, and April of each year presents a wondrous spectacle, for here Jews, Indians, merchants, jewellers, boatmen, conjurors to charm off the dreaded sharks, Brahmins, Roman Catholic priests, and many other professions and nationalities are represented, all in a state of speculation, hope, and excitement that fill their faces with animation and their frames with activity.

The fleet of boats leaves the shore at 10 P.M. on the firing of a signal-gun, and returns at noon next day, when again the gun is fired, flags are hoisted, and Babel immediately ensues.

It was noon when our Malay skipper landed. The gun had just been fired. Many of the boats were in, others were arriving. Leaving his boat in charge of his men, the skipper wended his way quickly through the excited crowd with the wandering yet earnest gaze of a man who searches for some one. Being head and shoulders above most of the men around him, he could do this with ease. For some time he was unsuccessful, but at last he espied an old grey-bearded Jew, and pushed his way towards him.

" Ha ! Pungarin, my excellent friend," exclaimed the Jew, extending his hand, which the skipper merely condescended to touch, " how do you do ? I am *so* overjoyed to see you ; you have business to transact, eh ? "

"You may be quite sure, Moses, that I did not come to this nest of sharpers merely for pleasure," replied Pungarin, brusquely.

" Ah, my friend, you are really too severe. No doubt we are sharp, but that is a proper business qualification. Besides, *our* trade is legitimate, while yours, my friend, is—"

The Jew stopped and cast a twinkling glance at his tall companion.

" Is *not* legitimate, you would say," observed Pungarin, " but that is open to dispute. In my opinion this is a world of robbers ; the only difference among us is that some are sneaking robbers, others are open. Every man to his taste. I have been doing a little of the world's work openly of late, and I come here with part of the result to give you a chance of robbing me in the other way."

" Nay, nay, you are altogether too hard," returned the Jew, with a deprecating smile ; " but come to my little office. We shall have more privacy there. How comes it, Pungarin, that you are so far from your own waters ? It is a longish way from Ceylon to Borneo."

" How comes it," replied the Malay, " that the
sea-mew flies far from home? There is no limit to
the flight of a sea-rover, save the sea-shore."

" True, true," returned the Jew, with a nod of
intelligence; " but here is my place of business.
Enter my humble abode, and pray be seated."

Pungarin stooped to pass the low doorway, and
seated himself beside a small deal table which,
although destitute of a cloth, was thickly covered
with ink-stains. The Malay rover was clad in a
thin loose red jacket, a short petticoat or kilt, and
yellow trousers. A red fez, with a kerchief wound
round it turban fashion, covered his head. He
was a well-made stalwart man, with a handsome
but fierce-looking countenance.

From beneath the loose jacket Pungarin drew
forth a small, richly chased, metal casket. Placing
it on the table he opened it, and, turning it upside
down, poured from it a little cataract of glittering
jewellery.

" Ha ! my friend," exclaimed his companion, " you
have got a prize. Where did you find it ?"

" I might answer, ' What is that to you ?' but I
won't, for I wish to keep you in good humour till
our business is concluded. Here, then, are the facts
connected with the case. Not long ago some
Englishmen came out to Hong-Kong to dive to a
vessel which had been wrecked on an island off the

coast. My worthy agent there, Dwarro, cast his
eyes on them and soon found out all about their
plans. Dwarro is a very intelligent fellow. Like
yourself, he has a good deal of the sneaking robber
about him. He ascertained that the wreck had
much gold coin in it, and so managed that they
hired his boat to go off to it with their diving
apparatus. Somewhat against their will he accompanied them. They were very successful. The first
time they went on shore, they took with them gold
to the value of about twenty thousand pounds.
Dwarro cleverly managed to have this secured a
few hours after it was landed. He also made
arrangements to have a fleet of my fellows ready, so
that when more gold had been recovered from the
wreck they might surround them on the spot and
secure it. But the young Englishman at the head
of the party was more than a match for us. He
cowed Dwarro, and cleverly escaped to land. There,
however, another of my agents had the good fortune
to discover the Englishmen while they were landing
their gold. He was too late, indeed, to secure the
gold, which had been sent on inland in charge of two
Chinamen, but he was lucky enough to discover this
casket in the stern-sheets of their boat. The
Englishmen fought hard for it, especially the young
fellow in command, who was more like a tiger than
a man, and knocked down half a dozen of our

men before he was overpowered. We would have
cut his throat then and there, but a party of
inhabitants, guided by one of the Chinamen, came
to the rescue, and we were glad to push off with
what we had got. Now, Moses, this casket is
worth a good round sum. Dwarro wisely took the
trouble to make inquiries about it through one of
the Chinamen, who happened to be an honest man
and fortunately also very stupid. From this man,
Chok-foo, who is easily imposed on, he learned that
the casket belongs to a very rich English merchant,
who would give anything to recover it, because it
belonged to his wife, who is dead—"

"A rich English merchant?" interrupted Moses,
"we Jews are acquainted pretty well with all the
rich English merchants. Do you know his name?"

"Yes; Charles Hazlit," answered the Malay.

"Indeed! well—go on."

"Well," said Pungarin, abruptly, "I have nothing
more to say, except what will you give for these
things?"

"One thousand pounds would be a large sum to
offer," said the Jew, slowly.

"And a very small one to accept," returned
Pungarin, as he slowly gathered the gems together
and put them back into the casket.

"Nay, my friend, be not so hasty," said Moses
"what do you ask for them?"

"I shall ask nothing," replied the Malay; "the fact is, I think it probable that I may be able to screw *more* than their value out of Mr. Hazlit."

"I am sorry to disappoint your expectations," returned the Jew, with something approaching to a sneer, as he rose; and, selecting one from a pile of English newspapers, slowly read out to his companion the announcement of the failure of the firm of Hazlit and Co. "You see, my good friend, we Jews are very knowing as well as sharp. It were better for you to transact your little business with me."

Knowing and sharp as he was, the Jew was not sufficiently so to foresee the result of his line of conduct with the Malay rover. Instead of giving in and making the best of circumstances, that freebooter, with characteristic impetuosity, shut the steel box with a loud snap, put it under his arm, rose, and walked out of the place without uttering a word. He went down to the beach and rowed away, leaving Moses to moralise on the uncertainty of all human affairs.

Favouring gales carried the Malay pirate-junk swiftly to the east. The same gales checked, baffled, and retarded the schooner *Fairy Queen* on her voyage to the west.

"Darling Aileen," said Miss Pritty, recovering from a paroxysm, "did you ever hear of any one dying of sea-sickness?"

"I never did," answered Aileen, with a languid smile.

Both ladies lay in their berths, their pale cheeks resting on the woodwork thereof, and their eyes resting pitifully on each other.

"It is awful—horrible!" sighed Miss Pritty at at the end of another paroxysm.

Aileen, who was not so ill as her friend, smiled but said nothing. Miss Pritty was past smiling, but not quite past speaking.

"What dreadful noises occur on board ships," she said, after a long pause; "such rattling, and thumping, and creaking, and stamping. Perhaps the sailors get their feet wet and are so cold that they require to stamp constantly to warm them!"

Aileen displayed all her teeth and said, "Perhaps."

At that moment the stamping became so great, and was accompanied by so much shouting, that both ladies became attentive.

A few moments later their door opened violently, and Mr. Hazlit appeared with a very pale face. He was obviously in a state of great perturbation.

"My dears," he said, hurriedly, "excuse my intruding—we are—attacked—pirates—get up; put on your things!"

His retreat and the closing of the door was followed by a crash overhead and a yell. Immediately after the schooner quivered from stem to stern, under the shock of her only carronade, which was fired at the moment; the shot being accompanied by a loud cheer.

"Oh horror!" exclaimed Miss Pritty, "my worst fears are realised!"

Poor Miss Pritty was wrong. Like many people whose "worst fears" have been engendered at a civilised fireside, she was only *beginning* to realise a few of her fears. She lived to learn that *her* "worst fears" were mere child's play to the world's dread realities.

Her sea-sickness, however, vanished as if by magic, and in a few minutes she and her companion were dressed.

During those few minutes the noise on deck had increased, and the shouts, yells, and curses told them too plainly that men were engaged in doing what we might well believe is the work only of devils. Then shrieks of despair followed.

Presently all was silent. In a few minutes the cabin door opened, and Pungarin entered.

"Go on deck," he said, in a quiet tone.

The poor ladies obeyed. On reaching the deck the first sight that met them was Mr. Hazlit standing by the binnacle. A Malay pirate with a drawn sword stood beside him, but he was otherwise unfettered. They evidently thought him harmless. Near to him stood the skipper of the *Fairy Queen,* with the stern resolution of a true Briton on his countenance, yet with the sad thoughtful glance of one trained under Christian influences in his eye. His hands were bound, and a Malay pirate stood on either side of him. He was obviously *not* deemed harmless!

The decks were everywhere covered with blood, but not a man of the crew was to be seen.

"You are the captain of this schooner?" asked Pungarin.

"Yes," replied the prisoner, firmly.

"Have you treasure on board?"

"No."

"We shall soon find out the truth as to that. Meanwhile, who is this?" (pointing to Mr. Hazlit.)

The captain was silent and thoughtful for a few moments. He was well aware of the nature of the men with whom he had to do. He had seen his crew murdered in cold blood. He knew that his own end drew near.

"This gentleman," he said, slowly, "is a wealthy British merchant—well known and respected in England. He has rich friends. It may be worth your while to spare him."

"And this," added the pirate captain, pointing to Aileen.

"Is his only child," answered the other.

"Your name?" asked Pungarin.

"Charles Hazlit," said the hapless merchant.

A sudden flash of intelligence lit up for a moment the swarthy features of the pirate. It passed quickly. Then he spoke in an undertone to one of his men, who, with the assistance of another, led the captain of the schooner to the forward part of the ship. A stifled groan, followed by a plunge, was heard by the horrified survivors. That was all they ever knew of the fate of their late captain. But for what some would term a mere accident, even that and their own fate would have remained unknown to the world—at least during the revolution of Time. The romances of life are often enacted by common-place people. Many good ships with ordinary people on board (like you and me, reader) leave port, and are "never again heard of." Who can tell what tales may be revealed in regard to such, in Eternity?

The *Fairy Queen* was one of those vessels whose fate it was to have her "fate" revealed in Time.

We cannot state with certainty what were the motives which induced Pungarin to spare the lives of Mr. Hazlit and his family; all we know is, that he transferred them to his junk. After taking everything of value out of the schooner, he scuttled her.

Not many days after, he attacked a small hamlet on the coast of Borneo, massacred most of the men, saved a few of the young and powerful of them—to

serve his purposes—also some of the younger women
and children, and continued his voyage.

The poor English victims whom he had thus got
possession of lived, meanwhile, in a condition
of what we may term unreality. They could not
absolutely credit their senses. They felt strangely
impelled to believe that a hideous nightmare had
beset them—that they were dreaming; that they
would unquestionably awake at last, and find that it
was time to get up to a substantial and very common-
place English breakfast. But, mingled with this
feeling, or rather, underlying it, there was a terrible
assurance that the dream was true. So is it through-
out life. What is fiction to you, reader, is fact to
some one else, and that which is *your* fact is some
one else's fiction. If any lesson is taught by this,
surely it is the lesson of *sympathy*—that we should
try more earnestly than we do to throw ourselves out
of ourselves into the place of others.

Poor Miss Pritty and Aileen learned this lesson.
From that date forward, instead of merely shaking
their heads and sighing in a hopeless sort of way, and
doing nothing—or nearly nothing—to check the
evils they deplored, they became red-hot enthusiasts
in condemning piracy and slavery (which latter is
the grossest form of piracy) and despotism of every
kind, whether practised by a private pirate like
Puugarin, or by a weak pirate like the Sultan of

Zanzibar, or by comparatively strong pirates like the nations of Spain and Portugal.

In course of time the pirate junk anchored at the mouth of a river, and much of her freight, with all her captives, was transferred to native boats. These were propelled by means of numerous oars, and the male captives were now set to work at these oars.

Mr. Hazlit and his daughter and Miss Pritty were allowed to sit idle in the stern of one of the boats, and for a time they felt their drooping spirits revive a little under the influence of the sweet sunshine while they rowed along shore, but as time passed these feelings were rudely put to flight.

The captives were various in their character and nationality, as well as in their spirits and temperaments. These had all to be brought into quick subjection and working order. There were far more captives than the pirates knew what to do with. One of those who sat on the thwart next to the Hazlits had been a policeman in one of the China ports. He was a high-spirited young fellow. It was obvious that his soul was seething into rebellion. The pirate in charge of the boat noted the fact, and whispered to one of his men, who thereupon ordered the policeman to pull harder, and accompanied his order with a cut from a bamboo cane.

Instantly the youth sprang up, and tried to burst his bonds. He succeeded, but before he could do anything, he was overpowered by half a dozen men, and re-bound. Then two men sat down beside him, each with a small stick, with which they beat the muscles of his arms and legs, until their power was completely taken away. This done, they left him, a living heap of impotent flesh in the bottom of the boat, and a salutary warning to the rebellious.

But it did not end here. As soon as the poor fellow had recovered sufficiently to move, he was again set to the oar, and forced to row as best he could.

The voyage along the coast, and up a river into which they finally turned, occupied several days. At first, on starting, Aileen and her companions had looked with tender pity on the captives as they toiled at the heavy oars, but this deepened into earnest solicitude as they saw them, after hours of toil, gasping for want of water and apparently faint from want of food. Next day, although they had lain down in the bottom of the boat supperless, the rest had refreshed most of them, and they pulled on with some degree of vigour. But noon came, and with it culminated the heat of a burning sun. Still no water was served out, no food distributed. Mr. Hazlit and his party had biscuit and water given them in the morning and at noon. During the latter meal Aileen observed the native policeman regarding her food with such eager wolfish eyes that under an impulse of uncontrollable feeling she held out her can of water to him. He seized and drank the half of it before one of the pirates had time to dash it from his lips.

Presently a youth, who seemed less robust than his comrades, uttered a wild shriek, threw up his hands, and fell backwards. At once the pirates detached him from his oar, threw him into the sea, and made another captive fill his place. And now, to their inexpressible horror, the Hazlits discovered that the practice of these wretches—when they happened to have a super-abundance of captives— was to make them row on without meat or drink, until they dropt at the oar, and then throw them overboard! Reader, we do not deal in fiction here, we describe what we have heard from the mouth of a trustworthy eye-witness.

In these circumstances the harrowing scenes that were enacted before the English ladies were indeed fitted to arouse that "horror" which poor Miss Pritty, in her innocence, had imagined to have reached its worst. We will pass it over. Many of the captives died. A few of the strongest survived, and these, at last, were fed a little in order to enable them to complete the journey. Among them was the native policeman, who had suddenly discovered that his wisest course of action, in the meantime, was submission.

At last the boats reached a village in one of those

rivers whose low and wooded shores afford shelter to too many nests of Malay pirates even at the present time—and no wonder! When the rulers and grandees of some Eastern nations live by plunder, what can be expected of the people?

The few captives who survived were sent ashore. Among them were our English friends.

CHAPTER XV.

SUDDEN AND BAD NEWS INDUCES SUDDEN AND GOOD ACTION.

ABOUT this time there hung a dark cloud over the pagoda in Hong-Kong. Even the bright eyes of Molly Machowl could not pierce through this cloud. Rooney himself had lost much of his hopeful disposition. As for Edgar Berrington, Joe Baldwin, and David Maxwell, they were silently depressed, for adversity had crushed them very severely of late.

Immediately after their losses, as already detailed or referred to, stormy weather had for several weeks prevented them from resuming operations at the wreck, and when at last they succeeded in reaching the old locality, they found themselves so closely watched by shore boats that the impossibility of their being able to keep anything they should bring up became obvious. They were forced, therefore, to give up the idea of making further attempts.

"It's too bad," growled Maxwell one morning at breakfast, "that all our trouble and expense should end in nothin'—or next to nothin'."

"Come, Maxwell," said Edgar, "don't say 'nothing.' It is true we lost our first great find that luckless night when we left it with Wilson, but our second haul is safe, and though it amounts only to eight thousand pounds sterling, that after all is not to be sneezed at by men in our circumstances."

"Make not haste to be rich," muttered Joe Baldwin in an undertone.

"*Did* we make haste to be rich?" asked Edgar, smiling. "It seems to me that we set about it in a cool, quiet, business-like way."

"Humph, that's true, but we got uncommon keen over it—somethin' like what gamblers do."

"Our over-keenness," returned Edgar, "was not right, perhaps, but our course of action was quite legitimate—for it is a good turn done not only to ourselves but to the world when we save property; and the salvor of property—who necessarily risks so much—is surely worthy of a good reward in kind."

"Troth, an' that's true," said Rooney, with a wry grin, "I had quite made up me mind to a carridge and four with Molly astore sittin' in silks an' satins inside."

"Molly would much rather sit in cotton," said the lady referred to, as she presided at the breakfast-table; "have another cup, Rooney, an' don't be talking nonsense."

"But it does seem hard," continued Maxwell in

his growling voice, " after all our trouble in this
venture, to be obliged to take to divin' at mere har-
bour-works in Eastern waters, just to keep body and
soul together."

" Never mind, boy," exclaimed Rooney with a successful effort at heartiness, "it won't last long —it's
only till we get a suitable chance of a ship to take
us an' our small fortins back to ould Ireland—or
England, if ye prefer it—though it's my own opinion
that England is only an Irish colony. Never say
die. Sure we've seen a dale of life, too, in them
parts. Come, I'll give ye a sintiment, an' we'll
drink it in tay—"

Before the hopeful Irishman could give the sentiment, he was interrupted by the sudden opening of
the door and the abrupt entrance of a Chinaman,
who looked at the breakfast party with keen interest
and some anxiety.

" If it's your grandmother you're lookin' for,"
said Rooney, " she don't live here, young man."

Paying no attention to this pleasantry, the Chinaman closed the door with an air of mystery, and,
going up to Edgar, looked him inquiringly in the
face, as he said interrogatively :—

" I's pleeceman. You's Eggirbringting ?"

"Not a bad attempt," exclaimed Edgar, with a
laugh. " I suppose that is my name translated into
Chinese."

"Took me muchee—long—time for learn him from young missee," said the Chinaman with a hurt look.

At the mention of a young lady Edgar's amused look changed into one of anxiety, for he had, through an English acquaintance in the port, become aware not only of Mr. Hazlit's failure, but of his sudden departure for England with his daughter and Miss Pritty, and a vague suspicion of bad news flashed upon him.

"You bring a message, I see?" he said, rising and speaking hurriedly. "Let me hear it. Quick."

Thus invoked, the Chinaman spoke so quickly and in such a miraculous jumble of bad English, that Edgar could not comprehend him at all;—only one thing he felt quite sure of, namely, that his anxiety was well found.

"Ho! Chok-foo!" he shouted.

The domestic entered, and to him the Chinaman delivered his message, which was to the following effect :—

He was a native policeman who had been captured on the coast when in discharge of his duties. Many others had been taken by the same pirates at different times, and among them an English gentleman named Hazlit, with his daughter and a lady friend. These latter had been spared, probably with a view to ransom, at the time the crew of their vessel was massacred, and were at that moment in one of the strongholds belonging to the pirates, up one of the intricate rivers on the coast of Borneo. He, the policeman, having resolved to make his escape, and being, in virtue of his wise, wily, and constabular nature, well able to do so, had mentioned the circumstance to the young lady, and, under promise of a handsome reward, had agreed to travel and voyage, night and day, by boat or vessel, as fortune should favour him, in order to convey immediate intelligence of these facts to a youth named "Eggirbringting,' whom the young lady described as being very tall and stout, and extremely handsome.

It may easily be imagined with what mingled feelings of anxiety and impatience the "tall, stout, and extremely handsome young man" listened to this narrative as it was volubly delivered by the "pleeceman" and slowly translated by Chokfoo.

When at last he was fairly in possession of all that the messenger had to relate, Edgar paced up and down the room for a few seconds with rapid strides.

"We must go into action at once, sir," suggested Joe Baldwin.

"Of course, of course, but *how?* that's the point," exclaimed Edgar, with a look of impatient vexation. " Borneo is a long way off. There are no steamers running regularly to it that I know of. However, it 's

of no use talking ; let 's go at once and make inquir
I 'll go see our consul—perhaps—"

"P'lhaps," interrupted the messenger, " p'lhaɪ
the pleeceman can talkee."

" If he can, let him speak," cried Edgar, with impatience.

"Pleece he nevir too muchee quick," returned
the man, coolly. " We knows what we 's can do.
Hai, yach !"

Edgar sat down with a sharp sigh of discontent,
and waited for more.

" Well ? "

"Well," repeated the policeman, " there be steam-
boat here now—go for Borneo quick."

"At once !" cried Edgar, starting up and seizing
his hat, " why did you not—"

"Sh! keepee cool, you no 'casion makes so fashion,"
interrupted the policeman, who thereupon went on
to explain that on his arrival in Hong-Kong he had
gone at once to head-quarters, before delivering his
message to Edgar, in order to make himself master
of all the news about town that was worth knowing,
or likely in any way to advance the interest of those
whom he sought to serve. Among other things he
had learned the important fact that, two days before
his arrival, a small gun-boat, belonging to a certain
Rajah of Borneo, and commanded by a certain Scotchman, and employed for the express purpose of hunting

up and rooting out the pirates of the China seas, had put in to the port for repairs. He had hurried down to the gun-boat in time to prevent her departure, had told his story, and had just come from her to say that her captain would like much to see Mr. Berrington.

On hearing this, Edgar again started up and eagerly ordered the native policeman to guide him to the gun-boat in question without another moment's delay. He was followed, of course, by his male companions, who were nearly as much interested in the matter as himself. They were soon on the deck of the gun-boat.

It was a neat trim screw-steamer of small size, 180 tons burthen, and manned by about sixty Malays and a few Englishmen. Everything on board was as bright and orderly as if it had been a British man-of-war. Her commander received the visitors on the quarter-deck. He looked like one who was eminently well qualified to hunt up, run down, cut out, or in any other mode make away with pirates. There was much of the bull-terrier in him—solid, broad, short, large-chested—no doubt also large-hearted—active, in the prime of life, with short black curly hair, a short black beard and moustache, a square chin, a pleasant smile, a prominent nose, and an eagle eye. Indeed he might himself have made a splendid chief of the very race against which he waged " war to the knife."

"Glad to make your acquaintance, Mr. Berrington," said the captain, holding out his hand. "The native policeman has told me all about your friends—I understand them to be such?"

"Yes—intimate friends."

"Well, this business is quite in my way. I shall be glad to take you with me. But who are these?" he added, looking at Edgar's companions.

"They are comrades, and might do good service if you will allow them to volunteer."

"My crew is complete," said the captain, doubtfully, "except, indeed, that my chief engineer is just dead, but none of your men look as if they could fill his shoes."

"That is true, but I can fill them myself," said Edgar, eagerly.

"Indeed!"

"Yes, I am an engineer by profession; my comrades are professional divers. We have been engaged on a wreck here for some time past."

"Good," said the captain; "are your dresses and apparatus at hand?"

"Some of them are."

"Then bring them aboard at once. I leave in an hour. Just bring what you have handy. Lose no time. I will take your men also. They may be of use."

Within an hour after the foregoing conversation

Molly Machowl was left disconsolate in the pagoda under the care of Chok-foo, while the Rajah's gun-boat was steaming out to sea with Edgar, Baldwin, Rooney, Maxwell, and Ram-stam added to her war-like crew.

CHAPTER XVI.

BEARDING THE LION IN HIS DEN.

STEAM has pretty well subdued time. Fifty years ago it was a mighty feat to " put a circle round the globe." Now-a-days a " Cook "—by no means a captain—will take or send you round it in " a few weeks."

Romantic reader, don't despair! By such means romance has undoubtedly been affected in some degree, but let not that grieve thee! Romance has by no means been taken out of the world ; nor has it been, to use an unromantic phrase, reduced in quantity or quality. Human inventions and appliances alter the aspects of romance, and transfer its influences, but they cannot destroy a Creator's gift to the human race. They have, indeed, taken the romance out of some things which were once romantic, but that is simply because they have made such things familiar and commonplace. They have not yet touched *other* things which still remain in the hallowed region of romance. Romance *is* a region.

Things crowd out of it, but other things crowd into it. The romantic soul dwells perpetually in it, and while, perhaps with regret, it recognises the fact that many things depart from that region, it also observes, with pleasure, that many things enter into it, and that the entrances are more numerous than the exits. The philosophico-romantic spirit will admit all this and be grateful. The unphilosophico-romantic spirit will not quite see through it, and may, perchance, be perplexed. But be of good cheer. Have faith! Do not let the matter-of-fact "steam-engine," and the "telegraph," and the "post-office," rob thee of thy joys. They have somewhat modified the flow of the river of Romance, but they have not touched its fountain-head,—and never can.

Why, what is Romance? Despite the teachings of the dictionaries—which often give us the original and obsolete meaning of words—we maintain that romance signifies the human soul's aspirations after the high, and the grand, and the good. In its fallen condition the poor soul undoubtedly makes wondrous mistakes in its romantic strainings, but these mistakes are comparatively seldom on the side of exaggeration. Our dictionary says that romance is extravagance—a fiction which passes beyond the limits of real life. Now, we maintain that no one—not even the most romantic of individuals—ever comes *up* to real life. We have been a child—at least we incline to that belief—and we have been, like other children, in the habit of romancing, as it is called, that is, according to dictionaries, passing "beyond the limits of real life" into "extravagance." We are now a man—it is to be hoped—have travelled far and seen much and yet we can say conscientiously that the wildest fancies of our most romantic moods in childhood have been immeasurably surpassed by the grand realities of actual life! What are the most brilliant fancies of a child or of a mere ignorant "romancer," compared to the amazing visions of the Arctic regions or the high Alps, which we have seen? "Fictions" and "extravagance"! All our wildest sallies are but *intravagance* and feeble fancy compared with the sublimity of fact. No doubt there are men and women gifted with the power of burlesquing reality, and thus, not going beyond its limits, but causing much dust and confusion within its limits by the exaggeration and falsification of individual facts. This, however, is *not* romance. We stand up for romance as being the bright staircase that leads childhood to reality, and culminates at last in that vision which the eye of man hath not yet seen nor his mind conceived; a vision which transcends all romance is itself the greatest of all realities, and is "laid up for the people of God."

We return from this divergence to the point which led to it—the power of steam to subdue time. No

doubt it was unromantic enough to be pushed, propelled, thrust, willing or not willing, against, or
with, wind and tide, so that you could gauge your
distance run—and to be run—almost to a foot; but
it was very satisfactory, nevertheless, especially to
those whose hearts were far in advance of their vessel,
and it was more than satisfactory when at the end
of their voyage of a few days they found themselves
gliding swiftly, almost noiselessly, up the windings
of a quiet river whose picturesque scenery, romantic
vistas, and beautiful reflections might have marked
it the entrance to a paradise instead of a human
pandemonium.

It was very early when the gun-boat entered the
stream. The mists of morning still prevailed, and
rendered all nature fairy-like. Weird-looking mangrove bushes rose on their leg-like roots from the
water, as if independent of soil. Vigorous parasites
and creepers strove to strangle the larger trees, but
strove in vain. Thick jungle concealed wealth of
feathered, insect, and reptile life, including the
reptile man, and sundry notes of warning told that
these were awaking to their daily toil—the lower
animals to fulfil the ends of their being, the higher
animal to violate some of the most blessed laws of
his Creator. Gradually the sun rose and dispelled
the mists, while it warmed everything into strong
vitality. As they passed up, clouds of water-fowl

rose whirring from their lairs, and luxuriant growth of weeds threatened to obstruct the progress of the steamer.

"Come here, policeman," said the captain to the native functionary; "how far above this, did you say, is the nest of the vipers?"

"'Bout tree mile."

"Humph!" ejaculated the captain, turning to Berrington, who had come on deck at the moment. "I never went higher up the river than this point, for, just ahead, there are reeds enough to stop the screw of a three thousand ton ship, but if you'll get your diving dresses ready I'll try it. It would be much better to bring our big guns to bear on them than to attack in boats."

"I'll have 'em ready directly," said Edgar. "Perhaps we'd better stop the engines now."

"Just so; stop them."

The engines were stopped, and the gunboat glided slowly over the still water until it came to rest on its own inverted image.

Meanwhile the air-pump was rigged, and Joe Baldwin put on his dress, to the great interest and no little surprise of the Malay crew.

"Ready, sir," said Edgar, when Joe sat costumed, with the helmet at his side and his friends Rooney and Maxwell at the pumps.

"Go ahead, then—full steam," said the captain.

Just in front of the vessel the river was impeded quite across by a dense growth of rank reeds and sedges; a little further on there was clear water. Into this the gun-boat plunged under full steam.

As was expected, the screw soon became choked, and finally stopped. Had the pirates expected this they would probably have made a vigorous attack just then. But the danger, being so obvious, had never before been incurred, and was therefore not prepared for or taken advantage of by the pirates. Nevertheless the captain was ready for them if they had attacked. Every man was at his station armed to the teeth.

The moment the boat began to work heavily Joe's helmet was put on, and when she came to a stand he went over the stern by means of a rope-ladder prepared for the purpose.

"Be as active as you can, Joe. Got everything you want?" said Edgar, taking up the bull's-eye.

"All right, sir," said Joe.

"Pump away," cried Edgar, looking over his shoulder.

Next moment Joe was under water, and the Malays, with glaring eyes and open mouths, were gazing at the confusion of air-bubbles that arose from him continually. From their looks it seemed as though some of them fancied the whole affair to be a new species of torture invented by their captain.

Joe carried a small hatchet in his girdle and a long sharp knife in his hand. With these he attacked the reeds and weeds, and in ten minutes or less had set the screw free. He soon reappeared on the rope-ladder, and Edgar, who had been attending to his lines, removed the bull's-eye.

"What now, Joe?" he asked.

"All clear," said Joe, coming inboard.

"What! Done it already?"

"Ay; steam ahead when you like, sir."

The order was given at once. The assistant engineer put on full steam, and the gunboat, crashing through the remaining obstruction, floated into the comparatively clear water beyond. The screw had been again partially fouled, of course, but ten minutes more of our diver's knife and axe set it free, and the vessel proceeded on her way.

Scouts from the pirate-camp had been watching the gun-boat, for they had counted on nothing worse than an attack by boats, which, strong in numbers, they could easily have repelled. Great therefore was the consternation when these scouts ran in and reported that the vessel had cleared the obstructions by some miraculous power which they could not explain or understand, and was now advancing on them under full steam.

While the operations we have described were being carried out on board the gun-boat, in the pirate village poor Mr. Hazlit was seated on a stump outside a rude hut made chiefly of bamboos and palm leaves. He wore only his trousers and shirt, both sadly torn—one of the pirates having taken a fancy to his coat and vest, the former of which he wore round his loins with his legs thrust through the sleeves. The captive merchant sat with his face buried in his hands and bowed on his knees.

Inside the hut sat Aileen with poor Miss Pritty resting on her bosom. Miss Pritty was of a tender confiding nature, and felt it absolutely necessary to rest on somebody's bosom. She would rather have used a cat's or dog's than none. Aileen, being affectionate and sympathetic, had no objection. Nevertheless, not being altogether of angelic extraction, she was a little put out by the constant tremors of her friend.

" Come, dear, don't shudder so fearfully," she said, in a half coaxing half remonstrative tone.

" Is he gone ?" asked Miss Pritty in a feeble voice, with her eyes tight shut.

She referred to a half-naked warrior who had entered the hut, had half shut his great eyes, and had displayed a huge cavern of red gum and white teeth in an irresistible smile at the woe-begone aspect of Miss Pritty. He had then silently taken his departure.

" Gone," repeated Aileen, rather sharply; " **of**

course he is, and if he were not, what then ? Sure.
his being dark and rather lightly clothed is not
calculated to shock you so much."

" Aileen !" exclaimed Miss Pritty, raising her head
suddenly, and gazing with anxiety into the face of
her friend; " has our short residence among these
wretches begun to remove that delicacy of mind
and sentiment for which I always admired you ?"

" No," returned Aileen, firmly, "but your excessive
alarms may have done something towards that end.
Nay, forgive me, dear," she added, gently, as Miss
Pritty's head sank again on her shoulder, with a sob,
" I did not mean to hurt your feelings, but really, if
you only think of it, our present position demands the
utmost resolution, caution, and fortitude of which we
are capable; and you know, love, that this shuddering
at trifles and imagining of improbabilities will tend
to unfit you for action when the time arrives, as it
surely will sooner or later, for my father has taken
the wisest steps for our deliverance, and, besides, a
Greater than my father watches over us."

" That is true, dear," assented Miss Pritty, with
a tender look. " Now you speak like your old self;
but you must not blame me for being so foolish.
Indeed, I know that I am, but, then, have not my
worst fears been realised ? Are we not in the hands
--actually in the hands—of pirates—real pirates,
buccaneers—ugh !"

Again the poor lady drooped her head and shuddered.

"*Your* worst fears may have been realised," said Aileen; "but we have certainly not experienced the worst that might have happened. On the contrary, we have been remarkably well treated—what do you say? Fed on rats and roast puppies! Well, the things they send us *may* be such, for they resemble these creatures as much as anything else, but they are well cooked and very nice, you must allow, and—"

At that moment Aileen's tongue was suddenly arrested, and, figuratively speaking, Miss Pritty's blood curdled in her veins and her heart ceased to beat, for, without an instant's warning, the woods resounded with a terrific salvo of artillery; grape and canister shot came tearing, hissing, and crashing through the trees, and fierce yells, mingled with fiend-like shrieks, rent the air.

Both ladies sat as if transfixed—pale, mute, and motionless. Next moment Mr. Hazlit sprang into the hut, glaring with excitement, while a stream of blood trickled from a slight wound in his forehead.

Uttering a yell, no whit inferior to that of the fiercest pirate near him, and following it up with a fit of savage laughter that was quite appalling, the once dignified and self-possessed merchant rolled his eyes round the hut as if in search of something.

Suddenly espying a heavy pole, or species of war-club, which lay in a corner, he seized it and whirled it round his head as if he had been trained to such arms from childhood.

Just then a second salvo shook the very earth. Mr. Hazlit sprang out of the hut, shouted "To the rescue! Aileen, to the rescue!" in the voice of a Stentor, plunged wildly into a forest-path, and dis-appeared almost before the horrified ladies could form a guess as to his intentions.

CHAPTER XVII.

RECOUNTS THE WILD, FIERCE, AND IN SOME RESPECTS PECULIAR INCIDENTS OF A BUSH FIGHT.

ALTHOUGH the pirates were taken aback by this unexpected advance of the Rajah's gun-boat to within pistol-shot of their very doors, they were by no means cowed. Malays are brave as a race, and peculiarly regardless of their lives. They manned their guns, and stood to them with unflinching courage, but they were opposed by men of the same mettle, who had the great advantage of being better armed, and led by a man of consummate coolness and skill, whose motto was—" Conquer or die !"

We do not say that the captain of the gun-boat *professed* to hold that motto, for he was not a boaster, but it was clearly written in the fire of his eye, and stamped upon the bridge of his nose !

The pirate-guns were soon dismounted, their stockade was battered down, and when a party at last landed, with the captain at their head, and Edgar with his diving friends close at his heels, they were driven out of their fortification into the woods.

Previously to this, however, all the women and children had been sent further into the bush, so that the attacking party met none but fighting-men. Turning round a bend in a little path among the bushes, Edgar, who had become a little separated from his friends, came upon a half-naked Malay, who glared at him from behind a long shield. The pirate's style of fighting was that of the Malay race in general, and had something ludicrous, as well as dangerous, about it. He did not stand up and come on like a man, but, with his long legs wide apart and bent at the knees, he bounded hither and thither like a monkey, always keeping his body well under cover of the shield, and peering round its edges or over, or even under it, according to fancy, while his right hand held a light spear, ready to be launched at the first favourable moment into the unprotected body of his adversary.

Edgar at once rushed upon him, snapping his revolver as he ran; but, all the chambers having been already emptied, no shot followed. Brandishing his cutlass, he uttered an involuntary shout.

The shout was unexpectedly replied to by another shout of " Aileen, to the rescue!" which not only arrested him in his career, but seemed to perplex the pirate greatly.

At that moment the bushes behind the latter opened; a man in ragged shirt-sleeves and torn trousers sprang through, whirled a mighty club in the air, and smote the pirate's uplifted shield with such violence as to crush it down on its owner's head, and lay him flat and senseless on the ground.

" Mr. Hazlit !" gasped Edgar.

The merchant bounded at our hero with the fury of a wild cat, and would have quickly laid him beside the pirate if he had not leaped actively aside. A small tree received the blow meant for him, and the merchant passed on with another yell, " To the rescue !"

Of course Edgar followed, but the bush paths were intricate. He unfortunately turned into a wrong one, when the fugitive was for a moment hidden by a thicket, and immediately lost all trace of him.

Meanwhile Rooney Machowl, hearing the merchant's shout, turned aside to respond to it. He met Mr. Hazlit right in the teeth, and, owing to his not expecting an assault, had, like Edgar, well-nigh fallen by the hand of his friend. As it was, he evaded the huge club by a hair's-breadth, and immediately gave chase to the maniac—for such the poor gentleman had obviously become. But although he kept the fugitive for some time in view, he failed to come up with him owing to a stumble over a root which precipitated him violently on his nose. On recovering his feet Mr Hazlit was out of sight.

Rooney, caressing with much tenderness his injured nose, now sought to return to his friends, but the more he tried to do so, the farther he appeared to wander away from them.

"Sure it's a quare thing that I can't git howld of the road I comed by," he muttered, as with a look of perplexity he paused and listened.

Faint shouts were heard on his left, and he was about to proceed in that direction, when distinct cries arose on his right. He went in *that* direction for a time, then vacillated, and, finally, came to a dead stand, as well as to the conclusion that he had missed his way; which belief he stated to himself in the following soliloquy :—

"Rooney, me boy, you've gone an' lost yoursilf. Ah, bad scran to 'ee. Isn't it the fulfilment of your grandmother's owld prophecy, that you'd come to a bad ind at last? It's little I'd care for your misfortin myself, if it warn't that you ought to be helpin' poor Mr. Hazlit, who's gone as mad as blazes, an' whose daughter can't be far off. Och! man alive," he added, with sudden enthusiasm, "niver give in while there's a purty girl in the case!"

Under the impulse of this latter sentiment, Rooney started off at a run in a new and totally uncon-sidered direction, which, strange to say, brought him into sudden and very violent contact with some of those individuals in whom he was interested.

Here we must, in hunters' language, "hark back" on our course for a few minutes—if, indeed, that *be* hunters' language! We do not profess to know much thereof, but the amiable reader will understand our meaning.

Just after the attack had begun, and Mr. Hazlit had sallied from the hut with his war-club, as already related, Aileen became deeply impressed with the fact that all the women and children who had been wont to visit and gaze at her in wonder had vanished. The rattling of shot over her head, too, and the frequent rush of pirates past her temporary abode, warned her that the place was too much exposed in every way to be safe. She therefore sought to rouse her companion to attempt flight.

"Laura," she said, anxiously, as a round shot cut in half the left corner-post of the building, "come, we must fly. We shall be killed if we remain here."

"I care not," exclaimed Miss Pritty, clasping her friend closer than ever, and shuddering; "my worst fears have been realised. Let me die!"

"But *I* don't want to die yet," remonstrated Aileen; "think of *me*, dear, if you can, and of my father."

"Ah, true!" exclaimed Miss Pritty, with sudden calmness, as she unclasped her arms and arose. "Forgive my selfishness. Come; let us fly!"

If the poor lady had owned a private pair of

cherubic wings, she could not have prepared for flight with greater assurance or activity. She tightened her waist-belt, wrapped her shawl firmly round her, fastened her bonnet strings in a Gordian knot, and finally, holding out her hand to her friend, as if they had suddenly changed characters, said, "Come, are you ready?" with a tremendous show of decision. She even led the wondering Aileen along a winding path into the jungle for a considerable distance; then, as the path became more intricate, she stopped, burst into tears, laid her head again on its old resting-place, and said in a hollow voice:—" Yes; all is lost!"

"Come, Laura, don't give way; there's a dear. Just exert yourself a little and we shall soon be safe at—at—somewhere."

Miss Pritty made a vigorous struggle. She even smiled through her tears as she replied:—" Well, lead on, love; I will follow you—to death!"

With her eyes tightly shut, lest she should see something hideous in the woods, she stumbled on, holding to her friend's arm.

"Where are we going to?" she asked, feebly, after a few minutes, during which Aileen had pulled her swiftly along.

"I don't know, dear, but a footpath *must* lead to something or somewhere."

Aileen was wrong. The footpath led apparently

to nothing and nowhere. At all events it soon
became so indistinct that they lost it, and, finally,
after an hour's wandering, found themselves hopelessly involved in the intricacies of a dense jungle,
without the slightest clew as to how they should get
out of it.

Aileen stopped at last.

"Laura," she said, anxiously, "we are lost!"

"I told you so," returned Miss Pritty, in a tone
that was not quite devoid of triumph.

"True, dear; but when you told me so we were
not lost. Now we *are.* I fear we shall have to
spend the night here," she added, looking round.

Miss Pritty opened her eyes and also looked
round. The sight that met her gaze was not encouraging. Afternoon was drawing on. Thick bushes
and trees formed a sort of twilight there even at
noon-day. Nothing with life was visible. Not a
sound was to be heard, save such little rustlings of
dry leaves and chirpings as were suggestive of snakes
and centipedes. The unhappy Laura was now too
frightened to shudder.

"What shall we do?" she asked; "shriek for
help?"

"That might bring pirates to us instead of friends,"
said Aileen. "Listen; do you hear no sound?"

"Nothing," replied Miss Pritty, after a few
moments of intense silence, "save the beating of my

own heart. Aileen," she continued, with sudden anxiety, " are there not serpents in these woods ? "

" Yes, I believe there are."

" And tarantulas ?"

" Probably."

" And tortoises ? "

" I—I 'm not sure."

" Darling, how *can* we sleep among tortoises, tarantulas, and serpents ?"

Even Aileen was at a loss for a reply, though she smiled in spite of herself.

" I 'll tell you what," she said, cheerfully, " if we *must* spend the night in the bush we shall get into a tree.   That will at least save us from all the venomous creatures as well as dangerous beasts that crawl upon the ground.   Can you climb ? "

" Climb !" repeated Miss Pritty, with a hysterical laugh, " you might as well ask me if I can dive."

" Well, you must learn.   Come, I will teach you. Here is a capital tree that seems easy to get into."

Saying this, Aileen ran to a gnarled old tree whose trunk was divided into two parts, and from which spread out a series of stout branches that formed a sort of net-work of foliage about eight or ten feet from the ground. Climbing actively up to these branches, she crept out upon them, and from that position, parting the twigs, she looked down laughingly at her friend.

Her bright spirit was contagious. Miss Pritty almost forgot her anxieties, smiled in return, and walked towards the tree, in doing which she trod on something that moved in the grass. A piercing shriek was the result. It was immediately replied to by a wild yell at no great distance.

"It was only a frog; look, I see it now, hopping away. Do be quick, Laura; I am sure that was the yell of a savage."

No further spur was needed. Miss Pritty scrambled up into the tree and crept towards her friend with such reckless haste that one of her feet slipped off the branch, and her leg passing through the foliage, appeared in the regions below. Recovering herself, she reached what she deemed a place of security.

"Now, dear, we are safe—at least for a time," said Aileen, arranging her friend's disordered dress. "Take care, however; you must be careful to trust only to limbs of the tree; the foliage cannot bear you. Look, you can see through it to the ground. Lean your back against this fork here; sit on this place—so; put your foot on this branch, there—why, it is almost like a chair—hush!"

It was quite unnecessary to impose silence. They both sat among the branches as motionless as though they had been parts of the tree. They scarce dared to breathe, while they peered through the foliage and beheld the dim form of a man advancing

Whoever he was, the man seemed to growl as though he had been allied to the beasts of the jungle. He came forward slowly, looking from side to side with caution, and, stopping directly under the tree of refuge, said—

"Musha!" with great emphasis, then placing both hands to his mouth he gave vent to a roar that would have done credit to a South African lion.

As neither of the ladies understood the meaning of "Musha," they listened to the roar with a thrill of unutterable horror. Miss Pritty, as if fascinated, leant forward, the better to observe her foe. Suddenly, like the lightning-flash, and without even a shriek of warning, she lost her balance and dived head-foremost into the bosom of Rooney Machowl!

Well was it for the bold Irishman that Miss Pritty was a light weight, else had he that day ended his career in the jungles of Borneo. As it was he went down like a shock of corn before the scythe, grasped Miss Pritty in an embrace such as she had never before even imagined, and proceeded to punch her poor head.

Then, indeed, she made herself known by a powerful scream that caused the horrified man to loose his hold and spring up with a torrent of apologies and self-abuse.

"Och! it's not possible. Baste that I am! oh ma cushla astore, forgive me! It's a gorilla I thought

ye was, sure, for I hadn't time to look, d'ee see. It's wishin' you had staved in my timbers intirely I am."

Rooney's exclamations were here cut short, and turned on another theme by the sudden appearance of Aileen Hazlit, who soon found that her friend was more alarmed than hurt.

"I *am* so glad you have found us, and *so* surprised," said Aileen, who had met Rooney in England during one of her visits to Joe Baldwin's abode, " for we have quite lost ourselves."

Rooney looked a little awkwardly at the fair girl.

" Sure, it 's glad I am myself that I 've found you," he said, " but faix, I 'm lost too ! I do belave, howiver, that somebody 's goin' to find us."

He turned his head aside and listened intently. Presently a cry was heard at no great distance. It was replied to by another.

" Pirates," said Rooney, in a hoarse whisper, drawing a cutlass from his belt.

As he spoke another cry was heard in an opposite direction.

"Friends!" exclaimed Rooney. " Sure we 're surrounded by friends and foes ! Come, git into the tree, ladies. I 'll give a hail, an' if the varmin should come up first, I 'll kape them in play. Don't show yer purty faces dears, an' be as aisy as ye can."

So saying, Rooney gave vent to a true British
cheer, while the ladies ascended once more into the
tree.

The cheer was instantly replied to by counter-
cheers and howls. A minute more and two half-
naked Malays, armed with spears and long shields,
bounded into the clear space and attacked the Irishman, but Rooney had placed his back to the tree
and was ready for them. Although he was scarcely
a match for two such men, whose peculiar and
bounding mode of fighting he did not understand,
Rooney nevertheless quickly disabled one by the
sheer strength of a blow, which cut through the
shield and wounded his enemy's head. The other
he sprang upon like a wild cat and grappled with
him. At that moment a third Malay glided on the
scene, brandished his spear, and stood by the swaying combatants awaiting a favourable opportunity to
thrust his weapon into the white man's back. He
stood right under the branch in which the ladies
were concealed. Miss Pritty saw his intention and
felt convinced he would succeed. In desperate
alarm at the danger of her protector, and horrified
at what she was about to do, she grasped the pirate
by the hair and tore out a large handful, at the same
time uttering shriek upon shriek mingled with
appalling bursts of hysterical laughter.

This saved Rooney, who turned just in time to

protect himself, but as he did so six more pirates leaped upon the scene and overpowered him. They also sprung up the tree, and quickly brought down the ladies.

Poor Miss Pritty had gone fairly off into violent hysterics by that time. She was carried down in the arms of a pirate, into whose hair she had permanently fastened her ten fingers, while she filled the woods with unearthly cries.

Before any advantage, however, could be taken of this success, a cheer was heard close at hand. Next moment, Edgar Berrington burst on the scene, followed by the captain of the gun-boat and a body of men. The pirates did not await them, but fled instantly.

"Fire a volley, lads," shouted the captain.

The men obeyed, and one or two yells told that it had not been without effect, nevertheless, all the miscreants escaped with the exception of Miss Pritty's captive, who, unable to clear himself from her close embrace with sufficient speed, was collared and throttled into submission by Edgar.

"We'll divide our force here," said the captain. "I'll follow them up a while with some of the boys, and you, Mr. Berrington, will return with the rest to the gun-boat, in charge of the ladies."

Edgar was about to object, but the captain silenced him at once with —

"Come, sir, you're under my orders. Do what I bid you."

There was no resisting this, so Edgar turned, not unwillingly, and gave his arm to Aileen, who seized it with a grateful eagerness that sent a thrill of delight through all his frame.

"Come along, my lads," he cried. "Take care of Miss Pritty, poor thing!" he added, turning to Rooney.

The Irishman obeyed. He stooped and lifted her in his arms. She had been lying in a state of semi-insensibility with her eyes tightly shut. The moment she felt herself being lifted, she clutched her protector by the hair, and held on, shrieking.

"Ay, tug away, cushla!" said Rooney, as he moved after his friends, "it's not much of *that* ye'll manage to root up."

"Have you seen my father?" asked Aileen, anxiously, as they moved on together.

"He is safe," answered Edgar; "I found him exhausted in the hut which he told me you had occupied, and had him conveyed on board the gunboat."

"Thank God!" exclaimed Aileen, fervently, "but," she added, with a slight shudder, "it seemed to me as if his mind had been unhinged—and—and he was wounded."

"A mere scratch on the temple," said Edgar

"yet sufficient, with surrounding circumstances, to account for the temporary madness that assailed him. Fear not, Aileen, he is safe now, through God's mercy, and you shall soon be safe beside him."

A feeling of deep gratitude and restfulness stole over the poor girl's spirit, and she almost wept for joy as they stepped into a small boat, and were rowed over the calm water to the gun-boat, which lay, black and still, under the deep shadow of a bank of luxuriant foliage.

"My child," said Mr. Hazlit, sadly, as they reclined together on the couches of the little cabin, while Edgar sat on a camp-stool near them, Miss Pritty having been consigned to the captain's berth, "they tell me that this fearful work is not yet over. There is to be more fighting and bloodshed."

"How? what do you mean, papa?"

"Tell her, Mr. Berrington."

"We have just had news sent us by a fast row-boat from a town about sixty miles along the coast that a large fleet of pirate-prows have been seen off the coast. They have taken several trading prows, and captured many men belonging to the Sarawak territory, besides several Chinamen. When our captain completes his work on shore here, he intends to start at once in chase of these pirates, in the hope of destroying them and freeing their slaves."

"God help us," said Aileen, "it seems as if men

in this part of the world, gloried in pouring out
blood like water."

"Some of them undoubtedly do. Perhaps it may
reconcile your mind to the destruction of these
miscreants to know that for every one killed there
will probably be saved the lives of dozens—if not
hundreds—of innocent men and women, whom he
would have murdered, or doomed to hopeless slavery,
in the course of his wicked career."

As Edgar spoke, the sound of oars was heard.
Presently the captain and his men leaped on deck.
The moorings were cast loose, our hero took his
station at the engine, and the gun-boat glided
swiftly down the river, leaving the pirate strong-
hold in flames.

CHAPTER XVIII.

LIFTS THE CURTAIN SLIGHTLY AS TO PIRATICAL DOINGS IN THE NINETEENTH CENTURY.

SILENTLY they glided on, until the shades of evening fell, and the brilliant stars came out Silently, for the gun-boat went at half speed; silently, for her engines were good and new, and worked softly without the jarring of age or mal-construction; silently, because those on board were in a tranquil mood, and did not raise their voices above a low murmur.

" How romantic," said Aileen, in a low tone, as she sat by the stern rail and watched the gleaming track left by the screw; " how enjoyable, if we could only forget what has just passed, and the object we have in view. The world is a mystery !"

" Is this the first time you have thought so?" asked Edgar, who leaned on the rail near her.

" Well, I think it is," she replied, with a sad smile ; " at least it is the first time I have been deeply impressed with the thought."

S

"It is a very old thought," returned the youth, musingly. "Philosophers from the earliest times have recorded it. Thoughtful men and women of all ages have expressed it. Young people of all generations fancy they have discovered it. The Bible is a key which opens up much of it, and makes it plain ; but much still remains in mystery, and I suppose will continue so to remain, till Time merges in Eternity."

"Do you think such mystery undesirable ?" asked Aileen.

"No. It is desirable, else God would not have left it there. 'Shall not the Judge of all the earth do right ?' There is a need be, I doubt not, for mystery, and there is no need for our being distressed by it, for what we know not now we shall know hereafter. But there is much cause for anxiety lest we, either through wilful ignorance, or carelessness, or stupidity, should allow that to remain involved in mystery which is made plain by revelation. The way of salvation was an insurmountable mystery to me once, but since you gave me that poor man's Testament, Aileen, it has become very plain and very dear to me, through Jesus Christ."

Aileen thanked God in her heart, and a thrill of gladness filled her, but before she could utter a word in reply, the captain came forward and said in a low tone :—

"Stop the engine, Mr. Berrington. We'll lie by in this creek till daybreak."

Edgar went below. The vibrating of the boat ceased, and an awful stillness seemed to sink down upon her as she glided into a little creek or bay, which was deeply shaded by mangrove trees.

But the silence did not last long. It was still three hours from day-light, and the captain employed the time in preparations for the action which he anticipated on the following day. The yards were sent down; the decks were cleared of all useless incumbrances; the guns were got ready; and an attempt was made, to some extent, to disguise the vessel, so that, in the event of the pirates being found, the gun-boat might get as near as possible without her true character being discovered. The men, meanwhile, who were not engaged in such work, busied themselves in sharpening cutlasses and cleaning small arms, while they conversed in an undertone. All was activity and order, without fuss or needless noise—the result of a man of the right stamp being in command.

"It's a brush we'll be havin' soon," said Rooney Machowl, with a flash of the eye which told that he inherited a little of his nation's love of fighting.

"Looks like it," replied Maxwell, who sat beside his friend in the midst of a group of the Malay crew, rubbing up his cutlass with much interest.

"Does anybody know how many of a crew we have altogether?" asked Rooney.

"I heard the captain say to Mr. Berrington," answered Joe Baldwin, who was busy cleaning a rifle, "that we've got ninety men all told, which is quite enough for a 180-ton vessel. With these and seven guns we should be more than a match for all the pirates of the eastern seas."

"Ho!" exclaimed Ram-stam, looking up from the weapon he was engaged on with an amused expression, "you know noting of pirits of dem seas. Hi! hi! wait."

Ram-stam said this with the air of one who held the decided opinion that when he *had* waited Joe would have his views enlarged.

"What, are they such bold fellows?"

"Ho yis, vely muchee bold. Ca'es for noting. 'Flaid of noting. Doos a'most anyting—'cept what's good."

"Swate cratures," murmured Rooney; "I hope we'll be introdooced to aich other soon."

As it is desirable that the reader should have a little more extended knowledge of the miscreants referred to, we will retrace our steps in time a little, and change the scene.

On one of those sweltering mornings in which the eastern seas appear to have a tendency to boil under the influence of the sun, three piratical junks might

have been seen approaching a small island which
lay on the sea as if on a mirror. They were propelled by oars. The largest of these junks was under
command of our red-jacketed acquaintance, Pungarin.
It was what is termed double-banked, and the oars
were pulled by "slaves," that is to say, the crews
of trading vessels recently captured.

Pungarin had more slaves than he knew what to
do with on that occasion. He had been unusually
successful in his captures. All the white men
taken had at once been slaughtered, also all who
attempted to give the pirates trouble in any way,
including those who chanced to be too weak, ill, or
old to work. In regard to the rest, each man was
secured to his place at the oar by means of a strip
of cane, called rattan, fastened round his neck, and
a man was appointed to lash them when they showed
symptoms of flagging. This the unhappy wretches
frequently did, for, as on a former occasion to which
we have referred, they were made to pull con-
tinuously without food or water, and occasionally,
after dropping their oars through exhaustion, it took
severe application of the lash, and the discovery of
some unusually sensitive spot of the body, to rouse
some of them again to the point of labour.

The junks were strange, uncouth vessels, of considerable size, capable, each, of containing a very
large crew. They might almost have been styled

"life-boats," as they had hollow bamboos wrought into their structure in a manner which gave them great buoyancy, besides projecting beyond the hulls and forming a sort of outside platform. On these platforms the slaves who rowed were fastened. In each vessel there were at least forty or fifty rowers.

Pungarin walked up and down his poop-deck as if in meditation, paying no regard to what was going on around him until a feeble cry was heard from one of the rowers,—a middle-aged and sickly man. The pirate captain looked carelessly on, while the overseer flogged this man, but the lash failed to arouse him, and the captain ordered the man to desist—but not in mercy.

"Over with him," he said, curtly, and then resumed his walk.

The slave-driver drew his knife, and cut the rattan that bound the man, who turned his dying eyes on him with an imploring look.

At that moment one of the pirates, who from his dress and bearing seemed to occupy a position of authority, stepped upon the platform and looked at him. He gave a brief order to one of his comrades, who brought a large piece of cork and fastened it to the slave's neck. He also brought a short spear with a little flag at its handle. This he thrust a few inches into the fleshy part of his shoulder, and then pushed him off the platform into the sea. Thus the wretched creature was made to float, and, as he went astern, some of the pirates amused themselves by shooting at him with their muskets.

Now, *gentle* reader, don't shut your eyes and exclaim, "Oh! too horrible." It is *very much* because of that expression of yours, and the shutting of your "gentle" (we would rather say selfish) eyes that these accursed facts exist! Yes, we charge it home on you so-called "soft ones" of the earth, that your action,—namely, shutting your eyes,—does probably as much, if not more, to perpetuate horrible evil as does the action of open godlessness,—that condition which is most aptly expressed by the world's maxim, "every man for himself and the devil for us all."

Do not imagine that we presume to invent such things or to exaggerate for the sake of "sensation." We relate well-authenticated facts. We entertain strong doubts as to whether devils are, in any degree, worse than some among the unsaved human race. There is great occasion for you, reader, whoever you are, to know and ponder such facts as we now relate. We are too apt to regard as being applicable only to the past these words, "the dark places of the earth are full of the habitations of cruelty." If we were to fill our book with horrors from beginning to end, we should only have scratched the surface of the great and terrible truth. Assuredly now, not less

than in days of old, there is urgent need of red-hot
philanthropy.

But we gladly pass from the cruel to the cunning
phase of piratical life. These villains had at that
time been about six months on their cruise. They
had made the entire circuit of Borneo, murdering,
and plundering, and striking terror and desolation
wherever they went. The scenes enacted by Norse
pirates in the tenth century were repeated in the
middle of the nineteenth by a people who, *unlike* the
Norsemen, had no regard whatever for law ; and now
they were returning home laden with booty.

The pirate chief's usual mode of procedure on
such occasions was to go to an unfrequented island
in the neighbourhood of Singapore, land all his war-
like stores and prisoners, and, leaving them under a
strong guard, proceed with two of his prows loaded
to the gunwale with merchandise, to the port. The
merchant-boats which he had previously sunk, and
whose crews he had murdered, provided him with
"port-clearances," which enabled him to personate
the trader and regularly enter and clear the customs
at Singapore, so as to cause no suspicion ; then,
returning to his place of rendezvous with a fresh
supply of guns, ammunition, etc., he divided his
ill-gotten gains and recommenced his piratical expeditions.

On the present occasion, however, Pungarin had

received intelligence which induced him to modify his plans. Hearing that a gun-boat was in pursuit of him, he determined to change his rendezvous for the time.

The weary slaves were therefore again set to work at the oars; but "kind Nature" took pity on them. A breeze sprang up and increased into a gale, under the influence of which the prows sped out to sea and soon left the islands far behind them.

It was while thus attempting to evade their enemy that the pirates had the misfortune to run at last into the very jaws of the lion.

CHAPTER XIX.

A FIGHT WITH MALAY PIRATES.

At six o'clock in the morning, the tide suiting, the gun-boat crept out to sea, and steamed slowly along the coast to the southward, keeping a good look-out. They soon discovered sundry prows, but, after ordering them to come alongside, found that they were legitimate traders. Thus the day was spent in a vain search, and at night they returned to their anchorage, as it was not possible to make any discoveries in the dark.

Next morning, at the same hour, they steamed out to sea again, intending to keep about twelve miles off the coast, so as to be able to command a broad expanse of water in every direction ; but before they had got two miles from the anchorage, three prows were observed about four or five miles to seaward.

" That looks like the rascals," observed the captain, as he surveyed them through the glass.

"Indeed," said Mr. Hazlit, who, rather pale and weak from his recent unwonted experiences, leaned in a helpless manner on the quarter rails.

" Yes ; they pull forty or fifty oars, double-banked,"
returned the captain, wiping his glass carefully.
" They've got heavy guns on board, no doubt. We
shall have to protect our boiler."

The gun-boat was so small that a portion of her
steam-case was unavoidably exposed above deck.
A shot into this would have been disastrous.
Orders were therefore given to surround it with bags
of coal, which was promptly done.

" And, one of you," said the captain, turning to
the man who chanced to be nearest him, " go into
the cabin and bring up the sofa cushions; we shall
want them to protect the legs of the men stationed
on the poop."

Rooney Machowl happened to be the man who
received this order. He at once descended.

" By your lave, Miss," he said, with a bashful air ;
" I 'm sorry to ask a lady to git up, but it 's the
capting's orders—he wants the cushions."

" By all means," said Aileen, with a smile ; " why
does he want them ? "

" Plaze, Miss, to protect our legs, savin' yer
presence."

Somewhat puzzled, and not a little amused by the
reply, Aileen rose and allowed the cushion on which
she sat to be removed. These cushions were placed
in the nettings on the poop, which was much exposed,
to arrest the enemy's bullets.

In a few minutes it was seen that the three prows were doing their best to get into shoal water, where the steamer could not have followed them. In this effort one of them was successful, for although the gun-boat's course was changed in order to cut her off, she managed to run on shore, whence the pirates immediately opened fire. The other two, seeing there was no possibility of accomplishing the same feat, ceased rowing, and also opened fire, at a distance of about five or six hundred yards.

"We shall attack from our port side," said the captain to his chief officer; "let the guns be laid accordingly."

The armament of the gun-boat consisted of two nine-pounder guns, one on the forecastle, and one on the poop; one twelve-pounder, just before the bridge; and four six-pound brass carronades. These were all soon ready, but the order was not given to fire till they had got to within a hundred yards of the pirates, who were now pelting them smartly with small arms.

The captain stood on the bridge, the most commanding and, at the same time, the most exposed position in the vessel. He wore a cap, from under which his black eyes seemed to twinkle with fire and mischief.

He soon observed that the two prows, wincing under his fire, were edging for the shore. With that reckless resolution, therefore, to which all true heroes give way at times—not excepting Nelson himself—he resolved to run them down.

The recklessness of this consisted in the fact that his vessel was not a " ram," but built of comparatively thin plates. The necessity for it lay in the certainty that a few minutes more would enable the prows to gain shallow water and escape.

" Besides," thought the captain to himself, as he walked up and down the bridge with his hands in his pockets, while bullets whistled round his head, " even a *thin* plate can stand a good strain when struck end-on. Never venture, never win !"

Giving the order " full speed " to the engineer, and " port your helm a little—steady " to the man at the wheel, the captain quietly awaited the result.

The result was most effective. The gun-boat went at the prow like a war-horse; her sharp bow struck one of the pirate vessels fair amidships and cut her in two pieces, launching her crew and captives into the sea !

She then backed astern, and made for the other prow, but she, laying to heart the fate of her companion, made for the shore as fast as possible. It was in vain. The gun-boat ran into her and sank her immediately, but so nearly had they succeeded in their intention, that there were only six inches of water under the steamer's keel when she backed out.

" Lower the boats," shouted the captain, the instant his object had been accomplished ; and it was not a moment too soon, for the sea all round was alive with human beings, some of whom evidently waited to be picked up, while others swam vigorously for the shore. In a short time, about a hundred men were rescued, most of whom were slaves—only ten being pirates. There was no difficulty in distinguishing between pirates and slaves, because the latter wore the "rattan" round their necks, in addition to which their spitting on the pirates, and furiously abusing them for past cruelty, and their falling down and kissing the feet of their deliverers, made the distinction abundantly clear.

Most of the other pirates gained the shore, but we may here finally dismiss them, and relieve the reader's mind by stating that they were afterwards hunted down and slain to a man by the natives of that district, who entertained a deadly, and very natural hatred of them, having suffered much at their hands in time past.

While the rescued captives were going about excitedly telling of the shocking barbarities that had been practised on them, the captain discovered among them a Singapore native who could speak a little English. Taking this man aft, he questioned him closely.

" Are there any more pirate junks hereabouts ?" he said.

" Yis ; tree more."

" Whereaway ?"

" Hout seaward. Not know how far. Longish way off, me tink. We was sent off from dem last night, after all de goods an' money was tooked out of us. What for, no kin tell. Where tothers go, no kin tell."

" They've got lots of captives aboard, I suppose?" said the captain.

" Ho ! great lots," replied the Singapore man.

" And lots of treasure too, no doubt."

" Ho ! very greater lots of dat."

After obtaining all the information he could from this man and from the other passengers, the captain steamed out to sea in a westerly direction, keeping a man at the mast-head to look out. The captives were in the meanwhile made as comfortable as circumstances would admit of, and the ten pirates were put in irons in the hold.

As the morning advanced, the sun increased in power and splendour. Not a breath of wind ruffled the sea, which shone like a mirror, reflecting perfectly the sea-birds that accompanied them. Everything was so calm and peaceful that the captain sent a message to Mr. Hazlit and his daughter to request them to come up and enjoy the fresh air.

During the brief action described, they had been sent below to be out of danger. They obeyed the summons, and even Miss Pritty was induced by Aileen to come on deck.

Poor Miss Pritty! Her hysterical fit was now quite over, but pale cheeks and a trembling exhausted frame told eloquently of her recent sufferings. Mr. Hazlit's limbs were also shaky, and his face cadaverous, showing that his temporary aberration of reason had told upon him.

"Oh *how* delicious!" exclaimed Miss Pritty, referring to the atmosphere, as she sank into an easy-chair which the captain placed for her. "Are these the pirates?" she added, shuddering, as her eyes fell on some of the rescued people.

"No, Miss Pritty," answered the captain, "these are the freed captives. The pirates are in irons in the hold."

"You had to fight, I suppose?" continued Miss Pritty, shutting her eyes and pursing her mouth with the air of one who braces herself to face the inevitable.

"Well, we could hardly call it fighting," answered the captain, with a smile, as he cleaned the glasses of his telescope and swept the horizon carefully; "we had a round or two of the guns, and a few bullets whistled about our ears for a little—that was all."

"Was any one wounded—k—killed?" asked Miss Pritty, opening her eyes with an anxious look; "and oh!" she added, with a sudden expression of horror, as she drew up her feet and glanced downwards,

" perhaps the decks are—no," she continued sinking back again with a sigh, "they are *not* bloody !"

At that moment the man at the mast-head reported three prows, just visible on the horizon ahead.

" I suppose we must go below again," said Aileen, sadly, after the captain returned from the bridge, to which he had gone to examine the prows in question.

" Not yet, Miss Hazlit. It will probably be an hour ere we come up with them. You 'd better enjoy the morning air while you may. I 'll warn you in good time."

Aileen therefore remained on deck for some time with her father, but poor Miss Pritty, on the first intimation that more pirates were in sight, got up hastily, staggered with a face expressive of the utmost horror into the cabin, flung herself into the captain's berth, thrust her head under the pillow, piled the clothes over that, and lay there--quaking!

She quaked for full half an hour before anything happened. Then she felt a hand trying to remove her superincumbent head-gear. This induced her to hold on tight and shriek, but, recognising Aileen's voice, she presently put her face out.

" Don't be so terrified, dear," said Aileen, scarce able to repress a smile.

" I *can't* help it," answered her friend, whimpering; " are the—the pirates—"

" They are not far off now. But don't give way

T

to needless alarm, dear. Our captain sent me below because he is going to fight them, and you know he is sure to win, for he is a brave man. He says he 'll run them all down in a few minutes."

"Oh!" groaned Miss Pritty, and with that, pulling her head in like a snail, she resumed quaking.

Poor Aileen, although talking thus bravely to her friend, was by no means easy in her own mind, for apart from the fact that they were about to engage three pirate junks, manned by hundreds of desperate men, she could not repress her shrinking horror at the bare idea of men talking coolly about shedding human blood. To one of her imaginative nature, too, it was no small trial to have to sit alone and inactive in the cabin, while the bustle of preparation for war went on overhead; we say alone, because her father, although there, was too much exhausted to act the part of companion or comforter in any degree.

Meanwhile the gun-boat approached close to the enemy, and it soon became apparent that they meant to fight—trusting, no doubt, to their very decided superiority in numbers.

"They mean mischief," said the captain, as he shut up his telescope.

"Faix, an' they'll git it too," replied Rooney Machowl, who chanced to be near at the time, though the remark was not addressed to him.

To this the captain made no reply, save by a grim curl of his black moustache, as he once more ascended to his exposed position on the bridge. From this outlook he could see plainly that the pirates were lashing their three prows together, and training all their guns on one side, where the attack was expected. As each prow mounted twelve guns, they could thus fire a broadside of thirty-six heavy pieces, besides small arms.

The men of the gun-boat were now all at their quarters, eagerly awaiting the order to begin. The captain descended and went round among them, so as to inspect everything with his own eye.

" Now, lads," he said, in passing, " remember, not a single shot till I give you positive orders."

He returned to the bridge. Although naturally disinclined to parley with scoundrels, he felt that he had a duty to perform, and resolved to go close up, and, if possible, induce them to surrender. But he was saved the trouble of attempting a parley, for while yet six hundred yards off, a regular volley burst from the sides of the pirate vessels.

Again the black moustache curled, but this time with a touch of ferocity, for the shot partly took effect, cutting the rigging to some extent, killing one man of the crew, and wounding several. A musket-ball also struck his own cap and knocked it off his head.

"Just hand that up," he said, pointing to the cap.

One of the men obeyed, and the captain, taking a look at the hole, replaced it. Still he gave no order to fire, although the pirates were seen to be busily re-loading.

Ranging up to within a hundred yards, the captain looked quickly at his men.

"Port, a little," said he to the man at the wheel.

"Are you ready?"

"Ay, ay, sur," from Rooney Machowl, in a deep bass undertone.

"Fire!"

As if but one piece had been fired the whole broadside burst from the side of the gun-boat, shaking the little vessel violently. Miss Pritty's voice came up responsive with an unearthly yell!

"Load!" was instantly ordered, and so quickly was it obeyed that before the enemy were ready with their second volley the gun-boat had charged and fired again, doing great damage.

There being no wind, a dense cloud of smoke from the three volleys settled down on the water and completely hid them and their enemy from each other.

"Steam ahead, full speed," signalled the captain to Edgar Berrington.

The screw instantly whirled, and under cover of the dense veil, the active little vessel moved away just in time to escape a murderous volley of shot, shrapnel, and ball, which was poured into the smoke she had left behind her! The pirates followed this up with a wild cheer and a brisk fire of musketry, which only ceased when, discovering their mistake, they beheld the gun-boat emerge from the smoke, steer round the end of their line, and, slewing to port, deliver another volley of great guns and small arms, that raked them all from stem to stern, doing terrible execution both to the prows and their crews.

Thus the gun-boat played round and round the enemy, always maintaining the distance of about a hundred yards, and keeping up the action as fast as they could load and fire. The pirates, on their part, fought with the courage of trained men of war and with the ferocity of tigers at bay—who ask and expect no mercy. And thus they fought for no less than three hours.

One reason why the pirates were able to hold out so long lay in the fact that their prows were surrounded by a thick matting made from a certain palm-leaf, which, although it could not prevent shot from passing through, concealed the men who lay behind it, and so prevented the riflemen of the gun-boat crew from taking aim. In order to get the better of this difficulty, the latter fell into the way of watching for the puffs of smoke that came through the matting, and firing at these puffs.

Conspicuous among the pirates for his coolness, daring, and utter disregard of his life, was one tall, powerful fellow in a red jacket. Every one guessed him at once to be a chief among the pirates, and this question was soon settled by some of the recently freed captives, who recognised him as being the great chief of the fleet—Pungarin.

He went about the deck of his prow, which occupied the centre of the line, encouraging his men to rapid action, and often pointing the guns with his own hands.

Many rifle-shots were fired at him, but in vain. He seemed to bear a charmed life.

"Can none of you pick him off?" said the captain of the gun-boat.

Twenty rifles replied to the words, and the man's red jacket was seen to be torn in many places, but himself remained unhurt!

At last the pirate guns were silenced in two of the prows, only the chief's maintaining an obstinate fire. This vessel would have been much sooner silenced, no doubt, but for the ferocity of Pungarin. When his men, driven at last by the deadly fire of the assailants, forsook a gun and sought refuge behind the matting, the pirate chief would promptly step forward and serve the gun himself, until very shame sometimes forced his men to return.

At last all the guns were disabled but one, and

that one Pungarin continued to serve, uninjured, amid a perfect storm of shot.

"The fellow has got the lives of twenty cats," growled the captain, as he turned to give directions to the steersman, which brought the gun-boat still closer to the enemy. The effect of a well-delivered volley at this shorter range was to cut the fastenings of the three prows, thus permitting them to separate.

This was precisely what was desired, the captain having resolved to run the pirates down one at a time, as he had done before. He would not board them, because their superior numbers and desperate ferocity would have insured a hand-to-hand conflict, which, even at the best, might have cost the lives of many of his men. The instant, therefore, that the prows were cut adrift, he gave the order to back astern. At the same moment Pungarin was heard to give an order to his men, which resulted in the oars being got out and manned by the surviving pirates and slaves, who rowed for the land as fast as possible. Their escape in this way, however, the captain knew to be impossible, for they were now fully twenty-five miles from shore. He therefore went about his work leisurely.

Backing a considerable distance, so as to enable his little war-horse to get up full-speed, he took careful aim as he charged.

It was interesting to watch the swart faces and

glaring eyeballs of those on board the first prow, as
the gun-boat bore down on them.   Some glared from
hate, others obviously from fear, and all seemed a
little uncertain as to what was about to be done.
This uncertainty was only dispelled when the prow
was struck amidships, and, with a tremendous crash,
cut clean in two.   Simultaneous with the crash arose
a yell of mingled anger and despair, as pirates and
prisoners were all hurled into the sea.

Again the order was given to go astern.   The
steamer immediately backed out of the wreck.   After
gaining a sufficient distance the engines were reversed,
and the little vessel bore down on another prow.

This one made violent efforts to evade the blow,
but the captain had anticipated as much.   His
orders were sharp; his steersman was prompt.
The cut-water did its duty nobly, and in a few
seconds another pirate vessel was sent to the bottom.

The sea was now swarming with human beings in
all directions, some clinging to any scrap of wreck
they could lay hold of, some paddling about aimlessly
and roaring for help, while others swam steadily in
the direction of the land.   These last were chiefly
pirates, who had evidently made up their minds to
escape or drown rather than be captured.

As it was evident that many of those struggling
in the water would be drowned in a few minutes, the
captain delayed his attack on the third prow, and

ordered the boats to be lowered. This was done promptly, and many of the poor victims captured by the pirates were rescued and brought on board. A few of the pirates were also picked up. These had jumped overboard with their "creases" and other weapons in their hands, and were so vindictive as to show fight furiously in the water when the sailors attempted to save them. Many of the men suffered from this. Poor Rooney Machowl was among the number.

He pulled the bow-oar of his boat, and hauled it in on drawing near to any one, so as to be ready to catch the hand of the swimmer, or make a grasp at him. As they approached one of the swimmers, Rooney observed that he had a short twisted sword in his hand, and that he looked over his shoulder with a fierce scowl. Nevertheless, as he leaned over to the rescue, it did not occur to the worthy man that the swimmer meant mischief, until he saw the twisted sword leap from the water, and felt the point of his nose almost severed from his face !

"Och ! you spalpeen," cried Rooney, with a yell of intense indignation and pain.

He was about to follow this up with a blow. from his powerful fist that would have sent the pirate at least a fathom of the way down to the bottom, but the sword again leaped upwards, causing him to start back as it flashed close past his cheek, and

went right over the boat into the sea. At the same
moment a Malay seized the pirate by an ear, another
grasped him by an arm, and he was quickly hauled
in-board and bound. "Here, Joe Baldwin," cried
Rooney to his comrade, who pulled an oar near the
stern of the boat, "for anny favour lind a hand to
fix on the pint o' my poor nose. It was niver purty,
but och! it's ruinated now past redimption."

"Not a bit, man," said Joe, as he bound up the
injured member by the simple process of tying a
kerchief right round his friend's face and head;
"it'll be handsomer than ever. There was always
too much of it. You can afford to have it reduced."

Rooney did not quite seem to appreciate this
comforting remark; however, after his nose was
bound he and the rest of the boat's crew continued
their work, and soon returned on board the gun-boat
with a mixed lot of pirates and captives. Of course
the rescuers were more careful in approaching the
swimmers after Rooney's misfortune, but in spite
of this many of them were wounded by the pirates
slashing at them with their swords and knives, or
flinging these weapons violently into the boats.

In a short time all were saved who yet remained
above water. Then the boats were hauled up and
the steamer gave chase to the prow in charge of the
pirate captain, which was by that time far away
on the horizon.

CHAPTER XX.

THE FIGHT CONCLUDED.

THE nautical proverb saith that "A stern chase is a long one;" but that proverb, to make it perfect and universally applicable, should have been prefaced by the words "All things being equal."

In the present case all things were not equal. The gun-boat was a fast steamer; the chase was a slow row-boat, insufficiently manned by tired and wounded men. But many of them were desperate men. Their leader was an arch-fiend of resolution and ferocity. He knew that escape, in the circumstances, was impossible. He was well aware of the fate that awaited him if taken. He therefore made up his mind to give his enemies as much trouble as possible, to delay their triumph and cause it to cost them dear, and, in every practicable way that might occur, to thwart and worry them to the end.

Animated by such a spirit, he managed to encourage his men, and to terrify and lash his slaves to almost superhuman exertions, so that before being overtaken

they approached considerably nearer to the shore
than would otherwise have been the case. This,
as it afterwards turned out, resulted in a benefit to
some of those in the gun-boat, which they did not
think of at the time. As they overtook the prow,
Pungarin ordered the starboard rowers to cease.
Those on the port side continued to pull, and in a
few seconds the prow's broadside was brought to
bear on the approaching enemy. Not till they were
within a hundred yards did the pirate leader again
speak. Then his powerful voice resounded through
his vessel :—

"Fire !"

At the word every piece on board the prow, great
and small, belched forth a volume of smoke, flame,
and metal, but the result was trifling. In his
anxiety to do deadly execution, the pirate had over-
done his work. He had allowed his foe to come too
close, and most of the discharge from the heavy
guns passed over her, while the men with small
arms, rendered nervous by prolonged delay, fired
hastily, and, therefore, badly. A few wounds were
suffered, and many narrow escapes were made, but
in other respects the discharge passed by harmlessly.
The captain, in his exposed and elevated position on
the bridge, felt, indeed, as if a thunder-shower of
iron hail had passed, not only round, but through
him ! He paid no regard to it, however, but held

straight on. Next moment there was a dire collision; the prow went under water, and the surface of the sea was covered with shouting and struggling men.

The boats were quickly lowered, as on the previous occasion, and most of the people were rescued, though, of course, some who could not swim were drowned.

The scene that now ensued was very exciting, and in some respects very terrible, for, besides the gurgling cries of the perishing, there were the defiant yells of the pirates, who, more fiercely than those in the other prows, resisted being taken alive, and used their creases and knives with deadly effect.

This naturally filled the conquerors with such indignation that in many cases they killed the pirates who showed fight, instead of disarming and capturing them.

At last every one in the water was either saved, killed, drowned, or captured, with the exception of one man, whose red jacket clearly pointed him out as the pirate chief. Being greatly superior to his fellows in mental and physical powers, it was natural that he should excel them in his efforts to escape. Even after the whole affair was over, this man, who might have been a hero in other circumstances, continued to baffle his pursuers.

In the boat which finally captured him was the Singapore man already mentioned. This man, for reasons best known to himself, had a bitter hatred of Pungarin, and was the chief cause of the boat in which he pulled an oar being kept in close pursuit of the pirate chief.

"Dis way," he cried, when the general *mêlée* was drawing to a close. "Yonder is de red-coat. He make for de shore."

The steersman at once turned in the direction indicated, which brought them close to the gun-boat.

Pungarin's keen eye quickly observed that they were making towards him, although the water around him swarmed with other men. He at once dived and came up close to the side of the vessel, under its quarter, and in dangerous proximity to its screw. The boldness of the course might have diverted attention from him for a time, but his one touch of vanity—the red jacket—betrayed him. He was soon observed. A cry was given. His sharp-eyed enemy the Singapore man saw him, and the boat was once more pulled towards its mark. But Pungarin dived like an otter—not only under the boat, but under the steamer also; coming up on the other side, and resting while they sought for him. Again they discovered him. Again he passed under the ship's bottom, and this time continued his dive onwards towards the shore. When his power of remaining under water failed, he came gently to the surface, turning on his back, so that only his mouth and nose appeared.

One full breath sufficed, and he dived again without having been observed. If Pungarin had adopted this plan while the boats were busy capturing his comrades, it is possible that he might have escaped, for his swimming powers and endurance were very great; but it was now too late. When he rose the second time to the surface, the affair was over, and men's minds were free to fix entirely on himself. Just then, too, he thought it advisable to put his head fully out of the water in order to see that he had kept in the right direction.

He was instantly observed by his Singapore enemy, and the chase was resumed.

It is almost unnecessary to say that it terminated unfavourably for the pirate chief. For several minutes he continued to dive under the boat while they tried to seize him, and wounded some of the men nearest to him; but his Herculean powers began at last to fail, and he finally floated on the surface as if helpless.

Even this was a ruse, for no sooner was the boat near enough, and the Singapore man within reach of his arm, than he raised himself, and made a cut at that individual with such good will that he split his skull across down nearly to the ears.

Next moment he was hauled into the boat and bound hand and foot.

The scene on board the gun-boat now was a very terrible one. Every man there was more or less begrimed with powder and smoke, or bespattered with blood and soaked with water, while all round the decks the wounded were sitting or lying awaiting their turn of being attended to, and groaning more or less with pain.

On calling the roll after the action was over, it was found that the loss suffered by the gun-boat crew was two men killed and eighteen wounded— a very small number considering the time during which the affair had lasted, and the vigour with which the pirates had fought.

And now was beautifully exemplified the advantage of a man possessing a "little knowledge"—falsely styled "a dangerous thing"—over a man who possesses *no* knowledge. Now, also, was exhibited the power and courage that are latent in true womanhood.

There was no surgeon on board of that gun-boat, and, with the exception of Edgar Berrington, there was not a man possessed of a single scrap of surgical knowledge deeper than that required for the binding up of a cut finger.

As we have already shown, our hero had an inquiring mind. While at college he had become intimately

acquainted with, and interested in, one or two
medical students, with whom he conversed so
much and so frequently about their studies, that he
became quite familiar with these, and with their
medical and surgical phraseology, so that people
frequently mistook him for a student of medicine.
Being gifted with a mechanical turn of mind, he
talked with special interest on surgery; discussed
difficulties, propounded theories, and visited the
hospitals, the dissecting-rooms, and the operating-
theatres frequently. Thus he came, unintentionally,
to possess a considerable amount of surgical knowledge, and when, at last, he was thrown providen-
tially into a position where no trained man could be
found, and urgent need for one existed, he came
forward and did his best like a man.

Aileen Hazlit also, on being told that there was
need of a woman's tender hand in such work, at
once overcame her natural repugnance to scenes of
blood; she proceeded on deck, and, with a beating
heart but steady hand, went to work like a trained
disciple of Florence Nightingale.

To the credit of the timid, and for the encouragement of the weak, we have to add that Miss Pritty
likewise became a true heroine!

No average individual, male or female, can by any
effort of imagination attain to the faintest idea of
poor Miss Pritty's horror at the sight of "*blood!*"

—"*human gore!*" particularly. Nevertheless Miss
Pritty, encouraged by her friend's example, rose to the
occasion. With a face and lips so deadly pale that
one might have been justified in believing that all the
blood on the decks had flowed therefrom, she went
about among the wounded, assisting Aileen in every
possible way with her eyes shut. She did indeed
open them when it was absolutely necessary to do
so, but shut them again instantly on the necessity
for vision passing away. She cut short bandages
when directed so to do; she held threads or tapes;
she tore up shirts, and slips, and other linen garments, with the most reckless disregard of propriety;
she wiped away blood from wounds (under direction),
and moistened many dry lips with a sponge, and
brushed beads of perspiration from pale brows—
like a heroine.

Meanwhile Edgar went about actively, rejoicing
in his new-found capacity to alleviate human
suffering. What the Faculty would have thought
of him we know not. All on board the gun-boat
venerated him as a most perfect surgeon. His
natural neatness of hand stood him in good stead,
for men were bleeding to death all round him, and
in order to save some it was necessary that he
should use despatch with others. Of course he
attended to the most critical cases first, except in
the case of those who were so hopelessly injured as

to be obviously beyond the reach of benefit from man. From these he turned sadly away, after whispering to them an earnest word or two about the Saviour of mankind—to those of them at least who understood English. To waste time with these he felt would be to rob hopeful cases of a chance. All simple and easy cases of bandaging he left to the captain and his chief officer. Joe Baldwin, being a cool steady man, was appointed to act as his own assistant.

From one to another he passed unweariedly, cutting off portions of torn flesh, extracting bullets, setting broken bones, taking up and tying severed arteries, sewing together the edges of gaping wounds, and completing the amputation of limbs, in regard to which the operation had been begun—sometimes nearly finished—by cannon shot.

"How terribly some of the poor wretches have been starved!" muttered Edgar as he bent over one of the captives, attempting to draw together the edges of a sword-cut in his arm; "why, there is not enough of flesh on him to cover his wound."

"There an't much, sir," assented Joe Baldwin, in a sympathetic tone, as he stood close by holding the needle and thread in readiness. "There's one man for'ard, sir, that I saw in passing to the chest for this thread, that has scarcely as much flesh on him as would bait a rat-trap. But he seems quite contented, poor fellow, at bein' freed from slavery, and don't seem to mind much the want o' flesh and blood. Perhaps he counts on gettin' these back again."

"Hm ! these are not so easily regained when lost as you seem to imagine, my friend," exclaimed a pompous but rather weak voice. Joe looked up. It was Mr. Hazlit, whose bloodless countenance and shrunken condition had become more apparent than ever after he had been enabled to reclothe himself in the garments of civilisation.

"Why, sir," said Joe, gently, "you seem to have bin badly shaken. Not bin wounded, I hope, sir ?"

"No,—at least not in body," replied the merchant, with a faint smile and shake of the head; " but I've been sadly bruised and broken in spirit."

Joe, remembering somewhat of Mr. Hazlit's former state of spirit, had almost congratulated him on the beneficial change before it occurred that his meaning in doing so might have been misunderstood. He therefore coughed slightly and said, "Ah—indeed!"

"Yes, indeed, my man," returned the merchant; " but I have reason to be supremely thankful that I am here now in *any* condition of mind and body worthy of being recognised."

As the amateur surgeon here desired Joe to assist him in moving his patient a little, Mr. Hazlit turned away, in a stooping attitude because of weakucss, aud, with his vest flapping against the place where his chief development had once beeu, shuffled slowly towards the quarter-deck.

It was at this time that the boat which captured Pungarin came alongside, and there was a general movement of curiosity towards the gangway as he was passed on board.

The hands of the pirate chief were tied behind his back, but otherwise he was free, the cords that had bound his legs having been cast loose.

A howl of execration burst from the captives when they saw him, and several ran forward with the evident intention of spitting on him, but these were promptly checked by the sailors.

Pungarin drew himself up and stood calmly, but not defiantly, as if waiting orders. There was no expression ou his bold countenance save that of stern indifference for the crowd around him, over whose heads he gazed quietly out to sea. His brow remained as unflushed and his breathing as gentle as though his struggles for life had occurred weeks ago, though the wet garments and the ragged red jacket told eloquently of the share he had taken in the recent fight.

"Take him below and put him in irons," said the captain.

"Please, sir," remarked the man whose duty it was to secure the prisoners, "we've got no more

irons on board.   We had only thirty pair, and there's
now thirty-eight prisoners in the hold."

"Secure him with ropes, then," returned the
captain;—"where is Mr. Berrington?" he added,
looking round hurriedly.

"For'ard, sir, lookin' after the wounded," answered
a sailor.

While the pirate chief was led below, the captain
walked quickly to the place where Edgar was
busy.

"Can you spare a minute?" he asked.

"Not easily," said Edgar, who had just finished
the dressing with which we left him engaged;
"there are several here who require prompt attention; but of course if the case is urgent—"

"It *is* urgent: come and see."

Without a word our amateur surgeon rose and
walked after the captain, who led him to the
companion-hatch, leaning against which he found
the Singapore man, with his head split across and
apparently cut down nearly from ear to ear.   From
this awful wound two small spouts of blood, about
the thickness of a coarse thread, rose a foot and a half
into the air.   We use no exaggeration, reader, in
describing this.   We almost quote verbatim the
words of a most trustworthy eye-witness from whose
lips we received the account.

The man looked anxiously at Edgar, who turned

at once to the captain and said in an undertone, but hurriedly, "I can be of no use here. It is quite impossible that he can live. To attempt anything would really be taking up time that is of vast importance to more hopeful cases."

"Sir, do try," faltered the poor man in English.

"Ha! you speak English?" said Edgar, turning quickly towards him; "forgive me, my poor fellow, I did not know that you understood"—

"Yis, me speak Engleesh. Me Singapore man. Go for vist me friends here. Cotch by pirits. Do try, doctir."

While he was speaking Edgar quickly took off the man's necktie and bound it round his head; then, using a little piece of wood as a lever, he passed it through the tie and twisted it until the two sides of the gaping gash were brought together, which operation stopped the bleeding at once. This done he hastily left him; but it will interest the reader to know that this Singapore man actually recovered from his terrible wound after a month of hospital treatment. He was afterwards taken over to Singapore as a natural curiosity, and exhibited there to several doctors who had refused to believe the story. For aught we know to the contrary, the man may be alive and well at the present day. Certain it is that his cure at that time was complete.*

* We were told this fact by a trustworthy eye-witness.

It was evening before all the wounds were dressed, and it was dark night ere the disorder caused by the action and its consequences were removed, and the gun-boat restored to somewhat of its wonted tidiness and appearance of comfort. But there was little comfort on board during the silence of that long night, which seemed to many as though it would never end; and which, in the case of a few, ended in Eternity.

Although silence began to descend on all, sleep was not there. Excitement, fatigue, and the awful scenes they had witnessed, drove it from the pillows of Aileen and her friend. Frequent calls for the aid of the surgeon put anything like refreshing rest —much though he required it—quite out of the question, and at whatever hour of the night or early morning he entered the temporary hospital where the sufferers lay, he was sure to be met by the white flash of the many eyes in haggard swart faces that turned eagerly and expectantly towards him—proving that sleep had little or no influence there.

There was less of this want of repose, strange to say, in another part of the vessel.

Down in the dark hold, where one feeble lamp cast a mere apology for light on the wretched surroundings, many of the pirates slept soundly. Their days were numbered—each one knew that full well—yet they slept. Their hearts ought to have been full of dark forebodings, but they slumbered—some of them with the profound quietude of infants! One might wonder at this were it not a familiar fact. This condition of "the wicked" has been observed in every age, and is stated in holy writ.

But *all* were not asleep in that dismal prison-house. There were among them, it seemed, a few who were troubled with fears—perhaps some who had consciences not yet utterly seared. At all events, two or three of them moved uneasily as they sat huddled together, for there was little room for so many in such a confined space, and now and then a bursting sigh escaped. But such evidences of weakness, if such it may be called, were few. For the most part silence reigned. In mercy the captain had ordered a chink of the hatch to be left open, and through this the stars shone down into the dark chamber.

Looking up at these, in statue-like silence, sat the pirate chief. No one had spoken to him, and he had spoken to none since his entry there. Sleep did not visit *his* eyes, nor rest his heart, yet he sat perfectly still, hour after hour. Perchance he experienced the rest resulting from an iron will that abides its approaching time for action.

The tending of the wounded, the cleansing of the ship, the feeding of survivors, the shutting up and arranging for the night, had passed away—even the groaning of sufferers had dwindled down to its lowest ebb—long before Pungarin moved with the intent to carry out his purpose.

The night-watch had been set and changed; the guard over the prisoners had been relieved; the man in charge of them had gone his rounds and examined their fetters; the careful captain had himself inspected them,—all was perfectly quiet and deemed safe, when Pungarin at last moved, and gave vent to one deep prolonged sigh that seemed to be the opening of the escape valve of his heart, and the out-rush of its long-pent-up emotions.

Slowly, but persistently, he began to struggle, and in the darkness of the place it seemed to those of his comrades who observed him as if he were writhing like a snake. But little did his fellow-pirates heed. Their hearts had long ago ceased to be impressible by horrid fancies. They could not help but see what went on before their eyes—it did not require an effort to help caring!

We have already said that some of the prisoners had been bound with ropes for want of irons. Pungarin was among the number, and his almost superhuman efforts were directed to freeing himself from his rope, either by tearing his limbs out of it, or by snapping it asunder. In both attempts he failed. Sailors are, of all men, least likely to tie a knot badly, or to select a rope too weak for its purpose.

The pirate at length made this discovery, and sank down exhausted. But he rose again ere long.

Those of the prisoners who had been secured by ropes were fastened to a beam overhead. The place was very low. None of them could have stood erect under this beam. While endeavouring to free himself, Pungarin had struggled on his knees. He now raised himself as high as possible on his knees. His hands, although tied in front of him, could be raised to his head. He quickly made a loop on the rope and passed it over his head.

Just then the guard removed the hatchway, and descended to make the last inspection for the night. Pungarin hastily removed the rope, sank down and lay quite still as if in slumber.

Night passed slowly on. The morning-star arose. The sun soon chased away the shadows, and brought joy to the awaking world. It even brought some degree of comfort to the comfortless on board the gun-boat. The sleepers began to rouse themselves, the wounded to move and relieve themselves, if possible, by change of position. The cook set about his preparations for the morning meal, and the captain, who, being dangerously close to shore, had taken no rest whatever during the night, gave up the charge of his vessel to the first officer, and went below to seek that repose which he had so well earned.

Ere he had closed an eye, however, his attention was arrested by a cry, and by a peculiar noise of voices on deck. There are tones in the human voice which need no verbal explanation to tell us that they mean something serious. He jumped up and sprang on deck. As if by instinct he went towards the hatchway leading to the hold.

"He's dead, sir!" were the first words that greeted him.

A glance into the hold was enough to explain.

The pirate-chief had hanged himself. With difficulty, but with inflexible resolution, he had accomplished his purpose by fastening the rope round his neck and lifting his legs off the ground, so that he was actually found suspended in a sitting posture.

His comrades in guilt, little impressed, apparently, by his fate, sat or reclined around his body in callous indifference.

CHAPTER XXI.

DIFFICULTIES OF VARIOUS KINDS, ALSO TROUBLES, AND A DISCOVERY.

"GENTLEMEN," said the captain of the gun-boat to Mr. Hazlit and Edgar as they sat that morning at breakfast, "it is my intention to run to the nearest town on the coast—which happens to be Muku— have these pirates tried and shot, then proceed to Singapore, and perhaps run thence to the coast of China. I will take you with me if you wish it, or if you prefer it, will put you on board the first homeward-bound passenger-ship that we can find. What say you?"

Now, reader, we possess the happy privilege of knowing what Mr. Hazlit and Edgar thought as well as what they said, and will use that privilege for purposes of our own.

In the first place, Edgar thought he should very much like to hear Mr. Hazlit's views on that subject before speaking. He therefore said nothing.

The course being thus left clear to him, the merchant thought as follows :—

"It's very awkward, excessively awkward and vexatious. Here am I, ever so many thousands of miles away from home, without a single sovereign in my purse, and without even the right to borrow of the captain, for I have nothing certainly available even at home—*Home !* why, I *have* no home !"

At this point the poor man's thoughts took form in words.

"Ahem !" he said, clearing his throat, "I am much obliged by your kindness ('Don't mention it, sir,' from the captain), and should prefer, if possible, to reach Hong-Kong and ship thence for England. You see, I have some business friends there, and as I shall have to replenish my purse before—"

"Oh, don't let that stand in the way," said the captain, promptly, "I shall be happy to lend what you may require, and—"

"Excuse my interrupting you, captain, and thanks for your obliging offer," said Mr. Hazlit, holding up his large hand as if to put the suggestion away; "but for reasons that it is not necessary to explain, I wish to recruit my finances at Hong-Kong."

"And I," said Edgar, breaking in here, "wish to go to the same place, not so much on my own account as on that of one of my companions, who has left two very pretty little pieces of property there in the shape of a wife and a child, who might object to being left behind."

This settled the question, and the breakfast party went on deck.

"Mr. Hazlit," said Edgar, "will you walk with me to the stern of the vessel? I wish to get out of earshot of others."

Mr. Hazlit replied, "Certainly, Mr. Berrington;" but he thought a good deal more than he said. Among many other things he thought, "Ah! here it comes at last. He thinks this a good time to renew his suit, having just rendered us such signal assistance. I think he might have waited! Besides, his saving our lives does not alter the fact that he is still a penniless youth, and I *will* not give my daughter to such. It is true I am a more thoroughly penniless man than he, for these villains have robbed me and Aileen of our rings, chains, and watches, on which I counted a good deal,—alas! but *that* does not mend matters. It makes them rather worse. No, it must not be! My child's interests must be considered even before gratitude. I *must* be firm."

Thought is wondrously rapid. Mr. Hazlit thought all that and a great deal more during the brief passage from the companion-hatch to the stern-rail.

"I wish to ask you to do me a favour, Mr. Hazlit," the young man began.

The merchant looked at him with a troubled expression.

"Mr. Berrington, you have been the means of saving

our lives. It would be ungrateful in me to refuse you any favour that I can, *with propriety*, grant."

" I am aware," continued Edgar, "that you have —have—met with losses. That your circumstances are changed—"

Mr. Hazlit coloured and drew himself proudly up.

" Be not offended, my dear sir," continued the youth earnestly ; " I do not intrude on private matters —I would not dare to do so. I only speak of what I saw in English newspapers in Hong-Kong just before I left, and therefore refer to what is generally known to all. And while I sincerely deplore what I know, I would not presume to touch on it at all were I not certain that the pirates must have robbed you of all you possess, and that you must of necessity be in want of *present* funds. I also know that *some* of a man's so-called 'friends' are apt to fall off and fail him in the time of financial difficulty. Now, the favour I ask is that you will consider me—as indeed I am—one of your true friends, and accept of a loan of two or three hundred pounds—"

" Impossible, sir,—im—it is very kind of you— very, Mr. Berrington—but, impossible," said Mr. Hazlit, struggling between kindly feeling and hurt dignity.

" Nay, but," pleaded Edgar, " I only offer you a loan. Besides, I want to benefit myself," he added, with a smile. " The fact is, I have made a little money in a diving venture, which I and some others undertook to these seas, and I receive no interest for it just now. If you would accept of a few hundreds —what you require for present necessities—you may have them at three or five per cent. I would ask more, but that, you know, would be usurious!"

Still the fallen merchant remained immovable. He acknowledged Edgar's pleasantry about interest with a smile, but would by no means accept of a single penny from him in any form.

Edgar had set his heart upon two things that morning, and had prayed, not for success, but, for guidance in regard to them.

In the first he had failed—apparently. Not much depressed, and nothing daunted, he tried the second.

" Captain," he said, pacing up and down by the side of that black-bearded, black-eyed, and powerful pirate-killer, " what say you to run back to the spot where you sank the pirates, and attempt to fish up some of the treasure with our diving apparatus ?"

" I 've thought of that two or three times," replied the captain, shaking his head ; " but they went down in deep waters,—forty fathoms, at least,—which is far beyond your powers."

"True," returned Edgar, " but the prow of the pirate chief was, you know, run down in only nineteen fathoms, and *that* is not beyond us."

" Is it not ?"

x

" No, we have already been deeper than twenty fathoms with the dress I have on board."

" There is only one objection," said the captain, pausing in his walk; " I have learned from the prisoners that before we came up with them, Pungarin had had all the money and chief treasure transferred from his own prow to another, which was a faster boat, intending to change into it himself, but that after our appearing he deferred doing so until the fight should be over. If this be true, then the treasure went down in deep water, and the chief's prow has nothing in it worth diving for."

" But we are not sure that this story is true; and at all events it is probable that at least *some* of the treasure may have been left in Pungarin's boat," urged Edgar.

" Well, I 'll make the trial; but first I must dispose of my prisoners."

So saying, the captain resumed his walk and Edgar went below to look after his engine, having, in passing, given Rooney Machowl instructions to overhaul the diving gear and get it into good working order.

This Rooney did with much consequential display, for he dearly loved to bring about that condition of things which is styled " astonishing the natives." As the Malays on board, seamen and captives, were easily astonished by the novelties of the western hemisphere, he had no difficulty in attracting and chaining their attention to the minutest details of his apparatus. He more than astonished them !

With the able assistance of Baldwin and Maxwell and Ram-stam, he drew out, uncoiled, rubbed, examined inch by inch, and re-coiled the life-line and the air-tube ; unscrewed the various pieces—glasses, nuts, and valves—of the helmet, carefully examined them, oiled them, and re-fastened them, much to the interest and curiosity of "the natives." The helmet itself he polished up till it shone like a great globe of silver, to the intense admiration of "the natives." The pump he took to pieces elaborately, much to the anxiety of "the natives," who evidently thought he had wantonly destroyed it, but who soon saw it gradually put together again, much to their satisfaction, and brought into good working order. Rooney even went the length of horrifying one or two of "the natives" by letting one of the heavy shoulder-weights fall on their naked toes. This had the effect of making them jump and howl, while it threw the others into ecstacies of delight, which they expressed by throwing back their heads, shutting their eyes, opening their mouths, and chuckling heartily.

Aileen and Miss Pritty, in the meantime, lay on the sofas in the cabin, and at last obtained much-needed refreshment to their weary spirits by falling into deep, dreamless, and untroubled slumber.

Thus the gun-boat with its varied freight sped on

until it reached Sarawak, where the pirates were sent ashore under a strong guard.

With these our tale has now nothing more to do; but as this cutting short of their career is not fiction, it may interest the reader to know that they were afterwards tried by a jury composed half of native chiefs and half of Europeans, who unanimously found them guilty. They were condemned to be shot, and the sentence was carried out immediately, in the jungle, two miles outside of the town. They were buried where they fell, and thus ended one of the sharpest lessons that had ever been taught to a band of miscreants, who had long filled with terror the inhabitants of Borneo and the neighbouring archipelago.

Some idea may be formed of the service done on this occasion—as estimated by those who were well able to judge—when we say that the captain of the gun-boat afterwards received, in recognition of his prowess, a handsome sword and letter of thanks from the Rajah, Sir James Brooke; a certificate, with a pocket chronometer, from the Netherlands-Indian Government; a commander's commission from the Sarawak Government; and letters of grateful thanks from the Resident Governor of the west coast of Borneo, the Council of Singapore for the Netherlands Government, and others—all expressive of his gallant conduct in utterly routing so large a body of pirates, liberating two hundred and fifty slaves—chiefly of the

Dutch settlements—and clearing the Borneon coast of a curse that had infested it for many years.*

Having disposed of the pirates, the gun-boat proceeded immediately to sea, and in a short time reached the scene of her recent victory. It had previously been proposed to Mr. Hazlit that he might remain in Sarawak, if he chose, during the short period of the gun-boat's intended absence, but the unfortunate man—owing to financial reasons!—decided to remain in the vessel.

It happened to be a calm, lovely morning, not unlike that on which the action had been fought, when they reached the scene of their intended operations, and began to drag for the sunken prow.

The difficulty of finding it was much greater than had been anticipated, for the land, although visible, was much too far off to be of any service as a guide. At last, however, it was discovered; the diving apparatus was got out; the anchor cast, and Maxwell, being esteemed the most enduring among the divers, prepared to go down.

"It feels quite like old times, sir, don't it?" said

* We may as well state here that our information on this subject was obtained from Captain John Hewat, formerly in command of the steam gun-boat *Rainbow*,—belonging to Sir James Brooke, K.C.B., Rajah of Sarawak,—in which he had six years' experience of pirate-hunting in the eastern seas, and now captain of one of Donald Currie and Co.'s magnificent line of Cape steamers. Perhaps we ought to apologise for thus dragging the gallant captain into fiction, but we trust he will find that, in regard to his own particular doings, we have stuck pretty closely to fact.

Joe Baldwin to Edgar Berrington, as he assisted to dress the diver, and manipulated the various parts of the costume with a fondness that one might feel towards a favourite dog from which one had been for some time parted.

"It does indeed, Joe," replied Edgar, smiling; "I almost envy Maxwell the pleasure of a dip—especially in such a clear cool sea in this hot weather."

"How is he to breathe?" asked Miss Pritty, who with Aileen and her father, as well as the captain and crew of the gun-boat, watched the process of robing with as much interest as if they had never before seen it performed.

"Sure, Miss," observed Rooney Machowl, with great simplicity of aspect, "he does it by drawin' in an' puffin' out the air through his mouth an' nose."

"Very true," observed Miss Pritty, with a good-natured smile, for even she could see that the Irishman was poking fun at her; "but how is air conveyed to him?"

"It is sent down by means of an air-pump," said Edgar, who took on himself the duty of explaining.

"Dear me!" returned Miss Pritty, elevating her eyebrows in surprise; "I always thought that pumps were used only for pumping up water."

"Och! no, Miss," said Rooney, "they're largely used for pumping up beer in London."

"Now, David, are you all right?" asked Joe.

" All right," said Maxwell, as he rose and shook himself to settle the weights comfortably on his back and breast.

" Come along then, me boy," said Rooney.

Maxwell went to the side of the vessel, where a rope ladder had been prepared, and his two attendants assisted him to get over.

" All right ? " asked Joe again, after giving the order to pump, which Ram-stam commenced with the steady coolness and regularity of a veteran.

" All right," replied Maxwell, who immediately afterwards slowly disappeared.

After an hour's absence he signalled that he was coming up. In a few minutes his helmet was seen far down in the depths. Then it emerged from the surface.

" I want a crowbar," he said on the glass being removed.

" If you 'd had on a helmet with a speakin'-tube," observed Rooney, " you might have said that without comin' up."

" True, lad," growled Maxwell, " but not havin' on a helmet with a speakin'-toobe, here I am, so please look alive."

" Any sign of treasure ? " asked Edgar.

"Not as yet, sir."

The crowbar having been brought, the diver again went down.

For some time all went on quietly, for it was expected that, deep though the water was, Maxwell's power of enduring pressure would enable him to remain below for at least two hours, if not longer. After looking for some time inquiringly at the spot where he had disappeared, most of the Malays resumed their various duties about the vessel, though a few remained a little to regard Ram-stam with much interest, as being one who, in a measure, held the life of a fellow-being in his hands.

Suddenly a loud hissing noise was heard over the side. It sounded to those on deck as if the great sea-serpent had put his head out of the sea close alongside and sent a violent hiss into the air.

Joe Baldwin was attending to the air-tube, while Rooney held the life-line. He looked quickly down.

"The air-pipe's burst!" he shouted, and both he and his comrade, without a moment's delay, began to haul up the diver as fast as they possibly could.

That the reader may properly appreciate what had happened, it is necessary to remind him that at nineteen fathoms Maxwell's body was subjected to a pressure—from *water*, outside his dress—of about 50 pounds to the square inch, and that to prevent such a tremendous pressure from crushing in and collapsing all the cavities of his body, an *equal* pressure of air had to be *forced* into his dress, so that the pressure of water outside the dress was met and counteracted by the pressure of air inside.   This highly condensed air of course tended to crush the diver, as did the water, but with this important difference, that the air entered his lungs, wind-pipe, ears, nose, etc., and thus prevented these organs from collapsing, and confined the absolute pressure to their walls of flesh so to speak, and to the solid muscular parts of his frame.   Maxwell, being a very muscular man and tough, was, as we have said, able to stand the pressure on these parts better than many men.   When, therefore, the air-tube burst—which it happened to do at a weak point just a foot or so above water—the diver's dress was instantaneously crushed tight round him in every part, the air was driven completely out of it, and also largely out of poor Maxwell's body !

The moment he appeared at the surface it was seen that he was insensible, for he swung about by his life-line and tube in a helpless manner.

Seeing this, Edgar, who had anxiously watched for him, got out on the ladder and passed the loop of a rope under his arms.   It was quickly done.   He was laid on deck and the bull's-eye was unscrewed by Rooney, who instantly exclaimed, " He 's dead !"

" No, he 's not; I see his lips move," said Joe Baldwin, aiding Edgar to unscrew the helmet.

This was soon removed, and a frightful sight was revealed to the spectators.   Maxwell's face and neck were quite livid and swelled out to an almost bursting extent; blood was flowing profusely from his mouth and ears, and his eyes protruded horribly, as if they had been nearly forced out of their sockets.

It is right to observe that the helmet worn by Maxwell on this occasion was an old-fashioned one which, in the haste of departure from Hong-Kong, they had taken with them instead of one of their new ones. Most of the helmets now in use possess a valve which shuts of itself in the event of the air-tube bursting, and prevents the air from being crushed out of the dress. A dress full of air will, as we have already said, keep a man alive for at least five minutes. He has time, therefore, to reach the surface, so that danger from this source is not nearly so great as it used to be.

Such restoratives as suggested themselves to the chief on-lookers were applied, and, to the surprise of every one, the diver began to show signs of return-ing life. In a few minutes he began to retch, and soon vomited a large quantity of clotted blood. After a time he began to whisper a few words.

"Cheer up, my lad," said the captain in a kindly voice, as he went down on one knee beside the pros-trate man; "don't attempt to speak or exert your-self in any way. You'll be all right in a few days. We'll have your dress taken off and send you below, where you shall be taken good care of."

With returning vitality came back Maxwell's in-bred obstinacy. He would not hold his tongue, but insisted on explaining his sensations to his comrades as they busied themselves taking off his dress—a rather violent operation at all times, and very difficult in the circumstances.

"W'y, messmates," he said, "I hadn't even time to guess wot 'ad 'appened. Got no warnin' wotsome-dever. I just felt a tree-mendous shock all of a suddent that struck me motionless—as if Tom Sayers had hit me a double-handed cropper on the top o' my beak an' in the pit o' my bread-basket at one an' the same moment. Then came an 'orrible pressure as if a two-thousand-ton ship 'ad bin let down a-top o' me, an' arter that I remembers nothin'."

It is probable that the poor fellow would have gone on with his comments, though he spoke with difficulty and in a feeble voice, in which none of his charac-teristic gruffness remained, if he had not been cut short by Joe Baldwin and Rooney Machowl lifting him up and carrying him below.

Rooney, who carried his shoulders, took occasion to say while on the way down :—

"David, boy, did ye find anny treasure?"

"No ;—see'd nothin'."

"Ow, ow, worse luck!" sighed Rooney.

Maxwell was made comfortable with a glass of weak brandy and water—hot—and his comrades returned on deck, where they found Edgar Berrington commencing to put on the diving dress.

"Goin' down, sir?" inquired Joe.

"Yes. We have fortunately another air-tube, and I want to complete the work we have begun."

"Is there not a risk," whispered Aileen to her father, "that the same accident may happen again?"

"Ah, true," answered Mr. Hazlit aloud; "the water appears to be very deep, Mr. Berrington. Do you not think it probable that the air-tube may burst a second time?"

"I think not," replied Edgar, as he sat down to have his helmet affixed to the dress. "The best made articles are liable to possess flaws. Even the most perfect railway-wheel, in which the cleverest engineer alive might fail to detect a fault, may conceal a dangerous flaw. There is no certainty in human affairs. All we can say is that, when we consider the thousands of divers who are daily employed all over the world, accidents of the kind you have just witnessed are not numerous. If I were to refrain from going down because this accident has occurred, I might as well refrain evermore from entering a railway-carriage. We *must* risk something sometimes in our progress through life, Mr. Hazlit. It was intended that we should. Why were we gifted with the quality of courage if risk and danger were never to be encountered?"

The screwing on of the bull's-eye put a stop to further remark, and a few seconds later our hero went over the side, while Ram-stam, smiling benignant indifference as to the event which had so recently happened, steadily performed his duty.

As Mr. Hazlit and Aileen watched the bubbles that rose in multitudes to the surface, the former repeated to himself, mentally, "Yes, we must risk something sometimes in our progress through life." He went on repeating this until at last he followed it up with the sudden reflection :—" Well, perhaps I *must* risk my daughter's happiness in this youth's hands, even though he *is* penniless. He seems an able fellow; will, doubtless, make his way anywhere At all events it is quite evident that he will risk his life anywhere ! Besides, now I think of it, he said something about lending me some hundred pounds or so. Perhaps he is not absolutely penniless. It is quite certain that I am. Curious sentiment that of his : ' We must risk something sometimes.' Very curious, and quite new—at least exhibited to me in quite a new light."

While Mr. Hazlit's mind ran on thus, and his eyes dreamily watched the bubbles on the surface of the sea, our hero was grubbing like a big-headed goblin among the wreckage at the bottom.

He moved about from place to place in that slow leaning fashion which the resistance of water renders unavoidable, but he found nothing whatever to repay him for his trouble. There were beams and twisted iron-work, and overturned guns, and a few bales, but nothing that bore the least resemblance to boxes or bags of money.

One or two large cases he discovered, and forced them open with the crowbar, which Maxwell had dropped when he was struck insensible, but they contained nothing worth the labour of having them hoisted up. At last he was about to leave, after a careful search of more than an hour, when he espied something shining in a corner of what had once been the pirate chief's cabin. He took it up and found it to be a small box of unusual weight for its size. His sense of touch told him that it was ornamented with carving on its surface, but the light was not sufficient to enable him to see it distinctly. His heart beat hopefully, however, as he hastened as fast as the water would permit out of the cabin, and then, to his joy he found that it was Aileen Hazlit's jewel-box! How it came there he could not guess; but the reader partly knows the truth, and can easily imagine that when the pirate chief sent his other valuables to the swift prow, as before mentioned, he kept this—the most precious of them all—close to his own person to the last, desiring, no doubt, to have it always under his own eye.

Not troubling himself much, however, with such

speculations, Edgar returned to the cabin, placed the box where he found it, and spent full half-an-hour more in plying his crowbar in the hope of discovering more of the pirate's horde. While thus engaged he received two or three signals to "Come up" from Joe Baldwin, who held his life-line; but he signalled back "All right—let me alone," and went on with his work.

At last there came the signal "Come up!" given with such a peremptory tug that he was fain, though unwilling, to comply. Taking the box under his arm he began to ascend slowly. On gaining the surface he was made at once aware of the reason of the repeated signalling, for a sudden squall had burst upon the eastern sea, which by that time, although perfectly calm below, was tumbling about in waves so large that the gun-boat was tossing like a cork at her anchor, and it was found to be almost impossible to work the air-pump. In fact it was only by having two men stationed to keep Ram-stam on his legs that the thing could be done!

With some difficulty Edgar was got on board, and the order was immediately given to weigh anchor.

Expressing great surprise at the state of things he found above water, and regret that he had not sooner attended to orders, Edgar placed the box on the deck. Then he unrobed, and drawing on his trousers and a canvas jacket, he issued from behind the funnel—which had been his robing-room—and went aft, where he found Aileen seated between her friend Miss Pritty and her father.

"Miss Hazlit," he said with a peculiar smile, "allow me to introduce you to an old friend."

He held up before her the carved steel box.

"My mother's jewel-case!" she exclaimed, with a look of intense surprise.

"My—my wife's jewels!" stammered Mr. Hazlit, in equal surprise; "where on earth—why—how—where—young man, did you find them?"

"I found them at the bottom of the sea," replied Edgar. "It is the second time, strange to say, that I have had the pleasure of fishing them up from that vast repository of riches where, I doubt not, many another jewel-case still lies, and will continue to lie, unclaimed for ever. Meanwhile, I count myself peculiarly fortunate in being the means of restoring *this* case to its rightful owner."

So saying he placed it in the hands of Aileen.

The captain, who had watched the whole scene with quiet interest and a peculiar curl about his black moustache, as well as a twinkle in his sharp black eye, uttered a short laugh, thrust his hands into his pockets, and walked away to give the order that the steamer's head should be laid precisely "sou', sou'-west, and by south, half-south," with a slight—almost a shadowy—leaning in the direction of "southerly."

CHAPTER XXII.

MISCELLANEOUS MATTERS, ENDING WITH A "SKRIMMAGE" UNDER WATER.

WE are back again in Hong-Kong—in the pagoda —-with our old friends seated comfortably round their little table enjoying a good supper.

Pretty little Mrs. Machowl has prepared it, and is now assisting at the partaking of it. Young Master Teddy Machowl is similarly engaged on his father's knee. The child has grown appallingly during its father's absence! Ram-stam and Chok-foo are in waiting—gazing at each other with the affection of Chinese lovers re-united.

"What a sight you are, Rooney!" said Mrs. Machowl, pausing between bites to look at her husband.

"Sure it's the same may be said of yoursilf, cushla!" replied Rooney, stuffing his child's mouth with sweet potato.

"Yes, but it's what a *fright* you are, I mane," said Mrs. Machowl.

"An' it's what a purty cratur *you* are that *I* mane,"

Y

replied Rooney, repeating the dose to Teddy, who regarded his father with looks of deep affection.

"Ah! go 'long wid you. Sure it's your nose is spoilt entirely," said Mrs. Machowl.

"An' it's your own that is swaiter than iver, which more than makes up the difference," retorted her lord.—"Howld it open as wide as ye can this time, Ted, me boy ; there, that's your sort—but don't choke, ye spalpeen."

There seemed indeed some occasion for the latter admonition, for Teddy, unused to such vigorous treatment, was beginning to look purple in the face and apoplectic about the eyes. In short, there is every probability that an attack of croup, or something dreadful, would have ensued if the child's mother had not risen hastily and snatched it away from the would-be infanticide.

"Now then, Ram-stam and Chock-foo," said Edgar Berrington, putting down his spoon, "clear away the rat's-tail soup, and bring on the roast puppy."

Grinning from ear to ear, and with almost closed eyes, the Chinese servitors obeyed.

While they cleared the table and laid the second course, the conversation became general. Previously it had been particular, referring chiefly to the soup and the free circulation of the salt.

"So, then," observed Joe Baldwin, leaning back in his chair, "we must make up our minds to be content with what we have got. Well, it an't so bad after all! Let me see. How much did you say the total is, Mister Eddy?"

"Close upon eight thousand five hundred pounds."

"A tidy little sum," observed Rooney, with an air of satisfaction.

"Eight thousand—eh?" repeated Joe; "hum, well, we'll cut off the five hundred for expenses and passage home, and that leaves eight thousand clear, which, according to agreement, gives each of us two thousand pounds."

Maxwell, who still looked pale and thin from the effects of his late accident, nodded his head slowly, and growled, "Two thousand—jus' so."

"An' that, Molly, my dear," said Rooney, "if properly invisted, gives you an' me a clair iucome—only think, an *income*, Molly—of wan hundred a year! It's true, cushla! that ye won't be able to rowl in yer carridge an' walk in silks an' satins on that income, but it'll pay the rint an' taxes, owld girl, an' help Teddy to a collidge eddication—to say nothin' o' pipes an' baccy. Ochone!—if we'd only not lost the first haul, we'd have bin millerinaires be this time. I wouldn't have called the Quane me grandmother."

"Come, Rooney, be grateful for what you've got," said Edgar. "Enough is as good as a feast."

"Ah! sur, it'll be time to say that when we've finished the puppy," replied the Irishman, as

Chok-foo placed on the board a savoury roast which bore some resemblance to the animal named, though, having had its head and legs amputated, there could be no absolute certainty on the point. Whatever it was, the party attacked it with relish, and silence reigned until it was finished, after which conversation flowed again—somewhat languidly at first. When, however, pipes were got out by those who smoked, and chairs were placed in the verandah, and no sound was heard around save the yelling of Chinese children who were romping in the Chinese kennel that skirted the pagoda, and the champing of the jaws of Ram-stam and Chok-foo as they masticated inside—then came the feast of reason, not to mention the flow of soul.

"I wonder what our friends at Whitstable will say to this ventur' of ours," said Maxwell.

"Have you many friends there?" asked Edgar.

"Many?—of course I has. W'y, I suppose every English diver must have friends there."

"Where is it?" asked Edgar.

"Why, sir, don't you know Whitstable?" exclaimed Joe Baldwin, in surprise.

"You forget, Joe," replied Edgar, with a smile, "that although I have learnt how to dive, and have read a good deal about the history of diving, I am only an amateur after all, and cannot be supposed to know everything connected with the profession. All

I know about Whitstable is that it is a port somewhere in the south of England."

"Right, sir," said Joe, "but it's more than that;
it lies on the coast of Kent, and is famous for its
oyster-beds and its divers. How it came to be a
place of resort for divers *I* don't know, but so it is,
an' I *have* heard say it was divin' for oysters in days
of old that gave the natives a taste for the work.
Anyhow, they've got the taste very decided somehow,
an' after every spell o' dirty weather they're sure to
have telegrams from all parts of the coast, and you'll
see Lloyds' agents huntin' up the divers in the public-
houses an' pakin' 'em off wi' their gear right and left
by rail to look after salvage.

"These men," continued Joe, "are most of 'em
handicraftmen as well as divers, because you know,
sir, it would be of no use to send down a mere
labourer to repair the bottom of a ship, no matter
how good he was at divin'; so, you'll find among
'em masons, and shipbuilders, and carpenters, and
engineers—"

"Ah!" interrupted Edgar, "I was just wondering
how they would manage if it were found necessary
to have the engines of a sunk steamer taken to pieces
and sent up."

"Well, sir," rejoined Joe, "they've got men there
who can dive, and who know as much about marine
engines as you do yourself. And these men make

lots of tin, for a good diver can earn a pound a day,
an' be kept in pretty regular employment in deep
water. In shallow water he can earn from ten to
fifteen shillings a day. Besides this, they make
special arrangements for runnin' extra risks. Then
the savin' they sometimes effect is amazin'. Why, sir,
although you do know somethin' of the advantages
of diving, you can never know fully what good they
do in the world at large. Just take the case of the
Agamemnon at Sebastopol—"

"Och!" interrupted Rooney, whose visage was
perplexed by reason of his pipe refusing to draw
well, "wasn't (puff) that a good job intirely (puff!
there ; you 're all right at last !) He was a friend o'
mine that managed that job. Tarry, we called him—
though that wasn't his right name. This is how it
was. The fleet was blazin' away at the fortifications,
an' of coorse the fortifications—out o' politeness if
nothin' else—was blazin' away at the fleet, an'
smoke was curlin' up like a chimbley on fire, an' big
balls was goin' about like pais in a rattle, an' small
shot like hail was blowin' horizontal, an' men was
bein' shot an' cut to pieces, an' them as warn't was
cheerin' as if there was any glory in wholesale murther
—bah ! I wouldn't give a day at Donnybrook wid a
shillelah for all the sieges of Sebastopool as ever I
heard tell of. Well, suddintly, bang goes a round
shot slap through the hull of the *Agamemnon*,

below the water-line! Here was a pretty to do! The ordinary coorse in this case would have bin to haul out of action, go right away to Malta, an' have the ship docked and repaired there. But what does they do? Why, they gets from under fire for a bit, and sends down my friend Tarry to look at the hole. He goes down, looks at it, then comes up an' looks at the Commodore,—bowld as brass.

" ' I can repair it,' says Tarry.

" ' Well, do,' says the Commodore.

" So down he goes an' does it, an' very soon after that the *Agamemnon* went into action again, and blazed away at the walls o' the owld place harder than ever."

" That *was* a good case, an' a *true* one," said Joe Baldwin, with an approving nod.

" And these divers, Mr. Edgar," continued Joe, "sometimes go on their own hook, like we have done this time, with more or less luck. There was one chum of mine who took it into his head to try his chances at the wreck of the *Royal Charter*, long after all hope of further salvage had been abandoned, and in a short time he managed to recover between three and four hundred pounds sterling."

" An immense amount of money, they do say, was recovered from the *Royal Charter* by divers," observed Maxwell.

" That is true, and it happens," said Edgar, sadly,

" that I know a few interesting facts regarding that
vessel. I know of some people whose hearts were
broken by the loss of relatives in that wreck. There
were many such—God comfort them : But that is
not what I meant to speak of. The facts I refer to
are connected with the treasure lost in the vessel.
Just before leaving London I had occasion to call
on the gentleman who had the management of the
recovered gold, and he told me several interesting
things. First of all, the whole of the gold that
could be identified was handed at once over to its
owners; but this matter of identification was not
easy, for much of the gold was found quite loose in the
form of sovereigns and nuggets and dust. The dust
was ordered to be sent up with the ' dirt ' that
surrounded it, and a process of gold-washing was
instituted, after the regular diggings fashion, with
a bowl and water. Tons of ' dirt ' were sent up and
washed in this way, and a large quantity of gold
saved. The agent showed me the bowl that was
used on this occasion. He also showed me sovereigns
that had been kept as curious specimens. Some of
them were partly destroyed, as if they had been
caught between iron plates and cut in half; others
were more or less defaced and bent, and a few
had been squeezed almost into an unrecognisable
shape. In one place, he told me, the divers saw a
pile of sovereigns through a rent in an iron plate

The rent was too small to admit a man's arm, and the plates could not be dislodged. The divers, therefore, made a pair of iron tongs, with which they picked out the sovereigns, and thus saved a large sum of money. One very curious case of identification occurred. A bag of sovereigns was found with no name on it. A claimant appeared, but he could tell of no mark to prove that he was the rightful owner. Of course it could not be given up, and it appeared as if the unfortunate man (who was indeed the owner) must relinquish his claim, when in a happy moment his wife remembered that she had put a brass 'token' into the bag with the gold. The bag was searched, the token was found, and the gold was immediately handed to them."

"Molly, my dear," said Rooney Machowl at this point, "you make a note o' that; an' if ever you have to do with bags o' goold, just putt a brass token or two into 'em."

"Ah! shut up, Rooney," said Mrs. Machowl, in a voice so sweet that the contrast between it and her language caused Edgar and Joe to laugh.

"Well, then," continued Edgar, "in many other curious ways gold was identified and delivered to its owners : thus, in one case, an incomplete seal, bearing part of the legs of a griffin, was found on a bag of two thousand sovereigns, and the owner, showing the seal with which he had stamped it, established his claim. Of course in all cases where bars of gold were found with the owners' names stamped on them, the property was at once handed over; but after all was done that could be done by means of the most painstaking inquiry, an immense amount of gold necessarily remained unclaimed.

"And I s'pose if it wasn't for us divers," said Maxwell, "the whole consarn would have remained a dead loss to mankind."

"True for ye," responded Rooney; "it's not often ye come out wid such a blaze of wisdom as that, David! It must be the puppy as has stirred ye up, boy, or, mayhap, the baccy!"

"Take care *you* don't stir me up, lad, else it may be worse for you," growled Maxwell.

"Och! I'm safe," returned the Irishman, carelessly; "I'd putt Molly betwain us, an' sure ye'd have to come over her dead body before ye'd git at me. —It wasn't you, was it, David," continued Rooney, with sudden earnestness, "that got knocked over by a blast at the works in Ringwall harbour two or three years ago?"

"No, it warn't me," responded Maxwell; "it was long Tom Skinclip. He was too tall for a diver—he was. They say he stood six futt four in his socks; moreover he was as thin as a shadow from a bad gas-lamp. He was workin' one day down in the 'arbour, layin' stones at the foundations of the noo breakwater, when they set off a blast about a hundred yards off from where he was workin', an' so powerful was the blast that it knocked him clean on his back. He got such a fright that he signalled violently to haul up, an' they did haul 'im up, expectin' to find one of his glasses broke, or his toobes bu'sted. There was nothin' wotsomedever the matter with 'im, but he wouldn't go down again that day. 'Owsever, he got over it, an' after that went down to work at a wreck somewhere in the eastern seas—not far from Ceylon, I'm told. When there 'e got another fright that well-nigh finished him, an' from that day he gave up divin' an' tuck to gardening, for which he was much better suited."

"What happened to him?" asked Edgar.

"I'm not rightly sure," answered Maxwell, refilling his pipe, "but I've bin told he had to go down one day in shallow water among sea-weed. It was a beautiful sort o' submarine garden, so to speak, an' long Tom Skinclip was so fond o' flowers an' gardens nat'rally, that he forgot hisself, an' went wanderin' about what he called the 'submarine groves' till they thought he must have gone mad. They could see him quite plain, you see, from the boat, an' they watched him while he wandered about. The sea-weed was up'ard of six feet high, tufted on the top with a sort o' thing you might a'most fancy was flowers. The colours, too, was bright. Among the branches o' this submarine forest, or grove, small lobsters, an' shrimps, an' other sorts o' shell-fish, were doin' dooty as birds—hoppin' from one branch to another, an' creepin' about in all directions.

"After a time long Tom Skinclip he sat down on a rock an' wiped the perspiration off his brow—a⁺ least he tried to do it, which set the men in the boat all off in roars of laughter, for, d'ee see, Skinclip was an absent sort of a feller, an' used to do strange things. No doubt when he sat down on the rock he felt warm, an' bein' a narvish sort o' chap, I make no question but he was a-sweatin' pretty hard, so, without thinkin', he up with his arm, quite nat'ral like, an' drawed it across where his brow would have bin if the helmet hadn't been on. It didn't seem to strike him as absurd, however, for he putt both hands on 'is knees, an' sat lookin' straight before 'im.

"He hadn't sat long in this way when they see'd a huge fish—about two futt long—comin' slowly through the grove behind 'im. It was one o' them creeters o' the deep as seems to have had its head born five or six sizes too big for its tail—with eyes an' mouth to match. It had also two great horns above its eyes, an' a cravat or frill o' bristles round its neck. Its round eyes and half-open mouth gave it the appearance o' bein' always more or less in a state of astonishment. P'r'aps it was—at the fact of its

havin' bin born at all! Anyhow, it swum'd slowly
along till it cotched sight o' Skinclip, when it went
at him, an' looked at the back of his helmet in great
astonishment, an' appeared to smell it, but evidently
it could make nothin' of it. Then it looked all down
his back with an equal want of appreciation. Arter
that it came round to the front, and looked straight
in at Skinclip's bull's-eye! They do say it was a
sight to see the start he gave!

"He jump up as smart a'most as if he'd bin in the
open air, an' they observed, when he turned round,
that a huge lobster of some unbeknown species was
holdin' on to his trousers with all its claws like a
limpet! The fish—or ripslang, as one of the men
called it, who said he knowed it well—turned out to
be a pugnaceous creetur, for no sooner did it see
Skinclip's great eyes lookin' at it in horror, than it
set up its frill of spikes, threw for'ard the long horns,
an' went slap at the bull's-eye fit to drive it in.
Skinclip he putt down his head, an' the ripslang
made five or six charges at the helmet without much
effect. Then it changed its tactics, turned on its
side, wriggled under the helmet, an' looked in at
Skinclip with one of its glarin' eyes close to the glass.
At the same time the lobster gave him a tree-
mendious tug behind. This was more than Skinclip
could stand. They see'd him jump round, seize the
life-line, an' give it four deadly pulls, but his com-

rades paid no attention to it. The lobster gave him another tug, an' the ripslang prepared for another charge. It seemed to have got some extra spikes set up in its wrath, for its whole body was bristlin' more or less by this time.

" Again Skinclip tugged like a maniac at the line. The ripslang charged ; the lobster tugged ; the poor feller stepped back hastily, got his heels entangled in sea-weed, and went down head first into the grove !

" The men got alarmed by this time, so they pulled him up as fast as they could, an' got him inboard in a few minutes ; but they do say," added Maxwell, with emphasis, " that that ripslang leaped right out o' the water arter him, an' the lobster held on so that they had to chop its claws off with a hatchet to make it let go. They supped off it the same night, and long Tom Skinclip, who owned an over strong appetite, had a bad fit of indisgestion in consikence."

CHAPTER XXIII.

MORE ABOUT THE SEA.

ONCE more we beg our reader to accompany us to sea—out into the thick darkness, over the wild waves, far from the abodes of man.

There, one night in December, a powerful steamer did battle with a tempest. The wind was against her, and, as a matter of course, also the sea. The first howled among her rigging with what might have been styled vicious violence. The seas hit her bows with a fury that caused her to stagger, and, bursting right over her bulwarks at times, swept the decks from stem to stern, but nothing could altogether stop her onward progress. The sleepless monster in the hold, with a heart of fervent heat, and scalding breath of intense energy, and muscles of iron mould, and an indomitable—yet to man submissive—will, wrought on night and day unweariedly, driving the floating palace straight and steadily on her course—homeward bound.

Down in the cabin, in one of the side berths

lay a female form. Opposite to it, in a similar berth, lay another female form. Both forms were very limp. The faces attached to the forms were pale yellow, edged here and there with green.

" My dear," sighed one of the forms, " this *is* dreadful ! "

After a long silence, as though much time were required for the inhalation of sufficient air for the purpose, the other form replied :—

" Yes, Laura, dear, it *is* dreadful."

" 'Ave a cup of tea, ladies ? " said the stewardess, opening the door just then, and appearing at an acute angle with the doorway, holding a cup in each hand.

Miss Pritty shuddered and covered her head with the bed-clothes. Aileen made the form of " no, thanks," with her lips, and shut her eyes.

" *Do* 'ave a cup," said the stewardess, persuasively.

The cups appeared at that moment inclined to " 'ave " a little game of hide-and-seek, which the stewardess nimbly prevented by suddenly forming an obtuse angle with the floor, and following that action up with a plunge to starboard, and a heel to port, that was suggestive —at least to a landsman—of an intention to baptise Miss Pritty with hot tea, and thereafter take a " header " through the cabin window into the boiling sea ! She did neither, however, but, muttered something about " 'ow she do roll, to be sure," and, seeing that her mission was hopeless, left the cabin with a balked stagger and a sudden rush, which was appropriately followed up by the door shutting itself with a terrific bang, as though it should say, "You might have known as much, goose! why did you open me?"

"Laura, dear," said Aileen, "did you hear what the captain said to some one just now in the cabin, when the door was open?"

"N-no," replied Miss Pritty, faintly.

"I distinctly heard some one ask how fast we were going, but I could not make out his reply."

"Oh!" exclaimed the other, brightening for a brief moment; "yes, I *did* hear him. He said we were going six knots. Now I do *not* understand what that means."

"Did you mean that?" asked Aileen, turning her eyes languidly on her friend, while a faint smile flickered on her mouth.

"Mean what?" said Miss Pritty, in evident surprise.

"No, I see you didn't. Well, a knot means, I believe, a nautical mile."

"A notticle mile, Aileen; what is that?"

"A *naut*ical mile; dear me, how stupid you are, Laura!"

"Oh! I understand. But, really, the noise of that screw makes it difficult to hear distinctly. And,

7

after all, it is no wonder if I *am* stupid, for what between eating nothing but pickles for six weeks, and this dreadful—there! oh! it comes ag—"

Poor Miss Pritty stopped abruptly, and made a desperate effort to think of home. Aileen, albeit full of sympathy, turned her face to the wall, and lay with closed eyes.

After a time the latter looked slowly round.

" Are you asleep, Laura?"

Miss Pritty gave a sharp semi-hysterical laugh at the bare idea of such an impossible condition.

" Well, I was going to say," resumed Aileen, "that we cannot be very far from land now, and when we do get there—"

" Happy day!" murmured Miss Pritty.

" We intend," continued Aileen, "to go straight home—I—I mean to our old home, sell everything at once, and go to live in a cottage—quite a tiny cottage—by the sea somewhere. Now, I want you to come and visit us the very day we get into our cottage. I know you would like it—would like being with me, wouldn't you?"

" Like it? I should delight in it of all things."

" I knew you would. Well, I was going to say that it would be such a kindness to dear papa too, for you know he will naturally be very low-spirited when we make the change—for it is a great change, Laura, greater perhaps than you, who have never been very rich, can imagine, and I doubt my capacity to be a good comforter to him though I have all the will."

Two little spots of red appeared for the first time for many weeks on Miss Pritty's cheeks, as she said in a tone of enthusiasm :—

"What! *You* not a good comforter? I 've a good mind to refuse your invitation, since you dare to insinuate that I could in any degree supplement *you* in such a matter."

"Well, then, we won't make any more insinuations," returned Aileen, with a sad smile; "but you 'll come—that 's settled. You know, dear, that we had lost everything, but ever since our jewel-case was found by—by—"

"By Edgar," said Miss Pritty; "why don't you go on ?"

"Yes, by Mr. Berrington," continued Aileen, "ever since that, papa has been very hopeful. I don't know exactly what his mind runs on, but I can see that he is making heaps of plans in regard to the future, and oh! you can't think how glad and how thankful I am for the change. The state of dull, heart-breaking, weary depression that he fell into just after getting the news of our failure was beginning to undermine his health. I could see that plainly, and felt quite wretched about him. But now he is comparatively cheerful, and so gentle too. Do you know,

I have been thinking a good deal lately of the psalmist's saying, 'It is good for me that I have been afflicted;' and, in the midst of it all, our Heavenly Father remembered mercy, for it was He who sent our jewel-box, as if to prevent the burden from being too heavy for papa."

Miss Pritty's kind face beamed agreement with these sentiments.

"Now," continued Aileen, "these jewels are, it seems, worth a great deal of money—much more than I had any idea of—for there are among them a number of very fine diamond rings and brooches. In fact, papa told me that he believed the whole were worth between eight and nine thousand pounds. This, you know, is a sum which will at least raise us above want (poor Miss Pritty, well did *she* know that !)—though of course it will not enable us to live very luxuriously. How fortunate it was that these pirates—"

"Oh !" screamed Miss Pritty, suddenly, as she drew the clothes over her head.

"What's the matter?" exclaimed Aileen ; "are you going to be—"

"Oh ! no, no, no," said Miss Pritty, peeping out again ; "how could you bring these dreadful creatures to my remembrance so abruptly ? I had quite forgotten them for the time. Why, oh why did you banish from my mind that sweet idea of a charming cottage by the sea, and all its little unluxurious elegancies, and call up in its place the h-h-orrors of that village-nest—pig-sty—of the dreadful buccaneers? But it can't be helped now," added Miss Pritty, with a resigned shudder, "and we have the greatest reason to be thankful that their hope of a good ransom made them treat us as well as they did;—but go on, dear, you were saying that it was fortunate that these p-pirates—"

"That they did not sell the jewels or take any of them out of the box, or send them into the other prow which was sunk in deep water, where the divers could not have gone down to recover them."

"Very true," assented Miss Pritty.

At this point the cabin door again burst open, and the amiable stewardess appeared, bearing two cups of fresh tea, which she watched with the eyes of a tigress and the smile of an angel, while her body kept assuming sudden, and one would have thought impossible, attitudes.

"Now, ladies, *do* try some tea. Really you must. I insist on it. Why, you'll both die if you don't."

Impressed with the force of this reasoning, both ladies made an effort, and got up on their respective elbows. They smiled incredulously at each other, and then, becoming suddenly grave, fell flat down on their backs, and remained so for some time without speaking.

"Now, try again; do try, it will do you so much good—really."

Thus adjured they tried again and succeeded. Aileen took one sip of tea, spilt much of the rest in thrusting it hurriedly into the ready hands of the all but ubiquitous stewardess, and fell over with her face to the wall. Miss Pritty looked at her tea for a few seconds, earnestly. The stewardess, not being quite ubiquitous, failed to catch the cup as it was wildly held towards her. Miss Pritty therefore capsized the whole affair over her bed-clothes, and fell back with a deadly groan.

The stewardess did not lose temper. She was used to such things. If Miss Pritty had capsized her intellect over the bed-clothes, the stewardess would only have smiled, and wiped it up with a napkin.

"You'll be better soon, Miss," said the amiable woman, as she retired with the débris.

The self-acting door shut her out with a bang of contemptuous mockery, and the poor ladies were once more left alone in their misery.

CHAPTER XXIV.

TAKING THE TIDE AT THE EBB.

WHEN things in this world reach their lowest ebb, it is generally understood or expected that the tide will turn, somehow, and rise. Not unfrequently the understanding and the expectation are disappointed. Still, there are sufficiently numerous instances of the fulfilment of both, to warrant the hope which is usually entertained by men and women whose tide has reached its lowest.

Mr. Hazlit was naturally of a sanguine temperament. He entertained, we had almost said, majestic views on many points. Esteeming himself "a beggar" on three hundred a year—the remains of the wreck of his vast fortune—he resolved to commence business again. Being a man of strict probity and punctuality in all business matters, and being much respected and sympathised with by his numerous business friends, he experienced little difficulty in doing so. Success attended his efforts; the tide began to rise.

Seated in a miniature parlour, before a snug fire, in his cottage by the sea, with one of the prettiest girls in all England by his side, knitting him a pair of inimitable socks, the " beggar" opened his mouth slowly and spake.

" Aileen," said he, " I 've been a fool !"

Had Mr. Hazlit said so to some of his cynical male friends they might have tacitly admitted the fact, and softened the admission with a smile. As it was, his auditor replied :—

" No, papa, you have *not*."

" Yes, my love, I have. But I do not intend to prove the point or dispute it. There is a tide in the affairs of men which, taken at the ebb, leads on to fortune."

Aileen suspended her knitting and looked at her sire with some surprise, for, being a very matter-of-fact unpoetical man, this misquotation almost alarmed her.

" ' Taken at the *flood*,' is it not, papa ?"

" It may be so in Shakespeare's experience. *I* say the ebb. When first I was reduced to beggary—"

" You never were *that*, papa. We have never yet had to beg."

" Of course, of course," said Mr. Hazlit, with a motion of his hand to forbid further interruption. " When I say ' beggary,' you know what I mean. I certainly do *not* mean that I carry a wallet and a staff. and wear ragged garments, and knock at back-doors. Well, when I was reduced to beggary, I had reached the lowest ebb. At that time I was led—mark me, I was led—to 'take the tide.' I took it, and have been rising with the flood to fortune ever since. And yet, strange to say, though I am now rich in a way I never before dreamed of, I have still an insane thirst for earthly gold. What was the passage, dear, that you quoted to me as being your text for the day?"

"'Owe no man anything,'" replied Aileen.

"Yes, it is curious. I have never mentioned the subject to you, my child, but some months ago—when, as I have said, the tide was very low—I was led to consider that passage, and under the influence of it I went to my creditors and delivered up to them your box of jewels. You are aware, no doubt, that having passed through the insolvency court, and given up all that I possessed, I became legally free. This box was recovered from the deep, and restored to me after my effects had been given up to my creditors, so that I might have retained it. But I felt that this would have been unjust. I respect the law which, after a man has given up all he possesses, sets him free to begin life again with some degree of hope, but I cannot avoid coming to the conclusion that moral duties cannot be abrogated by human laws. I take advantage of the law to prevent inhuman creditors from grinding me to death, but I refuse to take advantage of the law so as to escape from the clear duty that I ought to pay these creditors—gradually and according to my ability— to the uttermost farthing. Having been led to act on this opinion, I gave up the box of jewels. To my surprise, my creditors refused to take them. They returned them to me as a gift. I accepted the gift as a trust. On the proceeds, as you see, we manage to live comfortably, and I am now conducting a fairly successful business in the old line—on a small scale."

Mr. Hazlit smiled sadly as he uttered the last words.

"And the debts, papa, which you told me once were so heavy, do you mean to pay them all?" asked Aileen, anxiously.

"I do," replied her father, earnestly; "by slow degrees it may be, but to the last farthing if I live. I shall try to owe no man anything."

A glad smile lit up Aileen's face as she was on the point of throwing her arms round her father's neck, when the door opened, and a small domestic— their only one besides the cook—put a letter into the hands of her young mistress.

Aileen's countenance assumed a troubled look as she handed it to her father.

"It is for you, papa."

Mr. Hazlit's visage also assumed an expression of

anxiety as he opened and read the letter. It ran thus :—

" DEER SUR,—i thinks it unkomon 'ard that a man shood 'ave is bed sold under im wen anuther man oas im munny, speshally wen is wifes ill—praps a-dyin. the Law has washt yoo sur, but it do seam 'ard on me, if yoo cood spair ony a pownd or two id taik it kind.—Yoors to komand,   JOHN TIMMS."

" This is very much to the point," said Mr. Hazlit, with a faint smile, handing the letter to Aileen. " It is, as you see, from our old greengrocer, who must indeed be in great trouble when he, who used to be so particularly civil, could write in that strain to me. Now, Aileen, I want your opinion on a certain point. In consequence of your economical ways, my love, I find myself in a position to give fifty pounds this half-year towards the liquidation of my debts."

The merchant paused, smiled, and absolutely looked a little confused. The idea of commencing to liquidate many thousands of pounds by means of fifty was so inexpressibly ridiculous, that he half expected to hear his own respectful child laugh at him. But Aileen did not laugh. With her large earnest eyes she looked at him, and the unuttered language of her pursed, grave, little mouth was, " Well, go on."

"The liquidation of my debts," repeated Mr. Hazlit, firmly. "The sum is indeed a small one—a paltry one—compared with the amount of these debts, but the passage which we have been considering appears to me to leave no option, save to begin at once, even on the smallest possible scale. Now, my love, duty requires that I should at once begin to liquidate. Observe, the law of the land requires nothing. It has set me free, but the law of God requires that I should pay, at once, as I am able. Conscience echoes the law, and says, 'pay.' What, therefore, am I to do ?"

Mr. Hazlit propounded this question with such an abrupt gaze as well as tone of interrogation, that the little pursed mouth relaxed into a little smile as it said, "I suppose you must divide the sum proportionally among your creditors, or something of that sort."

"Just so," said Mr. Hazlit, nodding approval. "Now," he continued, with much gravity, "if I were to make the necessary calculation—which, I may remark, would be a question in proportion running into what I may be allowed to style infinitesimal fractions—I would probably find out that the proportion payable to one would be a shilling, to another half a sovereign, to another a pound or so, while to many would accrue so small a fraction of a farthing that no suitable coin of this realm could be found wherewith to pay it. If I were to go with, say two shillings, and offer them to my good friend Granby as part payment of my debt to him, the probability is that he would laugh in my face and invite me to dinner in order that we might celebrate the event over a bottle of very old port. Don't you think so ?"

Aileen laughed, and said that she did think so.

"Well, then," continued her father, "what, in these circumstances, says common sense ?"

Aileen's mouth became grave again, and her eyes very earnest as she said quickly—

"Pay off the green-grocer !"

Mr. Hazlit nodded approval. "You are right. Mr. Timms' account amounts to twenty pounds. To offer twenty pounds to Mr. Granby—to whom I owe some eight thousand, more or less—would be a poor practical joke. To give it to Mr. Timms will evidently be the saving of his business at a time when it appears to have reached a crisis. Put on your bonnet and shawl, dear, and we will go about this matter without delay."

Aileen was one of those girls who possessed the rare and delectable capacity to "throw on" her bonnet and shawl. One glance in the mirror sufficed to convince her that these articles, although thrown on, had fallen into their appropriate places neatly. It could scarcely have been otherwise. Her bonnet

and shawl took kindly to her, like all other things
in nature—animate and otherwise. She reappeared
before her sedate father had quite finished drawing
on his gloves.

Mr. John Timms dwelt in a back lane which
wriggled out of a back street as if it were anxious
to find something still further back into which to
back itself. He had been in better circumstances
and in a better part of the town when Mr. Hazlit
had employed him. At the time of the rich merchant's failure, the house of Timms had been in a
shaky condition. That failure was the removal of
its last prop; it fell, and Timms retired, as we have
seen, into the commercial background. Here, however, he did not find relief. Being a trustful man
he was cheated until he became untrustful. His
wife became ill owing to bad air and low diet. His
six children became unavoidably neglected and
riotous, and his business, started on the wreck of
the old one, again came to the brink of failure. It
was in these circumstances that he sat down, under
the impulse of a fit of desperation, and penned the
celebrated letter to his old customer.

When Mr. Hazlit and his daughter had, with
great difficulty, discovered Mr. Timms' residence and
approached the door, they were checked on the
threshold by the sound of men apparently in a state
of violent altercation within.

"Git out wid ye, an' look sharp, you spalpeen," cried one of the voices.

"Oh, pray don't—don't fight!" cried a weak female voice.

"No, I won't git out till I'm paid, or carry your bed away with me," cried a man's voice, fiercely.

"You won't, eh! Arrah then—hup!"

The last sound, which is not describable, was immediately followed by the sudden appearance of a man, who flew down the passage as if from a projectile, and went headlong into the kennel. He was followed closely by Rooney Machowl, who dealt the man as he rose a sounding slap on the right cheek, which would certainly have tumbled him over again had it not been followed by an equally sounding slap on the left cheek, which "brought him up all standing."

Catching sight at that moment of Mr. Hazlit and Aileen, Rooney stopped short and stood confused.

"Murder!" shrieked the injured man.

"Hooray! here's a lark!" screamed a small street boy.

"Go it! P'lice! A skrimmage!" yelled another street boy in an ecstasy of delight, which immediately drew to the spot the nucleus of a crowd.

Mr. Hazlit was a man of promptitude. He was also a large man, as we have elsewhere said, and by no means devoid of courage. Dropping his daughter's arm he suddenly seized the ill-used and noisy man by the neck, and thrust him almost as violently back into the greengrocer's house as Rooney had kicked him out of it. He then said, "Go in," to the amazed Rooney, and dragging his no less astonished child in along with him, shut and locked the door.

"Now," said Mr. Hazlit, sitting down on a broken chair in a very shabby little room, and wiping his heated brow, "what is the meaning of all this, Mr. Timms?"

"Well, sir," answered Timms, with a deprecatory air, "I'm sorry, sir, it should 'ave 'appened just w'en you was a-goin' to favour me with the unexpected honour of a wisit; but the truth is, sir, I couldn't 'elp it. This 'ere sc—man is my landlord, sir, an' 'e *wouldn't* wait another day for 'is rent, sir, though I told 'im he was pretty sure o' 'avin it in a week or so, w'en I'ad time to c'lect my outstandin' little bills—"

"More nor that, sur," burst in the impatient and indignant Rooney, "he would 'ave gone into that there room, sur,—if I may miscall a dark closet by that name—an' 'ave pulled the bed out from under Mrs. Timms, who's a-dyin', sur, if I 'adn't chanced to come in, sur, an' kick the spalpeen into the street, as you see'd."

"For w'ich you'll smart yet," growled the landlord, who stood in a dishevelled heap like a bad boy in a corner.

" How much rent does he owe you ?" asked Mr. Hazlit of the landlord.

" That's no business o' yours," replied the man, sulkily.

" If I were to offer to pay it, perhaps you'd allow that it *was* my business."

"So I will *w'en* you offers."

" Well, then, I offer now," said Mr. Hazlit, taking out his purse, and pouring a little stream of sovereigns into his hand. " Have you the receipt made out ?"

The landlord made no reply, but, with a look of wonder at his interrogator, drew a small piece of dirty paper from his pocket and held it out. Mr. Hazlit examined it carefully from beginning to end.

" Is this right, Mr. Timms ?" he asked.

The green-grocer examined the paper, and said it was—that five pounds was the exact amount.

" You can put the receipt in your pocket," said Mr. Hazlit, turning round and counting out five sovereigns on the table, which he pushed towards the landlord. " Now, take yourself off, as quietly as you can, else I'll have you taken up and tried for entering a man's premises forcibly, and endeavouring to obtain money by intimidation. Go !"

This was a bold stroke on the part of the merchant, whose legal knowledge was not extensive, but it succeeded. The landlord pocketed the money and moved towards the door. Rooney Machowl followed him.

"Rooney!" said Mr. Hazlit, calling him back.

"Mayn't I show him out, sur?" said Rooney, earnestly.

"By no means."

"Ah, sur, mayn't I give him a farewell kick?"

"Certainly not."

Mr. Hazlit then expressed a desire to see Mrs. Timms, and the green-grocer, thanking the merchant fervently for his timely aid, lighted a candle and led the way into the dark closet.

Poor Mrs. Timms, a delicate-looking woman, not yet forty, who had evidently been pretty once, lay on a miserable bed, apparently at the point of death.

Aileen glided quickly to the bed, sat down on it, and took the woman's hand, while she bent over her and whispered :—

"Don't be distressed. The rent is paid. He will disturb you no more. You shall be quiet now, and I will come to see you sometimes, if you'll let me."

The woman gazed at the girl with surprise, then, as she felt the gentle warm pressure of her hand a sudden rush of faith seemed to fill her soul. She drew Aileen towards her, and looked earnestly into her face.

"Come here, Timms," said Mr. Hazlit, abruptly, as he turned round and walked out of the closet, "I want to speak to you. I am no doctor, but depend upon it your wife will *not* die. There is a very small building—quite a hut I may say—near my house—ahem! near my cottage close to the sea, which is at present to let. I advise you strongly to take that hut and start a green-grocery there. I'm not aware that there is one in the immediate neighbourhood, and there are many respectable families about whose custom you might doubtless count on; at all events, you would be sure of ours to begin with. The sea-air would do your wife a world of good, and the sea-beach would be an agreeable and extensive playground for your children."

The green-grocer stood almost aghast! The energy with which Mr. Hazlit poured out his words, and, as it seemed to Timms, the free and easy magnificence of his ideas were overpowering.

"W'y, sir, I ain't got no money to do sitch a thing with," he said at last, with a broad grin.

"Yes, you have," said Mr. Hazlit, again pulling out his purse and emptying its golden contents on the table in a little heap, from which he counted fifteen sovereigns. "My debt to you amounts, I believe, to twenty pounds; five I have just paid to your landlord, here is the balance. You needn't mind a receipt. Send me the discharged account at your leisure, and think over what I have suggested. Aileen, my dear, we will go now."

Aileen said good-night at once to the sick woman

and followed her father as he went out, repeating—
" Good-evening, Timms, think over my suggestion."

They walked slowly home without speaking.
Soon they reached the cottage by the sea.   As they
stood under the trellis-work porch the merchant
turned round and gazed at the sun, which was just
dipping into the horizon, flooding sea and sky with
golden glory.

" Aileen," he said in a low voice, " I have commenced life at last—life in earnest.   I was a poor
fool once.   Through grace I am a rich man now"

CHAPTER XXV.

SHOWS HOW OUR HERO FORMED PLANS, HOW MISS PRITTY FORMED
PLOTS, AND HOW THE SMALL DOMESTIC AMUSED HERSELF.

On a certain cold, raw, bleak, biting, bitter day
in November, our hero found himself comfortably
situated at the bottom of the sea.

We say 'comfortably' advisedly and comparatively,
for, as compared with the men whose duty it was to
send air down to him, Edgar Berrington was in a state
of decided comfort. Above water nought was to be
seen but a bleak, rocky, forbidding coast, a grey sky
with sleet driving across it, and an angry indigo sea
covered with white wavelets. Nothing was to be felt
but a stiff cutting breeze, icy particles in the air, and
cold blood in the veins. Below water all was calm
and placid; groves of sea-weed delighted the eye;
patches of yellow sand invited to a siesta; the
curiously-twisted and smashed-up remains of a wreck
formed a subject of interesting contemplation, while
a few wandering crabs, and an erratic lobster or two,
gave life and variety to the scene, while the tempera-

ture, if not warm, was at all events considerably milder than that overhead. In short, strange though it may seem, Edgar was in rather an enviable position than otherwise, on that bleak November day.

Some two years or so previous to the day to which we refer, Edgar, with his diving friends, had returned to England. Mr. Hazlit had preceded them by a month. But Edgar did not seek him out. He had set a purpose before him, and meant to stick to it. He had made up his mind not to go near Aileen again until he had made for himself a position, and secured a steady income which would enable him to offer her a home at least equal to that in which she now dwelt.

Mr. Hazlit rather wondered that the young engineer never made his appearance at the cottage by the sea, but, coming to the conclusion that his passion had cooled, he consoled himself with the thought that, after all, he was nearly penniless, and that it was perhaps as well that he had sheered off.

Aileen also wondered, but *she* did not for a moment believe that his love had cooled, being well aware that that was an impossibility. Still she was perplexed, for although the terms on which they stood to each other did not allow of correspondence, she thought, sometimes, that he *might* have written to her father —if only to ask how they were after their adventures in the China seas.

Miss Pritty—to whom Aileen confided her troubles —came nearer the mark than either of them. She conceived, and stoutly maintained, that Edgar had gone abroad to seek his fortune, and meant to return and marry Aileen when he had made it.

Edgar, however, had not gone abroad. He had struck out a line of life for himself, and had prosecuted it during these two years with untiring energy. He had devoted himself to submarine engineering, and, having an independent spirit, he carved his way very much as a free lance. At first he devoted himself to studying the subject, and ere long there was not a method of raising a sunken vessel, of building a difficult breakwater, of repairing a complicated damage to a pier, or a well, or anything else subaqueous, with which he was not thoroughly acquainted, and in regard to which he had not suggested or carried out bold and novel plans and improvements, both in regard to the machinery employed and the modes of action pursued.

After a time he became noted for his success in undertaking difficult works, and at last employed a staff of divers to do the work, while he chiefly superintended. Joe Baldwin became his right-hand man and constant attendant. Rooney and Maxwell, preferring steadier and less adventurous work, got permanent employment on the harbour improvements of their own seaport town.

Thus engaged, Edgar and his man Joe visited nearly all the wild places round the stormy shores of Great Britain and Ireland. They raised many ships from the bottom of the sea that had been pronounced by other engineers to be hopelessly lost. They laid foundations of piers and breakwaters in places where old Ocean had strewn wrecks since the foundation of the world. They cleared passages by blasting and levelling rocks whose stern crests had bid defiance to winds and waves for ages, and they recovered cargoes that had been given up for years to Neptune's custody. In short, wherever a difficult submarine operation had to be undertaken, Edgar Berrington and his man Joe, with, perhaps, a gang of divers under them, were pretty sure to be asked to undertake it.

The risk, we need scarcely say, was often considerable; hence the remuneration was good, and both Edgar and his man speedily acquired a considerable sum of money.

At the end of two years, the former came to the conclusion that he had a sufficient sum at his credit in the bank to warrant a visit to the cottage by the sea; and it was when this idea had grown into a fixed intention that he found himself, as we have mentioned, in rather comfortable circumstances at the bottom of the sea.

The particular part of the bottom lay off the west

coast of England. Joe and a gang of men were hard at work on a pier when Edgar went down. He carried a slate and piece of pencil with him. The bottom was not very deep down. There was sufficient light to enable him to find his man easily.

Joe was busy laying a large stone in its bed. When he raised his burly form, after fixing the stone, Edgar stepped forward, and, touching him on the shoulder, held out the slate, whereon was written in a bold runing hand :—

"Joe, I'm going off to get engaged, and after that, as soon as possible, to be married."

Through the window of his helmet, Joe looked at his employer with an expression of pleased surprise. Then he took the slate, obliterated the information on it, and printed in an equally bold, but very sprawly hand :—

"Indeed ? I wish you joy, sir."

Thereupon Edgar took the slate and wrote :—

"Thank you, Joe. Now, I leave you in charge. Keep a sharp eye on the men—especially on that lazy fellow who has a tendency to sleep and shirk duty. If the rock in the fair-way is got ready before my return, blast it at once, without waiting for me. You will find one of Siebe and Gorman's voltaic batteries in my lodging, also a frictional electrical machine, which you can use if you prefer it. In the store there is a large supply of tin-cases for gunpowder and compressed gun-cotton charges. There also you will find one of Heinke and Davis's magneto-electric exploders. I leave it entirely to your own judgment which apparatus to use. All sorts are admirable in their way; quite fresh, and in good working order. Have you anything to say to me before I go?"

"All right, sir," replied Joe, in his sprawly hand; "I'll attend to orders. When do you start, and when do you expect to be back?"

"I start immediately. The day of my return is uncertain, but I'll write to you."

Rubbing this out, Joe wrote:—

"You'll p'r'aps see my old 'ooman, sir. If you do, just give her my respects, an' say the last pair o' divin' drawers she knitted for me was fust-rate. Tightish, if anything, round the waist, but a bit o' rope-yarn putt that all right—they're warm an' comfortable. Good-bye, I wish you joy again, sir."

"Good-bye," replied Edgar.

It was impossible that our hero could follow his inclination, and nod with his stiff-necked iron head-piece at parting. He therefore made the motion of kissing his hand to his trusty man, and giving the requisite signal, spread his arms like a pair of wings, and flew up to the realms of light!

Joe grinned broadly, and made the motion of

kissing his hand to the ponderous soles of his employer's leaden boots as they passed him, then, turning to the granite masonry at his side, he bent down and resumed his work.

Arrived at the region of atmospheric air, Edgar Berrington clambered on board the attending vessel, took off his amphibious clothing, and arrayed himself in the ordinary habiliments of a gentleman, after which he went ashore, gave some instructions to the keeper of his lodgings, ordered his horse, galloped to the nearest railway station, flashed a telegraphic message to Miss Pritty to expect to see him that evening, and soon found himself rushing at forty miles an hour, away from the scene of his recent labours.

Receiving a telegraph envelope half-an-hour later, Miss Pritty turned pale, laid it on the table, sank on the sofa, shut her eyes, and attempted to reduce the violent beating of her heart, by pressing her left side tightly with both hands.

" It *must* be death !—or accident !" she murmured faintly to herself, for she happened to be alone at the time.

Poor Miss Pritty had no near relations in the world except Edgar, and therefore there was little or no probability that any one would telegraph to her in connection with accident or death, nevertheless she entertained such an unconquerable horror of a telegram, that the mere sight of the well-known envelope, with its large-type title, gave her a little shock; the reception of one was almost too much for her.

After suffering tortures for about as long a time as the telegram had taken to reach her, she at last summoned courage to open the envelope.

The first words, "Edgar Berrington," induced a little scream of alarm. The next, "to Miss Pritty," quieted her a little. When, however, she learned that instead of being visited by news of death and disaster, she was merely to be visited by her nephew that same evening, all anxiety vanished from her speaking countenance, and was replaced by a mixture of surprise and amusement. Then she sat down on the sofa—from which, in her agitation, she had risen—and fell into a state of perplexity.

"Now I *do* wish," she said, aloud, "that Eddy had had the sense to tell me whether I am to let his friends the Hazlits know of his impending visit. Perhaps he telegraphed to me on purpose to give me time to call and prepare them for his arrival. On the other hand, perhaps he wishes to take them by surprise. It may be that he is not on good terms with Mr. Hazlit, and intends to use me as a go-between. What *shall* I do?"

As her conscience was not appealed to in the matter, it gave no reply to the question; having little or no common sense to speak of, she could scarcely expect much of an answer from that part of her being. At last she made up her mind, and, according to a habit induced by a life of solitude, expressed it to the fireplace.

"Yes, that's what I'll do. I shall wait till near the time of the arrival of the last train, and then go straight off to Sea Cottage to spend the evening, leaving a message that if any one should call in my absence I am to be found there. This will give him an excuse, if he wants one, for calling, and if he does not want an excuse he can remain here till my return. I'll have the fire made up, and tell my domestic to offer tea to any one who should chance to call."

Miss Pritty thought it best, on the whole, to give an ambiguous order about the tea to her small domestic, for she knew that lively creature to be a compound of inquisitiveness and impudence, and did not choose to tell her who it was that she expected to call. She was very emphatic, however, in impressing on the small domestic the importance of being very civil and attentive, and of offering tea, insomuch that the child protested with much fervour that she would be *sure* to attend to orders.

This resulted in quite an evening's amusement to the small domestic.

After Miss Pritty had gone out, the first person

who chanced to call was the spouse of Mr. Timms, the green-grocer, who had obviously recovered from her illness.

"Is Miss Pritty at 'ome?" she asked.

"No, ma'am, she ain't, she's hout," answered the small domestic.

"Ah! well, it don't much matter. I on'y called to leave this 'ere little present of cabbidges an' cawliflowers—with Mr. Timms' kind compliments and mine. She's been wery kind to us, 'as Miss Pritty, an' we wishes to acknowledge it."

"Please, ma'am," said the domestic with a broad smile, as she took the basket of vegetables, "would you like a cup of tea?"

"What d'you mean, girl?" asked the green-grocer's wife in surprise.

"Please, ma'am, Miss Pritty told me to be sure to offer you a cup of tea."

"Did she, indeed? That's was wery kind of her, wery kind, though 'ow she come for to know I was a-goin' to call beats *my* comprehension. 'Owever, tell her I'm greatly obleeged to her, but 'avin 'ad tea just afore comin' out, an' bein' chock-full as I can 'old, I'd rather not. Best thanks, all the same."

Mrs. Timms went away deeply impressed with Miss Pritty's thoughtful kindness, and the small domestic, shutting the door, indulged in a fit of that species of suppressed laughter which is usually indicated by a series of spurts through the top of the nose and the compressed lips.

She was suddenly interrupted by a tap at the knocker.

Allowing as many minutes to elapse as she thought would have sufficed for her ascent from the kitchen, she once more opened the door. It was only a beggar—a ragged disreputable man—and she was about to shut the door in his face, with that summary politeness so well understood by servant girls, when a thought struck her.

" Oh, sir," she said, " would you like a cup of tea ?"

The man evidently thought he was being made game of, for his face assumed such a threatening aspect that the small domestic incontinently shut the door with a sudden bang. The beggar amused himself by battering it with his stick for five minutes and then went away.

The next visitor was a lady.

" Is Miss Pritty at home, child ?" she asked, regarding the domestic with a half-patronising, half-pitying air.

" No, ma'am, she 's hout."

" Oh ! that 's a pity," said the lady, taking a book out of her pocket. " Will you tell her that I called for her subscription to the new hospital that is about to be built in the town ? Your mistress does not know me personally, but she knows all about the hospital, and this book, which I shall call for to-morrow, will speak for itself. Be sure you give it to her, child."

"Yes, ma'am. And, please, ma'am, would you like a cup of tea?"

The lady, who happened to possess a majestic pair of eyes, looked so astonished that the small domestic could scarcely contain herself.

"Are you deranged, child?" asked the lady.

"No, ma'am, if you please; but Miss Pritty told me to be sure to offer you a cup."

"To offer *me* a cup, child!"

"Yes, ma'am. At least to offer a cup to any one who should call."

It need scarcely be added that the lady declined the tea, and went away, observing to herself in an undertone, that "she *must* be deranged."

The small domestic again shut the door and spurted.

It was in her estimation quite a rare, delicious, and novel species of fun. To one whose monotonous life was spent underground, with a prospect of bricks at two feet from her window, and in company with pots, pans, potato-peelings, and black-beetles, it was as good as a scene in a play.

The next visitor was the butcher's boy, who came round to take "orders" for the following day. This boy had a tendency to chaff.

"Well, **my lady**, has your ladyship any orders?"

"Nothink to-day," answered the domestic, curtly.

"What! nothink at all? Goin' to fast to-morrow, eh? or to live on stooed hatmospheric hair vith your own sauce for gravey—hey?"

"No, we doesn't want nothink," repeated the lomestic, stoutly. "Missus said so, an' she bid me sk you if you'd like a cup of tea?"

The butcher's boy opened his mouth and eyes in mazement. To have his own weapons thus turned, s he thought, against him by one who was usually ather soft and somewhat shy of him, took him quite back. He recovered, however, quickly, and made rush at the girl, who, as before, attempted to shut he door with a bang, but the boy was too sharp for er. His foot prevented her succeeding, and there s no doubt that in another moment he would have orcibly entered the house, if he had not been seized rom behind by the collar in the powerful grasp of Edgar Berrington, who sent him staggering into the street. The boy did not wait for more. With a vild-Indian war-whoop he turned and fled.

Excited, and, to some extent, exasperated by this ast visit, the small domestic received Edgar with a one-third timid, one-third gleeful, and one-third reckless spirit.

"What did the boy mean?" asked Edgar, as he urned towards her.

"Please, sir, 'e wouldn't 'ave a cup of tea, sir,"

2 B

she replied meekly, then, with a gleam of hope in her eyes—" Will *you* 'ave one, sir ?"

"You're a curious creature," answered Edgar, with a smile. "Is Miss Pritty at home ?"

"No, sir, she ain't."

This answer appeared to surprise and annoy him.

"Very odd," he said, with a little frown. "Did she not expect me ?"

"No, sir, I think she didn't. Leastways she didn't say as she did, but she was very partikler in tellin' me to be sure to hoffer you a cup of tea."

Edgar looked at the small domestic, and, as he looked, his mouth expanded. *Her* mouth followed suit, and they both burst into a fit of laughter. After a moment or two the former recovered.

"This is all very pleasant, no doubt," he said, " but it is uncommonly awkward. Did she say when she would be home ? "

"No, sir, she didn't, but she bid me say if any one wanted her, that they'd find her at Sea Cottage."

" At Sea Cottage—who lives there ?"

" I don't know, sir."

" Where is it ?"

" On the sea-shore, sir."

" Which way—*this* way or *that* way ?" asked Edgar, pointing right and left.

" *That* way," answered the girl, pointing left.

The impatient youth turned hastily to leave.

" Please, sir—" said the domestic.

" Well," said Edgar, stopping

"You 're sure, sir—" she stopped.

" Well ?—go on."

" That you wouldn't like to 'ave a cup of tea ?"

" Child," said Edgar, as he turned finally away, " you 're mad—as mad as a March hare."

" Thank you, sir."

The small domestic shut the door and retired to the regions below, where, taking the pots and pans and black-beetles into her confidence, she shrieked with delight for full ten minutes, and hugged herself.

CHAPTER XXVI.

A CLIMAX IS REACHED.

WHEN Edgar Berrington discovered the cottage by the sea, and ascertained that Miss Pritty was within, he gave his name, and was ushered into the snug little room under the name of Mr. Briggington. Aileen gave a particularly minute, but irrepressible and quite inaudible scream ; Mr. Hazlit sat bolt up in his chair, as if he had seen a ghost; and Miss Pritty—feeling, somehow, that her diplomacy had not become a brilliant success—shrank within herself, and wished it were to-morrow.

Their various expressions, however, were as nothing compared with Edgar's blazing surprise.

" Mr. Hazlit," he stammered, " pray pardon my sudden intrusion at so unseasonable an hour ; but, really, I was not aware that—did you not get my telegram, aunt ?"

He turned abruptly to Miss Pritty.

" Why ye-es, but I thought that you—in fact —I could not imagine that—"

"Never mind explanations just now," said Mr.
Hazlit, recovering himself, and rising with a bland
smile, "you are welcome, Mr. Berrington; no hour
is unseasonable for one to whom we owe so much."

They shook hands and laughed; then Edgar shook
hands with Aileen and blushed, no doubt because
she blushed, then he saluted his aunt, and took
refuge in being very particular about her receipt of
the telegram. This threw Miss Pritty into a state
of unutterable confusion, because of her efforts to
tell the truth and conceal the truth at one and the
same time. After this they spent a very happy
evening together, during the course of which Mr.
Hazlit took occasion to ask Edgar to accompany him
into a little pigeon-hole of a room which, in deference to a few books that dwelt there, was styled the
library.

"Mr. Berrington," he said, sitting down and pointing to a chair, "be seated. I wish to have a little
private conversation with you. We are both practical men, and know the importance of thoroughly
understanding each other. When I saw you last
—now about two years ago—you indicated some
disposition to—to regard—in fact to pay your
addresses to my daughter. At that time I objected
to you on the ground that you were penniless.
Whether right or wrong in that objection is now a
matter of no importance, because it turns out that I

was right on other grounds, as I now find that you did not know your own feelings, and did not care for her—"

"Did not *care* for her?" interrupted Edgar, in sudden amazement, not unmingled with indignation.

"Of course," continued Mr. Hazlit, with undisturbed calmness, "I mean that you did not care for her sufficiently; that you did not regard her with that unconquerable affection which is usually styled 'love,' and without which no union can be a happy one. The proof to me that your feeling towards her was evanescent, lies in the fact that you have taken no notice either of her or of me for two years. Had you gained my daughter's affections, this might have caused me deep regret, but as she has seldom mentioned your name since we last saw you, save when I happened to refer to you, I perceive that her heart has been untouched—for which I feel exceedingly thankful, knowing as I do, only too well, that we cannot command our affections."

Mr. Hazlit paused a moment, and Edgar was so thunderstruck by the unexpected nature of his host's discourse, that he could only stare at him in mute surprise and unbelief in the evidence of his own ears.

"Now," resumed Mr. Hazlit, "as things stand, I shall be very happy indeed that we should return to our old intimacy. I can never forget the debt of

obligation we owe to you as our rescuer from worse
than death—from slavery among brutalised men,
and I shall be very happy indeed that you should
make my little cottage by the sea—as Aileen loves
to style it—your abode whenever business or
pleasure call you to this part of the country."

The merchant extended his hand with a smile of
genuine urbanity. The youth took it, mechanically
shook it, let it fall, and continued to stare in a
manner that made Mr. Hazlit feel quite uneasy.
Suddenly he recovered, and, looking the latter
earnestly in the face, said :—

"Mr. Hazlit, did you not, two years ago, forbid
me to enter your dwelling ?"

"True, true," replied the other somewhat disconcerted'; "but the events which have occurred since
that time warranted your considering that order as
cancelled."

"But you did not *say* it was cancelled. Moreover
your first objection still remained, for I was nearly
penniless then, although, in the good providence of
God, I am comparatively rich now. I therefore
resolved to obey your injunctions, sir, and keep
away from your house and from your daughter's dis-
tracting influence, until I could return with a few of
those pence, which you appear to consider so vitally
important."

"Mr. Berrington," exclaimed the old gentleman,

who was roused by this hit, " you mistake me.　My
opinions in regard to wealth have been considerably
changed of late.　But my daughter does not love
you, and if you were as rich as Crœsus, sir, you
should not have her hand without her heart."

Mr. Hazlit said this stoutly, and, just as stoutly,
Edgar replied :—

"If I were as rich as Crœsus, sir, I would not
accept her hand without her heart; but, Mr. Hazlit,
I am richer than Crœsus !"

" What do you mean, sir ? "

" I mean that I am rich in the possession of that
which a world's wealth could not purchase—your
daughter's affections."

" Impossible ! Mr. Berrington, your passion urges
you to deceive yourself."

" You will believe what she herself says, I suppose?" asked Edgar, plunging his hand into a breast
pocket.

" Of course I will."

" Well then, listen," said the youth, drawing out a
small three-cornered note.　" A good many months
ago, when I found my business to be in a somewhat
flourishing condition, I ventured to write to Aileen,
telling her of my circumstances, of my unalterable
love, and expressing a wish that she would write me
at least one letter to give me hope that the love,
which she allowed me to *understand* was in her breast

before you forbade our intercourse, still continued. This," he added, handing the three-cornered note to the old gentleman, " is her reply."

Mr. Hazlit took the note, and, with a troubled countenance, read :—

" DEAR MR. BERRINGTON,—I am not sure that I am right in replying to you without my father's knowledge, and only prevail on myself to do so because I intend that our correspondence shall go no further, and what I shall say will, I know, be in accordance with his sentiments. My feelings towards you remain unchanged. We cannot command feelings, but I consider the duty I owe to my dear father to be superior to my feelings, and I am resolved to be guided by his expressed wishes as long as I remain under his roof. He has forbidden me to have any intercourse with you : I will therefore obey until he sanctions a change of conduct. Even this brief note should not have been written were it not that it would be worse than rude to take no notice of a letter from one who has rendered us such signal service, and whom I shall never forget.—Yours sincerely,   AILEEN HAZLIT."

The last sentence—" and whom I shall never forget "—had been carefully scribbled out, but Edgar had set himself to work, with the care and earnest application of an engineer and a lover, to decipher the words.

"Dear child!" exclaimed Mr. Hazlit, in a fit of abstraction, kissing the note; "this accounts for her never mentioning him;" then, recovering himself, and turning abruptly and sternly to Edgar, he said: —"How did you dare, sir, to write to her after my express prohibition?"

"Well," replied Edgar, "some allowance ought to be made for a lover's anxiety to know how matters stood, and I fully intended to follow up my letter to her with one to you; but I confess that I did wrong—"

"No, sir, no," cried Mr. Hazlit, abruptly starting up and grasping Edgar's hand, which he shook violently, "you did *not* do wrong. You did quite right, sir. I would have done the same myself in similar circumstances."

So saying, Mr. Hazlit, feeling that he was compromising his dignity, shook Edgar's hand again, and hastened from the room. He met Aileen descending the staircase. Brushing past her, he went into his bed-room, and shut and locked the door.

Much alarmed by such an unwonted display of haste and feeling, Aileen ran into the library.

"Oh! Mr. Berrington, what *is* the matter with papa?"

"If you will sit down beside me, Aileen," said

Edgar, earnestly, tenderly, and firmly, taking her hand, " I will tell you."

Aileen blushed, stammered, attempted to draw back, but was constrained to comply. Edgar, on the contrary, was as cool as a cucumber. He had evidently availed himself of his engineering know-ledge, and fitted extra weights of at least seven thousand tons to the various safety valves of his feelings.

" Your father," he began, looking earnestly into the girl's downcast face, " is—"

But hold ! reader ; we must not go on. If you are a boy, you won't mind what followed ; if a girl, you have no right to pry into such matters. We there-fore beg leave at this point to shut the lids of our dexter eye, and drop the curtain.

CHAPTER XXVII.

THE LAST.

ONE day Joe Baldwin, assisted by his old friend, Rooney Machowl, was busily engaged down at the bottom of the sea, off the Irish coast, slinging a box of gold specie. He had given the signal to haul up, and Rooney had moved away to put slings round another box, when the chain to which the gold was suspended snapt, and the box descended on Joe. If it had hit him on the back in its descent it would certainly have killed him, but it only hit his collar-bone and broke it.

Joe had just time to give four pulls on his lines, and then fainted. He was instantly hauled up, carefully unrobed, and put to bed.

This was a turning-point in our diver's career. The collar-bone was all right in the course of a month or two, but Mrs. Baldwin positively refused to allow her goodman to go under water again.

"The little fortin' you made out in Chiny," she said one evening while seated with her husband at supper in company with Rooney and his wife, "pays for our rent, an' somethin' over. You 're a handy man, and can do a-many things to earn a penny, and I can wash enough myself to keep us both. You 've bin a 'ard workin' man, Joe, for many a year. You 've bin long enough under water. You 'll git rheumatiz, or somethin' o' that sort, if you go on longer, so I 'm resolved that you shan't do it—there !"

" Molly, cushla !" said Machowl, in a modest tone, " I hope you won't clap a stopper on *my* goin' under water for some time yit—plaze."

Molly laughed.

" Oh ! it 's all very well for you to poke fun at me, Mister Machowl," said Mrs. Baldwin, " but you 're young yet, an' my Joe 's past his prime. When you 've done as much work as he 's done—there now, you 've done it at last. I told you so."

This last remark had reference to the fact that young Teddy Machowl, having been over-fed by his father, had gone into a stiff blue-in-the-face condition that was alarming to say the least of it. Mrs. Machowl dashed at her offspring, and, giving him an unmerciful thump on the back, effected the ejection of a mass of beef which had been the cause of the phenomena.

" What a bu'ster it is—the spalpeen," observed Rooney, with a smile, as he resumed the feeding process, much to Teddy's delight ; " you 'll niver do for a diver if you give way to appleplectic tendencies o' that sort.   Here—open your mouth wide and shut your eyes."

"Well, well, it'll only be brought in manslaughter, so he won't swing for it," remarked Mrs. Baldwin, with a shrug of her shoulders.   "Now, Joe," she continued, turning to her husband, "you'll begin at once to look out for a situation above water.   David Maxwell can finish the job you had in hand,—speakin' of that, does any one know where David is just now?"

"He's down at the bottom of a gasometer," answered Joe; "leastwise he was there this afternoon —an' a dirty place it is."

"A bad-smellin' job that, I should think," observed Rooney.

"Well, it ain't a sweet-smellin' one," returned Joe. "He's an adventurous man is David.   I don't believe there's any hole of dirty water or mud on the face o' this earth that he wouldn't go down to the bottom of if he was dared to it.   He's fond of speculatin' too, ever since that trip to the China seas.   You must know, Mrs. Rooney, if your husband hasn't told you already, that we divers, many of us, have our pet schemes for makin' fortunes, and some of us have tried to come across the Spanish dubloons that are said to lie on the sea-bottom off many parts of our coast where the Armada was lost."

"It's jokin' ye are," said Mrs. Machowl, looking at Joe with a sly twinkle in her pretty eyes.

" Jokin'! no, indeed, I ain't," rejoined the diver.
" Did Rooney never tell ye about the Spanish
Armada ? "

" Och! he's bin sayin' somethin' about it now an'
again, but he's such a man for blarney that I never
belave more nor half he says."

" Sure ain't that the very raison I tell ye always
at laste twice as much as I know ?" said Rooney,
lighting his pipe.

"Well, my dear," continued Joe, " the short an'
the long of it is, that about the year 1588, the
Spaniards sent off a huge fleet of big ships to take
Great Britain and Ireland by storm—once for all—
and have done with it, but Providence had work for
Britain to do, and sent a series o' storms that wrecked
nearly the whole Spanish fleet on our shores.
Many of these vessels had plenty of gold dubloons
on board, so when divin' bells and dresses were
invented, men began to try their hands at fishin' it
up, and, sure enough, some of it was actually found
and brought up—especially off the shores of the
island of Mull, in Scotland. They even went the
length of forming companies in this country, and in
Holland, for the purpose of recovering treasure from
wrecks. Well, ever since then, up to the present
time, there have been speculative men among divers,
who have kept on tryin' their hands at it. Some
have succeeded ; others have failed. David Maxwell

is one of the lucky ones for the most part, and even when luck fails, he never comes by any loss, for he's a hard-workin' man, an' keeps a tight hold of whatever he makes, whether by luck or by labour."

"But what about the bad-smellin' job he's got on hand just now?" asked Rooney.

"Why, he's repairin' the bottom of a gas tank. He got the job through recoverin' some gold watches that were thrown into the Thames by some thieves, as they were bein' chased over London Bridge. David found ten of 'em—one bein' worth fifty pounds. Well, just at that time an experienced and hardy fellow was wanted for the gas-work business, so David was recommended. You know a gas tank, as to look an' smell, is horrible enough to frighten a hippopotamus, but David went up to the edge of this tank by a ladder, and jumped in as cool as if he'd bin jumpin' into a bed with clean sheets. He stopped down five hours. Of course, in such filthy water, a light would have been useless. He had to do it all by feelin', nevertheless, they say, he made a splendid job of it,—the bed of clay and puddle, at the bottom, bein' smoothed as flat a'most as a billiard table,— besides fixin' sixteen iron plates for the gas-holder to rest on. He was to finish the job this afternoon, I believe."[1]

---

[1] Something similar to the "job" above mentioned was accomplished by G. Smith, a diver on the staff of Messrs. Heinke and Davis, of London.

" Ah, he 's a cute feller is David," observed Rooney, reflectively, as he watched a ring of smoke that rose from his pipe towards the ceiling. "What d'ee intind to turn your hand to if you give up divin', Joe ?"

"If!" said Mrs. Baldwin, with a peculiar intonation.

"Well, *when* you give it up," said Rooney, with a bland smile.

" I 'm not rightly sure," replied Joe. " In the first place, I 'll watch for the leadings of Providence, for without that, I cannot expect success. Then I 'll go and see Mr. Berrington, who has just returned, they say, from his wedding trip. My own wish is to become a sort of missionary among the poor people hereabouts."

" Why, Joe," said his friend, "you 've bin that, more or less, for years past."

" Ay, at odd times," returned Joe, " but I should like to devote *all* my time to it now."

In pursuance of his plan the ex-diver went the following morning to the sea-shore, and walked in the direction of Sea Cottage, following the road that bordered the sands.

Near to that cottage, about two hundred yards from it, stood a small but very pretty villa. Joe knew its name to be Sea-beach Villa, and understood that it was the abode of his former master and

friend, Edgar Berrington.   There was a lovely garden
in front, full to overflowing with flowers of every
name and hue, and trellis-work bowers here and
there, covered with jessamine and honeysuckle.   A
sea-shell walk led to the front door.   Up this walk
the diver sauntered, and applied the knocker.

The door was promptly opened by a very small,
sharp-eyed domestic.

"Is your master at home, my dear?" asked Joe,
kindly.

"I ain't got no master," replied the girl.

"No!" returned Joe, in some surprise.   "Your
missus then?"

"My missus don't live 'ere.   I'm on'y loaned to
this 'ouse," said the small domestic; "loaned by Miss
Pritty for two days, till they find a servant gal for
themselves."

"Oh!" said Joe, with a smile, "is the gentleman
who borrowed you within?"

"No, 'e ain't," replied the small domestic.

At that moment Mr. Hazlit walked up the path,
and accosted Joe.

"Ah, you want to see my son-in-law?   He has
not yet returned.   I expect him, however, to-day.
Perhaps, if you call in the afternoon, or to-morrow
morning, you may—"

He was interrupted by the sound of wheels.
Next moment a carriage dashed round the corner of

the garden wall, and drew up in front of the house. Before the old gentleman had clearly realised the fact, he found himself being smothered by one of the prettiest girls in all England, and Joe felt his hand seized in a grasp worthy of a diver.

While Aileen dragged her father into the villa, in order to enable him to boast ever after that he had received the first kiss she ever gave under her own roof, Edgar led Joe to a trellis-work arbour, and, sitting down beside him there, said :—

"Come, Joe, I know you want to see me about something. While these two are having it out in-doors, you and I can talk here."

"First, Mister Eddy," said Joe, holding out his big horny hand, "let me congratulate you on comin' home. May the Lord dwell in your house, and write His name in your two hearts."

"Amen !" returned Edgar, again grasping the diver's hand. "My dear wife and I expect to have that prayer answered in our new home, for we put up a similar one before entering it. And now, Joe, what is it that you want ?"

"Well, sir, the fact is, that my old woman thinks since I smashed my shoulder, that it's high time for me to give up divin', and take to lighter work ; but I didn't know you were comin' home to-day, sir. I thought you'd been home some days already, else I wouldn't have come to you, but—"

"Never mind, Joe. There's no time like the present—go on."

Thus encouraged, Joe explained his circumstances and desires. When he had ended, Edgar remained silent for some minutes.

"Joe," he said at length, "you used to be fond of gardening. Have you forgotten all about it?"

"Why, not quite, sir, but—"

"Stay—I'll come back in a few minutes," said Edgar, rising hastily, and going into the house.

In a few minutes he returned with his wife.

"Joe," said he, "Mrs. Berrington has something to say to you."

"Mr. Baldwin," said Aileen, with a peculiar smile, "I am greatly in want of a gardener. Can you tell me where I am likely to find one, or can you recommend one?"

Joe, who was a quick-witted fellow, replied with much gravity :—

"No Miss—ma'am, I mean—I can't."

"That's a pity," returned Aileen, with a little frown of perplexity; "I am also much in want of a cook—do you know of one?"

"No, ma'am," said Joe, "I don't."

"What a stupid, unobservant fellow you must be, Joe," said Edgar, "not to be able to recommend a cook or a gardener, and you living, as I may say, in the very midst of such useful personages. Now,

Aileen, *I* can recommend both a cook and a gardener to you."

"You see, ma'am," interrupted Joe, with profound gravity, and an earnestness of manner that quite threw his questioners off their guard, "this is an occasion when you may learn a valuable lesson at the outset of wedded life, so to speak—namely, that it is much safer an' wiser, when you chance to be in a difficulty, to apply to your husband for information than to the likes of me; you see, he's ready with what you want at a moment's notice."

Aileen and Edgar were upset by this; they both laughed heartily, and then the former said:—

"Now, Mr. Baldwin, we won't beat any longer about the bush. We have not succeeded in getting a cook, being in the meantime obliged to content ourselves with a temporary loan of the green-grocer's wife, and of Miss Pritty's small domestic; therefore I want to engage *your* wife, who is at present, I believe, open to an engagement. We are also un-provided with a man to tend our garden, look after our pony, and help me in the missionary work, in which I hope immediately to be engaged in this town. Do you accept that situation?"

Aileen said this with such an earnest irresistible air, that Joe Baldwin struck his colours on the spot, and said, "I do!" with nearly as much fervour as Edgar had said these words six weeks before.

The thing was settled then and there, for Joe felt well assured that his amiable Susan would have no objection to such an arrangement.

Now, while this was going on in the bower, Mr. Hazlit, observing that his children were occupied with something important, sauntered down the sea-shell road in the direction of his own cottage. Here he met Miss Pritty.

The sight of her mild innocent face called up a thought. Dozens of other thoughts immediately seized hold of the first thought, and followed it. Mr. Hazlit was sometimes, though not often, impulsive. He took Miss Pritty's hand without saying a word, drew her arm within his own, and led her into the cottage.

"Miss Pritty," he said, sitting down and pointing to a chair, "you have always been very kind to my daughter."

"She has always been very kind—*very* kind—to me," answered Miss Pritty, with a slight look of surprise.

"True—there is no doubt whatever about that," returned Mr. Hazlit, "but just now I wish to refer to your kindness to her. You came, unselfishly, at great personal inconvenience, to China, at my selfish request, and for her sake you endured horrors in connection with the sea, of which I had no conception until I witnessed your sufferings. I am grateful

for your self-sacrificing kindness, and am now about
to take a somewhat doubtful mode of showing my
gratitude, namely, by asking you to give up your
residence in town, and come to be my housekeeper
—my companion and friend."

Mr. Hazlit paused, and Miss Pritty, looking at
him with her mild eyes excessively wide open, gave
no audible expression to her feelings or sentiments,
being, for the moment, bereft of the power of
utterance.

"You see," continued Mr. Hazlit, in a sad voice,
looking slowly round the snug parlour, "I shall be a
very lonely man now that my darling has left my
roof. And you must not suppose, Miss Pritty, that
I ask you to make any engagement that would tie
you, even for a year, to a life that you might not
relish. I only ask you to come and try it. If you
find that you prefer a life of solitude, unhampered
in any way, you will only have to say so at any
time—a month, a week, after coming here—and I
will cheerfully, and without remonstrance, reinstate
you in your old home—or a similar one—exactly as
I found you, even to your small domestic, who may
come here and be your private maid if you choose."

Miss Pritty could not find it in her heart to
refuse an offer so kindly made. The matter was
therefore settled then and there, just as that of the
diver and his wife had been arranged next door.

Is it necessary to say that both arrangements were found, in course of time, to answer admirably? Miss Pritty discovered that housekeeping was her forte, and that she possessed powers of comprehension, in regard to financial matters connected with the payment of debts and dividends, such as she had all her previous life believed to be unattainable anywhere, save in the Bank of England or on the Stock Exchange.

Mrs. Baldwin discovered that cooking was her calling—the end for which she had been born—although discovered rather late in life. Joe made the discovery that gardening and stable-work were very easy employments in the Berrington household, and that his young mistress kept him uncommonly busy amongst the poor of the town, encouraging him to attend chiefly to their spiritual wants, though by no means neglectful of their physical. In these matters he became also agent and assistant to Mr. Hazlit—so that the gardening and stable-tending ultimately became a mere sham, and it was found necessary to provide a juvenile assistant, in the person of the green-grocer's eldest boy, to fill these responsible posts.

The green-grocer himself, and his wife, discovered that Christian influence, good example, and kind words, were so attractive and powerful as to induce them, insensibly, to begin a process of imitation, which ended, quite naturally, in a flourishing business and a happy home.

The small domestic also made a discovery or two. She found that a kitchen with a view of the open sea from its window, and a reasonable as well as motherly companion to talk to, was, on the whole, superior to a kitchen with a window opening up a near prospect of bricks, and the companionship of black pots and beetles.

At first, Aileen travelled a good deal with her husband in his various business expeditions, and thus visited many wild, romantic, and out-o'-the-way parts of our shores ; but the advent of a juvenile Berrington put a sudden stop to that, and the flow of juvenile Berringtons that followed induced her to remain very much at home. This influx of " little strangers " induced the building of so many wings to Sea-beach Villa, that its body at last became lost in its wings, and gave rise to a prophecy that it would one day rise into the air and fly away: up to the present time, however, this remains a portion of unfulfilled prophecy.

Mr. Hazlit became rich again, not indeed so rich as at first, but comfortably rich. Nevertheless, he determined to remain comparatively poor, in order that he might pay his debts to the uttermost farthing. His cottage by the sea had comforts in it, but nothing that could fairly be styled a luxury, except, of course, a luxurious army of well-trained grandchildren, who invaded his premises every morning with terrific noise, and kept possession until fairly driven out by force of arms.

Rooney Machowl and David Maxwell stuck to their colours manfully. They went into partnership, and continued for years struggling together at the bottom of the sea. Mrs. Machowl tended the amiable Teddy during the early, or chokable period of infancy, but when he had safely passed that season, his father took him in hand, and taught him to dive. He began by tumbling him into a washing tub at odd times, in order to accustom him to water. Then, when a little older, he amused himself by occasionally throwing him off the end of the pier, and jumping in to save him. Afterwards he initiated him into the mysteries of the dress, the helmet, the life-line, the air-pipe, etc., and, finally, took him down bodily to the bottom of the sea. At last, Teddy became as good and fearless a diver as his father. He was also the pride of his mother.

One afternoon—a bright glowing afternoon—in the autumn of the year, Mr. Hazlit sat in a favourite bower in the garden of his cottage, with Aileen on one side of him, and Edgar on the other. At the foot of the garden a miscellaneous group of boys, girls, and babies, of all ages, romped and rolled upon the turf. In front lay the yellow sands, and, beyond, the glorious glittering sea rolled away to the horizon.

Mr. Hazlit had just been commenting on their happy condition as compared with the time when they "knew not God." The children having just romped themselves into a state of exhaustion, were reasonably quiet, and the sun was setting in floods of amber and gold.

"What a peaceful evening!" remarked Aileen.

"How different," said Edgar, "from that of which it is the anniversary! Don't you remember that this is the evening of the day in which we attacked the Malay pirates long ago?"

"So it is. I had forgotten," said Mr. Hazlit.

"Dinner, sir," said a boy in buttons, who bore a marked resemblance to the green-grocer's wife.

As he spoke a stout gentleman opened the garden gate and walked up the path leading to the bower. At the same moment Miss Pritty issued from the house and echoed the green-grocer's boy's announcement.

They were all silent as the stout gentleman approached.

"What! *can* it be?" cried Edgar, starting up in excitement.

"The captain!" exclaimed Mr. Hazlit.

"Impossible!" murmured Aileen.

"Pirates!" cried Miss Pritty, turning deadly

white, and preparing to fall into Edgar's arms, but curiosity prevented her.

There could be no mistake. The bright glittering eyes, the black beard and moustache, the prominent nose, the kindly smile, the broad chest and shoulders, revealed unquestionably the captain of the Rajah's gunboat.

"Miraculous!" cried Edgar, as he wrung the captain's right hand. "We were just talking of the great fight of which this is the anniversary."

"Amazing coincidence!" exclaimed Mr. Hazlit, seizing the other hand.

"Not so much of a coincidence as it seems, however," said the captain with a laugh, as he shook hands with the ladies, "for I made arrangements on purpose to be here on the anniversary day, thinking that it might add to the interest of my visit."

"And to come *just* at dinner-time too," said Miss Pritty, who had recovered.

"Another coincidence," observed Aileen, with an arch look.

"Come—come in—here, this way, captain," cried Mr. Hazlit, dragging his friend by the hand. "Welcome—heartily welcome to Sea Cottage."

The captain submitted to be dragged; to be placed by the side of Aileen; to be overwhelmed with kindness by the elder members of the family, and with questions by the younger members, who regarded him as a hero of romance quite equal, if not superior, to Jack the Giant-killer.

But how can we describe what followed? It is impossible. We can only say that the evening was one of a thousand. All the battles were fought over again. The captain came out strong for the benefit of the youngsters, and described innumerable scenes of wild adventure in which he had been personally engaged. And to cap it all, after dinner, when they went out into the garden, and were seated in floods of moonlight in the bower, two men opened the garden gate and made for the back kitchen, with the evident intention of calling on the cook. These were discovered to be Rooney Machowl and David Maxwell.

Of course they were made to come and shake hands with their old commander, the captain, and gradually got into a talk, and laughed a good deal at the recollection of old times, insomuch that the noise they made drew Joe Baldwin to the scene, and, as a natural result, this led the conversation into divers channels—among others to life and adventure at the bottom of the sea, and there is no saying how long they might have talked there if a cloud had not obliterated the moon, and admonished them that the night was at hand.

And now, good reader, with regret we find that our tale has reached its close. We may not have added much to your knowledge, but if we have, in any degree, interested you in the characters we have summoned to our little stage, or in the incidents that have been enacted thereon, we shall not have wrought in vain, for the subject into which you have consented to dive with us is not only an interesting, but a dangerous one—involving. as it does the constant risking of manly lives, the well-being of large communities, the progress of important industries, and the salvation of much valuable property to the world at large.

THE END.

www.ingramcontent.com/pod-product-compliance
Lightning Source LLC
Chambersburg PA
CBHW050901130726
47900CB00015B/1451